G. D. Benneke

PROMISED LAND

Book One

L O V E

— and —

H A T E

FriesenPress

Suite 300 - 990 Fort St
Victoria, BC, Canada, V8V 3K2
www.friesenpress.com

ISBN
978-1-4602-4842-3 (Hardcover)
978-1-4602-4843-0 (Paperback)
978-1-4602-4844-7 (eBook)

1. *Fiction, Historical*

Distributed to the trade by The Ingram Book Company

To the Old Folks,
God love 'em,
I dedicate this work!

Foreword

When the train rolled into York that very pleasant October afternoon in 1904, it carried the hopes and dreams of the Buechler family. Like most of the others who came to the Promised Land, they fled work and war, pestilence and poverty in a land that promised them nothing but more of the same.

When the trains rolled into York that bleak December in 1905, they carried exiles driven out of "Mother Russia" because they'd refused to die and because they believed and lived differently and practiced work instead of war.

Running from something or to something, many more walked or wagoned with everything they owned tied in, or on, or behind. The only things they had were hope and each other.

All it took was ten dollars and a commitment to a book of rules and they had land; the ultimate resource, the absolute prize, the gifts of hope and promise. They came by the thousands and after them came the scum — big land meant big money in high places. These were poor, desperate, and illiterate people; easy defenceless picking.

This is a fiction, yet a fiction fraught with reality. This is a story of people, our people. Many of the things told in this story did happen to them on one or the other side of the Atlantic and often on both sides. They came to build a better life, that we might live it- let us never forget that simple fact. Reality is a matter of record despite multitudinous attempts to change or disguise it. The rest; places, names, and events are coincidental.

Whether this was a **Promised Land** or not depends on who you ask. To some it was and to others the words of promise were empty. Your conclusions must be entirely your own.

In the Beginning

Torn and bleeding, he crawled away. For months he lingered in raging agony, his body spewing bits of infected flesh and rotting metal and always, the angelic eyes hovered over him, inching him closer to recovery.

Because his homeland offered him only more pain and persecution, when he'd recovered, he left to seek a better world; one with more promise.

He climbed off the boat penniless and worked his way west to the wheat fields of Kansas to do what he knew and what he longed to do, for he loved the soil. This was America — vast distances of it shimmered in the afternoon heat. Making his fortune was a virtual certainty.

Yet the land of "Milk and Honey" also proved unkind to the young man. What he found was fatigue not fortune, cruel taskmasters, and long hard days with little rest or mercy. The propaganda in the newspapers and the posters he had seen in his homeland, after the war, was a lie! He'd survived the mercies of the Prussian military, he could surely thrive in this. He worked his way to the fertile farms of Iowa and found conditions there a little better.

In a bid of desperate hope, he sent a letter home to his heart. For five long years he had yearned over her. She had come to see him off, kissed him in tears, and made him promise never to forget and he certainly had not. He imagined that she would surely have lost all hope by now and be married but she wasn't. She too had agonized over the dashing soldier whom she had helped to draw back from death and with whom she had unwittingly fallen in love.

His letters conveyed the truth. He was ragged and broke but he found enough for Frieda's passage. He couldn't meet the boat but he did meet the train. He'd left a pretty girl and now met a mature young woman with those same beautiful eyes and he loved every bit of her more than he imag-ined. Her beauty had grown upon his lonely spirit. He borrowed a suit and married her two days later.

Success was elusive; The Fates would not allow and the years brought little more than breaking toil and a meagre subsistence. The lands were never for themselves. Frieda never complained but she did agonize over the destiny and the desires of their children, for they produced five healthy, strong boys and a beautiful girl who was Papa's joy.

Then, one day Frieda was strong, vibrant, and healthy and the next, she was mortally ill. It was too late for her. Before she died, she told him not to despair; everything would shortly be well for their children. There would be good news soon. She knew!

The news, when it came, was homesteads; a quarter of land for ten dollars in Canada, the vast wilderness to the north; barren, empty, cold. Rumour had it peopled by untamed savages, much like in the American past, but it was land and ... affordable. The work meant nothing — it was the will that mattered.

I
"I promise!"

"All aboard!"

The stench of old, hot grease blended with the sharp, cutting tang of coal smoke, freshly applied. The harsh bark of the freight handlers and the clatter of the hand-powered freight wagon, the ear-splitting scream of the high-pitched steam whistle and the sequential, rattling crash of the car linkage and the town of Maynard dropped away. His father, his brothers, and his little sister, frantically waving their blessing, disappeared into the mist as the hot steam clashed with the cool October evening and he was so alone.

When Papa came to America, he came with a dream. He didn't fail but he didn't reach his dream either. The responsibility for that fell upon Carl, for he was the eldest — he carried with him the fortunes of his entire family and the spirit of his dead mother. That was an awesome burden for one of his age.

Heavy labours had grown Carl into powerful manhood yet, inwardly, he was still a child. He'd never been away from his home or his family for more than a week and then only because he had to be, as a consequence of his labours. This was very much different; this carried with it the pain of permanency. The lights of home were not yet below the horizon and he was horribly lonesome.

Yet within his youthful enthusiasm, the fire of the unknown burned, the spirit of adventure. Papa and Mama had often spoken to their children of the Canadian wilderness and longingly dreamed of its opportunities. They spoke of its dangers as well; its cold, its savagery. It wasn't that long ago they'd heard about rebellion and Louis Riel.

The Trail of Ninety-eight and the lore of sudden riches didn't appeal; it was the promise of land, for they were farmers. Somewhere, in a coach behind Carl, rode their entire resource; everything the family could beg, buy, or borrow; every tool, utensil, seed, and nail that they and their friends and neighbours could spare to guarantee his success.

The two hundred dollars that Papa and Max had gathered and the sixty that Carl had saved were concealed in several separate locations, even sewn into his clothing; he'd heard of pickpockets and flimflam men. He had everything and left his family behind, destitute, yet buoyed with hope and anticipation.

The aged rail car lurched and bounced along the equally aged rail bed. The seat was hard and cold but he had it to himself. The potbelly near him was dormant and the kerosene lamp flickered and died … out of fuel. Darkness, like his depression, descended into totality. His companions were as desolate and indifferent as he. They'd acknowledged him when he boarded, with a curt nod or "Evenin," then wrapped themselves; each within his own solitude.

He lifted his old grip, filled tight with his meagre wardrobe, placed it at the window end of his seat, curled up, his head upon it, and gave himself over to his anxiety. Sheer boredom, the hypnotic clatter of the rails, the sometimes not so gentle rock of the car beneath him, the stress of his adventure, and the very long day overcame him. He slept in spite of himself.

———

"Damnit! A guy pays one helluva damn ticket and he's got ta freeze his damn arse off 'cause they're too damn cheap to get some damn wood 'er stuff in here ta light this damn stove!"

Carl shot upright with alarm.

A burly, overweight man fetched the side of the potbelly a kick that rocked it and dislodged the bottom section of the stovepipe, precipitating a cloud of soot and an even more artistic expletive. The man shoved it back, turned to the door, yanked it open, head-rounded the corner and bellered at someone on the ground., "Git some damn coal er wood in here er I'll damn well come out there and build a damn fire under the whole damn lot of ya'! We paid pretty damn dear for this damn ride and by gad, ya'll damn well keep us from freezin' er I'll damn well know why!"

He was right, of course, it was freezing in the car and Carl was fully dressed, heavy mackinaw and all. Papa never minced words, but Carl had never heard so many "damns" put together so damn emphatically.

Dawn had cracked the horizon just enough for Carl to see as he wiped the crust of sleep out of his eyes. The train sat on a desolate siding, taking on water and coal. He pried the stubborn window open and looked past the car toward the locomotive.

Several smeared workmen shovelled coal out of a horseless wagon placed by the track for the purpose. Someone, out of sight on the engine, yelled something to someone else who was still obscured by the feeble light and the someone on the water tower yelled back. "There's still a helluva lot more in the well!"

A short distance from the tower, an enormous pump projected from the earth. Beside it stood a horse-powered treadmill. A length of pipe led to an enormous trough and behind the trough, through a barren grove of trees, Carl could see water glistening ... the local watering hole, all inclusive. The initiative impressed him.

A rutted trail, freckled out with horse manure, passed between a few forlorn shacks of some nowhere place that had a name though Carl didn't care enough to ask.

The door of the car jerked violently and an equally burly, sleep-faced trainman lurched through with a bucket of coal in one hand and the other arm piled to the absolute limit with kindling wood. The disgruntled patron took one look at the trainman's massive demeanour, wisely chose to remain silent, and resumed his seat somewhere behind Carl. Carl very discreetly closed the window.

The kindling crackled then roared to life and the trainman heaped coal on it. "There, ya' damn sissy girlies, shaddap and go back ta yer sweet dreamin'!" The door slammed violently behind him.

Again the stupid roar, "All aboard!" and the whistle screeched. Carl thought the procedure ridiculous, annoying, and unnecessary in a place like this. He was mildly surprised when the door opened and a woman, carrying a young, screaming child, stepped carefully through and scanned the dim interior. She selected the seat directly in front of Carl, as close to the glowing potbelly as occupancy would allow. A young man, somewhat older than Carl, struggled through after her, ox-burdened by a load of luggage. He dropped the collection to the floor and reached for the frantic child. The mother opened a case, which she carried with her, rummaged through it briefly and came up with a milk-filled bottle. She took the child, held him close and suppressed his wailing with its warmth. The man stuffed his burdens into any available cranny about the seat and above, in the luggage rack, then sat down silently beside his mate and offspring.

The train lurched, the linkage crashed, the child screamed. The young man cursed, then cradled the child and the mother with his long arm. The wailing amplified. The woman whispered something to the man, who rose, retrieved a case and again took the child. The mother took out a change and the man placed the child on the seat beside her, watching as the woman brought warmth and relief to the distressed, thoroughly saturated boy. Then he resumed his seat with an apologetic smile. The silence was deafening!

The domestic circumstance was so close to Carl's sympathy; he had witnessed the same scene many times with his parents and younger siblings and he saw in the young family, an image of his own. His eyes clouded embarrassingly with homesickness as he turned to the window and shaded his face with a hand, in the pretence of observing a distant object in the gathering light.

The car rattled to a jolting stop and Carl nearly fell out of the seat. In his reverie, he had again fallen asleep. The child whimpered but nothing more, then drifted off again, obviously exhausted. The burly trainman burst through the door and bellered, "Charles City!"

"Aw, shut-up! Ya'll wake the kid!" The outburst was kneejerk. Carl could hardly believe that it came out of him, but it did. He didn't like the attitude of the oversized lout.

"Oh! We got us a smart arse, ain't we? How'd ya like ta walk, girlie boy?" The trainman moved toward Carl threateningly. Carl vaulted to his feet to meet the assault just as Papa had taught him. The trainman stopped, hesitated for a moment, then turned and retreated without another word and slammed the door behind him. The young father, too, had risen. His and Carl's combined mass was approximately equivalent to the thug but that wasn't the motivation for the trainman's retreat. Carl heard a sharp click behind him and turned in time to see a lean, hard faced, older man returning a heavy revolver to the holster under his long coat.

"Gee, thanks mister! I thought sure I was done for."

"Been around the world, and on the train too long not to know and hate pushin' bastards like that. I been puttin' better'n him in jail all my life. No thanks necessary." He walked toward Carl and extended his hand. "Name's Brewster."

"Mine's Carl. I'm headin' for Canada, to see if I can find some land for us, me'n my brothers."

"Well, you're in the right company here, although, what I got to do ain't nearly so nice ... some real scum ta take back to Des Moines ... work for the State."

The car seemed to come alive; a loud murmur ran the circle. The young father smiled broadly and the mother, whitened by the near disaster, grinned foolishly with relief.

An older man in greased-over coveralls poked his smudged, handle-barred face through the door. "Might as well git off and walk a bit ... be a longer stop here ... maybe git some breakfast. We got us a helluva mess ta take care of on that old bugger agin."

"You comin'?" The Marshal looked back. Carl was starving and didn't realize it. He hadn't eaten since afternoon yesterday before Papa, the boys, and Bertha loaded him up for the short wagon ride to the train.

"Got a bunch of grub with me but nothin' to drink ... sure could use somethin' hot 'bout now."

"Well, bring your grub, coffee's on me." Carl grabbed the old school bag that had served him since his childhood and followed the Marshal. The rest all followed Carl. The Marshal seemed to be the only one who knew where to go.

Charles City wasn't anything like any place Carl had ever been yet in his secluded life. Maynard was just starting to build wooden sidewalks but those that Carl walked over here were old and worn and rotting and the new ones were all cement. So were all the watering troughs and the hitching posts were all of iron in a cement base. They'd never rot. The buildings were mostly made of bricks. In Maynard, only a few had enough money to afford to build with brick. The streets of Charles City were at least twice as wide and were all covered with gravel.

"What happened to all the horse manure? There's hardly any."

The Marshall told Carl that they had a crew to pick it up every couple days so the flies wouldn't get so bad. He led the others to a large, brick-faced building on Main Street, about three blocks from the station. None of them knew the place, not even the big guy who had cursed about the stove that morning.

The coincidence amused Carl; the big, hand-painted sign over the heavy door read "**Bertha's.**" His little sister, despite her fifteen years, already set an excellent table because she had to. That the first place Carl would stop to eat on this journey would be called after her was absolutely amazing.

"Hello ya great big beauty!" Carl was surprised that the stern-faced lawman had a sense of humour. The lady in back waddled out with the biggest smile and the biggest body Carl had ever seen on any woman and some of them in Maynard were big. She was about as opposite his Bertha as anyone could be. Carl didn't like big women but he just loved this one even before she spoke. When she spoke he adored her.

"Howdy, ya dirty old bugger! Where the heck ya bin so long? ... Hard fer a gal ta find any decent lovin' around here!" She waved her heavy hand at the assemblage in the room, now relatively crowded; the wagons and horses outside had predetermined the mass within. She gave the Marshal the heaviest hug and the biggest kiss on the mouth that Carl had ever seen.

"And where did ya find this beauty?" She looked straight at Carl. "Welcome sonny and ye'r welcome any time! ... Bout time somethin' good lookin' showed up 'round here 'stead 'a all this scrub!" She waved her heavy hand again.

"Honest-ta-God Bertha, if ya' didn't cook sa good and ya' weren't sa funny, we'd have ta take our business somewheres else."

The entire room erupted with laughter at the mysterious joke.

"Aw, go over ta Mable's ya' scrawny little stud — we know yer goin' tanight anyway!"

The room erupted again. The embarrassed little patron sat and ate quietly.

"Sit down, sonny!" Her big hand seized Carl, dragged him to a table and forced him down. "I'm gonna feed ya' the best damn breakfast ya' ever et!"

"But I ain't got much money and I brought my grub with me." Carl thought he was being set up, like Papa had warned.

"I ain't asked ya' for nothin' but to eat all that I give ya', that's all. Yer lucky that ya' got the Marshal with ya' or I'd keep ya'; yer sa darn cute!" She gave his cheek a pinch that stung for half an hour and turned to retrieve the coffee pot from the small stove and two of the big cups. She filled them without a word and bounced to the kitchen with fantastic, unpredictable agility. The smile was gone. Now she was serious; this was business.

"What's Mabel's?" Carl asked. The room again erupted with laughter, even the straight-faced Marshal.

"Mabel's has two stories," he said. "She'll feed ya' downstairs. What she does to ya' upstairs, well, that's another story!" Again the laughter. The red-faced little patron left his breakfast, threw a coin on the counter near the door, and left hurriedly amongst even more laughter. Carl was embarrassed by the response but thoroughly confused. He'd heard about such questionable places. He'd have liked to ask where Mable's was but he knew what that would do. He just wanted to see if those places looked like what his friends in Maynard said they were, that's all.

Golly! The hot coffee was good. He wolfed it down so quickly that the Marshal anticipated his gagging but it never happened. "When ya' said ya'd like somethin' hot, ya' weren't kiddin'. When did ya' say ya' ate last?"

Carl was embarrassed. He didn't answer.

The Marshal drank, then went to the stove and filled their cups again and a few others on the way. He was well known and liked here. Carl could tell how the people reacted to him.

The breakfast was the biggest Carl had ever seen on one plate at one time. Bertha wasn't kidding but Carl hardly noticed; his attention was distracted by the prettiest girl he could ever remember seeing, as she carried the loaded plates. She was everything Carl imagined an angel could be. She dropped the plate on the table in front of the startled Marshal with a cold and abrupt gesture, then placed Carl's in front of him with gentle care. She looked into Carl's eyes for a few moments and her cold expression melted. She hesitated, smiled, and blushed.

He was very conscious of his expression. It was likely stupid; it always was at times like this. His face felt hot. "My name's Carl!" he blurted and then felt even stupider.

"I'm Milly," she said, faltering a bit.

"Aw' right you two!" the Marshal growled unpredictably, destroying the spell. "How's your folks Milly? ... Ain't seen them in a while."

"And whose fault is that?" she snapped. "We didn't know where you were for almost a year. We thought maybe something happened to you; you and your stupid gun and badge! Wilbur saw you in Cedar Rapids a couple months ago and told us when he got back, otherwise we wouldn't have known. Now you want to weasel your way back in as if you're part of the family? You got to do better than that and you know it! Grandma didn't die! You and your damn marshalling, your holier-than-now law-makin'; you were never around when she needed you! Even when she took sick, you were after that Worley bunch and your wife, my grandma, who I never got to know because I was just a baby, was dyin'! Your bein' gone and all, that's what killed her!"

Her eyes flashed, her face reddened and her body shook with emotion. Carl felt uncomfortable; this was personal — this was family. He was amazed at the connection and looked for familiarity.

"And when Mom needed you because she was with child and she and Dad weren't married yet, you said hateful things to her because you were so pure and abiding. Well my mom and my dad are a family now. We've got a right and proper home. Wilbur and I don't know what a grandpa is 'cause you've never been around. Dad hates you because of what you called him before and what you said to Mom. I've seen her when she thought no one was around. She looks at your and Grandma's picture and cries because, somehow, she missed having a proper home when she was a kid.

"Now you breeze in here on some mission or other, not intending to stop, even to say hello. Last time you were through, we heard you stopped at Bertha's so we knew you didn't care enough. Now I work here and you didn't know that and weren't you surprised? But maybe not; you maybe didn't recognize me; you've seen me all of twice in the last ten years. Tell me, what do I tell Mom and Dad tonight when I go home? 'Oh, by the way, Grandpa dropped in for breakfast this morning and I caught him at it?'" Tears ran down her pretty cheeks. Carl's admiration for the Marshal changed to doubt.

The room fell to dead silence. Everyone looked uncomfortable at hearing what they shouldn't have.

Bertha, hearing the confrontation, had come up and stood behind Milly for the last little while. "Sorry darlin'," she said to Milly. "I didn't know. Every time he passed through here I thought he came to see you and the family." She turned to the very disturbed Marshal. "Ya heartless old bastard, 'stead a kissin' ya' I should 'a kicked yer ass!"

Bertha's big hand came around hard and caught the Marshal on the shoulder with such force that his hat flew from his head. The Marshal stared at the floor, in shame. "The only way I'll ever let ya' come back in here agin is if ya' come in with your family first, ya' miserable old sonuvagun! Yer badge ain't scarin' me neither. Now ya' got lots a fence-mendin' to do and if yer atall smart and I think ya' are, ya'll get started right now."

Milly had almost instinctively moved beside Carl with her back turned to the table. She was crying quietly. Carl found himself holding her hand and he was surprised by his unusual boldness; he didn't know when he'd taken it.

The Marshal rose slowly, picked up his hat and placed it on the table. Bertha motioned Carl to the kitchen, leaving the Marshal with his grand-daughter. Carl followed, leaving his untouched breakfast, his hunger forgotten. When he glanced back, the Marshal, his arm around Milly, was leading her to the door and the sidewalk where they could talk without all the ears.

"Her grandma, she was my best friend when we were girls," Bertha said from the stove, where she filled Carl another plate. "Are ya' takin' the train out with the Marshal?" she asked.

"Yes!" Carl responded. "I'd like to stay a while but I can't. Everything my family and I got's on that train headin' for Canada. We're awful poor and our only hope is gettin' some land."

"Well, if I can't keep ya', then I better feed ya' fast, 'cause the train will be leavin' in about ten minutes." Bertha had already forgiven and resumed her old humour. Carl swallowed without chewing to get it all down. He usually ate that way but never in a circumstance such as this. He felt so much a part of this that it could have been his personal problem.

Milly came back in, wringing her hands in her apron. She stood looking at them for a moment, unsure what to say, and smiling awkwardly. "Said he had a job to do ... said to apologize to you for him and to talk to Mom and the family tonight and tell them that he'd be back in a few days." She shrugged her shoulders with doubt. "God, I hope he ain't just talking to make me feel better. Mom would sure be hurt!"

Bertha gave Milly one of her hugs and said something about how she knew the Marshal and that this time she was sure that he meant it. She took two plates that she had filled with eggs and ham and hustled out, back to business. Carl was alone with Milly.

They looked at each other and Carl could feel his face flush; her smile reached right into him. He searched desperately for something appropriate to say. He knew that whatever it would be, would likely sound foolish.

"Golly, I'm so ashamed that you had to see me do that, just meeting you and all. It's been gnawing at me so long just watching Mom." She flinched nervously, very unsure of herself and the anticipated response to her heartfelt apology.

Carl responded without forethought or hesitation. He walked to her and wrapped her in an innocent, sympathetic hug. It resulted in a whole lot more than he expected or hoped for. She closed her arms around his waist and just held on. Strangely, Carl wasn't surprised; it seemed to be so perfectly natural. Despite the fact that he'd met her hardly a half-hour ago, she put her head on his shoulder almost like she'd always done it and whispered again, "I am sorry!" He felt her trembling. She remained that way for some time, her breath gentle on his neck. Then she stiffened, lifted her head and look into his eyes.

"Oh my, what am I doing? You must really think that I'm nuts! You hardly know me and here I am holding on to you and telling you all my troubles." She didn't let go and neither did Carl. Her eyes were reddened from her bout with tears but wide with question and anticipation and it wasn't about her grandfather. She stuttered, "A-Are you goin' out with Grandpa?"

"Yes, I guess so!" he said, almost tongue-tied and very conscious of it.

"...You sure you can't stay a while so I can get to know you? It feels like I've known you for a long time already and we just met and I'd sure hate to see you go."

Carl regained his composure and told her what he had told Bertha, and her eyes fought back the tears again. She didn't want her feelings to show but they did. Carl was enthralled; he couldn't imagine something like this happening to him with such a beautiful young lady so unexpectedly, so quickly. He was puzzled and pleased; he had only fantasized about something like this and here it was, real, and he had to leave — no alternative.

"But the train's broke or somethin' and it's goin' to take a while to fix. I've got until then."

Bertha heard his remarks as she waddled back in. "Good! Ya' can help by carryin' in some water from out back, into that big crock by the stove until it's full, then ya can help Milly. Mind, now, ya' do exactly what she wants ya' to!" she said with a sly smile.

Milly's face blushed the prettiest smile and Carl felt his own burn at the inference.

"Grandpa went to the train to see how long and if he could help. He said he'd be back for everyone when it was ready." Milly's eyes glistened with question as she looked at Carl. He was back in with a pail full before he even realized that he had started.

"You can stop now. The crock's full and so is the pail." Milly touched his arm as she spoke. She was a bit amused and very pleased with the hypnotic effect she was having on this very good-looking young man.

Bertha chuckled, shaking her head, as she walked out with another order. "I'll be damned! I ain't seen nothin' like that in a while," she said, as if to herself, yet loud enough for them to hear.

"Can you give me a hand with all of these dishes?" Milly asked. She didn't order him like she was supposed to. A large, cast-iron sink was just heaped, with many more dishes piled on a counter beside it.

He rolled up his sleeves, dove in and asked nothing. Milly washed right beside him. She noted his every move and took every precaution to be sure that they touched very frequently. The pile diminished rapidly so after scalding the dishes with more hot water, she took up a towel and started to dry..

Bertha called Milly out into the nearly vacant dining room. Carl watched her departure over his shoulder. Through the glass, he saw Milly talk to an attractive middle-aged lady with her back toward him. Milly's eyes teared over again and she and the woman held each other and talked for quite a while. Then the lady turned and looked into the kitchen at Carl, who tried his best not to notice. He saw Bertha interject and Milly's bright blush. He knew who this was before she turned and came into the kitchen with them.

"Mom, this is Carl who I was telling you about."

Mom stared at him, quite deliberately, for what must have been a minute. "Mom, you're embarrassing us!"

"Us?" She twirled her finger downward, directing Carl to turn a full circle, then whistled softly. "You know, Bertha, you're right! He is a real beauty!"

"Mom! Really!"

Carl's extended hand crumpled under her advance and rolled up into one of the biggest hugs that Carl had, other then Bertha's. "You may have gathered, I'm Mom!"

She was definitely Milly's mother and she behaved exactly like Carl would have expected. She was bold, abrupt, and daring. Her features carried a bit of the Marshal and her moves were all Milly.

"Oh God, you must think we're awful! I have to apologize for my mother!"

"No you don't! I like her! She's nearly as pretty as you and she's lots of fun!"

"Well, I guess 'nearly' is about as close as I should get. You're right Milly, he is as nice as you said!" And to Bertha, "You're right, my girl really knows how to pick 'em! Welcome son! I hope to see a lot more of you. Better get him over for supper soon. Your dad is going to approve of this one." She walked over again and gave Carl a big motherly kiss on the cheek.

"Mom!" Milly's jaw dropped with annoyance and her mother giggled.

"What? You mean you haven't done that, yet?" She emphasized the "yet." "... Got to go now. Bye, see you soon, I hope." And she was gone.

Bertha left with her and Carl went back to the dishes. Milly dried quietly for a while; she was annoyed with her mother and didn't know what to say other then, "I'm sorry!"

"Don't be silly, she's just great ... a lot like you."

Milly stopped and looked a long time at Carl. "I was scared that maybe she was too bold and I don't want to scare you away like some of the others." She stopped abruptly, realizing what she had revealed.

"Look, don't be afraid to say what you want to me. I know a girl as pretty as you must have a lot a' fellas calling on her. I'd expect to have to earn my way with you."

She laid down the towel, put her arms around his shoulders as if pleading for understanding, then gave him a very unmotherly kiss on the same cheek. "There, that's the first. I sure hope you don't want it to be the last. I was only foolin' with them. I liked you from the minute I first saw you and I really hope you like me."

Carl dried his hands and held her even closer than he had before and much more deliberately. She had her answer.

How was this going to work? He had to continue for his family's sake. They went back to work and talked about his plans and his family until the dishes were all done.

The big roasts were starting to smell wonderful. Milly checked them and Carl threw a few more sticks into the big firebox. He checked the ashes but there was lots of room; somebody'd cleaned them out that morning. He looked around and found a pail of potatoes near a big boiling pot, pulled out his jackknife, and started to peel. Bertha and Milly noticed. "That's what you do when there's work and everybody's busy." Carl explained.

He finished the potatoes and looked around for something else. Milly, who had been busy with vegetables and a huge pot of stew, had them all boiling. She found his hand and led him to the small kitchen table and two of the big cups she had already poured. "Sit!" she ordered.

They drank quietly, never taking their eyes off each other. This girl was serious about him and he found himself very nervous. How was that possible? He wasn't the least bit worried about those other guys and didn't know why. He was going to have to leave her very soon and he was worried about how he was going to miss her and think about her all the time. He didn't know what was going to happen out there and how he could get around the loneliness and the distance and the isolation gap.

"Don't worry, we'll figure it out somehow. If we have to, we'll make it work; I know we can." Milly had spoken before he could. How did she know?

"I'm thinking exactly the same thing."

Carl got up, walked around the table and she rose to meet him, again anticipating his intention. She held out her arms. How long they stood, not saying anything, they didn't know or care.

The gentle voice beside them said, "Sorry kids, but the train is goin' ta leave in a few minutes. Most of the passengers are gone back already.

Marshal's waitin' for ya. Take off your apron and get ta the train with him ... least ya' can see him off."

Carl pulled on his mackinaw. Milly took off her apron and pulled on her coat.

"I want ta hear from ya' again, sonny. Only address ya' need is 'Bertha's, Charles City." She pinched the same cheek again, this time, not so hard and she laid a big kiss on the other one. "I can't figure how anyone can make such an impression on so many folks in so short a time. Just look at the smile on Milly's face. Now, can ya' beat that? ... in only a couple hours? I don't know what you got but I wish you could bottle it; I'd sure be able to sell it 'cause there's so little of it around here." She gave Carl her famous hug and nearly winded him. Milly squirmed and blushed, then took Carl's hand and pulled him away through the doors and out into the street.

The Marshall walked pensively, ahead, out of earshot, not wanting to interfere. He was very concerned about the unexpected turn of events. It was too fast and frightening and he wasn't at all sure of Carl.

Milly grasped Carl's arm and thrust hers through just as if they'd always done it. They looked at each other as they walked, as if they could learn everything about each other that way instead of taking their time; they didn't have any more of that.

They found their way up to the car door. All the way, they didn't say a word; they said it best by saying nothing at all. They held each other while everybody in the car watched and smiled. Her flush became a gleam. His awkward manner gave way to realization and confidence. He felt very good about what was happening.

She spoke first as had become the habit. "Are you sure you can't stay for just a little while? There's so much more to talk about. I've got so much more that I'd like to say but I can't think right now. I want you to meet my dad."

"I know what you want to say but you're so much better at it. I have to go and you know why. Now I've got even more reason 'cause I have to make somethin' for us."

She took her hands from his waist, placed them behind his neck and drew his head slowly toward her. Her kiss told him everything he really needed to know. He held her so tightly that he could feel her warm, young form and she responded willingly.

The conductor blared, the whistle screamed, and the dream was over. They held on. The vulgar trainman squirmed but kept silent because the Marshal watched.

Her eyes filled again. "Please don't forget me and write often. When you're settled, send your address, I'll write lots. I've always liked writing and I'll love doing it to you."

The conductor now stood beside. "We've got to go son. We can bring ya back just as easy as take ya away."

Carl turned and climbed the step, holding her hand all the way.

"Don't you ever forget me. Promise?" she said. "Because as quick as this all is, I can say that I love you!"

The steamer roared and Carl had to let go. "I promise!" he answered. "And I always keep my promise."

He stood on the train step, for longer than he imagined, just remembering the smell of her beautiful hair and the feel of her pressed against him. How could so many things happen to him so quickly? In two days, his life had totally changed. He howled with joy.

II

"Count me in."

Carl struggled against the toss of the accelerating train. He flopped with gratitude into the safety of his seat and arranged himself, nervously trying to avoid the grinning faces. This was new to him, there were just no words he could think of. The best he could do was to shut up and take the kidding.

"Ah, hush up! The lot of ya!" The car fell silent; the words had come out of the Marshal. "... Figured I'd sit with ya' for a talk, seein' as how Mason City ain't that far and seein' as how we both got an interest in my grand-daughter. Everything Milly said in there was the truth, about me bein' gone most a' the time. When I do my job, it gets to be like a disease and I forget about everything else. I figure it has to be done quick and I'll make up for it soon, when I can. It's just that I never found the time to do it yet. After I'm done this, I'll hang it up. I told her I would and I will. I'll lose 'em sure if I don't, I could see that when she said it. That's one thing about Emily, just like her grandma, she says what she means and she does what she says. You'd best do the same. I wouldn't care to see her hurt if you catch my meanin'. I'm ashamed of myself for what I didn't do. I'd hate ta have to be ashamed a' you too."

"I've never done anything like this before and I've never felt like this before either. Seems like I've known Milly all my life and all I've been doin' 'til now is lookin' for her. Now I've found her and I did just what I was supposed to when that happened. She's not like a stranger; she knows what I think because she says exactly that before I can figure out how to. She can't hide what she thinks about me either because I'd know, so she doesn't try. I don't know if that's the way it's supposed to be but that's the way it is."

"Oh, that's the way it's supposed to be alright." The words came from the young man seated in front of them. The woman smiled at her husband nervously, while the shy, wide-eyed, round, little face, with a white-knuckled grasp on the seat back, stared at the two behind him with unbridled curiosity and question.

The Marshal smiled, "That's right, son."

"I'm sorry for our eavesdropping. We couldn't help it. Your situation is not too much different than ours. Paul was gone for over three years, building a place for us. He came back last year to see if I still cared and wanted him. Boy, did I ever!" She elevated the child to exemplify her remarks. "He was all I could think about. We got married right away and Paul went back alone, to finish the house. He saw his son for the first time just a week ago." The woman smiled at Carl's misinterpretation of her remarks. "I'm not saying the same thing is going to happened to you and your girl, Milly's the name I heard, but from what I saw, I wouldn't be too surprised."

The listeners giggled behind their concealing hands and the Marshal roared with laughter, revealing his amusement at Carl's stuttering, fumbling blush. Then, mercifully, he came to Carl's rescue with a thorough explanation of recent events to the listeners.

The young woman displayed an incredulous expression. This was too good to pass up. "Well, if that's what happened the first time you met her, I predict a whole lot of these!" She hoisted the baby again and Carl cringed.

"Aw Mildred, give the poor guy a break. I know just how it feels and so do you." The young man silenced his teasing wife. "That's right, her name's Milly too. Strange, ain't it?"

Marshal-Grandpa interjected again. "Well now, if ya'd care to listen long enough for me to tell ya' a few things, you might learn somethin. Ya' been so darn occupied with the look of her and the sound of her that you never bothered to find out the facts. First off, Milly ain't for Mildred. She couldn't quite say 'Emily' when she was learnin' to talk, so 'Milly' became her name. There's things you got to know 'bout her that you ain't had time to learn. You saw her temper side, not really her good side."

Carl thought that he liked every side of her that he'd seen and that embarrassed him but nobody noticed.

"She can be stubborn and strong-willed but she's smart and will try anything if it don't hurt too much and I'm sure hopin' it don't. She's a very good student and her folks have the kind of money it takes to send her further. She didn't want to and said so. I ain't even heard her but I was told that she plays a pretty good piano. Her mother saw to that." The Marshal stopped for breath.

It was clear that he had an admiration for his granddaughter. He knew more about her than she realized; he cared very much. "And I'm real ashamed of myself for not bein' there for her grandma' or her or her brother and her mother when I was so badly needed. When Lena died, that's her grandma, I wasn't there. After the funeral, her mother lit into me and I was so hurt and ashamed that I left and hardly ever got up the need to see 'em once-in-a-while. I'm even proud a' their pa; he's done the right thing by 'em in spite of what I thought. He brings home pretty good and they've got a good life. I'm about the only bad thing in it and by-God, I'm gonna have to make things right even if they never trust me again." The Marshal's features stayed hard but his eyes softened.

Carl placed his hand on the grandfather's shoulder with understanding. "I didn't find the time to ask her full name and I didn't know about the piano thing and thank you for that. The rest I already know, you didn't have to tell me. I don't know how 'cause she didn't say much about herself. Somehow she told me everything I wanted to know."

The Marshal searched for recognition. "Say, you wouldn't be one of Fred Buechler's boys would you?"

"Why yes, I'm Carl, I'm the oldest. How'd you get to know us?"

The Marshal turned to the onlookers. "... Must be at least a dozen years ago, the law in Maynard quit and the state sent me in there 'til they could find another one. One mornin', about three or four-o-clock, two young fellas, one with a swoll-up mouth and the other a bloody nose, came into the office, where I was sound asleep, screamin' 'bout a big man and stealin' chickens and their ma and a gun and shootin' heads and scared the blazes out a' me. This guy was one of 'em. Well it took me all a' ten seconds to get into my pants and shoes and grab a pair a' cuffs and light out after 'em. I guess I was too slow, 'cause they came back a couple of times to hurry me up. It had to be near a mile or more, clear across town and then some in the country. By the time we got there, I was seein' double.

"Was the damndest thing! Here was this woman, with a gun longer then she was, standin' over a great-big, son-of-a-moose, all trussed up, hands to feet, behind his back, out cold, head all bloody, half the top of one ear lopped off and three or four wide-eyed kids standin' around. I remember a little girl who couldn't a' been more'n three or four, settin' on a tipped-up bucket, tryin' to sooth down a poor old squackin' hen she'd pulled up onto her lap. I was scared that her ma had made good on the promise to 'shoot' his head, but she only gave him one hellish wallop when he started dirty-mouthin' her."

Carl's mind reached back. "Well I'll be darned! Was that you?"

"I'm here tellin' ya', ain't I?"

"Max heard the racket in the henhouse and woke me. We crawled out the window 'cause those chickens were valuable to us and we figured there was somethin' after 'em. Well, there sure was and he'd wrung about a half dozen necks already. He wasn't satisfied to take one to eat; he intended to clean up. With all that racket he must'a been nuts or somethin'. I drove my teeth into his leg and Max made for his ugly face. I saw Max bounce off the roost and I ain't sure if he knocked my teeth out or they stayed in his leg. We ripped in again when one awful explosion stopped everything. Mama stood about five feet away with the Mauser stuck into his face. 'You steal my chicken and hoort my boy? I tink maybe I shoot you head!' We lit out after the sheriff."

"I hauled 'im in and locked 'im up. Didn't tie 'im loose 'til daylight, then I took 'im to the town and they made 'im pick horse shit off a' the street for a month 'til he'd paid for more chickens then he killed and then some. When he was done, I took 'im out to your folks to give your ma the rest a' the money and apologize. Your pa was home then and he took and gave 'im a demonstration a' how to cut stove wood ... Never seen anything like that before! ... Brought his arm 'round over top a' his head so fast, you could hear it whistle, and knocked off a three-foot piece of a fence rail, slick as an axe, with nothin' but his bare hand. Both a' us took the louse and kicked his arse out a' town so hard, I think he's still runnin. I'd sure like to know how your pa did that rail."

"Easy, with the speed. You have to hold your hand just right though, or you can bust it up pretty good." Carl held his up to show the Marshal the scars.

"You can do that?"

"Sure! Papa showed all us boys how. I'll show you some time."

"Well it's sure-'n-blazes a good thing that lard-pot, this mornin', didn't get at you or he'd a' got one hellish surprise." The Marshal laughed.

"Well Papa told us never to use it to purposefully hurt people; he said that he didn't teach us everything."

"How'd your folks get over to Pawlowich's? I met your pa when he was in the throws a' gettin' kicked off Ingmar Thorvaldson's place by that no-good son after Ingmar died."

"Papa went to work for Ingmar for over fourteen years. He and Mama were married there when she came over. Ingmar's wife died some time before that; birthin' that no-good Lars. I sure hated him ... got a-way too many lumps from him when I was growin' up. It's really strange; Ingmar and his Hilda had a girl, 'Angie', a lot older then Lars. Mama called her a perfect angel compared to that miserable kid. Anyway, Mama got over here because Ingmar told Papa that he'd best get that girl that he was making himself sick pining over, as quick as he could because there was a real need for her. I think he gave Papa the money. We were all born over at Ingmar's. Papa mentioned how grateful he was for Ingmar many's the time. How'd you meet Papa then?"

The little face in front of them came to a rest, first on its tiny chin and then on its cheek. The big round eyes flickered and closed. A good uproarious laugh was inspiring but that had quit happening and all this idle chatter was terribly dull. He slept upright and hanging on. Carl nodded to his mother, who broke his feeble grasp, then cradled him on the seat between her and her husband.

"Well, right after Ingmar died," the Marshal continued, "Lars ordered your pa off the place right then. Your pa said he wouldn't, 'cause he had to have time to pack up and find another place for his family and more work. Lars grabbed him and was for throwin' 'im right off. Well, after Lars came-to, he called me and I told 'im your pa was right and that he was very lucky; I'd have done worse. I'd locked Lars up a couple a' times before that, for bein' drunk and goin' after women. I told your pa that it might be best to get out a' there quick 'cause Lars was nuts and could hurt some of you. Anyway, you were gone before he healed up. Did you go to Pawlowich's after that?"

"No not yet! We had nowhere to go and no money so we set up a kind of a camp alongside the creek for most of that summer 'cause Papa couldn't find work right then. Things were pretty slim 'cause Mama had to leave most of her garden at Ingmar's when that louse kicked us off."

"If I'd 'a known, it wouldn't 'a happened. She came to me over the garden and we went out to get some of it but there wasn't much left after that louse and the weeds got through. God, I wish she'd 'a told me how bad things were for you."

"Anyway, Max and me always looked after the chickens for all the eggs and meat that we wanted at Ingmar's and we sure missed them. One night we decided that we could sure use some eggs so we went over to Ivan Pawlowich's. They had lots of chickens and we figured it wouldn't hurt if we took a few eggs. Well, wouldn't you know, Ivan caught us and was for whippin' us good but Mary stopped him. 'Kids steal apples and candy for devilment,' she said. 'They steal eggs because they have to.'

"Thank God for the Pawlowiches. They had an old yard on the land Ivan bought near town. It was pretty run down but they moved us into it and helped fix it up to be liveable. It was a lot better than where we were. Ivan was gettin' old and the work was too much for him. He'd have to give up some of his land because their only kid, a girl, was married and had moved away.

"Papa needed work, we needed a place to call home, Ivan needed help; it was ideal for both. Little sister Bertha, the one sittin' on the bucket, took awful sick right after that because of the hellish summer and would surely have died because we couldn't afford the doctor or medicine. Ivan helped us there too. We've been there ever since. They were the ones who gave us the chickens to look after, if we gave 'em the eggs that they needed, and the two little egg thieves would look after 'em. That's why we fought so hard. Ivan died a short time after my Mama."

"She's dead? She was always so healthy and active. God, I'm sure sorry to hear that. You maybe didn't know, 'cause you kids were in school, but the day after the chicken thievin', your ma had me out for the best damn chicken dinner I'd ever ate ... Said she didn't plan it that way but that's what happened and would a' been worse if I wasn't there ... Said she'd be in jail now 'cause she'd a' shot 'im, no doubt. She was quite the woman. God, that's too bad! Why is it only miserable buggers live forever?"

"We ran Ivan's place for Mary this year," Carl added, "but Mary said that there's no point in her hangin' on to it, so she wants to sell. She offered it to us but the banker threw Papa out when we went to him, miserable smart talkin' sonuvagun. We had to keep Papa off 'a him. So we're about to be nowhere again and Papa's too old and had too much hurt — that's why I'm here now. Ain't got much left. It's all up to me now." His voice broke.

"Well, where are ya headed?"

Carl heard that the plains of the western Canadian Territories were unpeopled and as open and good-producing as Kansas, with a lot more moisture. The ads said that anyone could file on a hundred and sixty acres of land for ten dollars if you lived on it and broke it.

Carl didn't have any specific location in mind and his first job was to look around and see what was to be had until the money was gone. He heard that there was lots of work in the territories on the railroad and stuff, so maybe he could find some to keep him for the winter and start looking again in the spring. His family was hoping he could latch on to something yet this fall, before the snow flew, but they heard winter comes early up there. Papa had warned Carl not to take any foolish risks. If he couldn't find anything, he wasn't supposed to stay because his life was worth more than any land.

Coming back home a failure was not an option; Carl'd promised everyone.

Paul, the young father, listened without a word. When Carl had finished, Paul looked to Mildred, who obviously read his thoughts because they hadn't discussed anything. "We've got some room in the house. You can bunk in with us until you find something and get a place built."

Mildred's response was one of anticipation. "You bet you can and we'd be glad to have you."

Paul resumed what he was about to say before Mildred's invitation. "You won't have to look far for land neither. There's still a lots a' land available and some of it's pretty good lookin' too. I'm sure there's a real good quarter, just a mile or so away, that's still for the taking. I've hunted over it the last couple of years. It runs up against some of the Doukhobor land.

"They're really good neighbours, very helpful if you need 'em and they're more than willing to give you the loan of tools and stuff if you need it, or if you're hard up ... not much meat but they sure know how to spread a table. They've never seen me hungry 'til I got somethin' to grow ... matter of fact, they're lookin' to the care of my teams and they gave me the loan of a milk cow until I can pay them somehow. I've helped them quite a bit with harvest and wood cuttin' and stuff for doin' mine because they've got a steam outfit. They got a sawmill set up with the same engine and they sawed all of the lumber for our house and the barn and helped build 'em too. You can't go far wrong with them.

"I'm sure you won't find anything better, no matter where you look, and we're hopin' you'll agree. You can use a team and I'll give you a hand to get started — so will they. Nobody can make it alone without a little help out there. We need another good neighbour."

"I hate to be a nuisance!"

Mildred interjected. "I haven't even seen my own home yet, but Paul drew me a picture and I've even got plans already for where I'll put you."

"Hey son, ya' can't get a better offer than that. You'll have to take it." The Marshal smiled at the fortunes of the young man who looked enthusiastic about becoming a permanent appendage to his small family.

Carl couldn't remember another time in his life when anyone, other than the family and the Pawlowiches, ever gave a damn about what happened to him. He hesitated no further. "Count me in." Everyone cheered! They couldn't help but hear. Carl had become the center of considerable interest that afternoon.

Paul shook Carl's hand and Mildred with her beautiful big smile said, "Welcome to our humble home. I am not really sure what it is yet, but I'll make it nice and homey really quick."

"Some of the Doukhobor gals gave me a hand with some of that," Paul stated, "but they didn't have much of a variety of paint. They sure are lookin' forward to greetin' you, Mildred. I'm afraid I done a lot a' talkin' and thinkin' about you, out loud. They've made a beautiful quilt for our bed and a nice crib for Jimmy and a few of the guys were workin' on some more furniture when I left to bring you back so I don't know what there'll be by the time we get there. Now they'll be really tickled because, instead of two, I'm comin' back with three. Everybody out there gets real anxious for a new face."

"We're going to have to really get on it pretty quick and get you built and settled. I hear that it gets lonely out there for a woman during the winter. Paul tells me that there's only one Doukhobor girl who speaks

English and I'm going to need another woman to talk to pretty soon. I'm really counting on you to get me one. Just imagine — two Millys."

"Wait a minute, there's a whole lot more then Milly waitin'. You might just get more company and neighbours then you're bargaining for. I've got four brothers and a sister waitin' and Papa's been waitin' all his life for land that we could call our own. Before Mama died, she made me promise I'd try real hard. I don't know how I can ever thank all of you for the promise you've already given me and the hope; yesterday I didn't have any."

They had a very early morning. Mildred rested her head on Paul's shoulder and was soon asleep. Paul had been nearly sick with anxiety when her letter told him that she was pregnant. It really hurt but he just couldn't be there. Now they were here with him and on their way to their new home and their new life together. He realized how much he had been alone and how he never wanted to be and wouldn't be ever again. God, they were beautiful! He stroked the sleeping child, kissed his wife's hair, then rested his head on the top of hers and dozed off with her.

Carl watched all of this with poorly clad emotion and intense gratitude. How could everything work out so right so fast? Was this real or was it dream that would fall apart if he woke up, and leave him back where he was? Nothing good ever happened to him or his family so easy.

"Papa was all alone in the old country. His family died of the plague or some such. He never really wanted to talk about it very much. Mama told me most of what I know. She met Papa during the war when he was in the hospital. I guess they dragged 'im off the street when he was a starving kid and slaved 'im from one farm to another and kicked 'im around an awful lot. The army just took and grabbed him one day, right out of the field and forced him to fight the French. That's how he got so badly hurt. Well, after he got blown up and shot a couple of times, he finally decided that it was hopeless and they were surely going to kill 'im if he stayed there so he left and had to hide or they'd 'a shot him as a deserter. He got a chance to get out of the country and come here. You know just about how good it's been here for us," Carl concluded.

———

The ancient locomotive, since the band-aid repair, had apparently gained new vigour and strove to excel. The speed increased alarmingly on the rolling old track and the trees and telegraph poles flashed by. The crew was intent on making up some of the lost time and the train rolled into Mason City with record speed, screeching to a violent stop. The sleepers didn't doze through that even if they managed to keep their seats.

Almost before the engine stopped, crews went at it to finish the partial repair. Again, they would lose a little time but it was unavoidable. Mason City was far better equipped to deal with locomotive repair and had some of the parts. A greased-over workman told the passengers that it would be nothing less than two hours so they might just as well walk around a bit. There'd be three consecutive whistles when they were just about ready to leave. He apologized for the delays and hoped nobody was too badly put out. Other than a few disappointed grunts and repressed curses, nobody complained too loudly.

Carl and Paul climbed off with the Marshal. Little Jimmy was still asleep, despite the bone-shuddering stop, so Mildred stayed put. This was the Marshal's stop so they walked with him, through the newly built station to the front and out into the street. The large clock on the face of the building told them that it was nearly half-past two and they would have to find a suitable place to get something. Carl's big school lunch bag sat forsaken on a bench by the door of Bertha's back in Charles City, a victim of Carl's romantic encounter and lapsed memory. He hadn't even realized that until they talked about eating.

The main street of Mason City was in many ways very similar to Charles. Because it was mid-afternoon, the place bustled. A large freight wagon moved across their vision and headed around the building to give as well as take.

"Whatta samhill happened t' ya' loafers?" the driver roared. "I heard a' late but, jeez, half-a day? When the samhill they gonna git ya' an engine 'stead a' that museum piece?"

Somebody roared back an obscene answer but with all the rattle the exact epithet was, thankfully, inaudible.

The popular traffic was all in their direction. The train was very important to the town and when it was so very late, it generated anxiety. The train carried no ice and fresh vegetables and fruit were very perishable and of great concern to the merchants. The shelf life would be reduced and so would the take. Apparently, the aged engine had achieved an undeniable reputation and was clearly nearing the end of its service.

The Marshal led them up the main street for several blocks, then down a prominent side street, to a large, brick-faced building fronted by a blind-folded lady holding a balance beam aloft. Carl knew this was the court-house. The Marshal suggested that they could enter with him but that they would have to stay in the lobby while he went to acknowledge that he was there to escort the "scum" back to Des Moines. He wanted to check the wares, to know what he had to "see, hear, and smell" all the way back.

They sat on a big, carved, wooden bench and stared up at the elegantly painted figures on the grand, vaulting ceiling. Carl'd read about Da Vinci and a fellow named "Angelo" and how they'd done so much of the same thing so long ago and he was fascinated. He really wondered how it was possible. He got all cramped up and kinky-necked painting the ceilings at home and at the Pawlowich's.

The Marshal returned quickly, muttering about the "… ugliest son of Satan!" he'd ever seen and how he'd have to be on his guard with this one.

They headed back to find Mildred sitting in the bustling station, the bright-eyed cherub on her lap, grasping gleefully at a wisp of cigar smoke floating just out of reach. Mildred didn't ask, she just thrust the baby into Carl's arms and stated, with an impish smile, "Might as well get the feel of it now." She was a bit surprised.

"Had five of 'em at home … all younger'n me."

Mildred finished doing up the buttons on her vest. "Sure beats soured bottles and a sick baby." Paul was startled by the lack of discretion on the part of his risqué wife. He'd been alone most of his life and he lacked the parental nonchalance.

"What? I covered him and myself with the blanket!" she snapped, almost annoyed with Paul's implied accusation. "Let's go eat." She left Jimmy with Carl. The kid was enthralled by the varied and peculiar expressions he observed on the face of his newfound friend as they made their way down the street.

"Well," Mildred noted, "I've got myself one sure-fired, good babysit-ter and somebody's goin' to have an awfully good daddy some day."

Carl didn't respond or react. He didn't even hear them chuckle. He was busy entertaining.

Carl didn't order all that much because of the heavy breakfast and the fact that he wasn't working. He excused himself and handed Jimmy back to his mother on the pretence of going to the biffy out back. He dug five dollars from one of his multitude of hiding places. The Marshal worried about his light appetite and offered to pay again but Carl declined politely.

Paul had noticed a large plot filled with machinery on the way in, so he and Carl went to have a look while the Marshal, whose return train wouldn't leave until tomorrow morning, went window shopping with Mildred for as long as Jimmy stayed awake.

————

It was like a walk through Wonderland. The face of farming was changing so very quickly. The world of technology had already surpassed the ability of the average producer to cope. Carl was just in the process of trying to establish himself on some land in a nowhere place that no one but the desperate and destitute had even heard about and before his eyes sat the destiny of his industry ... machines, huge beyond his imagination! Threshing machines dwarfed anything the Pawlowiches had and Carl thought they were equipped better than most. Pictures showed these monsters in action ... up to twenty men to keep them filled ... ten teams ... up to a hundred acres in a day ... steam tractors capable of pulling up to twenty plough bottoms with a crew of ten men just to set them in and out of the ground and keep the engine watered and fed.

Even more amazing was an absolutely new concept that Carl and Paul had only heard about and now here it was — no more water, no more coal and no more steam; power by exploding gasoline. The ones here were stationary engines but they had pictures of gasoline-powered traction engines as big as the steamers, capable of running the big separators. They were being built no farther away than Charles City by Hart and Parr. To the boys it was nothing more than a dream but it was something they would have to talk about and imagine.

————

They found Mildred back in the car with sleeping Jimmy and a warm crackling fire in the potbelly. Her dismal expression alarmed Paul.

"What happened?"

"Nothing ... to us. One of the repair men just told me that it didn't look like this locomotive was going to take us anywhere without some major repair and that it was amazing that it brought us this far."

"So what now?"

"They're going to try to find another engine and run it up tonight ... Marshal's talking to them right now to see what we should do. He'll be back right away to tell us."

Carl had some bedding in his packs that would help. He walked back to the freight car to check on all his stuff but the door had a big railroad padlock on it and nobody was around with a key. When he got back, the Marshal was there, surrounded by disgruntled passengers, with Calvin, the heavy gentleman, as the spokesman. "When ta hell kin we git goin'?"

"They told me that we should be rolling again by dark and if not, the rail road'll stand good for whatever we need," the Marshal responded.

"That ain't the point, dammit! Some 'a us just got ta git back awful quick. I just come ta bury my Pa 'cause there's only my sister and her two kids and she ain't well. Wife and kids are back home with fifty acres a' crop still waitin' and winter ta be got ready for. This flea-bit outfit would do better with at least a shoestring ta run on. Aw hell, what's the use? Might just as well take 'er easy. Cussin' ain't goin' ta help." Calvin threw up his hands with a disgusted snort, and along with some of the others, turned and walked back up town.

"Sorry folks! Not many strings I can pull for you in this case."

The railroad treated everybody to supper at the same place they had eaten that afternoon. They said that they'd found an engine and it was on its way. Nobody seemed to know when it would get here but if it wasn't before ten this evening, they'd make things good for the night. Carl took real advantage of the big meal because he hadn't eaten very much that afternoon and was beginning to wish that he had.

The locomotive didn't get there and accommodations weren't all that available. A few of the fairer people opened their homes and that helped. The Marshal got the family a room in the small hotel and even offered his bed to Carl.

"No sir, but I thank you kindly. I've got everything I need in my packs. I'll get them to open up and I'll be just fine in the car with the other fellas. You've got that 'son of Satan' to worry about in the morning and you're goin' to need your rest. Besides, you're the closest thing to a grandpa I'll ever have."

The Marshal was grateful, not for the inference, but for the fact that he was dead tired. His age was beginning to burden him. He'd only slept a couple of hours last night.

Carl slept hard, even when the locomotive roared up at two-thirty. He'd asked the time and then dropped off again. They weren't going to leave until eight the next morning anyway.

———

"What ta blazes!"

The car slammed violently. Carl found himself between the seats.

"Gad dammit!" Calvin charged past in a black rage and didn't stop at the door. He wrenched it open and barrelled through. Carl upped himself and hurried after, fearing the worst for the perpetrator of this rude awakening. The door was swinging back and hurried as he was, it caught him on the side of his head and dropped him with stunning force. He crouched on his knees, waited for his head to clear, then rose and wobbled off the car step into the cold half-light. The fury was just about to begin when he got to the rescue; Calvin had a crewman pinned to the side of the car.

"Quit this! Good Lord! Ain't things bad enough?"

Both combatants looked over with a frozen stare, their dispute forgotten. They took Carl by both arms and dragged him to a bench on the platform.

"What happened to you?"

"What happened?" Calvin roared. "Ya' slam ta' hell out a' us and throw everybody out a' their seat! 'T'a hell d' ya' think happened? Jeez, what a mess! Set down 'fore ya' fall down."

Carl was, at first, frightened, than puzzled. "What are ya doing?"

"What are we doin'? Jest look at yerself!"

Carl did, he was a sheet of blood all the way down his shirt and his pant leg. He touched the side of his head where it hurt and his hand came away covered with it. The crewman yanked off his scarf and twisted it around Carl's head so tight that it seemed to crush.

By the time the family boarded, a doctor had stitched the bloody gash, bound it with a tight bandage, given Carl a powerful pain killer and ordered him off his feet for two days. "If the headache doesn't quit in the next couple days, you've likely got a concussion and you'll need a hospital."

Burly Calvin had lifted Carl both on and off the freight wagon that hauled him to the small hospital and had personally carried him back to his seat in the car, covered him as gently as a baby, then sat on the next seat, fretting openly, wishing he hadn't been, "... sa damned stupert!"

Carl was the happiest of the lot. The powerful medication left him blissfully unconcerned.

The train jolted to a start. Carl hadn't heard the usual beller because the intimidating Calvin had pacified the belligerent trainman. It didn't happen. Carl dropped into a hollow, fitful sleep; aware, yet not aware. Sounds echoed. Someone had obviously grabbed him by the feet and was swinging him in wide circles and he struggled desperately against them, then ... nothing.

III
"What a place this is!"

"Whoa! Whoa! Take it easy!"

His brain exploded into a multitude of cracks and hisses, colours and swirling faces. He shut his eyes and lay back to wait for the melee to subside. The circumstances began to filter back.

His eyes opened to stability and the face of the angel. He stared in disbelief. No, no angel; it was little Jimmy. Mildred leaned directly over Carl with the child under one arm, his face just inches away from Carl's.

"Boy, you certainly had us worried. You were out a long time. You started to toss around so much that Calvin and Paul had to hold you to keep you from hurting yourself some more."

"How's yer head?" Calvin's big face blotched in.

"You can bet I know it's still up there!" It throbbed wildly. "It's better to suffer a bit then to have to put up with what that stuff did to me. That stuff is wild crazy. I've never felt like that in my entire life and I hope to never have it happen again. Hey, where are we?" Carl sat up again. The clatter of the wheels and the abrupt rocking were gone. "Why ain't we movin'? Busted again?"

"We're just out a' St. Paul. Had ta stop 'cause some jack lost a herd a cattle on the track. You just started to wake up when we stopped ... can see the light from here, we're that close."

"St. Paul? God, did that stuff dope me! How long was I out?"

"You've been sleeping since eight this morning — it's six now, so you can guess. You hungry?" Mildred asked.

"More thirsty then anything." He rose to his feet and hung on. His head still hurt but not the deep hurt, just the surface pain around the cut

{ 34 }

and bruise. He reached up to a very heavy bandage. "You got a mirror?" Mildred obliged from her shoulder bag.

He looked a lot worse than he felt. The bandage seeped through with dried blood over the cut. He saw why he was having difficulty seeing out of that eye; there wasn't much room left to see out of. The entire side of his face was welted an ugly blue-green with an angry red bruise running down past his cheekbone where the door hit but didn't cut.

"I didn't think that I hit that hard."

"Well boy, yer head sure rocked and ya' dropped like a stone. Ya' were runnin' after this hot-head."

"You got a change of clothes? You're all bloody."

Carl dug faded overalls out of the grip and an equally bleached smock. His modesty crawled him under the old blanket to change; there was nowhere else. The shirt stuck to his skin when he tried to remove it ... soaked right through and dried. He had to pry it away in a few places. "Just like a stuck pig!" he joked. "Wonder what Milly'd think a' me now?"

Mildred smiled. "Well you sure threw us when we first saw you; the floor near the door was covered with blood. We thought that somebody had clubbed you for your money."

"My money, oh Lord!" Carl grabbed under the seat for his mackinaw. It wasn't there — he verged on panic.

"Easy! Marshal said that would be one of the first places a thief would look ... told me to watch it until you woke up. Here it is. For goodness sake, you never 'put all your eggs in one basket.' If somebody lifts it, you're broke as well as cold."

"The Marshal? Ah shoot! I never got to talk to him before I passed out. Did he say anything?"

"He was sure sorry to see this happen. He said to tell you if the choice was his, you'd be it. He wished you all kinds of better luck than this. He said he wouldn't worry Milly or your folks about this ... figured you were so damned hard-headed that you wouldn't even remember this by next week and he left this for you." Paul handed Carl an envelope.

A greying fur-ball with ears and a wildly, waving Stetson, "Hayaa'ed!" past the window and another followed. Cattle bawled. Hooves pounded.

"Never heard of a fence?" Calvin's big head barely framed through the opened window and rolled with the action. "Need some lessons on lookin' ta cattle?" He stopped in disbelief and his humour changed to disgust. "Ah fer Gad sake, put 'at horse in the saddle and you git under it. He's sure'n hell smarter'n you!"

The linkage crashed violently, throwing Calvin off balance. His hands flailed out wildly, losing their purchase on the panel that dropped him into a violent headlock, which must have hurt to beat blazes. He regained his balance but lost his composure. The already blue air changed to a vivid scarlet. His powerful arms pistoned the panel up with such force that the frame separated at the corners, then he rammed it back down with an equivalent emphasis. The glass cracked but remained in place. It would no longer function as an entity.

Black with rage, Calvin turned toward the shocked and disapproving stares of his cohorts. He stood a moment, contemplating his verbiage and he was embarrassed. "Jeez, I'm sure sorry fer the way I swear!"

He leaned/struggled his way back to his seat, fighting the insane acceleration. The brakes screamed and he catapulted toward the open door and the back of the next coach. He dropped to his knees to avoid the consequence and would have skidded past his seat had his big hand not grabbed the post on the way by and slingshot himself forcefully into it. If that alone didn't set him off again, what he saw happen to the others surely did.

People and property flew from everywhere. A large grip left the shelf above, barely missing Carl's bandaged head and bounced forcefully off his shoulder, striking Mildred squarely on the back of her neck, driving her violently toward the seat ahead with Jimmy trapped between. Paul's arm, with lightning speed, waist-rounded her and alone averted the disaster. Jimmy remained glued to her grasp, screaming wildly.

Mildred's desperate, "No!" fell on deaf ears. Paul squeezed through the door just ahead of Calvin.

"You alright?" Carl asked on his way by, despite his screaming head. She was stronger than she looked or he was weaker. She held him fast. Her words were emphatic and clear. "Sit down! You may wish you were dead but I don't! You will be if you try!" She pulled him into the seat beside her and went to quieting the frightened child.

After his head cleared and the enraged rush passed, Carl and Mildred left the car to view the consequences. The fireman and the engineer left the cabin air-borne, both landing in the midst of the angered male passengers who yanked them upright. Paul and Calvin followed. The station crew's timely intervention stopped the blow that Calvin sent in the direction of the engineer and the stationmaster held Paul in check.

Again the forceful "No!" held Carl back.

"Ya' were mad over the cattle were ya'? I'll show you mad!" The crew held Calvin. "All the way from Des Moines, ya' bin slammin' us around. Look at ta' head on that young fella." Calvin nodded toward Carl. "An' that woman all covered in blood." She was, so Mildred moved to help. "And what about that screamin' baby? If he's hurt you can be damn sure this bastard ain't seein' mornin'."

"Your threats ain't scarin' us, ya' big bag a' shit!"

The hand of an elderly man, near the vulgar trainman, caught him full on the mouth and despite his size, rocked him backward into the crowd. The man followed, intent on blood, but the assemblage stopped him. The trainman never said another word. He feared far worse.

"That woman covered in blood is my wife. Now I'm goin' to say this only once." He turned on the conductor, who'd just gotten there. "If either a' them bastards are on this rig, let alone on the controls, we ain't throwin' them off near as nice as those two fella's did and I'm takin' over. I run these damn things before you were born and I can do it better in my sleep. Get 'em ta hell away from us and this train. Just see to it!" He drew his finger right up under the conductor's nose. Then he turned away toward Mildred and his injured wife. The crowd and tempers dispersed and the nerves steadied. Mildred would have reprimanded Paul for his rash action but the expression on his normally tranquil features warned her. Paul had a long fuse but the force at the end of it was formidable.

The injury didn't cripple Carl's appetite. The proprietor of the small cafe observed, with concern, the extent of Carl's capacity and questioned the wisdom of his, "on the house" contribution to the hero's well-being.

A doctor, bag in hand, appeared mysteriously, commenting on, "One hell of a train ride!" and insisting on viewing the injury, compliments of the railroad. Mildred told him about their concerns all that afternoon.

It hurt horribly when the doctor stripped off the dried bandage, tearing at the cut and starting it bleeding again. He checked the wound carefully, swabbed it with a disinfectant and ointment and bound it again with a smaller bandage. He checked Carl's vision then stated that there was no sign of a concussion. "What medication?"

Carl didn't know, so Mildred produced the small bottle.

"Damnation! Little wonder he slept all day. Lucky he didn't sleep forever. Where in hell did they teach that guy?" To Mildred he said, "As soon as you get back on that train, you pitch that as far as you can throw. Give him only as many of these as he needs for pain, there shouldn't be too much from here on, and make sure the baby doesn't get near this stuff." He produced a smaller bottle of innocent-looking white pills. "Good luck!" He patted Carl on the back, packed his bag, and disappeared as mysteriously as he had come, to tend to the other injuries.

This was a coal stop so they'd be here a while. The city, twinned with Minneapolis, was large and bright. It piqued Carl's curiosity but he headed right back to the car with Mildred and took it easy. He thought it wise not to push his luck. Mildred administered the "little white pill," while Carl clashed wills with her son over the issue of sleep. He had wanted to get, at least, a passing view of the "Twin City" and the Mississippi but Jimmy was a formidable opponent. Carl didn't even get to observe the two forlorn figures, standing on the platform, watching their former charge steam away.

———

Mildred plunked Jimmy on Carl's chest and watched him wiggle up to Carl's face. The eyes focused on the bandage, the little hand shot out, and Mildred hoisted Jimmy clear. "Good morning! How are you feeling now? We're pulling into Fargo so I thought I'd better wake you."

Jimmy resented the intrusion into his enterprise with a sudden temperous wail. Carl sat up, took his hard and fast friend, and the problem as quickly righted itself. "A whole lot better than I did after that dope I took yesterday. My headache is gone and I can see and hear straight again."

Without asking, Mildred handed him the mirror. The gross discolouration remained but he looked a little more like himself.

"Where did you say ...? Oh yeah ... Fargo! I guess I'm not quite all here yet. Wish I could have seen the lakes."

"Don't feel too bad ... bet ya'll be back this way soon Was pitch black, couldn't see a damn thing anyway. Brewed some coffee a while back

— think it's still warm. Want some?" Calvin handed Carl a quart jar half full of the toxic-looking brown fluid. It was still warm and tasted a lot better than it looked. He drained it under the watchful eye of his lap mate, who reached to sample anything that was left. Jimmy didn't really react too well to refusal but he forgave and forgot, quickly.

Fargo was a junction. Carl and the family had to head north along the old Pembina route to Winnipeg. Carl had hunted up and read a lot about the early days of the place; the Selkirk settlers, the fight for wealth and power between the two trade giants, the North West and the Hudson's Bay Companies, and the Red River uprising at Fort Garry; now Winnipeg. He was fascinated by living history and anticipated actually being where this stuff happened.

This was Louis Riel's ground. Carl couldn't understand how it was possible for Louis Riel, who fought only to keep what already belonged to his people, to be so villainized. As near as Carl could tell, what Riel did had kicked the country awake; Manitoba came in, they organized a police force and built the railroad that would carry settlers like him out there. And for all that, they tried and hung Riel in a backward place with the ironic name of "Pile of Bones."

They said Riel was crazy. Well, based on all of Carl's experience, as far as he could tell, if those were the actions of a crazy man, then the world could do with a lot less brains.

Paul said that the Canadian Government claimed they had to do all of that for only one reason and that was the threat of American expansion. "All we want is some land and a chance. There sure ain't any where we were. When you're as broke as everyone is here, it don't matter on which side of a line you are."

The back freighter and a flatcar, were loaded with the property of the people who had to head west and that included Calvin. They'd hook on to another, sleeker outfit for the trip to Bismarck and beyond.

Calvin was predictable. Carl appreciated the genuine nature of the man. There was never any doubt where Calvin stood on every issue. If he liked something, you knew it, if he didn't and you pushed it, chances were you would feel it. The bump on the head gave Carl a solid and dependable friend. He hated to see Calvin going off.

Calvin was the hand-shaking kind. There was nothing sentimental in his nature. "If, by some chance, yer ever in the Bismarck country and ya' don't look me up, ya'd best not let me find out about it. So long young fella."

Carl had been exceedingly fortunate until now. He had spent little of his own on feeding himself. The envelope from the Marshal had contained five ten-dollar bills with a note implying that this was merely an investment in the future of his great grandchildren.

Would he ever see Milly again? God, he sure wanted to.

Tracked by questioning stares, Carl bought biscuits, bread, a jar of strawberry jam and some smoked sausage at a small store near the station. Jimmy was asleep again and they couldn't see any eating place close by. It would be too long to Grand forks. Paul said that there wouldn't be much between the "Forks" and the "Peg" as he called them. He'd gotten caught that way his first trip out.

This train would haul them right through, then return the way it had come with whatever there was to bring back. Usually, a large part of the cargo was human; those who had tried and were broken by the effort. The trainman commented that they had done this, "Too ga'-damn many times! … bunch a' damn traitors! Best they git ta hell out'a the States and stay there! Good riddance!" Obviously, the Marshal and Calvin were gone and the thug was again intent on re-establishing his domain but he steered clear of Carl.

Other than Calvin and a few they added from the west, the people in the car stayed the same. Canada was a common destiny.

Paul was surprised when they got to Grand Forks. He had passed through in the dark, coming down, so it was over a year since he had last seen it in daylight. The main street had had a considerable facelift and an astute businessman had seen fit to build a neat, sizeable restaurant right next to the station and was capitalizing handsomely on the wisdom of the location. The place was packed, the service and the food were superior and the setting offered an excellent view. Carl thought he'd bring Milly here someday soon, when he came to get her.

Carl insisted on treating Paul and Mildred to a large meal at a very reasonable price but they ate quietly. Carl was there only in body; his responses were as abstract as his state of mind. This time, Mildred interjected when

Paul attempted to break the spell; she knew exactly what it meant. Paul had lived through it too and now they saw themselves in Carl's eyes. Everything was so fast, so insecure, so indefinite.

The whistle screamed a crude reality, and they hurried back from their anxieties.

... Next stop, Canada and the "Promised Land."

———

Other than the inevitable question of who they were, where they were heading, and to do what, the actual border crossing was hardly worth noting, yet inflicted an odd, unforeseen emotional reaction.

Mildred had a secure life before Paul strode into it — now she was leaving its security with her baby and his strange father, for a new country that she knew nothing about; an open, blank future filled with question and anticipated promise. She loved it! She leaned over the face of their child and delivered a kiss to the mouth of her life-mate that should have been more discreetly delivered in the intimacy of their bedroom. Everyone saw and smiled and dropped into their own anxiety.

Carl felt again like a child. He needed security, yet security was his to build and to offer to his own. He stared everybody's destiny in the face. It was blank, expressionless, unforgiving; his to mould. His determination was rock-solid — his emotions, on the other hand, shook with uncertainty. He couldn't fail. He'd die first!

He saw Mildred's kiss. He felt Milly's warm, soft lips, he tasted a hint of lip rouge, he smelled her perfume and he felt her warmth. He had to find and build a life. With her, he knew he could do what had to be done; she'd be his security. Here, at least, maybe he had a chance. This was urgent, this was real, this was necessary and immediate.

Paul was right, the distance between the border and Winnipeg was long, naturally wild, bursting with fertility and potential, filling with life and green and production. Yet it had a long way to go and it was in a hurry. The train wasn't.

It was very late when they rolled into the ragged, burgeoning "Gateway to the West" and everything had to be off-loaded, then reloaded. That, thankfully, wouldn't happen until morning.

Carl had done little but sleep the last two days and the thought suddenly occurred to him, *What have the others done?* It was October, he had his bed-roll, and he had often slept in stables and on hard floors wrapped in its warmth. There were enough seats so that most could stretch out on one. Miraculously, quilts, or sleeping rolls, or horse blankets, and duffle-bag pillows appeared from underneath, or above, or in, or behind and everyone settled down. There had to be hotels or boarding houses but it was too late and too dark and nobody knew the town or had much money.

The potbelly blazed; not the doing of the very disagreeable trainman. Carl wasn't sure just how it got there but he knew that Paul had become fairly adept at enforcing the need.

Jimmy, who slept on their seat, wrapped in a barely adequate wicker basket, which served to carry all their bedding for the trip, was strangely silent all evening. His mother was a good and generous provider. She and Paul slept fully clothed, with the exception of jackets and vests and shoes, between a heavy feather ticking and an ample woollen quilt stretched out under the seats ahead of theirs so that they wouldn't get stepped on and could attend to Jimmy, if he woke up, without disturbing anyone unnecessarily.

Carl lay awake for a long time, just thinking and wishing and dreaming. Finally, the little pill kicked in and he drifted off until the sun broke.

———

"What a place this is!"

Trains sat nearby, building steam for the day's journey. People took from one and gave to another, mostly east to westbound ... The world before their incredulous eyes, the "Melting Pot", the "Promised Land" ... Hope and opportunity, joy, anticipation, fear, anxiety, certainty and uncertainty, reckless abandon, tearful departure; nothing stable, predictable, guaranteed, all bound for the "Last Best West."

Carl was up before the others and took a quick look around the station, which was already bursting with strange life and dress that Carl had never seen or even imagined in his sheltered life. The huge building echoed languages that Carl couldn't imagine as understandable, just a rambling babble that came so fast!

How they loved colour and volumes of cloth. There were men with slouched hats, fur hats, pointed hats, tall and short, pulled well down or sitting on top, men with baggy pants and heavy jackets, men with high, leather, military looking and short, heavy work boots or flat sandals, pointed or rounded, even moccasins. There were men with moustaches, just pencil lines or heavy handlebars, rarely one without and men with big and small beards. There were women, shaped like walking triangles, who swayed past, wrapped in all that yardage, in keeping with custom and against the morning cold, with shawls and elaborate, often ridiculous hats of every variety, all marked with culture, style, nationality, class, and status.

"Golly!" Mildred stood on the platform by the car step, her eyes bulging just as Carl's were. The tempo and the volume increased drastically. Paul, standing behind her, had anticipated the response and found it humorous to see; he'd done exactly the same.

The rest of the bread and jam, biscuits and sausage, without coffee or even water disappeared quickly and with gratitude. Jimmy, fed first, was as bug-eyed as his mother, too fascinated by all the action to be frightened or even very hungry. They had to move fast; one wanted to be rid of them, the other wanted them on quickly ... all hurried, impatient, demanding.

Paul just had Mildred's volume of luggage. It was amazing how much a baby needed. Carl helped them to their assigned car, then they went after his as directed. There was lots but it was carefully and cleverly packed, compact and heavy. The car and the space were carefully assigned according to destination. These guys were very well organized.

Within a half an hour everything had been moved, assigned, and secured, even their seat in the car, now heaped with Jimmy's immediate needs. This would be a tight, uncomfortable ride. Now they would have a bit of time while the heavier things were loaded. It would be far less than Carl's historic inquisition desired.

They'd have to take most of the food they'd need for the next couple of days because most of the stops would be short and there wouldn't be much opportunity or place. Paul had found that out the hard way the first time. There'd been nobody to warn him. Carl regretted forgetting his lunch bag at Bertha's but it would likely be stale or mouldy by now anyway. Besides, he had a real need to go back and get it as soon as he could.

They bought stuff that was mostly dry or canned and would keep ... plenty of bread, more than enough. They wouldn't be hungry. There'd always be water. They filled up as much as they could hold at a little, close-by, Chinese restaurant. Paul even filled a couple of two-quarters with sugary tea ... no time for history this trip.

Paul said this was an ideal connection. "Comin' back this way, you'll have a longer wait. You'll have a chance to look around some, but experience tells me that you won't be interested; you'll have other things on your mind. I sure hope she'll do for you what mine did for me." Carl blushed but he saw Paul wasn't kidding. It put a huge smile on Carl's face but an ache in his heart.

There was more stuff and people to contend with than even the railroad anticipated and it took longer than expected, so they had a bit of time to wander around the station area. Paul took them around the building to show them the first locomotive to cross this country. It sat, still functional, behind the station. Somebody had assigned it the title, "The Countess of Dufferin." Just who the lady was and what she had done to deserve the honour, nobody knew or cared. She'd be moneyed and influential.

The place just boomed ... buildings going up everywhere. A big hotel not that far from the station, determined the faith and intention of the place. Broad thoroughfares, already marked out, indicated foresight and planning. An architect's drawing on the wall of the station indicated the likelihood of a new and elaborate structure very soon. Piles of freshly dug earth indicated that the intent was already becoming reality.

Carl had never been that close to this kind of industry. It was very much different than he'd imagined. There was no stockade surrounded by log shacks and tepees, no history to be seen, only the promise of the future.

Was this the nature of this country? Would he be as successful? Then why were all those guys who came before, throwing up their hands and coming back? What was the danger, the trap? Carl was very worried. He wished that he hadn't gone and seen. Some were very excited and others, like Carl, walked back to the train very quiet and thoughtful.

Paul didn't seem concerned and that gave Carl renewed hope and courage.

"Just don't expect to see this kind of stuff when you get there," he told Mildred and Carl.

"Well just what should we expect to see when we get there?" she asked in an accusing tone marked by her impish smile.

"Bush and grass, hot and cold, wet and dry, light and dark, work and very darn little rest and less reward, day after day 'til you lose track of days and time. Work, sleep, and work again. Very little time and very few people to talk to and then you have a heck of a time because they don't understand you and you can't understand them but they are learning and so will you. I've picked up lots of Russian in the last couple of years and I've taught even more English. We've all developed a system of sign language that, it seems, everybody understands.

"We're all in the same trough out there so we understand what others think because we've all got the same problems, the same thoughts, and the answers are always the same. When it gets too big we have to depend on one another for help to get through it. That's the way it is. Have I scared ya' enough yet?"

"Heck no! This sounds like it's going to be lots of fun. You'll soon find that there are still lots of things you're going to learn about me that you don't already know." Mildred delivered one of her promising kisses on the people-filled street and caught Paul totally off guard.

Carl could well imagine what went through people's minds when they saw the display. He stood there, an equivalent spectacle, with his battered face and bandaged head, his mouth open and a squirming baby in his arms.

Mildred bounced down the gravel street singing happily to herself, pleased with her delivery. Paul abandoned his embarrassment; it served no purpose around this woman whom he adored. He strode up behind, slapped her bottom in kind, and said with fictitious determination, "Don't you ever think your goin' to get away with that without revenge." It startled her. He wrapped his long arm around her and steered them in the direction of the station. "You realize you're going to have to deliver on the consequences of that first meeting?"

She stopped, turned, took Jimmy from Carl's arms and said, "Does it look like I have any intention of doing otherwise?"

"That wasn't all that I meant."

She reached out and brushed his cheek affectionately. "I'm with you through whatever we have to face to make a life and a family. I'm not afraid of much except things that are out of my control and things that might hurt any of us."

Jimmy had found his way back into Carl's arms. This was so interesting and personal that Carl was all ears and he didn't remember when it had happened. "Should I be hearin' all of this?"

"Why not? Look, listen, and learn. Get back there as quick as you can. Don't wait as long as I did. Love and loneliness make people do funny things. Borrow if ya have to but don't be away too long. Mildred's letter really scared me. I dropped everything and ran to salvage it, if it wasn't too late. Now I think it was a tactic, because I know her better."

"Here's another thing that I thought I would never tell you. I loved you so much and you were gone so long that the hurt very nearly made me do something that I will thank God forever, you saved me from. Why do you think a girl who has known a fella for only a few days before he goes away and stays away for over three years, would take him into her bed a few hours after she sees him again?" Mildred pointed to Jimmy. "I wanted you and any part of you that I could get, whether you'd have me or not. I took that chance and I'm forever grateful that I did because I sure wanted all of you."

Carl was glad that he'd heard all of this; they had become almost as much family to him as his own. He saw first-hand how two people should act in a family from a love point and what it really meant. That was the depth of something that as a child, he had never recognized between Mama and Papa. Yet now he realized it was always there, despite the hardship. He realized that it hurt Papa greatly that he couldn't provide more. It wasn't until now that he realized it really didn't matter to Mama; she had what was most important.

He handed Jimmy back to Paul and excused himself. He went directly to a little store they had passed and bought a big bundle of writing paper, some lead pencils, a good pen, that he thought was too expensive but very important, and a bottle of black ink, then he headed back to the train.

It wasn't until nearly eleven when the load, bursting at the seams, laboured out of the station and Winnipeg. Carl heard them say that it was the heaviest they'd ever remembered. They'd have hooked on more passenger space if they had it but there just wasn't any more around. Paul too said this was the largest load he'd seen but spirits were high and the atmosphere was bubbling; this was the final leg of the journey to the land and the promises Carl'd made.

IV

"The search for El Dorado!"

It was hot and muggy and they packed three to a seat made for two. With the back door of the coach closed, the breeze through the opened windows set up a turbulence that had nowhere to go and only created more discomfort. Carl rose and tried to prop the door open but had nothing heavy enough to hold it there. It swung erratically with the rock of their motion and just slammed shut again.

Tired and irritable, Jimmy fretted and fussed. He bounced from one set of arms to another and none of them proved satisfactory. When he rejected the bottle, Mildred nose-tested the rancid fluid with disgust but when she covered herself and him to try to nurse, it only compounded his discomfort and he reacted even more emphatically. There were other mothers with children in the car, but none as young as Jimmy. To their collective disgust and to Mildred's dismay, the crude mentality of some of the male passengers became apparent through the colour of their remarks. Finally, it became excessively abusive on the part of an obnoxious, middle-aged crude.

Despite Mildred's plea, Paul stood and turned to face the sloth. Carl was more than half of the way to him when two younger men, sensing the impending, rose from their seats. Without a word, each seized the man by an arm, lifted him bodily from his seat, locked his arms behind him and waltzed him, despite his vulgarisms and futile attempt at resistance, past Carl and out of the door. Both Carl and Paul followed, in case of the event of a further problem.

Pinning the man to the door of the next car, the two young men introduced themselves as police officers. "Nobody has to tolerate your filth. You are very close to a set of handcuffs. If you continue to resist, you'll be wearing them for as long as it takes this train to get to Portage. I understand they've got a nice new jail there and you could well be among its first residents. Is that absolutely clear? Is there anything I've said that you don't understand? Good! Now, you're riding the rest of the way with the freight and if that's not to your liking, we can handcuff you to a horse in livestock and you can argue with him."

"Thank you gentlemen, for your concern. He won't be bothering you or your wife or anybody else anymore."

"That's an ugly bruise. You'd better have a doctor look at it."

Curiosity is a more powerful human emotion than most. It took Carl and Paul a while to make their way through the gauntlet of questions to their seat. "Boy wasn't he surprised. Those two fellas are police officers." The obnoxious mannerisms of the marginal irritants in the car changed abruptly to cordiality. Two of them rose from their seats, hats in hand, swallowed their egos and shame-faced their way over to voluntarily apologize to Mildred and ask a few awkward questions about Jimmy, before returning to their seats.

"I should say so!" The stout, older lady handed the sleeping child back to Mildred and rose to clear the seat for Paul and Carl. She looked with puzzlement at both of them.

"His!" Carl pointed.

"You're a lucky fella ... sure got a nice family. You brothers?"

"No! We just ran into one another on the train but we're headin' for the same place."

"That's real good. You can't do it out there without some support. I'm goin' out to see my son and grandkids; they lost their mother a couple of years ago to some infection. They've got a doctor an' hospital now, but too damned late. Good thing the kids are a little older. It's a hell of a place, but he loves the freedom and I can see why. I'd move out there if I could but Paw says it's a bit late now. He hasn't been feeling well lately so I came alone this time. I guess I'll have to be happy with comin' out when I can. If you need a babysitter again, just ask. I love little fellas like this." She stroked the sleeping forehead. "I'd a' cracked that bastard myself if I was closer ... talk again before we get there."

"She's fantastic! As soon as she sat down and started talking to Jimmy he settled right down. When she took him, he went to sleep right away. I wish I had that touch." Then Mildred's demeanour and her voice changed. "What would you have done if that idiot pulled a knife or a gun? Words can hurt but they don't kill. What you two started sure can. You're worth an awful lot more to us alive." She was right and they knew it.

Carl thought about all that had happened the last few days. If the trend continued he really wasn't sure how long he was going to survive out here but it was better than just taking it and sitting and thinking and being homesick all the time.

The bruise and cut were irritating Carl more than usual so he thought maybe he should take the officer's advice and have somebody look at it as soon as they got to Portage. That wouldn't be too long now. That could cost a lot of money and he didn't know what the real cost of what he was doing would be. Maybe Mildred or somebody on the train could check and re-bandage it.

The two officers came in and sat down again without a word. Amazingly, there wasn't a single question.

The country they were rolling through was still largely undeveloped. Farms appeared every once-in-a-while but seemed to be fewer the farther away from Winnipeg they got. It looked good though. Carl looked for the tell-tale large straw piles and he could see the potential of the land by what nature put on it. Heavy bush wasn't always the best sign because it was too hard to clear. If it grew good grass with open bushy areas, it was probably the best ... an awful lot easier to develop. The country was flatter and opener then Minnesota. It was getting a lot like Iowa. Carl wondered what Assiniboine Territory would be like.

The train began to slow and a few claptrap buildings slid past. The whistle screamed its greeting and they were in the first car behind the locomotive. All of the windows were open and the noise cut right through. Along with a multitude of "gadammits", the interior of the car was shocked out of its lethargy. Carl hated to think what the result would have been had Calvin been there.

"Portage!" the red-faced conductor announced.

"Already?"

"Already, he sez. We're slower'n molasses! One awful big load for the old wheezer ... likely need ta take on more coal and water too. She'll be eatin' 'er up purty good. It's a heavy pull. We'll be here a spell. Maybe up ta an hour. Lots ta eat inside now." The conductor moved on to the other cars.

The train ground to a slow and careful stop. The load would allow for nothing else and this engineer was very exact. He'd rolled past the station and under the tower to take on water.

———

The town was a bit scattered and disorganized, like it had just happened. Portage, too, was an offshoot of the fur trade days and the constant need for supply depots ever deeper into the interior in the never-ending search for "El Dorado."

The station was the most impressive building in immediate view, heavily constructed to last, with lots of windows and a bright, welcoming interior. An enterprising lady, somewhat younger then Charles City's Bertha, yet very nearly equally proportioned, had won the right to establish a lunch counter and she served up sandwiches and coffee because they wouldn't allow her a kitchen. But this service was more than appreciated and it was utilized to the full.

Paul said she hadn't been there when he'd come a couple of weeks ago but the need was apparent. The station agent said that there were so many folks coming through lately and they were always hungry so they had asked her if she could do this to help. There was only one cafe in town, at the hotel, and it couldn't handle the crush.

She was a widow, desperate for a living. Her home was here and her kids had taken up land, or found jobs and were all nearby so she jumped at the opportunity. She wasn't as brazen as Bertha but she clearly liked working around people. The agent had chosen well.

A long counter was piled high with egg and chicken salad sandwiches. It was tomato season, so fresh tomato-lettuce reigned supreme. "Help yerself!" She had scavenged every free cup she could lay her hands on, every shape, size, colour or pattern were there. A young man and woman, with a big washtub kept the cups clean and the counter stacked.

"Take yer coffee from the big crock with the dipper. All I ask is try not ta get yer hands in, or spill too much. Milk and sugar are there too. It may not be the hottest, but we try our best. We got ta bring it over a block away but we just done that and it was real hot. It's a bit warm to have the heater goin' here."

People filled the tables, the benches and the room. Many stood and ate and drank out on the platform and along the sidewalk out front. The sandwich mills, a couple of teen-aged girls with lightening fingers cranked out the product relentlessly and stayed ahead of the game. Two half-grown boys, with a fair sized, pulley-wheeled, homemade wagon, roared back and forth over the wooden sidewalk to the house and the coffee flowed non-stop. They all knew what they were doing.

"Been cooking fer road and threshin' crews all ma' life. Know how ta feed lots a' people in a hurry." Carl was fascinated by the efficiency, so he had to ask. "Cafe down the street's overloaded too ... got a lot more room here when the trains come through ... can't figure where all these people are goin' ... know the country is big but this's been goin' on fer the last year or more."

The crowd thinned gradually, yet the pile of sandwiches grew. "Why?"

"There's another train through here this evening and there's a road buildin' crew comin' in after that. We ain't goin' to waste nothin'. Out here folks have ta look to one another 'cause not too many got much else."

Carl paid for the food out of the Marshal's contribution; one flat rate, eat all you want. He was glad of it too; it filled to capacity. Paul had to be running thin by now and Carl would need everything he had brought from home. He walked out of the station with Mildred and Jimmy to see if there was a store nearby.

"Just t'other side a' the hotel."

Mildred needed more milk so she left Jimmy with Carl and went to get some. Paul jumped on an opportunity and helped shovel a wagonload of coal into the tender on the engine. They were shorthanded and he needed every penny he could get.

He was anxious to get back because the weather was still warm and he hadn't dug his potatoes yet. There was no fieldwork done and the weather could change at any time. He had enough hay for the cow and the teams but he wanted to haul up some straw before the snow, while it was still easy. They needed a lot more wood too.

There'd be two more, no ... three more, but Carl wouldn't take something for nothing. They'd help one another and it would go better with the heavy jobs. Paul really appreciated the co-operation he had with the Doukhobors. It would be even better now; he was alone most of his life and now, suddenly, his home would be crowded.

Mildred found Carl and her son watching his dad finish the last of the coal. Paul went back into the station to wash off some of the grime. They all would have enjoyed a good wash but other than the odd "damp-mopping," they would have to suffer each other until they got home or found a place. There were plenty of spots along the road at places they had stopped but October was too cold for impromptu trough-dipping.

The "All Aboard!" was as emphatic as the previous but with much less gusto. The afternoon was beginning to wane and the prospect of the night, in this press was not at all inspiring. It would only be for the one night. Thank God a few had already climbed off at Portage.

The conductor and one of the train crew went back to the first of the freight cars to arrange and secure things and to see if they could get a bit more accommodation for the more daring to bed down in, to free up a bit more space in the Passenger. It was dangerously against railroad liability but these guys didn't seem to care and the willing were more than happy to take the risk.

Carl and Paul volunteered and were accommodated so Mildred could have the seat with Jimmy. She'd wrap herself in the quilt and let Paul and Carl have the ticking against the floor and the cold. Carl's bedroll would do well for a cover.

Carl had never seen freight cars with end doors as well as the big side "sliders." Somebody had been thinking when they made these. Their load of sandwiches had occurred at midafternoon so no one suffered too much. Carl drank some of Paul's tea, and with a small block of cheese, retired to the freighter and an impromptu card game under a secured barn lantern. It was a warm night and they were as comfortable as they were boisterous.

Paul stayed with his family and talked about their plans and expectations. He'd come with very little, accomplished a great deal and what he had was all theirs. He'd met every requirement and filed for title. Next year he would patent on an adjoining quarter.

It was nearly ten when their eyes started to droop and the yawn factor determined sleep. He tucked both of them in and kissed them. The car, much relieved by the crew's initiative, fell silent and his family was asleep.

"Grand! Ain't they?" the stout lady whispered as Paul walked quietly by.

Everyone was asleep in the freighter when Paul blew out the lantern and crawled in.

———

Carl woke to desperation, a consequence of the large drink of tea. It was hard to see and impossible to tell time in the blackened interior but the light filtering in through the cracks around the ill-fitting "slider" assured some daylight. The car was naturally noisy so Carl had little problem leaving without waking anybody. Stepping on a sleeper in the semi-darkness was a different matter. He got out with only one minor mishap and a brief, uncomplimentary dressing down.

He checked the Passenger for observers and then stood carefully on the step to accomplish his purpose. The morning light was still feeble but sufficient to encourage good vision.

The country was surprisingly cleared and settled. Fences crossed it here and there and many fields cradled cattle and straw piles. The buildings looked recent but not hurried; these were good signs. One of the fields confined a steamer with a thresher directed at a sizeable straw pile. Its stack smoked directly upward into the dead, still, morning air; the fireman was at it.

It was warm for this late; like summer and it inspired Carl to get at something. He walked quietly through the sleeping Passenger and onto the coal-tender platform. He climbed over through the stiff breeze and coal smoke of their propulsion and onto the cabin deck.

The fire door was open and the shovel flew. Most of Paul's load of coal, from yesterday afternoon, was gone and they would clearly have to stop for more soon. The fireman was startled but receptive and grateful for something new after the dreary night of labour. Carl had to cup his hands over the man's ear to convey his message. "Never been on one of these yet ... thought I'd come and take a look, if you don't mind too much."

"Mind? 'ell no! ... even do better'n that! 'Ere 'ave a go; me back's killin' me!" The engineer, who was lost in reverie, only now realized his fireman was speaking to someone, turned on his small, uncomfortable perch and acknowledged Carl with a nod and little more. He smiled, so he wasn't put out.

Carl went at his voluntary duty with his typical vigour until the fireman interjected with an, "Ere, that's bout enough!" and slammed the firebox door. Presumptuously, the fireman went on to explain everything about the bodily function of the locomotive and what each gauge foretold. Carl was polite and nodded with understanding but had extreme difficulty interpreting with all the noise. He'd run steamers and been on threshing crews since he was old enough to remember, so much of this he could comprehend merely by observation.

The engineer turned, looked at Carl, then said with a powerful, audible voice evolved over years of this deafening clatter, "I know! I still have one hell of time after all these years. Talks the hind leg off a horse and I catch 'bout half of it. I like to be called Hank." He extended a powerful handshake.

The fireman responded with, "'Ell of a 'ard chap to teach. Slow as blazes!" and continued undeterred.

By the time Carl had the grand tour and a detailed analysis interspersed with personal opinion, it was time to "coal up." He "cracked" the door and filled the "fire pot" in record time.

"Ere, want me job? I'm gettin' a might old anyway."

"Next stop off the beam," the engineer roared. He pointed past the bulk and through the steam-filled morning air at the distant disarray of buildings, visible now in the full light, around a turn in the rails. He cranked around on a valve lever and the pressure gauges corresponded with a sudden jump. The massive machine, followed by its horrendous load, coasted while its pistons strove to achieve equilibrium in the reduced reality, then caught and coughed again with much slower deliberation. They eased, delicately, into the town, to a precise stop beside the water tower.

Carl had observed a master at work. The engine was a part of him. He could read his load, his power and the distance with absolute precision.

Carl thanked the fireman and engineer for their tolerance and instruction. They invited him back any time. They said they'd have to "blow off some steam," because Carl had done his voluntary duties too well. "It surely don't hurt to learn a little about steam power. Maybe even get your papers 'cause you never know where life leads you. Steam's the way in this country. Got a ways to go in the Territory before you get to where you're goin'. You can learn quite a bit and we don't mind the help for the teachin', even though we're not supposed to. We'll tell 'em we're trainin' you and that ain't no lie neither." Hank invited.

"Sure thing, I'll be here. I'm anxious to know all I can learn because I think I'll need it all. I never had much schoolin' 'cause my folks and brothers and sister needed every hand and nickel all of us could bring home."

"Well, shake hands with your first cousins. That's just about the same story with all of us. I got my start and so did Archie just the way we're startin' you right now."

"Climbed on the bloomin' boat and off again without a bloomin' penny in me' pocket. ...learned ta fire a boiler and ta read a bloomin' gauge all the way across and that's 'ow I got me start. Been doin' it ever since ... 'aven't been 'ome in the last twenty years ... 'ad ta 'elp 'em some. Bleedin' good country if yer a 'big swag. Me paw died a year ago and I didn't 'ave the bloomin' time er money ta go back." His eyes moistened and he choked back.

"Best let the friends back in the Passenger know. They'll be wonderin' where I got to ... be back in a while and I'll gladly take you up on your offer."

Carl climbed back over the tender again and through the Passenger door to an unexpected reception by an angry Mildred and a stern lecture from Paul.

"Fella in freight said you stepped on him, early this morning, on your way out and then you disappeared without a trace. The conductor and the crew are searching the train even now. We thought sure that you fell off or got crushed a ways back."

"We've been frantic for over half an hour. Where in God's name have you been, to disappear so completely?" Carl told them and Mildred slapped him across his back hard enough not to be playful. "Well, it's just as simple as lettin' somebody know so you don't scare the hell out of all of us."

Carl humbled himself. "I didn't even think about it. I got so tied up with what they were teaching me, I didn't realize. I come from a large family and I know better 'n that." Carl hoped the revelation wouldn't get the engineer and fireman into trouble and ruin his opportunity when the conductor found out.

One of the police officers came in, retreated to call off the search, then returned and delivered a warning along with a clear indication that Carl's action had put a lot of people out.

Carl was really disturbed; he hadn't meant to, he just hadn't thought. He couldn't even explain his thoughtless action to himself. This wasn't like him. He just got wrapped up and careless. He'd never do that again. He'd been uncharacteristically negligent this entire trip and he would have to do better but then, he'd never really been so much amongst people he didn't grow up with and he had taken too much for granted. They didn't know him so well.

The officer took Carl into the station that was smaller and older than the one at Portage. Unlike Portage, there was no welcoming smell of coffee and food. They sat him down and ordered him to stay put until they could get someone to look at his head or at least find a first aid kit, so someone there could check and re-bandage it. Carl looked at his reflection in an inner window and noted, with satisfaction, that the bruise was still apparent but most of the discolouration was gone. It itched horribly but he didn't dare scratch it.

"We didn't have to look too far; your friend's wife knows her way around a bandage." Mildred pulled the bandage off carefully. It still hurt over the cut but it didn't bleed anymore. It appeared to be very red but didn't look to be infected. She thought it was beginning to heal and that's why it itched.

Mildred swabbed it and re-bandaged it lightly and carefully with extensive equipment and an apparent ease that amazed Carl. The window again served well to display the result. She clearly knew what she was doing.

"I spent eight years training and working in the Des Moines hospital before I met Paul. I'm a bit of a hand at this. You'd be surprised how many people I've patched up, even Paul. That's why I always carry most things with me." Paul rolled up his sleeve and displayed a neatly stitched scar on his forearm.

"How did that happen?"

Both Paul and Mildred blushed vividly. Paul smiled at her accusingly.

"Well I didn't mean to and I did a good job didn't I? It was only a couple of years old. Who'd ever expect a spring to break?" She stopped dead. "Oh my!" The listeners giggled, Paul squirmed uncomfortably and Mildred turned a bright crimson. The tension resulting from the search for Carl melted, a consequence of her incrimination. "I'm sorry about that! I wish I could learn to watch what I say," she leaned over and whispered into Paul's ear.

"For what happened, the cut was a small price to pay. You suppose we could do that again sometime? Maybe we could leave the cut out and I'm hoping, this time, we won't have to wait a couple years." Mildred delivered a promising kiss to his cheek.

Carl didn't hear the exchange but knew enough about her and her sense of fun to enjoy their embarrassment. He openly displayed his glee.

"Oh shut up, not a single word out of you lover-boy!"

"Bring us some hot coffee if you can find some. Crew asked me to help 'em again." Paul handed Mildred the empty two-quarter and left quickly. "No time to eat now." He returned and handed her some change to pay for it. Jimmy stayed with the stout grandmother.

There was plenty of help on the engine so Carl stood out of the road and took mental note of every action and reaction. By the time the auxiliary tank was filled, Paul and a station employee had the tender well stocked and they were ready to go.

The steam was up and Carl checked all the gauges after the engineer and memorized the pressure readings. He followed them down the ladder and around the engine to every wheel, bearing, and valve. Carl had learned, very young, not to touch parts that were clear of steam or coal heat. Moving parts pulling a heavy load tended to become hot. He learned what to check and why. They took a minute to explain a few things, then nodded to the waiting conductor who roared his warning. Hank yanked the steam whistle cord and they were off.

Carl observed and asked about every step of the start-up sequence, then watched the steady climb of the gauges and learned about how the engineer judged his speed by the steam pressure and the sound and action of the engine. It was instinctive and it was something that had taken the engineer many years to master. "It's different for every load and for every engine, even the same model. Haulin' big loads can really throw you, until you do it a while and know what can happen.

"Sometimes you've got to be able to judge the grade if you're on a new route. You can usually do that by the country that you're rollin' through. Sometimes you think you're rollin' flat but you're losin' power and speed. Quick-check the pressures, the throttle, even the brake. If it ain't that, look for tell-tale signs in the land you're rollin' through; you're usually on a gentle upgrade. If it ain't that and you ain't losin' pressure, you'd best know a lot about your machine.

"On down-grades you have to feel the motion and hear the sound. The pistons are pushin' the steam rather than the other way. Never use the brake unless you have to and then only for a short time. Your cars are braked too, or should be, but there's no guarantee because you can't check everything and you can't always trust somebody else to do it. Repair crews are as lazy as anybody so you got to be sure of your engine. Sometimes it can mean your life and all the others'. Always check the way I did and learn the danger signs. The ability to do that is what makes a steam engineer."

Carl relieved Archie again and learned from him how to judge a fire and its consequences. You could always tell the heat by the colour and the intensity of the flame. That told you when to fuel and when to stop; you didn't always trust the gauges. You trusted your ears, eyes and instincts, because gauges and pressure-relief valves stick shut. You could tell good coal from poor by the look and the feel and the flake and the same when you were burning wood, but it was never as good. You got to know your furnace; each one has its own character and you learned how to set the draft to generate just the right heat and conserve your coal.

Carl's brain and senses were so busy that he forgot his need; it was pushing eleven and he hadn't eaten anything since last night.

The Passenger looked a lot emptier. The last stop hosted a large eastern European population. Many people were coming over to join relatives already here.

By two that afternoon, they rolled into the "Territories" and Carl was again on the engine. "You're now in what's called 'Assiniboia.' They ain't joined up yet but I think it won't be too long."

The train dropped into a beautiful little valley almost as soon as they had crossed. Carl noted that very little of the flat table land on either side was worked but there were fences and cattle and buildings that still had the nature of immediacy about them, indicating a recent birth and an open future.

"In an hour or so, we're rollin' into York. Here, you're takin' 'er in." Hank cleared the perch and pushed Carl onto it. "I'm right here so watch your gauges and remember, feel your speed and your machine. You've got to keep your mind on it all the time."

Carl didn't object; he was surprised by the unexpected opportunity but he welcomed it. He sat down, hands free and observed the gauges. Everything was just as it should be. He listened to the sound … uniform and steady. He checked, with quick glances, the trees and foliage streaming past and sensed the wind direction by the lean and sway of the branches and the few leaves left. He checked the smoke stream for verification and speed of departure and related it to the wind. The sense of speed came with experience but he could sense the change in speed. Hank watched and did nothing.

It came subtly, a gradual change in the vibrations and the sound. Carl checked the gauges, the smoke stream and the foliage. He eased back on the steam throttle valve.

"Why'd that happen?"

"You had it set for the climb out of the valley. When we reached the top the extra power became more speed.

Now, you did just right and in good time, before it got ahead a' ya'. Ya' ain't no greenhorn, I'll tell ya that! Ya know how ta use the steam on your engine to control the load. Farm boy, ain'tcha? If it tried to get away, like on a steeper downgrade, what would ya do?"

"I'd use the engine as much as I could, then I'd have to brake I guess."

"Try it!"

Carl eased the lever back until he could hear the screech of contact and felt the resistance, then returned it to the neutral position as he had already reduced speed enough.

"You bin watchin', that's good. Now remember, between here and York you're not going to get much grade change so you don't have to worry about it too much. I know the road, so I'm tellin' you but if it's just you and the road's strange, keep your eyes and ears open. The thing ta do is ta recognize it early enough so ya' don't get the problem. Ask about the road, if you can, from somebody that's been or take a fireman that knows. A runaway's a real bugger! Happened only once to me and I'm damn lucky to be here."

"I'm still 'ere, but, bleedin' Christ, mine wasn't sa lucky." Archie pulled his shirt up to reveal an ugly, scarred patch of discoloured, purple skin. "Engineer flew and got crushed. We didn't 'ave a Passenger, just freight so weren't any but the crew. We're all hurt but 'e was the only one gone." His eyes reflected the anguish. He buried it in his shovel.

They approached a small village. "No freight for here but there may be some to take. We'll stop 'cause there's a wagon sittin' there, see it? ... maybe a passenger. Should have a flag up but these ain't. They'd get madder'n hell if we rolled right through." Carl backed off on the throttle and expected Hank to take over but he didn't move. "Bit too fast yet, back off more. Now, a bit more ... More! ... More! Feel the push of the load and judge your distance ... More! Now throw on a bit of brake, but don't leave it on. Harder!" Carl could feel the jolt of resistance and the sudden reduction of speed. The linkage clashed behind him.

"I ain't worried; I'll tell 'em all that you did it."

Carl brought the machine to a meagre roll well short of the wagon with its large wrapped bundle and passenger. He had to apply a bit more steam to make up the distance, then had to brake embarrassingly to stop just right. Hank smiled. "A hell of a lot better'n my first try."

"That was an 'ell of a lot better than the first time I fired fer ya."

"Keep the brake on; there's a bit of a grade here. You could roll and hurt somebody or smash somethin'. Don't forget that it's there because if it's not full-on you can start without knowin' and things could get pretty hot. It was rubbin' a bit when you touched the driver a while back."

"Be sure they're all clear ... two short whistles. Now wait a bit for the conductor to do his part. Okay, off brake! Throw on the steam ... More!" It just roared. "Try not to throw the wheels like some do; it ain't necessary and does nothin' but raise hell with the wheels and puts too much pressure on the drive. We're movin'. Give 'er more but do it with sense ... Easy! Keep on opening just so the wheels grab until you're up to speed. You can just feel a machine when it's workin' easy and when it's slavin'. Keep an eye on the gauges. Usually Archie's got a surplus head built up so you don't have to worry, but they all ain't Archie.

"By gosh, I think you're a natural, you've got a calling ... one more short stop before you're there."

Carl handled the next one a lot better but he had to stop quicker to be where he should be than he liked to. It was a lot better than some he'd felt on the trip up to Winnipeg. Carl handled the start with perfect precision and without one instruction from Hank. He was a bit worried about a few minor grades but handled them with no noticeable variation in the speed. The time flew as did the distance. It seemed only minutes, until with a smile, he rolled the engine to a stop under the York tower.

He would boast in years to come, how he'd brought his people into "The Promise Land."

V

"The dream of generations!"

"What's it look like?"

"Hurry! Let's get our stuff and let's go." ... No time! ... Grab and run!

"I can't wait!" Hope! ... So near!

... Friends! ... Family! ... Lovers!

"Hurrah!"

Just a few days ago he'd been a scared kid stepping onto a train to a new, strange world and here he was in that strange, new world and it wasn't nearly so strange; it carried hope and inspired confidence but ... no time now ... must hurry.

Within seconds, the machine had disgorged its human cargo to mass confusion. A living wave, joined by many more from the town, rolled up to the freighters. Despite the assurance that the train had to take on just about everything it needed to continue and that there would be more than enough time for everyone and everything, the hoard, with unbridled enthusiasm, pounded on the doors.

Carl climbed off the engine then right back on when he saw the frantic mass. Wisdom and Paul helped him choose the car route; maybe they could help. There were about a dozen in this Freighter already but there were three other Freighters without the end doors and they would prove more of a challenge to get to. Nobody refused their offer of help so they pitched in. The sliders would remain closed until order was restored. The two police officers proved invaluable in this capacity.

The conductor shouted the precise location of articles according to the way they were loaded. It was a useless effort as most of the passengers were there and had even helped to load. They knew exactly what was where.

As the names on the articles were called, the station crew and the police allowed only so many through to collect their valuables. Some were not tagged and would have to be identified personally later on.

Paul's problem was minor. ... just the family, himself and their luggage but Carl had a considerable volume to disentangle. During the turmoil, Carl, with Paul's help, moved all his things to the end of the car until he was free to get them out.

There was logic behind pushing Paul and Carl to the last car and it had everything to do with youth and strength. People dispersed with the bundles and packages small enough to handle, then the wagons rolled in for the crates and the furniture. When this was completed, the remaining freight had to be moved back and secured. Carl and Paul were both tired and sore. They lugged Carl's heavy bundles into the freight shed as instructed, for safe storage, until they knew what to do. Daylight was already fading.

The engine required further servicing, the cars were checked and additional freight, bound further west, had to be loaded, so much of the train crew remained. The rest, volunteers included, were escorted through the thinning station crowd and into an adjoining shed, to tables again stacked with an assortment of food. Thank goodness for the thought and the common decency. Nothing much more then the station had been here when Paul first came. He'd gotten so hungry that he felt sick. Nobody told him or gave a damn.

Mildred elbowed into a large basin of soapy water and the clean cups flourished. "First decent dipping I've had in a week! Wish I could jump right in." The pretty young lady next to her, flicked soap into Mildred's face and got as well as she gave. Jimmy slept, wrapped in a strange, colourful blanket, on the lap of the stout lady.

Carl and Paul ate while the physical caught up. The crews swarmed in and ate silently and quickly. The train was loaded and fuelled and with only a fraction of the human cargo, the passengers were much relieved. York was the crest of the rolling frontier ... the scream and roar of steam and they were gone.

Carl stretched his cramping muscles and carried both cups back to Mildred. Paul stayed put a while longer, nearly asleep.

Carl was worried about the land Paul told him about. He hoped it wasn't taken with this rush because he wanted anything of his to be close to theirs. He left the station to seek the Land Titles office; Paul said it had moved to a new building but he wasn't sure where.

The town was crude and clumsy, with growing pains, desperately trying to find itself. York had gotten its start in the wrong place so it up-rooted and moved to meet the railroad and here it was, such as it was. There was lots of room; the buildings hadn't bunched up yet. Businesses scattered loosely along the Main, opposite the tracks and side streets angled north from the Main. Most were nothing but trails with only the odd, hurried constructions on them. Hammers and saws echoed with determination to nurture the flood of home, business and land seekers.

York serviced a vast area. Until tracks were laid on the branches everything wagoned out of here. There was no shortage of work as there was of workers ... never enough time or hands or material.

"Hey! Ya lookin' fer work?"

"Kin ya' give us a hand here a while?"

Work as long as you can stand it, early and late. "There's still light."

A victim of his own desperate need, Carl was forced to decline although he'd like to have taken the offers. It was his nature.

Wagons loaded beyond logic with their charges, human and material, creaked their burdens to the sites or down the rutted trails from the station and out of town; each on its independent odyssey with no concern for the approach of darkness. The evening was indescribably beautiful.

Carl found a substantial building, still in the birth process, forced into premature labour, with a makeshift, hand-painted sign over an out-of-place, elaborate door and vaulting windows, set into a barren, unfinished, shiplap wall. The human wall extended well over half a block down the street and grew by the minute. There was no time to waste.

Carl rushed back to the station and found Paul elbowed in with Mildred. Because Carl's urgent request took priority, the stout lady handed a wide- awake Jimmy to Paul and dove in beside Mildred. There was still a fair line of people to feed.

Carl showed Paul where the new office was, then stepped into line until Mildred was done and could look after Jimmy. There was the night to worry about, they'd have to find a place. The town was crawling with people, all of them looking.

Even though they stayed open later, there was absolutely no chance that Carl would get in before they'd close. It was confusing and he was worried but Paul didn't seem to be. Paul went back with Jimmy but he'd return later to explain things. Carl couldn't be sure what was claimed and what wasn't. Paul would know where the quarter was in relation to his to get the right land description and to see if there was anything better or closer. The country was huge and there was a lot still available the last time Paul had asked but this was a heavy rush and land was being swallowed fast. Carl had four brothers who'd need claims within a fair distance.

As soon as the sun went down, the air turned cool — it could be a miserable night. Carl was grateful for what they had this late in the season.

It was dark when Paul and a younger boy, wrestling a large wheelbarrow fronted by a feeble, barn lantern and loaded with a well wrapped crock of hot coffee rolled up the line to warm the determined and the patient. They kept a fire going in the station and The Hotel just across the street all night and friend or Samaritan could hold a place in line to spell the cold. Most had blankets or covers of some kind and would sit or lie on the wooden sidewalk. As long as you held a place or someone else held it for you, you were safe. Place jumpers were not tolerated. Justice was swift and usually painful for anyone attempting to defy it.

There were all kinds of shysters around. You kept an eye open for them and warned others when you saw them or had a bad experience with one. Many of the dangerous ones were in positions of authority or legal advantage. They'd trick people. Lots of the folks here who couldn't speak English, let alone read or understand, were vulnerable. Together they were safe — alone, many fell victim to the "flimflam" men Papa had warned about. They were slick, dangerous, dirty and universally hated. Carl's every sense was alert. He'd watch for them and use the force Papa'd taught him if he had to.

Paul spelled him once. Carl was fine but he was tired and sleep was nearly impossible. He welcomed the relief and the warmth for an hour before he went back. There weren't any in his life, other than his family, Ingmar or the Pawlowiches, who cared enough like Paul did. Most wouldn't lose five minutes for him let alone a night's sleep.

The line behind him kept growing. They came off and on throughout the night, exhausted teams and drivers and families from "God knows where," with everything tied in or on or behind. Some led cattle or an extra team. Some came with two rigs, even crated chickens and pigs. Some came up from the States that way, driving a herd to stock their land. They'd stop and one would feed the line while the families or friends looked for a place to rest or feed themselves. Most had no money, they couldn't afford a ticket, or they'd had to bring too much. How long they drove, nobody could tell. The footsore teams hung their heads while their flanks heaved and quivered ... near to physical exhaustion, all worn thin and desperate. But for the first time in their lives, they'd found hope.

It was well after ten that morning before Carl, with Paul, got to an attendant. They questioned a map of the township, located Paul's, then traced the route Paul had advised and found the quarter open, as were most of the adjacent quarters. They were quite a bit farther from town. Paul had scouted the area thoroughly and advised on the land quality as he saw it and the possibilities for the boys and later opportunities. Paul had taken the time to know. He had done the smart thing but now things were a lot different. Everybody was desperate and in a hurry, they filed blindly. ... not the best.

They couldn't seem to find any quarter with a better location to suit Carl's need so Carl filed. It didn't take all that long after he decided. He left the Land Titles with anticipation, joy, and energy. He didn't feel any exhaustion from the night-long vigil. He was the first in his family to fulfill the dream of generations; he had land that he could call his own — their own. Papa would live to see it. He headed right back to the station to send a telegraph, no, two telegraphs. He didn't worry about the cost.

Mildred and Jimmy appeared, back at the station, fresh and clean, with the stout lady and a couple of sturdy boys, her grandsons. They'd spent the night out at her son's, a scant five miles away. She'd insisted and saved Paul some desperately needed money.

"You two fellas look a sight! Best come on out and get cleaned up a bit and get some rest." Carl hadn't seen himself in a while. Paul didn't look very good either; the coal dust, sweat, grime, beard and sleepless night had transfigured him. Carl found a tell-tale window to get a look. None of the people he'd met even seemed to notice; there were so many with wrapped-up heads or hands or feet, all very makeshift. Mildred could have a lively business around here.

The coffee and sandwich mill was running full tilt; there was another passenger-freight due around noon, if it was on time. Along with the steady construction trade, the "Hotel Cafe" just couldn't begin to handle it; the demand was constant. Such was not to be Paul and Carl's fare this time 'round.

Grandma ordered the boys to bring the team and the wagon to the grassed-in area between the rails and the street, to the west of the tower and the coal shed. It seemed to be a favoured rest area for teamsters and water was plentiful. It was equipped with stone-circled fire pits and top-flattened, poplar logs, for seats, to discourage cooking fires just anywhere. The grass was well packed and smooth. The boys hauled a large, heavily packed, wooden box, obviously constructed for the purpose, out of the wagon and set it beside the red and white checkered cloth that Mildred spread on the grass, well clear of the team.

The boys and Carl had to restrain an obviously spoiled-brat filly colt that had followed its mother into town. It'd developed an amazing attraction to the smell of food and people with food that usually led to a good tasting treat when the boys were around.

The "girls" weren't fooling. Since last night there was fresh bread and butter, a large roast chicken and boiled potatoes and carrots and gravy warming on the fire. The teakettle was nearly boiling; tea was something Carl had nearly forgotten about.

The surprise of the picnic was something totally new to both Carl and Mildred. Neither of them had ever tasted a Saskatoon berry pie. Pie of any kind was something Carl hadn't eaten much since Mama had taken sick.

This was the best and the most Carl had eaten since the meal at the other Bertha's. He shut his eyes and leaned back to see and think about Milly. There wasn't an hour went by without her being around in his head.

Jimmy latched himself instinctively onto the two younger members, who were equally entertained by his baby-ness; they hadn't been around one much. They had him filled with mashed up potatoes and gravy and his once clean, fresh clothing and face showed it. They wiped him off a bit and indulged his baby glee with a roll in the grass and the warm sunshine.

————

"Carl!" Somebody shook him.

"Carl!" He sat up with startling anticipation.

"Honestly, you're one of the funniest people to wake up. Now come, so you guys can get cleaned up. Our ride is here but they won't leave until tomorrow; they've got to put on several loads of bricks so travel will be slow. They know McPherson's and it's not out of their way."

Paul stood some distance away, talking with exaggerated gesture, to a giant of a man with a heavy handlebar and a pert light cap set at an angle on top of his round, good-natured face. He wore a pair of tall leather boots, baggy pants and a loose pullover shirt, bound by a colourful, homespun sash, drawn tight around his middle-aged girth.

"Carr-rroll!" he pronounced and extended a huge, hard-calloused hand. "Alexsay! Pavlowa tyellink you us? You comink. Vwe nyaybours. You hort youself?" he eyed Carl's head.

Carl shook his hand and found it a bit hard to disengage. He understood everything Alexsay had said. He indulged in a bit of an explanation and judged the man's understanding by the expression on his face.

Both Paul and Carl offered to help load brick but they declined emphatically. "Vwe got lots help. You go! You sleep! Vwe comink." Alexsay turned abruptly and strode to the heavy wagon with giant steps; there was nothing slow about him. He climbed with amazing agility, onto a make-shift plank seat, puckered his lips and produced a loud, clear, kissy sound. The uniform Percherons lunged into the harness and lumbered off to the kiln.

The boys pulled the Clydes up to the freight shed so Carl could load his bundles. All the fellas climbed to the top and arranged themselves on the softer ones. Jimmy, to his absolute delight, sat propped in their midst.

Carl's most valiant effort to observe the countryside on the brief journey ended in dismal failure. He awoke when the gentle roll of the wheels stopped and two excitable mongrels welcomed them into the McPherson yard.

A tall, thin, weather-scarred man, not in any way resembling his portly mother, helped the ladies down. Paul extricated his sleeping son and handed him down to Mildred. The boys, with the fortitude of youth, vaulted, while Paul chose a more discretionary dismount.

At the request, Carl guided the docile team to a shed and they unloaded his bundles. Then he steered them, more at their insistence then his foresight, to the water-filled trough.

"Al McPherson!" He extended a badly gnarled hand. "I take it you're the Carl that the women talked about last night? The other fella must be Paul?"

"I sure thank you for this chance to get cleaned up a bit ... spent last night on the sidewalk beside Land Titles and I'm beginning to feel it. Been one heck of a long trip. Hope things quiet down a bit once I get to the homestead."

"I can tell you not to plan on it. Be real careful though and don't get crazy. Ya' got three years, don't try ta do it in one; you can only do so much without hurtin' yourself." He held up the hand. "Brought my family when I first came out and that's a mistake. Don't ever do that. I still think the helluva time we had's what killed my woman, especially when I got hurt and she tried to do everything herself. Now she's layin' over there and we're here and it's as hard for me without her to talk to as it is for the kids. It wasn't necessary. We could have stayed in Hamilton but I had dreams. I still got dreams but now they're more like nightmares and I wish I could shake 'em." A large, well-painted, white cross in a carefully groomed, secluded spot, up against a natural grove, clearly marked his direction.

"Alice is seventeen and I want her to have a life of her own. It's better now with more people around but there still ain't no school closer'n York and I ain't had no time to teach her or the boys like May did. Mother's always after me to drop this and go back but it was May's wish as well as mine and I'd have to leave everything we'd done together and I sure couldn't leave her. I love the openness of this place and the freedom. I always hated the crowd of the city and the damn rush to get nowhere, to swing a bloody hammer and stoke a forge, like Pa did, all my life, with nothin' in it for me or the kids. But as hard as it's been, I'm still building this place, more for her then for the rest of us."

Carl was a stranger to the man yet what he said struck deep. You have to unload your soul on somebody and sometimes you recognize an understanding listener by just looking at him. Carl had often heard his parents when they'd thought he was asleep and they could talk privately. When he got older, they brought him into their discussions and concerns. After Mama died, he and Papa had many more discussions just like this one, because Papa viewed him as a man and a friend. He was the oldest and he always did have a degree of understanding founded in his nature and based on hardship. Al had guessed right.

They led the team to the stable, unharnessed and fed them and talked, this time, about Carl's situation and concerns. Al offered good advice and warnings about the dangers, what to avoid and what to do at all costs. He'd been through it, mostly the hard way and made the mistakes. He was a tired looking, worn-out man, before his time and the place showed why. Carl would be proud if he could point to his place in so few years and say, "I did this!" He told Al so.

"Al, get that young fella in here so we can get at him. What the heck ya' doin' out there? He's got to be dead tired! You're not workin' the blazes out of him are ya'?"

They walked out through the double doors and past the sleeping colt to the large, two-story house. It wasn't painted but it was clearly recent. A few places weren't finished yet, casualties of a great loss and the resulting loss of will. "Nearly had it finished when the wife took sick. I'm glad she got to spend a bit of time in it before she died. She was sure happy to get out of that sod hole we lived in for too long. That's probably what started her trouble. I sure hate myself for not borrowin' and tryin' sooner. Maybe she'd still be here." He wiped his eyes.

Al had put a large, metal barrel on top of a circle of stones. The boys kept it filled and it was a simple matter to light a fire under it and produce a large supply of hot water. He wanted to put a shelter of some kind around it for winter use but he had to find something out of metal because it was so close to the house and there was a danger of fire.

He displayed more of his creative ability just inside the porch of the rear entrance. A narrow door revealed a small room with a window, high up, out of reach of prying eyes. In the ceiling, a large tin can peppered full of tiny holes served to disperse the water into a fine spray and above that, a tank that held four good sized pails of water. He planned a second tank, joined to the first so that you could regulate it with a valve to mix the hot and cold and you didn't have to be so careful not to scald yourself. He laddered the water up through a small-doored opening in the outside wall of the house. He explained that he was going to try to make a pump of some kind, or maybe he could find one out of an old steamer that he could fix up to get the water up there a lot easier. Maybe he could do it on the inside so the winter wouldn't be a problem.

While the boys carried the water to Al, Carl peeled off in a small room next to the shower. He left his clothing in a large wooden box to hold the wash. The clothes soaking in the washtub were Paul's.

Wearing nothing but a large towel, he rounded the corner after carefully checking for witnesses. Once securely inside, he hung up the towel and recklessly reached up and turned on the valve. He learned very quickly that it was a foolish thing to do while standing underneath. Fortunately, there was escape room.

A strange female voice just outside the door laughed. "Should have warned you about that but I didn't get to you on time. It'll take a while for it to cool enough. Might as well come out and have some coffee." She yanked the door open without warning and handed in what looked like a light coat. Carl didn't have a hurried line on the towel so he grabbed the coat desperately and she closed the door giggling. "By the way, I'm Alice." He could hear Mildred's good-humoured laughter in the background, and Grandma's reprimand of her younger kind.

Carl obeyed, but felt very naked, despite the security of the coat. "Good gracious, I don't know what to think of these younger girls nowdays ... liable to do any darn thing. Shame on you! I'll say 'I'm sorry' for them, because I know they ain't." Both Paul and Al remained silent, smirking observers. Grandma poured Carl a cup and then buttered a slice of fresh bread for him.

Mildred pulled the disgustingly dirty bandage off Carl's head and found the cut well on the mend. She took small, menacing scissors and tweezers out of her handbag and dropped them into a small boiling pot on the kitchen stove.

By the time Carl had finished, she had the stitching out and lying on the table beside him. All he'd felt was the odd little tug. She was good at this stuff. Despite her warning, it still stung like hell-fire when she swabbed it with iodine.

Alice had lots of length and a limited girth. Structurally, she took after her father. From the picture on the living room wall, Carl judged that she carried her mother's good-natured look and shocking red hair. She was as "full of the dickens" as Mildred, maybe more. They communicated constantly, with look and word. Carl resolved to watch his step and his words around these two.

The shower was wonderful! Carl had never experienced anything as relaxing and cleansing. It was certainly better than some of the horse troughs he'd often washed in. He turned the valve back a bit to make it last longer.

To Grandma's dismay, Alice offered to "... come in there, scrub your back and wash behind your ears." Carl got the feeling that Alice usually got directly to the point.

He was even more dismayed when he was done. Wrapped in the coat, he went into the small laundry room to find his clothes soaking in the tub. He didn't question, much, just which one had done that. He realized that his duffle bag was out in the shed with the rest of his stuff and Paul and Al had gone out to do the evening chores. Thoroughly humiliated, Carl called for "Missus McPherson!"

Followed by his two tormentors, she responded. Their faces displayed their glee, but discretion and Grandma seized command. Alice, with suppressed giggles, was ordered out to retrieve Carl's bag. Mildred kept a straight face; she knew better.

Rejuvenated, Carl went out to see how the guys were doing and found them just finishing four large, very docile shorthorns so he fed the team for the night. Al took one pail to the house to cool and separate while Carl and Paul troughed the other two pails to the four half-grown, wildly enthusiastic calves, in the pen behind the barn. Al brought the pail with the cream skimmed off, from this morning and along with some grain, poured it to four mammoth porkers, rail-fenced into a sizeable pasture beside the calf pen.

At least a part of one of the fresh pails of milk should have gone to a flock of fully-grown eating chickens but Al forgot to mention it. They'd do very nicely with water tonight; they were "too fat already!" They'd all be dispatched after freeze-up so the meat would keep. Al would raise a new flock with a ready batch of clucking hens and a rooster kept over with the layers until the spring. Some of the crosses made good layers as well as eaters, so the rooster had a free rein and an exhausting schedule.

Carl gathered the eggs and then went with the boys to check the herd of beef cattle and the Clyde crosses on the next quarter. The boys had made such disgusting leeches out of all of them that it was hazardous to enter the enclosures. Bulky pockets produced edible splendours of admirable variety for the horses. The cattle, resenting the snub, reacted with a deafening clamour, much to the delight of the boys. They always threw some grain to the cattle but only in the morning. The concept of time escaped the bovine sensibilities.

Carl noted several large straw piles in the surrounding fields and one that nearly covered the cattle shed, which extended into the pen that the calves were in. Two very long stacks of hay stretched beside the corral and one side of the barn. The huge volume suggested no small degree of mechanization. Carl wanted to find out more, but it was nearly dark.

Carl objected to displacing the boys, until he found that they were indulging in an odyssey of "roughing it in the bush" in a makeshift tent for much of the summer. Alice, intent on offering her bed to Carl, bowed to Mildred's suggested bit of moderation. Mildred told Alice about Milly, then followed with the glad tiding that Carl had four very good looking brothers, who would be following in short order. Without discretion or hesitation, Alice asked Carl if he had a picture, because "I can hardly wait!" The girl was as totally uninhibited as she was personally charming.

The bed was old and sagged a bit but compared to the way Carl had slept in the last few nights, it was floating on a cloud. Alice stuck her bright, curly head through the door into his darkened room and sighed an alluring "Good night!" She'd got Mildred at her hair again and Carl noted that she looked really nice. His thoughts and her actions didn't bother him anymore. He'd react to her just like he did to Mildred; he expected it. He was so tired that it hurt and he couldn't think or even dream anymore.

———

He woke, suddenly, to a wet, disgusting drool. His eyes focused on the beast and his heart and bed fell away from under him. The doorway erupted into laughter. Three young McPherson redheads, with the curly one on top, projected through to gain a first-rate view of the reaction that their invitation to Duke, the more adventurous of the two dogs, would evoke.

First, stark naked, and now in his long underwear — Alice surely had a way of getting to know him. The humour ended abruptly with the smack of a flat hand, Carl couldn't tell who it fell on, and Grandma's exploding voice. The door slammed and the tirade continued down the hallway and downstairs, into the kitchen.

Carl dressed securely, under the scrutinizing eye of Duke and both of them walked into the kitchen, to find Alice, at the stove, her face straight and sober, cracking a few eggs into the frying pan. Carl had a strange feeling that she was the recipient of the slap because she should be "old enough to know better!" Yet, despite Grandma's stern observance, Alice delivered a glaringly apparent come-hither wink on the off-side, followed by the "Wait 'til I get you alone!" look — Milly or no Milly. Carl realized that she was even worse after she'd learned about Milly. He didn't know how much Mildred had told her. She loved fun and people and was so starved for human companionship that she was going to make the most of this opportunity. If something came out of it, so much the better.

Grandma McPherson was angrily mixing up a batch of pancakes when Carl came in. "Not one single word out of you young lady. Should be ashamed of yourself!"

Paul and Mildred hadn't moved yet. There wasn't a peep out of Jimmy and the boys were filling the wood box early, as retribution. Al had taken the milk pails off their customary hooks in the porch, so Carl said his pleasantries and with Duke and Duchess, headed for the barn to help.

He spoke to Al about every aspect of his farm and learned more about the pitfalls and progressions. After breakfast Al would show Carl and Paul what he could of his machinery. His threshing outfit, as yet substantially entailed to the Western Loan and Trust Company, was some distance away and was waiting for drier conditions. The investment was a man saver and increased his productive capacity.

Al bought a large, thirty-two inch Waterloo separator and his neighbour, a horse drawn J.I.Case steamer. It was a bit under-powered, but it did all of theirs and much of the surrounding country. It was paying its way very nicely.

It had rained heavily but Al figured they could get rolling again, maybe even this afternoon, on the stacks that were up before the rain. Maybe even do some more field threshing in a few days and save a lot of work if they could get back the teams and man-power. They'd had a good six-week run with only a few breakdowns but nothing major, so they had done very well. Everybody needed a rest too.

Al had a good older gang-plough and he'd bought a newer one a couple years ago, along with a seven-foot double disk. He had a home built cultivator that had taken him all winter to manufacture in a vented, forge-heated granary converted for that very purpose. He'd bought a wall-mounted drill press, with a good set of bits, from the railroad. He had the necessary forge tools from his work and his factory was complete. The skill, knowledge and talent came from the mills and forges of the east. He said he didn't have the money at the time because he was starting on the house, but he needed the cultivator. He'd developed on it a hand-operated trip lever with a cam attached to heavy springs. With help from a foot pedal, he could lift the cultivator out, or hold it in the ground when the cammed lever was thrown over center. Most of the time, he left it in on a turn. Four horses handled it nicely.

The boys were already doing all of the harrowing with a five-section diamond harrow bar chained to a converted set of light wagon wheels, seat and all. A single team could handle it. Al had invested in a good shoe seed drill that paid for itself quickly with the superior germination and crops he got from its accuracy. Al had everything that the Pawlowiches had, except their binder was better; the knotter on the used McCormick binder sometimes gave him trouble.

The stooking was the hardest and took a lot of manpower. Sometimes, if the weather was dry and help was short, they'd haul the sheaves from where the binder dropped them without stooking.

Paul realized that he had a long way to go and he felt a bit self-conscious. Mildred reminded him that it was only four years since he'd first axed his way into the high bluff that was now the sheltered yard site, and he'd done it with hardly a nickel. Al was here fourteen years this summer. Somebody had started here before and given up. They had a soddy over their heads and some land broke and he had a few dollars to start. It would take time, work and luck and she hoped it wouldn't do to them what it was doing to Al.

———

Alexsay and two other teams pulled into the yard shortly after ten. He and Al had met a number of years before when both drove spikes on the Grand Trunk as it passed through this part of the country and because of their namesake, had established a solid friendship. Alexsay's power and speed had earned him the pseudonym, "Malatok" (hammer) amongst the Doukhobors. Alexsay'd brought a crew down and helped Al throw up his barn in a few days, a couple of years ago. Many were skilled carpenters and wood workers. The ornate bed that Mildred and Paul slept in, was a gift from Alexsay.

On winter trips, Alexsay and others had often nighted over. Alice took great pleasure in boasting that much of the English Alexsay learned was due to her efforts and he let her think it. He called her his "Crasna Hallawvaya" (red-headed girl) and fascinated her for hours with his accounts of his youth in the old country and how they'd been persecuted and driven out to this country. He told her many of the legends and folktales of his people. Alice knew more about them and their language then most in this country.

In a matter of minutes, Mrs. McPherson had a big lunch ready. A host always fed her guests. It was a mark of hospitality common to all nationalities and races and out here, it went without question. It was a sin of gross proportion to turn a guest away hungry and it was unforgivable for a guest to refuse to eat and nowhere more so than in the Doukhobor culture.

Starvation and pestilence had overpopulated far too many cemeteries in the old country and even here in the first year. Hunger was painful and unforgiveable, even to animals

Alice was clearly upset when Carl climbed onto the wagon without something more than just "Good-bye." He climbed back off and wrapped her in a Bertha-type hug. "Alice, you're a really nice girl, pretty and everything, but I'm committed to the Milly that Mildred told you about and I'm really sorry it can't be any other way. I'll be back through again, soon, because there'll be lots of things I'm goin' to need before freeze-up, that I won't know about 'til I get there. I'll see you again then. You're lots of fun to be around and I'm sure there'll be some fella along who'll latch on to you. You don't have to hurry because you're young yet. Take your time! Life is for a long time and you'd best spend it with someone you really love."

Alice's tearful look changed slowly to a look of gratitude. "Honest!" she said, "I wasn't so much worried about that as I was that you didn't like me because of all of the silly things I did to you and the way I looked and all, with my funny hair. I'm out here all the time with the boys and I hardly ever get to see a fella and I get awfully anxious to know if they'd think that I'm pretty enough. Shucks, I'm comin' eighteen in a few months and most girls are either taken or married already and I've never even had a fella call on me. I ain't nearly as silly as I act some times but it's because I ain't around guys much and it may be silly but it's a worry to me. I sure like what you said though; nobody's ever said anything like that to me except Pa and he's got to think I'm pretty; he's my father. You're a strange new fella, with a fella's eyes and you're real good looking too and I sure thank you. I sure hope you don't mind too much if I keep on liking you because I ain't going to stop, you know! See you soon!" She gave Carl a parting kiss on the cheek that hinted at a little more than friendship. It would bother him once in a while when he thought about it.

———

Carl rode up front with big "Alyosha" and learned as much as he taught. Carl was surprised at how well he was able to communicate with his hands when words would not work and how easily he understood. Alexsay was

very eager to learn about Carl's background and family because commonality, out here, was strength and survival and a major binding force. Race
and language took a back seat to most but there were still plenty of the
elitest small minds. Alexsay re-enforced Papa's warnings and he advised Carl
to avoid them like the plague, even be prepared to tolerate a lot more then
he should for the sake of peace and order. "Vwork an' mine you business!"

They stopped only to water and feed the horses at midafternoon. Two
of the wagons carried the bricks and a few items that the men had bought
for home, the other carried all of Mildred's and Carl's stuff.

The steady, slow pace rolled them up the street of the quaint, little, old
world village as the sky darkened.

It was like a step back in time. Thatched roofs were something Carl had
only read about and seen drawings of in some of the history books he'd
looked at. The place was a beehive! Every human being, even the dogs and
late geese were excited.

"Vzdobram Vetchurum!" It was indeed, a very good evening.

The women flocked around "Mill-der" with elaborate greetings, hugs,
handshakes and kisses on the cheek, even for "Car-roll." "Pavlowa" got
handshakes, but he was old news. And "Jee-mee," they adored him and
his wide-eyed stare of fascination and just couldn't get enough. They had
even confiscated one of the few pictures that Mildred had gotten done and
sent to Paul. They'd been anticipating the arrival of "Pavlowa's" wife and
child for months and they found it very difficult to contain themselves and
their enthusiasm.

Carl offered to help unhitch and care for the horses. "Nyet! Vwe do!
You goink!" He pointed to a house close by. "Missus geew you to wash.
Den Vwe go supper, meet willage."

Candles and coal-oil lamps shone a bright greeting in almost every
window and lit up the darkening street. Delicious smells emanated from
every doorway. Heavily skirted, fully shawled, finely embroidered women,
in their very best, scurried with steaming pots to a large central bare
lumber building, the only one with a shingled roof, which they called
"Doughwam," where they met for their special occasions and prayers.

"Told you there'd be a few surprises when we got here. I thought about
you, out loud, an awful lot around these good listeners. I was expecting

this but I thought I'd surprise you." Mildred leaned a smiling kiss to Paul's cheek, much to the delight of some of the young observers and the approval of the elders, then followed her luggage and Loosha, into the house to wash and change for the event to which she would be central.

———

"Slavim ee bloh da rim Boha za yavo milest!"

"We praise and thank God for his mercies!" Paul translated for Mildred and Carl. The Doukhobors had become his trusted friends for more than four years. Of course he knew.

The elaborately prepared meal began with Mildred's first move. She occupied the seat of honour and all of the eyes in the entire room. She was an impressive woman in size, appearance, dress and manner, the kind that everyone noticed. It's what had caught Paul on first sight.

"Absolutely no meat!" They served a very filling, thick vegetable "borscht" with thickly sliced, buttered bread as a staple. The dish wasn't new to Carl or to Mildred because it was common to all of central and eastern European origin. Mama made hers a little bit differently, with different proportions of the same vegetables. Both of them had grown up on it and never lost the taste. Meat, too, was often absent, though not by choice, from many tables in the hard and lean days that were a given to many of the people who sought better lives in Canada's west.

Perogies, plain dough wrapped around a variety of vegetables, usually potatoes and sometimes a surprise fruit when it was available, were boiled and served with either melted butter or sour cream. Perashky, a variety of fruit wrapped in dough and baked, were often eaten smothered in fresh cream. There were vegetables of every sort, lots of cabbage prepared fresh or as sauerkraut and wrapped around a variety of vegetables or rice if they could get some and oven roasted and served smothered in butter or tomato sauce. Fresh cucumbers were finely ground and seasoned, usually with nothing but salt and sometimes a bit of onion for flavour, then blended with nothing more than fresh, cool water. Carl loved it. It was almost like a cool drink with substance, and lots of tea, strong and black with sugar, if they had it, but usually honey the way Carl liked it.

Today was special. They'd acquired a variety of dried fruit; apples, prunes, raisins, and apricots and boiled them together into a rich, thick broth that they served cold as a dessert. Prussians prepared something similar on occasions, which were extremely rare in Carl's family. Dried fruit, or fruit of any kind, other than what they grew, or picked wild, was a luxury that most simply could not afford. Carl had been a big boy when Mary Pawlowich gave him his first orange. He'd only heard about them until then.

The meal clarified exactly the physical proportions of most of the Doukhobors. Food was a godsend to these people. Alexsay told Carl a little bit of the travails they'd suffered during the ostracism, exile and expulsion from their homeland and the extreme deprivation they'd experienced until they could clear and settle and produce for themselves when they got here. Their only crime was their religious determination to live and work onto themselves, peacefully. They'd refused to fight in the Czar's conflicts and burned their guns.

A large group of men and women arranged themselves on opposite sides of one of the cleared tables, set only with a loaf of bread, a pitcher of water and a salt shaker. A beautiful, shawled, young woman delivered a brief introductory explanation with clear, remarkable English.

"A tribute and a welcome to Paul, Mildred, Jimmy and their very good friend and our new neighbour Carl." She repeated her statement in the Russian language.

The room fell to absolute silence. Her uniquely contralto voice echoed singularly, slowly and deliberately, but only briefly as an introduction to the harmony. With absolute precision, bred of years of finesse and tradition, the entirely a cappella harmony exploded upon the silenced anticipation … bass, alto, tenor, soprano; on the note, absolute and confident. Carl could feel the precision by the very vibrations in the room, as well as hear the harmony. There was no accompaniment now, nor had there ever been. The tempo was slow paced, concise and deliberate. The words were totally clear and unprotracted. This was not only a unique style, it was totally creative.

No one in the choral group knew anything about the mathematical precision of the science of music; they just went out and did it to absolute perfection. There were no grand masters, composers or arrangers here. These people did it and did it so well because they loved it. It was their pleasure, their prayers, their balm and their salvation in times of tribulation.

It was their tribute to their God, to their friends, to themselves and to the beauty of nature.

Carl felt the emotion of the tribute and noted Mildred's misty eyes. He had never before been recognized, let alone acknowledged with a tribute of this calibre or magnitude. Both of them didn't recognize a word, yet they understood all of it. It was a plea for friendship, understanding, respect, and harmony and it was the nicest thing anybody had ever done for them. They were really equal and welcome.

The chorale ended abruptly and the room fell to dead silence once again. Carl found himself on his feet and for the first time in his life, he wiped a tear of gratitude out of his eye.

As Carl spoke, the young lady translated. "My very good and dear people, other than Alexsay, I know not one of you. Yet, because of what I have heard and felt and seen tonight, like amongst my own family, I feel perfectly safe and at home. Like so many of you, I and my family have known little of the good times and most of the bad. My father slaved on the farms of Prussia and very nearly died on its battlefields and dreamed always, of land of his own. He, like some of you, was forced to serve in the Kaiser's pointless wars. Under threat of execution, he too fled his homeland for a better world and went right back to slavery on the farms, this time in America. The results differed very little. His longings and his best efforts went as unanswered as they did in the old country.

"There are many ways to be beaten. We, like you, have suffered all but the one. I am to be my family's only salvation. I am very grateful and much more confident just knowing that I do not stand alone against the wilderness and hardship in this awesome task. I thank you for the welcome, the food, the fellowship, the friendship, the offer of help, the security and the confidence that you have given me, my family, and someone very dear. They will be joining me as soon as it is possible for me to build a roof over our heads. From my heart's core, I thank you more than I can possibly say."

Both Paul and Mildred were awestruck at the level of Carl's God-given oral ability. It was hard to acknowledge, knowing his rustic style. He sounded like anything but a backward country boy. Carl remained blissfully unaware of what he had just accomplished.

A lean, stooped, old gentleman, of some obvious knowledge, respect and authority, rose from amongst the choir and responded.

Again the young lady translated. "My son, it is not for you but rather for us, to be grateful. New life, for us, is a major blessing, for we have lost so many and we thank and praise our creator for you and your family and Paul and his.

"Your strength will be very severely tested, hopefully not to the degree that mine, that all of ours, was. In the many years to come, we will protect and support you and yours in any way we can. The land is hard and sometimes savage but we know that we can defeat it and you can well see that we have. What is unpredictable and often unmanageable is mankind, for he is extremely cruel. In this we have much knowledge and experience and we will share it with you, for neither we, nor you, have seen the end of it. Praise God for his blessings and his mercies and for all of you and yours."

The very staid and respected old man was recognized as the epitome of the Doukhobor odyssey. His entire family had perished during the many great travails of his people and he never spoke openly about it. His suffering had been horrendous; defying human endurance.

"Brotee, ee syostree, Brothers and sisters ... Oche Nash, the Lord's prayer."

Again the choir, with the same precision, evoked similar emotion with a style unfamiliar to either Carl or Mildred. This was their tribute to their God. Some of the assemblage joined the choir with equal precision. They bowed their heads in worship.

The prayer did not end as expected. The room had hardly fallen silent, yet before a word was spoken, the prayer began again. This time singularly, with amazing power and vocal flexibility. This time, in the English language, and the singular voice was a revelation to Paul, for it was his life partner's. He had absolutely no idea that she had this superior ability. He knew she had an excellent voice, as he had heard her singing to herself in her work yet neither he nor Carl expected this degree of barrel-chested professionalism from slim and trim Mildred. She smiled at their surprise. She'd often sung the "Lord's Prayer" during her childhood and throughout her teens in her church and at public events and she was clearly its master. She'd sung most of her training and working years in on-stage productions and had even taught voice to her younger protégés.

The Doukhobor faces beamed with admiration and gratitude for they understood and respected vocal ability. She had achieved their absolute respect. In years to come, they would often sing for her to hear and ask for her advice on the style.

Paul fell in love all over again. He couldn't understand how any woman with the talent, promise, and ability of this beautiful human being could be so infatuated with the rustic likes of him. When they were alone again she would tell him that he was sadly lacking in his ability to recognize himself. "Don't you ever sell yourself short to me or to anyone else again. Besides, I know you've got one awfully good singing voice that you don't seem to realize. I've heard you!"

The rest of the amazing evening passed in conversation, light-hearted song, stories of the past, more food, and fellowship. One of the women draped a beautifully embroidered Doukhobor shawl over Mildred and showed her how to tie it. It would prove valuable against the "bite" of winter.

Mildred refused, graciously, the offer of accommodation for the night. She was just a mile from the home of her life that she had ached to get to for more than four years. She was a bit surprised when she found a team ready and hitched; they knew and understood.

Carl would stay with Alexsay for the night. Mildred and Paul needed their home to themselves.

VI

"God and nature ruled."

"Is this really happening? Is this really me?"

She felt like a giddy schoolgirl but the sleeping child cradled on her lap told her she wasn't. She felt like a teen going out on her first date but the man sitting beside her was her husband and the only one she'd ever really love. She felt like running, she felt like standing and screaming with joy, she felt both like laughing and crying. She couldn't really explain how she felt; she didn't know. She didn't even vaguely resemble the shallow, dreamy personality who fell off a horse to attract this man. For three long years she'd lived with fear. Where would she be now if he hadn't come back when he did? She couldn't express in words how much she loved both of them. She didn't care about the hardships she knew would confront them; this was a beginning. Everything she'd ever done, ever wanted, led here.

"Gosh you're quiet. Are you alright? When you're so quiet, I start to worry. You're not having second thoughts are you?

"Am I having second thoughts? I just thank God and you for making this happen. This is where I want to be."

The team turned, instinctively, into the well-worn cutline through the bush and the light did indeed come from the kitchen window. The beautiful, old, kerosene lamp blazed a cheerful greeting as they rolled up to their home. No one appeared to be around now but someone must have been recently. The smoking chimney foretold the warmth within.

Paul climbed down to take their sleeping child and help Mildred. He had to show her to the door and he wasn't sure why; the design of the building was such that the light from the kitchen window cast a clear reflection on the wooden walk up to the door. She seemed to fumble for the latch, so Paul opened it.

"What's wrong?" He looked around the shadow cast by the recent gift that she wore against the chill and saw her eyes filled with tears. "Oh my!" They stepped through, into the warmth of their home. Again, "Oh my!"

"What?" she asked, her joy and anticipation mixed with concern.

"They found some paint. I have to tell you that the place wasn't nearly so clean when I left to get you. All I could do was to think what the two of you looked like. I used to lay awake nights picturing, in my mind, the two of you sitting at this table talking to me and now you're really here." He kissed her tear-wet cheek and then her wide, smiling mouth. "The team will wait a bit, let's put Jim to bed." He passed the sleeping child to Mildred, picked up the lamp and led them into their living room, again stopping with his stereotypical "Oh my!"

Again, "What?"

"They've papered the walls and painted the ceiling. They were just unfinished lumber when I left. God bless those people! I saw Anastas working on this before I left ... certainly had no idea it was a gift for us." An ornate, two-seater bench with a hand carved, decorative, backrest and a cushioned seat faced the large, warm, enameled heater and the living room window beyond.

"It's bigger than I expected and much nicer than I imagined. I'm almost jealous that I wasn't part of the building. I thought I'd be roughing it as a pioneer wife and you bring me to this? It's beautiful! Did I tell you today, just how much I love you? Thank you for my wonderful home!"

"This is our room." He led to the door, left ajar, to allow warming air in. An enclosed stairwell passed over it to the second floor. "It was one big room, like upstairs, until your letter about Jimmy, so I partitioned it and put a door between, so we can hear and get to him without having to come out and around here." He pointed to the other door, at the end of the stairs. I'm afraid that my, that our, bed isn't the best you've ever slept in. It's not very big and it sags, so we'll sure sleep together."

"Well, if that's your idea of uncomfortable, I don't know what you'd call comfort." Mildred, first through, pointed to the newly built replica of the heavy bed they'd slept in at Al McPherson's.

"Alyosha!" Paul stated, recognizing the handiwork. "He built Jimmy's cradle too." They passed through into their son's smaller bedroom. The cradle was plain and simple but more than adequate for some time to come. Alexsay often said that he didn't like cribs for children once they were able to walk. It was from the cradle to the bed. He knew what it was like to look out between imprisoning bars and he wouldn't impose that on any human being, especially a tender and precious child.

They unwrapped their offspring, pulled off his tiny boy's cap and laid him on his side in the feather-ticked security of his own cradle, in his own room.

Mildred helped Paul with the luggage and groceries, then went in to start a pot of coffee while Paul unharnessed the team and fed them in the small corral beside the barn. The night was chilly, though bright and clear and Mildred was anxious to see all of her new home but it would have to wait until tomorrow. She couldn't really take much more tonight; it must have been near midnight. Paul's old alarm clock, demanding his firm, winding hand, sat dormant on the counter of the kitchen cupboard. There was an awful lot that needed doing tomorrow.

She was very grateful for Carl's discretion. They really needed to be alone this first night in their new home. They blew out the lamp and sat for a time, on Anastas's bench in front of the heater, with the moonlight pouring through the window.

They awoke, smothered between the feather-tick mattress and heavy woollen quilt, to a bright, clear morning and their son's inquisition regarding his mysterious location and his demand that he be changed immediately and fed quickly.

———

Carl insisted, despite all the objections that he help clean up and carry some of the trappings of the evening's event back to their rightful locations. It most have been nearly midnight by the time they closed the door behind them. Alexsay and his Loosha were gracious hosts and his bed was superior to any he'd ever had the pleasure to rest in. He nearly drowned in its feather-ticking depth.

Despite the comfort, Carl's night was a restless vigil. For generations eternal, Buechlers had slaved and slugged and fought and died of war, work, starvation and pestilence, since none could remember. Now, here he was, the very first, less than a mile from Buechler land. Within the crowded confines of his European forbearers, one-hundred and sixty acres would have netted him status, prestige, wealth, power, and authority. Many, like him, would have cowered at his will. He could have directed their destiny just as his had always been directed. What would it mean here? How would he fare? Where would he start?

The fire crackled in the stove yet he neither heard nor saw anyone. Either Alexsay was very silent for his size or Carl had actually slept a bit. Only a full-length blanket separated him from the neighbouring kitchen and its colouration depicted the glow of the kerosene lamp without.

It was still very dark outside. Apparently "early to rise" was a part of Alexsay's credo. Carl was up, dressed and out, with a speed that amazed even him.

"Forst, vwe lookink you place. Vwery close. Vwe mwilkink and fyeedy-ink, den vwe go." He pointed the exact location out of the window. "Vwe putyink you thing 'shala-shok'(storage shed). Is good dere. You tyakyink vwhat nyeedyink. Pavlowa shala-shuck neemah (no got). Vwe close you. You comink vwhen nyeedyink."

Carl understood the instructions clearly. He was a bit worried about the substantial supply of garden seed he had well packed but Alexsay assured him that they would keep dry and very well where they were. The village stored their garden seed in the same building and it always grew.

The entire village was awake and about before Carl and Alexsay got out. Barn lanterns flickered and waved but the horizon was already bright. They wouldn't long be needed; kerosene cost money. Most of them either turned their lamps down or sat by firelight when they didn't really need light. Carl had learned the art of night dwelling for the very same reason.

Within short order, the chores were done and Alexsay hitched the team to the wagon, despite Carl's objection. He knew better as Carl would well learn. "Vwalkynk lots, ridyink vwhen could." He picked up his axe and grub hoe. Carl already had his aboard and they were off. The team, at Alexsay's command, moved like he did.

Carl was excited beyond belief. In little more than a few minutes, Alexsay stopped the team and acknowledged Carl's puzzled look. "Toot!" (Here!) He pointed to his right.

Carl vaulted carelessly, off the wagon and dropped to his knees to kiss the ground. "Nyet!" Alexsay said, standing beside him and smiling appreciatively. He pointed to a thin, metal rod that stuck out of the ground. Carl was twenty feet off. He repeated his previous procedure and grabbed his hands full of the grass, tossing it wildly over his head, screaming with sheer delight. The startled team would have left them but Alexsay had firm command. Carl didn't even notice.

To this strange, big man, Carl's statement to the assembly the evening before, took on meaning. Carl wasn't a Doukhobor, he hadn't suffered their tribulation. Yet what Alexsay saw, took him back, emotionally, to that great moment when he first realized that he was free. His eyes filled, but not to the extent of Carl's. He placed his great arm around the young man.

Carl was embarrassed when he recovered. This very large, strange man knew nothing about him, or he of this man, yet he knew everything about the feeling because deprivation and suffering stood a common plane.

The exploration began. They tied the team, shouldered their axes and then walked the perimeter. Alexsay knew that the road allowance would lead directly south from their village, the way that they had come, so Carl had best seek a yard site along that side.

There was the matter of water in the determination. It was dry now, so Carl would have to depend on the advice of people like Alexsay and Paul, who knew the runs in the spring. He'd need a good well and the Doukhobors had considerable experience at finding likely well sites. Carl had, himself, spent many days, shovel in hand, digging for it. Now it would be his and he anticipated the chore with glee.

It took them the entire morning to trace the four corners of the property and mark them clearly so as not to require a repeat. It was early afternoon when they once again came upon the restless team, tied for over four hours.

Alexsay wasn't big without considerable re-enforcement. He consumed prodigious amounts of food and he hadn't replenished his store since early that morning. Carl would have foregone dinner but Alexsay threatened to eat a horse if he didn't get something soon so they headed back to food in abundance and Loosha's reprimand for being late.

Alexsay warned Carl not to become too anxious as he would be there for a long time. They faced the long, cruel winter and it was very wise to get on with the preparation before its arrival. He indicated that it was likely that Paul was in desperate need of assistance as his trip to get his family had cost him valuable time. They had already done just about all they could to help, without jeopardizing their own preparations. Paul's second team was still in their corral and Paul would surely have need of them soon as he hadn't done any of his fall fieldwork. It would be appropriate if Carl rode them back as quickly as possible.

Before Paul left, the team came over, dressed in nothing but halters and the ropes that led them. Alexsay stuck a bridle on the Percheron mare and leading the bay behind him, Carl was off in the westerly direction that Alexsay pointed.

Following the crudely cut but well-used trail, through the broken bush prairie, Carl couldn't help but ride into Paul's yard ten minutes later. The sun was already creeping down the horizon.

The barn and a granary were the first to cross his vision, both of them clearly recent. A small corral on the west side of the barn encircled the first team, harnesses still intact. A larger fenced area restrained the very friendly, roan milk cow.

The familiar animals echoed an uproarious greeting. The road turned toward the house, which sat some distance to the right, three-sided by the dense bush, with a clear view of the barnyard. A pile of rough-sawn lumber marked another as yet unfulfilled initiative.

The house chronicled Paul's progress. All one had to do was observe the colouration of the unpainted lumber to know the history. The smaller gabled, weathered structure, which now housed the kitchen, was Paul's first habitation. The newly constructed, much larger, two-story portion marked the happy man anticipating the arrival of his love. Two large posts, pointing upward to nothing, demanded a roof and the wooden sidewalk to the future veranda was so recent that it suffered no sun or rain stain and still smelled fresh-lumbery. The remnants of a depleted woodpile, lying just to the right, foretold an urgent necessity. The wagon sat right up beside the house, its tailing board leaning lazily against a wheel. Two forks worn shiny and a sizeable mound of potatoes in the box, displayed the initiative of the recent arrivals.

Carl tied the team to a post while the pairs on either side exchanged adoring nuzzles and soft conversant grumblings. The cow leaned through the tight wire to express her desire for at least an affectionate rub, or better yet, a tasty treat. Carl accommodated her initial desire.

The small voice, with a screech of glee, welcomed his trusted friend. Paul, with Jimmy under one arm and a slice of something in the other, waved Carl in. The racket the livestock made at Carl's arrival could have roused the deaf.

Carl was as impressed with the interior of the house as Mildred was. It was so arranged, as to depict a size greater than it really was. The kitchen accommodated the table easily, with lots of room for expansion that would be so necessary at harvest times, but there wasn't time now for the grand tour.

Mildred's hair was tied back with a scarf. She wore dirt-spattered overalls, two sizes too big and her face radiated joy and a fresh-washed look. They'd left the house for the potato patch at mid-morning, had forgone their dinner and only now came in with their burden.

Jimmy slept and was fed out there and seemed thoroughly revitalized. He crawled his way over to Carl and clawed up the pant leg, anticipating his reception on the welcoming lap. Carl knew the boy would soon be on his feet giving account of himself. While he carefully drank the coffee Mildred poured, Carl responded with an expressive conversation and a firm grasp on the strap of Jimmy's tiny overalls. Carl'd eaten just over an hour ago so he declined the food.

"Where's the patch? I'll go dig. Don't look like it'll freeze tonight so even if they don't get put down, we can cover 'em good, just so we get 'em out quick."

————

By the time Paul got the load down the chute and drove back to the patch, Carl had nearly half of what remained, on the surface. Mildred stayed back to make a decent supper.

Paul was amazed at the technique Carl used. He had dug, in the short time, nearly as much as Paul and Mildred did all morning. Carl stepped the fork in, then leaned the handle back, while at the same time, pulling on the dead vegetation and flipping the whole sideways, the way Papa had taught them.

It was pitch dark when they rolled up to the house with the job done. Mildred, wondering what was keeping them, wouldn't believe the story until she personally looked into the wagon.

"Raised a couple of acres every year, since I was twelve, to sell for grocery and spending money ... matter of fact ... just did two wagon loads a couple of weeks ago, before I left."

They ate quickly. Mildred knew her way around the kitchen too. By ten o'clock, they had everything down in the cellar and the outside lid closed. Somehow, Mildred had stopped the leak in the stove-boiler and had warm water for them. They were tired and didn't waste any time contemplating their achievement. Carl rolled out his bedding in the big, upstairs room and crawled in.

"As long as you're thinking about her, why not roll over and invite her in. I used to do that and look what it got me." Mildred called, jokingly, up the stairs.

Early next morning, Carl was awake and down again before daybreak. He was refreshed and thoroughly alive. The fire roared almost immediately; the old, large stove had an excellent draft. While the water heated, he had the large wood box filled. The morning was mild and the warm wind predicted a glorious day.

He found the coffee and had it on. He got out a large pot, for want of something smaller and poured it about half full of the hot water, then put in three cups of oatmeal from the older, opened bag. For a bachelor, Paul was well stocked.

The oatmeal was popping merrily when Mildred stumbled out to see what the racket was about and saw almost everything ready. Carl thought he'd been very quiet but she had "the mother's ear." Paul woke when she got up and now he too was out.

"Do you eat in the middle of the night?" she asked. The now functional, old alarm clock read six-ten. "Gee whiz! It stays dark here longer then back home. I got up at six the day we left and it was lighting-up already. Here it's not even showing. I didn't think we'd come that far north."

"Just wait!" said Paul. "By mid-December the sun'll be up at the crack of nine and down before four in the afternoon. You'll learn to use your night-eyes. It's a damn nuisance when you're tryin' to get somethin' done during the nice days but it's a blessing too 'cause you get a bit of time to rest and think and plan. You'll wish you could have some a' that rest time during the summer when the days run on forever and you've everything to do to get ready for this.

"It's a good thing you're here Carl 'cause we didn't get much sleep night before last and yesterday was a big day. There's an awful lot to do yet."

"Quit your grinning! It wasn't for the reason that you're thinking! I'll bet that you haven't even thought about such things have you? Don't you wish she could be here?"

Carl's embarrassed blush remained but his eyes revealed that Mildred hit a tender spot.

"Oh gosh, I'm so sorry! I, of all people, should have known better. Did you even contact her since you left? I can tell you, that as bad as you feel, she's having at least as hard a time and she's got no way of working at putting things together to help. You're going to sit down tonight and tell her about everything. We'll find some way of getting it off to her soon."

"I sent her a telegraph, 'bout the land, the same time I sent one home so she'll likely have it by now and have some idea where I am."

"Paul had no real address for nearly two months and I was scared silly that I was past-history, so to speak, but when I got a letter with a location, I felt better and could send off mine."

"Yeah, all eight of 'em! I think she'd have liked more from me but I was so damned caught up in work, I couldn't get to the mail every week. I think I averaged 'bout one a month and some of them were pretty short but I hope they helped."

"I'm here ain't I?"

It was fully daybreak now and everything had to be done. Paul milked the cow and Carl fed the teams and harnessed the ones he'd ridden over, hitched them to the wagon and pulled it over to the rack that sat on two heavy rails across forked posts. Paul had two higher posts with a similar rail across, all set up for a winch because the box was heavier and needed it. Carl drove the wagon under and Paul brought the homemade winch from the barn. They lifted the front of the box clear and slid it back onto big blocks of stove wood, then drove up to the rack. Alone, Paul would have backed the wagon under with the team but that was a demanding task on him and the team and required a multitude of attempts. With Carl's help, it was easier to unhitch and wheel-roll the wagon under. Then they simply lifted the rack, one corner at a time, and pulled the rail away, setting the rack on the wagon bunk. Paul secured it with a length of chain, already tied to the rack and they were done.

The straw pile was around the bush behind the house but some distance into the open pasture. It was a miserable chore in the dead of a cold winter so Paul wanted some hauled into the yard. He'd threshed a very heavy oats crop this year; a lot of it was on last year's breaking. It filled the granary in the yard, a new one in the field by the straw, and two stalls in the barn. He had one awfully big straw pile, two really, because the first pile blew up too, and would have plugged the blower if they didn't crank it over to the second pile. He'd wagoned the rest of the grain into the yard because there wasn't really any room there for huge straw piles that would have to be disposed of every year and fire was surely not an option like it was in an open field. He preferred this way, as long as there was enough help during threshing.

They had two loads in and stacked beside the hay, before dinner. Paul offered to go over to Carl's and help him find a yard location but Carl liked getting a job finished before another filled his mind. They went hard all afternoon and it was after dark when they finally quit with the last load still on the rack for morning. Paul hadn't dreamed that help could make such a difference. He'd done most things alone.

By two the next afternoon, they had the fenced-off hay yard heaped; more than enough for security. Spring could come in June.

Paul hadn't yet fenced the entire quarter because barbed wire cost money he didn't have. He had succeeded in fencing a pasture, which included a slough and an open, wild, hay meadow. It rounded the straw pile so the animals could rummage in it during the warmer winter days and the spring and summer. That saved a lot of work and feed.

People often let livestock wander in the fall without a problem if they checked on them daily and didn't let them get too far or do damage for a neighbour. They could wreck existing fences to get at one another but everybody took that in stride. You simply fixed a fence that your cattle damaged.

He had over eighty acres under cultivation already and another twenty broke, ready for the spring. It would clearly be a major challenge to handle all of it without a large expenditure on equipment but he didn't have the money. The house had nearly tapped him but he hadn't borrowed yet and didn't really want to.

He'd talked about it with Mildred and she told him that they wouldn't have to; all the years she'd worked hadn't exactly left her penniless. She made it totally clear that anything she had was his just as much as his was hers.

Paul didn't doubt that he'd be in over his head if he'd had to buy all the lumber. He could have log and sodded something temporary but there was Mildred and a desperate hope of something he'd never really had. He paid with his strength. He'd try to do something to help Carl and he knew the village would too. They respected everyone who respected them because too many viewed them with scorn and a racially, literate contempt.

Livestock were always a part of Carl's life and always would be, they'd need lots of water. A large part of his youth and early back muscle was expended on the never-ending pursuit of the vital fluid. They were not about to deny its powerful influence in opposition to a site with nothing more than an aesthetic attraction; there had to be a respectable equilibrium. Cattle could walk to water. A yard site couldn't run for cover.

They crossed the quarter several times at a variety of angles and finally established a location that satisfied, at least partially, all of the variables. It consisted of a natural clearing, which sat on a shallow ridge that ran northwest to southeast alongside a gully that showed clear evidence of plenty of water. It still held a good pool after the dry autumn. A nearby dig would surely bring in a shallow water table. The drainage would be good and the ridge led several hundred yards to the road allowance, offering a clear dry access. Much of the village was clearly visible and a short walk would put him in view of the bluff surrounding Paul's.

Paul had pointed out that his site, in the thick of the bush, offered excellent shelter as a consequence of several years of backbreaking work. This site wouldn't be quite as weather tight, but it offered fair security from the storms of winter and would likely be reasonably snow safe. More sheltering bush could be planted.

Carl couldn't express his feelings. Joy and enthusiasm gave way to stone-cold determination and ambition. He was silent on the darkening walk back. The ballasting axes hadn't left their shoulders but both appreciated the real extent of their accomplishment.

Paul had no one, other than the Doukhobors, to offer support. He had often floundered with indecision and lack of the knowledge acquired with experience. Even now he was often tormented by thoughts of all the "roads not taken." Carl would suffer some of the same indecisiveness yet Carl was founded on years of hands-on experience.

The lantern flickering quickly across the yard and the crisp, clear flute of Jimmy's voice in the dead-still air determined, to Paul's gratitude, that he now had a family for support. The animals were secured for the night. That had never been done for him before.

Though city-born, Mildred had the unique experience of a grandfather whose livelihood had centered around livery livestock so they became a part of her childhood. After school, unlike all of her classmates, she cared for them, just as she did now.

The smell wafting out of the door woke an emotion that Paul hadn't experienced for a long time; somebody cared enough to prepare the very best. In the right hands, even the rustic foods of the prairie bachelor could become a delicacy. Eggs were a staple, if he could get them or had a few hens, with only two options, either fried or boiled. These were scrambled, not unusual, but the flavour favoured the woman's hand. Mildred had sliced potatoes, with a bit of onion for flavouring, into a roaster and had slowly ovened them in a bit of milk, with salt and pepper, nothing more. The odour and flavour awoke, within them, an entirely new appreciation of the lowly vegetable and an alarming degree of restrained gluttony.

"You got any sisters?"

"No! Just two mean and ugly brothers, both of whom cook about as well as they look. Your Milly will surprise you too. Better stick to her." The response sounded like a reprimand.

"Not for me. I've got four brothers, all of them love their food and I've got to find a way to get them out of our kitchen and into their own, as soon as possible. I just thought I'd ask."

"Our kitchen? You are really talking to her. Wow! But I still think she'd really appreciate that letter that you haven't yet written." She laid a bundle of paper and a beautifully engraved fountain pen, a parting gift from the hospital and staff, on the table beside him. His own lay forsaken at Alexsay's with the rest of his stuff.

"Write it now."

She picked up the barn lantern, the only other source of light on the place and escorted Carl to the small table in the living room, then turned without a further word and walked back into the kitchen and took up, again, the train of conversation where she'd left it before Carl's indiscriminate question.

Carl was no stranger to words because he loved to read, more than most, but he was uncomfortable with putting thoughts on paper. His handwriting was scratchy and his spelling was only as predictable as the sound of the word and he wrote like he spoke to the villagers the other night. He'd tell her everything he could think of from the jumble of his mind, as eloquently as he could. Mildred came in to see how he was doing.

"Do you love her?"

"I sure do!"

"And I think, from what I've seen, that she loves you too. Write like you'd talk to her and tell her that way. She's taking you for what you really are and this isn't really you. You don't have to impress her, just tell her everything, even if you think she won't understand all of it. It'll show her your faith and trust in her and she'll work at figuring everything out, or she'll ask until she does. It'll keep her involved. Ask her things. Let her find things out for you. I'll bet you that she's got a couple letters written already, just waiting for an address. Believe me; I know!" She turned and left again. She'd never even attempt to interfere, or read his letters again.

He was on his own and he wrote long after the others had cleaned up and gone to bed. He told Milly and asked her and poured out his thoughts and concerns and dreams and plans and drew a map to show her the way the yard would look and where it was.

Hours later, he signed, "Remember, I love you!" and viewed with disbelief, the stack of paper and the hour. He enveloped the many pages and floated off into a blissful sleep with them lying beside the pillow.

He was up and out, again before daybreak, addressed the letter from memory and leaned it on edge, in obvious view, atop the warming chamber of the stove.

"It must have been near midnight before you got done and you don't want it goin' up in smoke. Either one of us or somebody from the village will be heading into town, usually every week, to take care of things like that. They usually pick up stuff like the mail and the odd things that others need so everyone doesn't need to run all the time. We ain't that far away from each other out here now but it's a hellish distance to York."

The nights, so far, had been frost-free, highly unusual for this country. Paul had to get some of the land ploughed that he would seed next spring, so he got at it. Carl could harrow but there wasn't anything worked yet and they'd be knocking together for a few days.

All Paul had was an ancient single furrow sulky that someone in the village no longer used, so they'd let him use it. They'd seen him walking endlessly and fighting with his walker, day after sweltering day. They had several nearly new ploughs and the teams and manpower to keep them working for long hours so they didn't really need it anyway. One team could pull it in the worked ground but it took both teams to turn new sod. That was already done for this year so one team was free.

Paul knew the free team could pull the walker in the open areas so he instructed Carl to take them and the rack over to the village and pick up the plough. The villagers were using it to turn some light brush because their gangs were too heavy to pull in that stuff.

Carl found the village in a flurry. The two loads of brick that had followed them in from York were nearly done covering the naked dougham. Not two, but three ploughs rolled and a disk followed. In so few days, the virtues of communal labour manifest themselves to an amazing degree. Human nature and group psychology made labour far less burdensome when everyone carried a portion of the load.

Carl found the old walker scoured and well greased-over to keep the rust off. It was someone else's property and was to be treated with care and respect, just as they trusted others to care for and respect theirs. The breakage was repaired with a hardwood handle and was as good as new.

They lay several long, heavy planks cross the rack. It took four to lift it on so Carl wouldn't get it off by himself. The planks could serve as an incline and Carl could hook the team to the protruding hitch end and pull it off without dropping it and maybe breaking a handle again.

They filled Carl with as much tea as he could hold and two slices of fantastic, fresh bread, then informed him that they would be sending a team into town for, as they joked, "Mails and nails."

Carl picked up some of his tools and cooking utensils, including several pots and pans and his only washtub. He had to unpack it because it was packed full to save space. Paul's was too small and things, including themselves, needed washing.

His explanation evoked a good humoured response and they trundled him off in another direction to personally inspect a small, hitherto, inconspicuous building, centered around a sizeable, barrel-like stove piled over with large stones and surrounded with two-tier benches. It was a steam bath like what Carl had read about from Roman and Greek times. He didn't think anybody had those things now, but here it was.

"You comink! Vwe vwashink togedar!"

He was totally blindsided; he was surrounded by women and he characteristically misunderstood. His reaction and expression was obvious in any language. They didn't try to explain, they just roared with laughter and embarrassed him even more. Mercifully, the eloquent young lady who had translated everything into both languages the other night, came along and clarified the fact that it wasn't co-gender at all. She left him with a day and a time.

Close-up and hidden under all the traditional garb, Carl recognized a very pretty girl, hardly his age, shy and nervous around him. She interpreted his blush and produced one of her own.

Where were they all coming from? Around Maynard, none of the women even gave him a second look — here, they tried not to look too interested but it showed. He was flattered but steadfast.

He'd thought of going right out to his place to start the ploughing but he had to get back and tell Mildred about the offer and see if she needed anything. Besides, it was a chance to mail his letter. He took the plough out to his site and pulled it off along with the tools he thought he'd need right away, then headed back with the rack. It would take some time but things like that could often save time in the long run.

Mildred had all she needed right now and wouldn't have much time to do anything with it if she had more. The windows surely needed curtains but that was a winter job and they'd lots to get in before the snow flew so Carl left the rack and headed back with the team and his letter.

The plough was a real sod-turner. It worked beautifully in these soft, deep, prairie soils, rolling the grass and light brush right under and the rich, virgin black ribboned out behind him. There weren't many dangerous stones to knock him flying. This one was a lot easier to handle than the Pawlowich's because there wasn't as much side-draft that he'd have to fight with — far less exhausting for both him and the team. Paul said the Doukhobors just loved it and had often used it for that very same reason.

The team was clearly accustomed to this procedure and knew instinctively how to perform. They were work-hardened and well fed and they stepped along about as fast as Carl could handle. Animals like these were God-sent. Their value was well beyond their price and Carl hoped that he could find his own as well trained. A baulking, high-spirited team was alright on the racetrack but out here they were a time waster and dangerously unpredictable.

The horses seemed to sense Carl's determination and responded with their own. In an hour's time they had an area turned that would grow enough to feed Carl and a dozen others next fall. Carl loved the smell of freshly turned soil even better now because it was his own.

He steered the team over to the depression and watered them and himself. It must have been noon, judging by the sun but this was new territory so he wasn't really sure. He wasn't hungry yet so they went at it again.

All that afternoon, Carl's mind centered on the wisdom of his alternatives. He couldn't keep depending on the good graces of Paul and the villagers and he was, by nature, strong willed and independent. He had no idea how much the basic machinery would cost up here but he had to get a lot done in a hurry without killing himself in the process. A desperate family depended on him. He knew the money would disappear fast and he'd need a lot more. There wasn't anything left at home that he could count on.

He hoped Max and August could find some work that paid better than the farm subsistence they got around there. Maybe there'd be some in the machinery plants at Charles or Waterloo. There was no way for him to get them up here for a year or so, yet he knew that if Mary sold, they could very well wind up back at the creek.

He'd heard some pretty disturbing stories about winters up here. It was hard to believe with the beautiful weather he'd seen so far but everybody talked about the unusually beautiful fall this year. He was worried about when the snow would come and how hard.

If he took Hank and Archie up on their offer, then how would he get anything done around here? This was what he'd come for and what he and Papa and the family always wanted. There were no quick and easy answers. Only time would tell. If only he had the wisdom to make a half-decent guess at the fortunes and misfortune of every action he took.

It was nearly dark when exhaustion and hunger pulled him back to reality. He'd overdone it. The team, willing to give all on demand, flagged heavily. He felt ashamed of himself; he knew better. They'd put in a day's work in an afternoon and tomorrow would bring more.

He pulled the plough out of sight into the bush and unhitched. His feet ached horribly and his muscles trembled from the exertion. He led the team back because they were as tired as he was. The mile seemed an awful lot longer. It was totally dark by the time they'd drained the trough and Carl had the harnesses off. Paul had a pail of oats waiting.

Next morning, despite the cramping, a bit of stiff aching and lingering exhaustion, Carl was off at daybreak. This time he left the team for the axe. He'd trim out some of the tougher areas so that he could keep the field straight.

Again he struggled with his thoughts and emotions; the magnitude of the job began to overwhelm him in all of its stark reality. Yesterday's progress was fantastic but every day would not be the same. If he could keep the pace, he'd have a sizeable field in next spring. Now, if only the weather'd hold!

He worked desperately, almost futilely and tired faster than yesterday. Early afternoon found him verging on physical collapse and knowing his endurance, he was puzzled. He sat back against the hard reality of the plough.

"Sinok!" (Sonny) ...A gentle nudge and Carl shot to his feet, fully awake and embarrassed. He startled the older man.

Anastas, seeing the blackened strip and disappearing bush, had come out of curiosity. He saw the extent of the accomplishment and came upon the lone, exhausted figure. He had seen such desperate hope and deadly ambition pronounce the downfall of too many. Anastas was very much afraid for the young man.

"Seadie!" (sit) he directed. He had only a minute grasp of the English language but an aptitude for making himself understood. He pushed Carl's shoulder down beside the plough and sat himself. He unwrapped a simple cloth bulging around a clay-moulded jug of personal vintage, filled with strong, black and heavily honeyed tea. Carl shook as he drank.

As the old man watched, his mind filled with painful, horrid reminiscence. Carl's sugar-bagged dinner sat nearby, still tightly wrapped. Anastas drew a brown paper bag from the large inner coat pocket that would keep it warm against his chest and handed it, opened, to Carl. Neither said a word. Carl ate as the two observed each other.

Anastas saw the fine, rugged features and the powerful frame of the young man and the fear in his eyes and remembered the travail of his own youth. Carl saw the concerned eyes and the livid scar that ran down the side of the old man's head, behind his ear and somewhere under the collar of his shirt and he recognized physical and emotional pain hidden beneath.

The piroshky were filled with a paste that Carl was certain was crushed, well-cooked beans, flavoured with something that Carl failed to recognize. His shaking stopped and his anxiety waned. He felt a strange peace settle upon him. He knew that the old man understood and he knew what the old man was doing. He saw Al McPherson and the white cross, he saw his father's concerned and anxious eyes and the anticipation in the faces of his siblings, he saw the pleading hope in his mother's fading eyes and he saw Milly's beautiful, smiling, confident face. "The peaceful life" extended to the emotional and the mental, as much as the physical. This fanatic drive would certainly guarantee him his own white cross.

With hardly a word, Anastas had achieved his intent. He pointed to the setting sun, to his mouth and to the village. Carl declined the unspoken offer and pointed to Paul's, all the while expressing his thoughts in English with the hope that the old man would catch much of it. He grasped both the old man's hands as an expression of gratitude, then went his way carrying an undeniable and clearly understood bond.

Carl dragged back with extreme effort. His chest ached, his head throbbed and his stomach churned. He was powerless to deter the affliction that he knew was upon him.

"Man, you look like hell! Are you sure you're alright? Tree didn't fall on you did it?"

"No! I'm just very tired." Carl washed himself slowly, enjoying the relaxing elixir of warm water. He ate very slowly and quietly and he didn't pack it in as he usually did at day's end.

"You're not feeling very well are you? You read like a book, you know. You're not going to get anywhere by working or worrying yourself sick. You'd better take it a bit easy for a day or so, or I can promise you, you'll wish that you did."

Paul brought his former swaybacked bed back in and carried it up the stairs, one piece at a time and set it up as close to the door, for warmth, as he could put it. Mildred wrapped Carl in a heavy blanket and sat him close to the living room heater while Paul got the bed ready.

"Do you have any tightness or pain in your chest?" Carl shook a silent, lying "No!" Strangely, he couldn't get warm and he began to shake violently, as if he was freezing.

Mildred was very concerned by what she saw. Carl heard her go up the stairs and speak quietly to Paul who came down with her. She prepared a warm drink for him, which smelled, pleasantly, of some medication and then topped it with one of the white pills that the doctor had given for the head injury. "Now we'd best get ya' up to bed."

Carl rose and found himself without the strength to stand. He slumped back and Paul had to help him up the stairs. He'd never felt so helpless before. Paul helped him into the bed and covered him tightly. Mildred followed up and told him that the drink plus the pill would help him sleep and that he would likely develop a high fever.

"Don't worry about it, because we'll be watching. I have more medication to help with that and I've learned a few tricks over the years that I know work. Call if it gets worse and don't wait. You are a very sick boy."

Carl collapsed into a tumultuous sleep fraught with horrific imagings and a scorching heat. Voices echoed, faces flashed and blurred. Someone lifted him and poured a cool liquid down his parching throat. He vaguely felt the cooling effect of something damp and aromatic on his burning skin and he heard Mildred's voice saying "pneumonia."

There was no sense of time, nor did it matter. The voices continued infrequently and so did the cool bathings. Somebody forced pleasant tasting, warm broth into him on a regular basis and he heard strange new voices that he couldn't all identify or understand. He remembered hearing Alexsay and he knew he had acknowledged him by name. He saw a worn face that he recognized as Anastas and he heard a part of what he thought was a prayer. A very strange tranquility settled over his turmoil and he knew he was alright. He slept long and peacefully.

VII

"Look who's back!"

"Well for goodness sake, look who's back!"

Mildred's voice echoed down a long, hollow tunnel. A gentle pressure wriggled up his thigh, squirmed onto his aching chest and amplified into his face as Carl's mind's eye flickered, focused, flashed off and then on again and he was awake. The miserly airflow was restricted further and then mercifully, the burden lifted as the protesting child vaulted from view and Mildred's tired features focused in.

Something cool and camphorous swabbed down his face and neck and onto his shoulders. The little face appeared again, inches from his, with curious question about the lack of the accustomed affection. The towel fell onto Carl's chest and the tiny hands smothered Carl's features with it. "Hold it fella!" She pulled him clear again as Carl struggled to clear his vision and congestion.

"No tightness in your chest, eh? You're not a very good liar you know. You had everybody scared to death. It's a good thing that you're as tough as you are dumb. I think you're a little bit dumber then you're tough," she scolded.

The old bed creaked under him as he turned toward the enamelled heater with a kettle purring contentedly on its back. "Paul and Alyosha carried you down here, bed and all, so you wouldn't get another chill. I'm surprised that you don't remember; you grouched all the way. It got pretty cold the last couple of nights."

"... Couple of nights? Good Lord, how long have I been down?"

"You got sick Friday night and today's Tuesday. You were about as sick as I've ever seen. Thank God for Anastas! He and Helen spelled us off keeping

G. D. Benneke

an eye on you. He had some type of broth … didn't say what was in it but it tasted unusual and it surely worked. There's certainly something to be said for the old grandmother home remedies. Paul and Alyosha made him go home this morning because he was exhausted. Are you hungry?"

"I'm not really sure but I could use a cold drink."

"Nothing colder than room temperature. I've got some fresh soup on. I'll get some of that."

Carl felt wet and sweaty so he lifted the blanket to get some air. "What the heck!" He sucked it back tight; he was stark naked.

"Alice ain't the only one," she teased. "Now, there's me and Helen. Oh, don't worry! You haven't got anything I haven't seen a thousand times. Honestly! You country boys are so well put together! Milly's sure lucky!" She planted Jimmy back onto the bed beside him and chuckled his embarrassment all the way back to the kitchen for the soup while Jimmy got the attention he craved.

The soup was substantial and Carl wolfed it down. "You're definitely on the mend and it's a good thing too; I'm almost worn out so hurry up! Don't you think all this is going to be free. I'll find a way to get it out of you somehow." She playfully shoved him down so Jimmy could get at him and she would be free to get back to the supper. The sun was down and it was darkening. Paul was still out on the plough and would be cold and hungry.

Carl's strength returned quickly. In a couple of days he was up and about but the ragged cough and shortness of breath persisted for some time.

As long as his chest bothered him, Carl restrained his ambition. The invincibility of youth had to surrender to the common sense of adulthood. He had responsibilities such as never before, well beyond his singular independence. He didn't know how to react to the care and attention of this couple who were barely familiar with each other. He wished there was some way he could repay them to the extent that they deserved but he had nothing other than himself so that's what he offered.

As soon as he was able and Mildred judged the issue, he assumed the household duties and the care of their child. He freed her up to do some of the things she enjoyed and she ploughed like she'd grown up doing it while Paul cut and cleared and added to the woodpile.

Carl's meals were simple but wholesome; what he made, he made well. Mildred complimented him and threatened to surrender her obligation entirely if he saw fit. In less than a week he cared for the animals as well as the house and his little charge was a constant companion. While Jim slept each afternoon, Carl tried his hand at baking and with a few attempts produced tolerable bread and a decent batch of oatmeal cookies. Mildred had a very good cookbook that he referred to constantly. He found the mannerisms of the stove the key to the quality of his products.

His concern over the status of his land and the need for rapid progress was constant and he tried desperately to envision a plan of action that would earn him the most progress with the least effort in the shortest time. This inopportune illness had really thrown things off but it couldn't be helped and he'd have to first think, then work his way around it. The persistently beautiful weather only added to his anxiety so he busied himself any way he could while his lungs healed and his strength returned.

He assumed an obligation to repair whatever he could find. Paul's tired old bucksaw was the first to experience his talents. He'd never done it before himself but he'd always watched Papa sharpen and set saws so he'd do his best. By the time he was done, the miraculous tool floated gently down through the hard, dry wood with little effort and the woodpile grew. He always liked the smell of fresh-sawn wood and the effort helped build his strength.

Every tub, boiler, and pail resisted the temptation to leak, including the built-in reservoir on the kitchen stove. Every door hinge worked solidly, the corral rails were all back in place and the pasture fence sang fiddle-string tight when he plucked it. He actually found some time to do something foreign to his nature; he rested a bit.

Jimmy had an insatiable curiosity and a magnetic attraction to dirt. At about four o'clock each afternoon, the ritual bath took place before Mother came in and witnessed the shocking little grime-ball. At noon Carl always saw to it that Jimmy was washed and his clothes usually weren't too bad yet.

Carl sought another source of endeavour and the growing pile of laundry caught his attention. He found an old scrub board, filled his large tub, and went at it. The humidity helped to clear his congestion, and did wonders to his desire for revenge. Mildred had insisted that the laundry be left to her but Carl wasn't feeling particularly obedient. Paul hadn't yet found the opportunity to manufacture a clothesline, so convenient, lower bushes served the purpose. When the couple came in that evening, Mildred's instinctive response was, "Why that bugger!" Her undergarments fluttered merrily at the forepeak of each.

That evening, as they sat around the living room heater, Carl announced that he and Jimmy had been preparing an event for them. He lifted Jimmy from Mildred's lap, took him into the center of the room and left him standing alone, then returned to his seat to observe their amazement as Jimmy waddled quickly after as if he'd been doing it for some time. After the hugs and kisses Carl apologized; he realized how very important the milestone first steps could be to the parents. It didn't really matter to them, the fact that their son was now on his feet was all that really mattered.

To this young family Carl had become more than just a friend and a fellow in need, he'd become a part of their lives.

Anastas came to see how Carl was coming along and insisted that he and the family come and spend some time in the "Bawnyah." Paul recommended it strongly. He explained that it was so pleasant that he didn't find it necessary to get a larger washtub to keep himself clean. Mildred had wondered about that but didn't ask. She wondered, too, about the communal bath style but didn't quite make as big a fool of herself as Carl did.

———

The stones, heated since early afternoon, exploded into intense, hot steam that penetrated every pore, even deep into Carl's grateful lungs. The water barrel stood near the heater and gathered some of the warmth; very cold water could cause some of the stones to crack when it was poured on.

The warmth and humidity was hypnotic. Carl found it hard to stay awake. Everyone in the room just sat and enjoyed the relaxing, cleansing, steam; it had become an event among these people and was sacred to their communal life. Here they could relax and socialize and plan and contemplate their lives, past, present and future. It served both governance and spirituality.

Occasionally someone would rise and pour another dipper on the stones and the steam filled the room to the point of invisibility. After the better part of an hour it got to the point where the heat was telling and it was time to leave. They rinsed themselves off with water from the barrel and went severally, into a tiny, adjoining room, to dry off and avoid a chill, before they dressed and went out into the cool night. Usually they went home but tonight, because of their guests, they gathered at the doughwam. The women and the few smaller children had finished earlier so they could put the children to bed.

The experience did marvellous things for Carl's cough and lungs; he didn't even feel like himself ... like he was on the outside looking in. He wished he'd done this earlier. Mildred remarked that she couldn't ever remember feeling so good and so clean. They had to acknowledge the spiritual reality of the experience. They were at peace with themselves, and their world.

God, he wished he could see her! He went to sleep with the sound of her voice.

Fearing Carl's recent illness, the crew put him at the saw to see if he could take the exertion of keeping the wood clear. He threw for two days at the village and they did all of Paul's in an afternoon. The experienced steamer and the crew performed flawlessly, with speed and precision, built on years of practice.

Because the community was scattered and few power saws existed yet, the sawing would continue to some distance from the village until the weather brought things to an end. Carl and Paul were invited to leave, of necessity, because of the demands of their own work.

Paul hooked both teams to his sulky and worked the open areas while Carl cleared as much as his growing strength would permit. Part of the advantage Paul saw on Carl's land was the fact that it consisted of larger open and light brush areas that would allow for breaking at least half of the quarter without the extreme effort of cutting and piling heavy bush. Carl lacked bush land experience because most of Iowa had been long since cleared and his meticulous nature had to be taught to forego aesthetics in favour of immediate gain and physical necessity.

By the time the afternoon temperatures would no longer allow the ground to thaw enough, they had turned and harrowed well beyond the required acres. Carl would have his first crop in the ground next spring.

Cooperation had and would continue to ensure the survival of many vital friends and neighbours in the harsh yet fertile landscape.

The weather stayed clear and the afternoons were fresh and relaxing to work in. The scattered pile of lumber shaped up into another granary-like structure that would serve for the necessary storage and Carl's bundles were among its first occupants.

Mildred got her clothesline, with a stout smooth wire, one very pleasant afternoon as great, gentle flakes of snow began to drift down.

The next morning was clear and warm again. Nearly a foot of slushy snow formed into puddles and then into streams. Carl walked over to his place and was more than pleased with his choice of a yard location as the runs were clearly evident and were performing much as Paul and Alexsay thought they would.

————

The huge, long-legged beast, many times larger than any deer, calmly walked out of the bush only yards ahead of him. It shook its enormous antlers, threateningly, in Carl's direction, as it blew a grunting hiss of warning. Carl froze, with wonder as much as discretion, as they observed each other carefully.

The animal decided that Carl posed no threat and continued its determined, ungainly trot across what would be Carl's yard and into the bush to the northeast. Carl had seen pictures of bull moose but he'd never seen one alive. They were common in the lake districts of Minnesota, but rare in Iowa and Carl didn't realize that they were so large. One of those would set a grand table for the winter but the Mauser still lay, wrapped in its oilskin, in the newly built shed. He could kick himself for not bringing it.

It would be a shame to kill such an impressive animal but the lack of meat was one of the very few virtues of the Doukhobor teachings that Carl could not willingly appreciate! A steak or a roast would really be nice tonight. The only meat they'd had since their arrival was canned or dried and then only in small quantities, usually as a base for soup or in a stew. Meat was always readily available in the barnyard at home but this was home now and there wasn't anything yet.

When he got back he told Paul and triggered an enthusiasm that surprised him. He was forced to unroll his weapon and retrace his steps to show Paul the track. It was indeed "the prize" that Paul had sought for several years. It seemed that Paul had crossed this same set of tracks at about this same location for the past several years and had never yet seen the creature that made them. He pumped Carl's memory for an accurate description and for anything else Carl could remember; he seemed almost envious.

They tracked the creature for some distance, placing themselves in danger of a very late return but never once caught even a distant glimpse. The animal was wary and old and it had gotten that way based on its ability and instinct. The stretch of its stride indicated its size and the speed of its movement. It was headed for the winter security of the lakes and heavily · wooded hills, miles to the east. Paul would miss it again. Secretly, Carl was glad but Paul was the inveterate hunter.

The weather turned even colder for the next several days and it became clear that the "big one" was on the way and there was a lot they would need. The neighbourhood was in the throes of organizing a joint trek to York to stock up; the weather was very unpredictable this late and there was always safety in numbers.

Carl could only look for, but he couldn't buy a team because there wasn't any feed put up to keep them. With the oats in the stalls there was restricted room in the barn and he couldn't get anything built now. Paul told him he would need better mitts and a heavier mackinaw to stand the rigours of winter out here, so Carl gave Paul some cash to buy that for him and he'd stay back with Jimmy to allow Mildred to get all that she needed.

Carl's pneumonia had made it apparent to Mildred that her medical background thrust upon her a responsibility beyond what she had anticipated. She'd need, at least, the rudimentary medical necessities to look to the care of her immediate vicinity and she needed to make arrangements to have her savings wired to the bank at York.

Carl wrote another letter to Milly and a briefer one home to tell them what had already been accomplished. They'd be very anxious to know.

For some time Carl looked forward to the possibility of a response to his first letters.

VIII

"It screamed like myriad demons!"

By the light of the low, cold, early-morning moon, Carl waved a well-equipped mother and father off to join a caravan of wagons. The morning proved beautiful beyond seasonable expectation so Carl loosed the livestock to the welcoming distraction of the straw pile. Because the cow was getting close to delivery and was subject to a once a day milking, Carl was concerned about the use of the enriched milk that she would be producing but Jimmy needed milk. It didn't seem to bother him in any way so far but Carl chose to take a late morning walk over to the village to get some of the leaner, skimmed product. Jimmy always enjoyed a good "piggy-back" and the welcoming reception he always got every time he was there. Besides, he had learned a new skill that Carl wanted to show off.

There was no way they were allowed to return without a huge, filling dinner. Carl's selective timing was not at all ignorant of that certainty. Jimmy, always the center of loving attention, had been so well fed that he fell asleep almost immediately and the sun was beginning to dip in the horizon before they left for home. The temperature remained warm yet the ominous wind was picking up and Carl was anxious to get going; it could get too cold for the child.

Despite the concerns of some of the women, he left the village and witnessed an ominous wall of white rolling in from the west. He'd have to turn back or risk Jimmy yet he'd have to get home to the livestock.

They had a team ready and the attractive young lady, despite her blushing, was delegated to drive the two home. All of the younger men were gone and the responsibility for the large herd fell to the women and the elders.

The team and the light buggy covered the short distance in a matter of minutes, yet the time was too long. The white wall shrouded them first with extremely heavy snow squalls before the rumbling roar, audible at a distance for some time, consumed them with horrendous compression. The driven flakes seared the exposed flesh and the wind ripped their breath away. Carl opened his mackinaw and buried the terrified child against him.

Everything was instantly immersed in a torturous field of white. He could barely see the face of panic on the young lady and the team disappeared. For the first time in his life, Carl was shocked into an all-consuming fear. The extent of this fury was totally foreign to him, yet he'd been warned about such things.

The white dissipated noticeably, as the experienced team struck the treed lane to the sheltered yard and walked up to the door. The girl grasped the screaming child and ran into the house as Carl headed the team for the barn and tore them free of the buggy. Paul's livestock stood at the rear entrance with frantic anticipation. The snow swirled crazily in the sheltered yard and visibility was restricted but still functional.

Hurriedly he tied the team to the cribbing of the oats bin and opened the back door. The horses paid no heed to the interlopers and rushed into their stall with gratitude, whinnying wildly with fear. The cow staggered into hers with difficulty, well into the pangs of delivery. "Jeez! That's all I need!"

Carl unharnessed the company and fed the establishment, guessing his way around the familiar barn in the diminished light.

Despite the shelter, the only evidence of the house was the reflection of the window light and he struck for it as the wild currents buffeted him with insane fury. The sheltering bush amplified the roar beyond hearing. It was more like a deafening flood.

Jimmy sat, tear-stained, on the young woman's lap, trying to eat one of Carl's oatmeal cookies with his one, almighty tooth. The cook stove was crackling but the house was still very chilled so Carl got the living room heater going. By the time he returned to the kitchen, the mirrored windows rattled white and the house seemed to vibrate.

The situation could have been very dangerous had they not been so close and the team as experienced and dependable as they were. Carl thanked God and the young woman for the kind offer of the ride. He and Jimmy would have perished in this. He hoped that Paul and Mildred and the others hadn't encountered a delay and had gotten at least as far as the McPhersons'. The clock read a quarter after four.

"I don't even know your proper name," he said.

"Helen!" she replied. "The Doukhobors call me 'Hawnya.'"

Carl blushed wildly and she reflected a response. So this was the Helen that Mildred teased about. "Ain't you Doukhobor?"

"I am, but I'm Prussian; Doukhobor is a spiritual following. My folks followed the teachings of Menno Simon. We all lived in the Caucasus region of southern Russia and were all kicked around for the same reasons. There seemed to be something more to motivate the persecution then our refusal to fight in their ridiculous wars. They seemed to be afraid of both our communal lifestyle and our refusal to cave to their denial of our religious teachings."

"I don't mean to pry but how'd you wind up here and knowing English so well?"

"Mother was English. Father met and married her in England. She taught us very well."

"You have brothers or sisters?"

"One of each." Her beautiful face began to distort. "I can hardly remember what they looked like any more. I was only eight when they disappeared. I don't even know if they're still alive. The Doukhobors cared for and raised me. I've been part of them ever since. They're the only family I've got now."

Carl questioned no further.

The soup he'd put on was hot, so they drank its warmth. The stove made its presence felt and Jimmy had drifted off again, after his fright. Carl put him into his cradle and dressed to check the cow.

It was pitch dark by now, so the light would serve him well. The lantern rocked and flickered wildly but thankfully remained alight, ringing Carl into a tube of white. The house-light behind stayed a constant beacon and he was surprised when the barn wall rose, suddenly, in front. He was grateful for its security. The temperature had dropped alarmingly.

The hooves and snout had emerged but the cow was exhausted by the effort. Carl ringed the hooves with hayme straps and pulled when she pushed. The calf was large but manageable and very much alive. In a few minutes the wet, helpless creature lay gasping at life. Carl wiped the face and probed the nostrils free of obstructions, then pulled her to the head of the anxious, adoring mother for the thorough cleansing and bonding. He drew some of the first milk from the understandably fidgeting beast and forced some, as best he could, into the reluctant, sputtering, calf. The experienced, trusting cow accepted Carl and the process as part of the natural order and went on with her licking.

The barn was nearly new, double-lumbered and very airtight so Carl didn't worry about the likelihood of frost-bite. He threw the resting horses more feed and braved his way back to the beacon and the warm kitchen. If anything, the fury without seemed to intensify with the darkness.

From the outset, Carl was just a bit suspicious that he and Helen were being set up. She was, by no stretch of the imagination, the only one who had been capable or free to drive him home. The older men were at the village; Carl saw them, yet here she was. None were aware of his circumstance and he hadn't spoken very much of Milly to anyone here.

He wasn't overly surprised because the typical, old, motherly matchmaking obligation was not unique to any specific culture. Helen was, after all, of the same Germanic stock as he and she spoke English fluently. Why not open wide the doors of opportunity?

She was growing uncomfortable with the situation because they were alone together with a small child in Carl's care. There was absolutely no way she had any option but to night over. She wasn't at all worried about Carl's intention any more then he was about her but she knew there would be consequences and incriminating questions would be a certainty.

Carl as well knew that the word would get out and he wouldn't be viewed quite the same in the village. It would be taken from an attitude of good humour but he was serious about Milly. What if she found out? "God, what'll Mildred say when she finds out?" Carl knew the village would be worried to distraction by their overzealous ploy. They certainly hadn't anticipated a result to this extent.

Helen's naturally fair complexion only served to amplify her lustre. She spoke comfortably and openly about her concern, but the blush was an uncontrollable part of her being. Carl wasn't much better. They kidded each other about their common fallibility.

He'd brought back some eggs with the milk and there were plenty of boiled potatoes so the typical "bachelor's friend," the frying pan and the large pot of soup served to throw together a delicious meal in a hurry. Helen was overly familiar with strong tea but coffee, in her household, was rare at best. It was a treat.

Carl prepared a bottle for when Jimmy woke up; he'd be a bit disturbed even though he was very comfortable and familiar with Carl. He'd never been away from his mother for so long. She was always there at bedtime and first thing in the morning.

Carl dressed to go check the cow and calf and Helen's warning against it proved valid when he opened the door. Driven by the furies, it very nearly left his strong hand and he slammed it back shut.

"I've seen this before in this country but never this bad, especially this early," she said. They spent the evening in the living room, soothing the disturbed child and swapping life's stories.

Helen was disturbed by Carl's lengthy account of his circumstance and his family. She appeared pleased by his relationship with Milly and told him so, wishing him the very best, then flattered him with her wish that someday she would meet someone like him.

Helen's story wasn't nearly as passive. She didn't remember all of it but what she did, she saw through eight-year-old eyes. Her father, no different than Carl's, left the same army, during the same war, for the same reasons and in the same way. To avoid a hangman's rope or a firing squad, he fled to Britain where he'd met and married her mother. He'd found work quickly with a British merchant company. Because he spoke German, Russian, and a fair degree of English, they shipped him and his family over to Caucasian Russia.

Because of his wartime experiences, he soon adopted the principles of the German-speaking Mennonites living in that region and became a hard and fast proponent of the passive religion. The company, receiving complaints, dumped him for his refusal to drop the following and as a consequence, the family lived with the Mennonites and suffered with them.

They too had been rounded up like cattle and persecuted into starvation. She'd seen her father beaten to the threshold of death and her mother raped by the Czar's finest, in front of her terrified children, simply because they too refused to acknowledge Russian Orthodoxy, or to fight in the Czar's wars. She remembered the starvation and the day when she'd last spoken to her very sick father, then she saw him no more. They ran and hid with their displaced community, always afraid, always hungry, always sick and very tired.

She remembered the cold, the wind, the snow, the dark, and the death. She remembered the guns and the fire and the screaming and the bloody remains ... Abe, that's all she ever knew him as, grabbing her and running on and on until morning and hiding all day, for days on end. She remembered stealing and begging for food and shelter ... the hunters and the dogs and that horribly cold morning when she awoke, wrapped against Abe in his large coat and found him cold and dead of his wounds.

She wandered in the snow for as long as sense and sensation continued, then she lay down to surrender to death. She remembered the voices, the Russian faces, and the pain. She remembered little of her lengthy, torturous recovery, yet she was old enough to recognize and appreciate the compassion of these people whom she recognized as the Doukhobors she'd often heard her parents speak about. She became the willing obligation of Anastas and she learned that he'd lost his entire family to the same evil that had taken hers.

As she grew, she listened and she learned that although they'd saved her, none of them were safe in Russia. They spoke of Verigin and Tolstoi and the Quakers and Canada.

She spoke of the cold, damp, stormy, sickness-ridden journey that went on forever and the bodies of the old and sick and weak, wrapped in blankets, consumed by the cold, blue-black, frothing ocean, the broken young mother, hiding the body of her dead baby for weeks, because she didn't want it thrown into the ocean, the quarantine in isolation that deprived them even further, the human barn and then the sod hole they crawled into for that first horrible winter. Worst of all, though they cared for her needs as they cared for their own, she spoke of the sense of no family, of not really belonging.

She, like Anastas, was alone and she grew up with him. Although he loved her like his own and she, like a father, they lived under a terrifying, emotional shadow that everything either of them had always loved, always perished horribly, painfully, and certainly. Because of his age, she now returned the care, with the overriding fear, that soon she would, once again, be all alone. Like Anastas, she hadn't opened her tortured soul for anyone to see until now, to this strange and appealing young man.

She sobbed intermittently throughout and coiled herself into a fetal position on the padded bench. Carl cradled her head and shoulders on his lap. Then she was asleep, quietly, peacefully, with a confidence she'd never felt before.

Carl carried her to Paul and Mildred's bed, taking great pains not to jar and waken her. He removed the shawl from around her shoulders, where she wore it constantly. Carl had never seen her without it. He removed her shoes and covered her. The heavy sweater would wake her, so he left it on. He picked up the lamp, looked in, re-covered the sleeping child and placed the half-empty bottle where he knew Jimmy could find it in the darkness.

He went back into the bedroom again and looked long and thoughtfully at her. Why anyone so perfect should have to harbour such horrors was more than he could comprehend. The degree of her torture would often haunt his thoughts.

He dragged his mattress and quilting down the stairs and beside the heater for the night where he could better hear Jimmy. The upstairs was freezing cold behind the closed door so he left it open a crack to let a bit of heat up but not enough for it to cool the downstairs. He carried the lamp into the kitchen, turned it down a bit and left it in the window, just in case. He banked the fires against the dramatic temperature drop, then crawled into the quilting and lay awake, thinking long and hard about everything and everybody and listening to the roar of the storm. He prayed that Mildred and Paul were safe.

He rose again and wrote beside the lamp, far into the night. When again he'd get to see Milly, he didn't know but he knew that he'd have to. He told her everything he'd seen and experienced, how he felt and what he thought. As soon as he could, he'd go back to her, if she'd have him, and bring her here because he didn't think he could stand living without her. He didn't even think about what he had just said and what his words meant.

Carl slept fitfully and got up twice to check on both and stoke the stoves. Jimmy fretted a bit, but Carl dried him, gave him a warmed bottle and soothed him back to sleep. There wasn't a sound out of Helen. Outside, it screeched like myriad demons and the house shook.

Something gentle, but noisy, woke him to a room full of daylight. Jimmy was already taking full advantage of his newfound propulsion. Obviously he was quite capable of climbing out of his cradle and finding his way. They'd have to be careful about leaving things around, especially if they were sharp or hot.

The room was very cool so Carl pulled Jim under the quilt beside him. He smelled coffee and oatmeal and the kitchen stove crackled so he ordered Jimmy to stay, pulled on his pants and shirt then got the heater going from the live coals still there.

Helen walked in, her "Good morning" as cheery as any he'd ever heard. She picked up the anticipating child and carried him into the bedroom to change him, as naturally as if she'd always done it. "A child is everyone's obligation when the need arises," she commented in response to Carl's query. "I've seen herd animals do it many times. Only mankind would question the motive." Carl had meant it in a teasing fashion but children were never a matter of levity.

Carl ate quickly because the wind had subsided and he was anxious to get to the barn to care for the animals; especially the newborn. He was all for taking Jim and his guest out to see the calf but Helen warned against it. She knew the dangers of this climate. "And you'd better be careful too — watch the wind. It can change so awfully fast."

The animals were fine, even the beautiful, fully dried heifer calf. Apparently she'd been up and had sucked herself full and was now lying just out of tongue-stroke of her reaching mother. Carl prodded the calf closer. Some, after feeding their calf naturally, became unreceptive to human hands but this creature understood her role clearly. Paul had chosen her well.

Carl managed to get several pails of water to each of the animals before Helen's concerns became frightening reality. The wind roared back with renewed vigour, as quickly as it had the day before. He opened the doors to a wall of white. He could see nothing. "If you're sheltered and secure, stay where you are until it breaks. It's bound to sooner or later."

Only insanity could motivate him to attempt the house. He knew the direction but without a reference point he would lose direction and not even know it. Death would be certain. The barn, with all the animals, was warm enough. Even the ammonia-filled environment wouldn't hurt his lungs. He threw several arms full of hay on top of the oats, then crawled into it, covering himself.

Hour after disgusting hour he waited, impatiently. ... always the wild howl. Helen would be frantic with worry. He'd have to find his way back somehow. Maybe the light after it got dark?

"The wire!" He remembered the roll of barbed wire he had leaned against the barn a few days ago, just to the right of the door. He could tie the end to the door handle and then roll his way toward the house. There'd be enough on the roll to get him there. Then, if he couldn't find the house, he could pull his way back to the safety of the barn. He'd give it a try. It was late afternoon and getting dark. Maybe now he could see the light from the window. The milk was alright but it wasn't solid food and he was getting hungry.

The storm wall was just as white and the vacuum force wanted to pull him out into it. He couldn't believe the power. He couldn't have imagined weather this violent. He bent down, protecting his eyes from the stinging sleet, rummaged in the snow behind the door and pulled the heavy roll in. The leather mitts would protect his hands, but he wasn't sure how he'd fare in the deep snow. He wrapped it several times around the door handle and then tied it, securely, so that there was no way it would come loose under strain. He wrapped his scarf tightly around his mouth and face and slit his eyes, then stepped out into it and braced himself against the unbelievable force. He shuddered to think of the sheer power on the open prairie.

With his back to the wind, he reeled his way out in the general direction of the house. The snow, away toward the middle of the yard, was hip deep and he had great difficulty backing his way through it and carrying the roll. He struggled on slowly, his weakened lungs aching from the exertion and the cold. He hoped he wouldn't pay dearly for this foolery.

The heavy roll lightened and dwindled. He felt he should be very close if he'd stayed on course. Already the sharp cold cut through his trusty mackinaw. Paul was right; it wasn't warm enough.

He reached the end of the wire ... no house. Cold and disappointed, he began pulling his way back toward the barn, leaving the wire to trail out behind him rather than carrying its weight.

Something hit the side of his face, hard, piercing through the scarf and into his cheek. Instinctively, he loosed his grip to protect his face and too late realized his fatal error. The hard, steel wire, rolled at the factory, had assumed the nature of a coil, and rather than trailing out behind, as it gained length, it sprang back, the end slashed into his cheek and now it was gone, coiling rapidly, despite the depths, closer to the barn. He grasped wildly, with panic desperation. It wasn't there. He flailed frantically after it, to no avail.

Where was he? For the first time in his thoughtful life, Carl lost all reason. He lunged, more swimming then running, frantically, in what he was sure was the direction of the barn. After several minutes of this insane logic, it too wasn't there. When reason returned, it was too late. He was totally lost to this hell.

———

She stood there clearly, directly in front of him. "Mama!" he screamed. Sensations had long since ceased. He felt tired and warm and reached out frantically for her welcoming, comforting embrace, just as he had as a child. She shunned his advance. Very hurt, he pleaded for her comfort. Stern faced, she turned from him and pointed to the despairing image of Papa and all the kids. She stepped to one side and out of the picture, revealing the pretty, anxious face. Milly's hand reached for him but she was too far away. Then she beckoned to him, "Come!" and he struggled after.

Something solid struck him hard. The image exploded and the pain of reality returned. He struggled back to his feet to grasp the offending obstacle as thought and sensation returned. "It has to be!" He reached up for the line wire that he couldn't feel but the resistance told him it was in his freezing fingers. "It's the clothesline post!" He knew where he was. His feet had disappeared but they carried his weight. It would lead him to the unfinished veranda and the door. He couldn't see the light from this angle yet he knew he was safe.

———

Hour after fateful hour, Helen waited in despair; the roar and vibration of the most violent weather she'd seen in her lifetime shook the house. Where was Carl? He was a careful and cautious young man yet she knew the often misplaced and fickle courage she'd witnessed in so many, somehow, she knew he'd be trying something and it terrified her.

Helen heard the pounding on the side of the house and saw the shadow flit across the frosted pane. She jerked the door frantically, until it tore from its frozen socket and the frost-bound, snow-clogged figure fell through and onto her, nearly felling her as well. She eased Carl to the floor and dragged him the rest of the way through, then barehanded the offending snow back out and slammed it shut.

This one was still alive! This time there was hope.

Carl wasn't unconscious, but he wasn't aware either. He was so exhausted that he couldn't reason any more than the knowledge that he was now inside the warm house. He cared about little else.

Carl was very far from safe and Helen knew it. Fighting for life on the barren steppes, many had perished from exposure. His core body temperature was, likely, dangerously low and she knew the trend would continue to the point where many of his organs could simply shut off and he could die. Somehow, she'd have to try to stop the slide. She knew of only one way and she had to do it very gradually.

She thought of filling the large tub with warmed water but it was too small to get him into it and there wasn't enough water in the house if she could. She pulled off his boots and socks. His toes were discoloured yet they weren't frozen; they were still very pliable. When she flexed them and rubbed them rapidly, a hint of normalcy began to appear. His hands were the same. She unwrapped the scarf and was pleased to see that only the exposed areas showed the white of frostbite. She rubbed these vigorously for several minutes until the white began to fade.

With some coaxing, Helen got Carl to sit up and help take off his mackinaw and sweater. She had to humour him out of his pants by letting him believe that she was who he imagined her to be and that he had an obligation to the family. She got him up with some difficulty and noted that he walked strongly and was still reasonably coordinated, that was very good. She got him into his bed, opened the draft on the heater to a danger-ous level and hung a blanket over a chair beside it to heat, then wrapped it tightly around him while she heated another.

When the circulation started to bring life and sensation to the limbs, he'd be in agony and she didn't know how she'd deal with that; sleep would be the best, but how? Anastas or Mildred would know what to do.

She rushed into the bedroom but Mildred had taken the bag from which she dispensed the white pills. She had instructed Helen to give him one, only if he woke up during his pneumonia delirium and Helen hoped to find them and do the same now.

She searched the kitchen cupboard and found only Paul's common remedies for the day-to-day aches of too much physical strain. They'd have to do. She changed the blanket, than got some lukewarm, very sweet tea into him. She rubbed his hands and feet with red liniment and pulled his mitts and socks back on, then wrapped them with snow-filled towels to slow the warming. She brought the steaming kettle back onto the heater, hoping his delicate lungs weren't affected by this. Then all she could do was sit and wait and pray. Mercifully, the child slept through all of it.

His sudden shout startled her awake. The room was chilling so she piled in more wood, grateful for the fact that she'd had the presence of mind to fill everything she could that morning, during the lull. She checked the child and found him asleep but completely saturated. She changed him and the bottle silenced his lament. The kitchen clock read two-thirty. The storm raged on. She was exhausted.

Carl shivered uncontrollably. "God I'm cold! I just can't warm up. I'm sure glad you found me. I thought I was gone, sure. Hold me a bit, just 'til I warm up."

Helen looked into his eyes. They were wide open, but clouded. That scared her. He was delirious again.

"You there?"

"I'm right here!" She crawled in next to him and held him tightly.

"Thanks!" he whispered. The shivering continued for a time, then he relaxed and began to breathe heavily, again in sleep.

She wasn't certain who she was. God knows what was going on in his deluded mind. He was just lucky to be alive.

When she'd first seen Carl at the Doughwam, her heart had nearly jumped out of her throat. She'd searched his face for tell-tale signs, hope against hope. She searched her mirror that night for similarity ... his hair, his face, his bone structure, his mannerisms, and his speech. It was amazing! Only last night had she finally put her hope to rest. She'd love him and everything he loved, like the brother she knew she'd lost. He'd unknowingly administered a miraculous balm to her emotional agony. She slept, holding him like a lover. He'd never know.

She awoke to silence. It was nearly daybreak. Carl slept peacefully and she listened to his breathing for signs of congestion. He felt warm and peaceful. Maybe, by some miracle, this strong, young man would defy the fates.

She pulled off the soggy towels, socks and mitts, then rubbed the hands and feet dry. They looked discoloured but that could only be superficial. It looked like the circulation was alright. They weren't turning dark at all. She knew there would be a lot of pain yet he was unusually calm.

She got up and rebuilt the fires, put the kettle on the cook stove, hung up Carl's wet clothing beside it to dry, and dressed herself in what she had with her. It wouldn't be enough to stop this onslaught so she crawled into Carl's large mackinaw. She found a pair of smaller boots that must have been Mildred's and pulled on several pairs of Paul's socks. She wrapped more scarfing around her head and pulled Carl's big mitts over her thin knitted gloves, to tend to the livestock in any way she could. She fought again, with the stubborn door and had to shovel it clear when she got it open. The clouds and the temperature told her it was far from over.

———

Carl woke with a start. He reached over and found no one there, yet the dream had been so real. Cold realization filtered slowly back and he recognized where he was and what had happened. He felt like hell. His face was burning hot and itched painfully. His toes and fingers screamed agony. He could withstand pain without complaint but this was verging on about as much as he could take. They moved freely yet hurt so badly that they'd lost all the normal sensations. The tips felt thick and leathery.

Jimmy was crying. Carl sat up and nearly lost his balance, he stood when his head cleared. His feet felt like his body weight would crush them. He called for Helen but received no answer. Jimmy met him at the door, crying harder with recognition. He knew something dreadful had happened but his friend had not deserted him. He reached up for the comforting embrace as Carl crouched to his knees, fearing his own stability. When he rose again, with the child, he had to steady himself. The crying stopped as the puzzled child looked with question at the discoloured, dishevelled features of his friend.

Carl stepped very unsteadily into the bedroom but Helen wasn't there, she had already made the bed. He called again and again received silence. He knew what she was trying to do and he feared for her. With painful difficulty he changed Jim and struggled to the kitchen window to look out.

The snow had stopped but a haze of deathly cold hung over the silent yard. The open barn door steamed violently from the warmth within and the barbed wire stretched from the veranda post to the barn door, she'd read his intent. He turned and warmed some milk for Jimmy then sat with him near the stove as Helen came through the door carrying the milk pail.

She was surprised and relieved to see him up. He would be alright. She'd fed the horses and cow and cleaned and bedded them. "Wasn't much milk. That's a healthy calf ... got a big appetite. How are you feeling?"

"Well, I've felt better! What I thought was goin' to happen to me last night, I'm just glad I'm here to feel anything. If you weren't here I'm sure both of us would be gone. There's an awful lot I've got to know about this country and I'm sure glad that people like you and the Karmadys and the good Lord are lookin' out for me."

Helen prepared a heavy breakfast; Carl hadn't anything to eat for a day and a half. "The human body does strange things when there is a will and a reason to live. I've seen, too often, what happens when people have no hope," she smiled. "Maybe you don't realize it but you, as well, have given me the only good reason I've ever had." Carl wondered what she meant but he didn't ask.

She tried valiantly to carry some water to the animals until Carl told her just to turn them loose. They'd head for the well if she could get the water up for them. They'd head back without trouble later, because they weren't used to the extreme cold and depth.

She did well and the beasts co-operated. She had a bit of difficulty getting her team into their rightful place but she managed. By the time she was finished, she was tired from the deep, loose, powder and very cold.

The wind was blowing up again but it wasn't snowing so it wasn't swirling in over the trees and they could see in the yard. Yet the devil himself shouldn't have been out in it. What had happened outside the yard? They didn't want to know.

Carl hoped nobody was desperate enough to try to drive home in this. He was sure they wouldn't be able to use the wagons. What was happening to the men in the bush? Helen said the shacks weren't very big or well insulated. She hoped they wouldn't try to get back to the village until this blew over.

Carl was subject to unexplainable bouts of chilling and shivering several times that morning and afternoon. Helen wrapped him with the warmed blankets and kept the heater blazing until they passed. His respiration seemed to be alright yet the chills were replaced by bouts of fever and they exhausted him. Helen tried to get him to rest but he found sleep impossible. She wished out-loud, that Mildred hadn't taken the pills. Mildred had put them up in their bedroom closet and told Carl that any medication he or Jimmy might need would be there.

Helen administered the pill that afternoon, put both her charges into Carl's bed, and left to check the livestock and replenish the wood. Jimmy thought it was great but found his companion very poor entertainment. In short order, both were asleep.

———

Helen lay on Anastas's cushioned bench, covered by a heavy quilt, sound asleep. She needed their presence. Jimmy still slept, though very actively. The abrupt little foot, driven directly below Carl's ribs was what brought Carl fully awake. Carl tucked the child back under the blanket and sat up quietly; he felt immeasurably better.

He sat a long time, just watching her sleep. She'd make a perfect life-mate, beautiful, intelligent, concerned, hardworking, experience in every aspect of the pioneering life, and she desperately needed a place in her tumultuous life. Helen had saved both of them by her presence and caring and she was here now. Her nature and mannerisms were as perfect and lovable as her appearance but she wasn't Milly. He adored Milly and he knew just how Milly felt about him too, even though he knew far less about her then he did about this woman. He thought how strange it was that life would cast into his emotions, two such fantastic creatures. He'd do everything within his power to see to the well-being and happiness of this woman because he loved her too, in a special way that did not evoke passion or desire.

He stoked the fires quietly. His feet and fingers pulsed wildly and they appeared to be swollen a bit but the violent, irrepressible pain had subsided and he could walk and grasp more comfortably. He covered himself with several extra pairs of socks, mitts and scarves. With his problems and Jimmy he didn't know just how much rest she'd got. He'd try to give her a break and look to the livestock. The visibility was again growing murky and the snow was starting to come. He'd be far more alert this time.

It was dark by the time he got back and the storm was more threatening. The two slept on. This was unusual for Jim but it was hard to tell just how much the child mind understands and how this had affected him.

Bread dough was rising on the cupboard counter so Helen had done a lot today. She had a large pot of potatoes peeled and on the back of the stove along with a smaller pot of carrots, so they wouldn't boil too quickly. Paul had a number of tubes of homemade sausage, well cured and wrapped, hanging down in the vegetable root cellar to keep it cooler. Carl wasn't sure if Helen would eat any but he'd bring some up anyway.

Her face appeared at the head of the ladder with Jim's sleepy wonder a bit higher up. "What on earth are you doing in your shape?"

Carl came up with the sausage and a couple of onions. "I've got a lot more life in me than you think. I've never set out to be a burden and I never will." She'd never reprimand or question his judgment or capacity again but his attempt to roll a loaf out of the bread dough ended in pain and he had to apologetically acknowledge the degree of his incapacity. He contented his pride by feeding Jimmy some of the well-mashed potatoes covered with the flavourful gravy Helen put together from the sausage. His trembling, senseless fingers actually got most of it into the child. He was feeling very much better. Mama often said that life meant a lot more after you came close to losing it.

———

The unusually severe weather continued its assault for three more days and prompted desperation and panic-ridden concern. Communication of any kind was impossible and part of human nature that demanded redress was the need to know, despite the fact that if something unfortunate had happened to the travelers or the timber crew or the two German children, it was not only impossible to respond but far too late. The villagers met daily to discuss possibilities and options. They could dispatch a rider to the Karmadys' during a lull and risk a life. The others were just too far away to consider. They'd have to content themselves with the knowledge that they were all dependable, intelligent, human beings. None could remember anything so severe and prolonged during their entire time in this country. All they could do was prepare a search-rescue and wait for this to end. They could endure the cold if it was quiet. Their enclosed vans were readied and waiting and they could pray.

———

It was clear, calm, and deathly cold all morning. Carl had just led the last of the teams to the well when he heard the shout. He responded in kind. The bebundled figure swam through the huge drifts piled in the lane. He had to leave his horse tied on the outside to prevent the animal from being immobilized in the depths. Carl tied the team and went out to meet him. He was unrecognizable, swathed as he was, and he spoke little English so Carl took him into the house to Helen. He unwrapped to warm himself and they filled him quickly with hot tea, soup, and bread. Carl had seen him in the village but didn't know him by name.

He was clearly too old for this kind of exertion but the relief at their safety was evident in his smile. He indicated that they would be sending several vans with extra teams toward York and to the bush next morning.

They anticipated a horrible trip so they'd need all the man and animal power that they could get. He ruled Carl out when he saw the condition of Carl's face and hands, then advised them to be prepared for the worst. Carl had difficulty understanding the degree of fatalism common to these people.

Carl helped to get the man back to his blanket-covered mount and he was gone. The world on the outside was very much different than Carl imagined. The open areas were stripped bare and the slightest tuft or bush nurtured a horrendous drift. The larger bushed areas revealed only the peaks of their patrons. Travel could jigsaw yet would require a lot of shovelling to get teams through some the bushed-in areas. He could see why they'd need the manpower.

The lane was thoroughly plugged and it was on the leeward side of the storm front; what was the western entrance like? He struggled and shovelled as much as his endurance would allow, to clear passage. He got one of the horses and tortured him through several times until both were "all in," then went in for rest and warmth. He returned later and rode another until he had a sizeable, canyon through. He'd pushed his limit; he could stand no more. His feet and hands screamed.

Carl thought of throwing caution to the wind and joining the rescue but the results of his daylong endeavours led to an agonizing night. Helen had pilled him as much as she dared. Nothing really helped, they hurt and that was the long and the short of it. A few of them showed signs of inflammation.

Carl had managed to stay in one piece so far and he'd like to remain that way. Papa carried the scars of several major wounds and God knows how many chunks of metal but he was still a complete unit. Carl would once again need Mildred's assistance and he was certain that he wouldn't be the only one. Thank God for her abilities. Helen had him soak his hands and feet in a lukewarm solution of strong saltwater and then bathed them with the red liniment to try to reduce the consequence of infection.

Her fatalism worried Carl. It seemed that somewhere, someone had robbed her of her will to try to alter circumstances. "Your old life is gone, never waste your time trying to re-imagine the course of consequence. It was far too painful then and is even more painful and defeating every time you try to live it over now. Take what you have and what you know you can get and start from where you are and build anew. You have to leave the past behind and live with hope. That's why I left my home and came here and look, now I've met you and Jimmy and I'm still alive as a result and just look at the fun that we've had!" Her sombre expression broke into a gentle smile. The advice was unnecessary. In her entire life that's all she'd ever done.

———

Carl awoke to a dog barking excitedly. He closed his eyes and listened hard. Yes, it was a dog and then he heard the rattle of trace chains as the team struggled up the canyon. When the team drew up beside the house, both he and Helen were up and at the door with both the lamp and lantern blazing.

The box was the same, except it was now a sleigh box. The dog was frosted from tip to tail, young, big, hairy and thoroughly excitable. If he didn't seem the worse for wear as a consequence of his adventure, he was the only one. The team was white with frost and ice and completely exhausted. Paul was the first to rise up out of the depths and shed the heavy horse blanket wind-break that had sheltered them throughout the ordeal.

"Jeez, what a mess! What in hell happened here?" Paul lifted Mildred to her feet just as Helen climbed over the low tailing board to help them or carry something. They were both very tired but as far as Carl could see, they seemed alright.

"What happened? Is he alright?"

"He's fine, he's lonesome, and he's asleep. Don't worry about him. The other him is a different matter!" Mildred's alarmed questioning trailed her through the door and out of earshot.

"I'll get them looked to. Get to the house and warm up." Carl, at the traces, had the team free of the sleigh, it could stay here for now. He'd get some water into them.

Helen's team had to be tied in the alley between Paul's other team and the cribbed oats stalls, to free their stall. The returning team plunged into the feed as Carl lifted the slippery, iced-over harnesses off and hung them, then headed for the house.

"Where'd you come from?" The dog took the time to shed some of his frost and have a drink from the rapidly freezing water left in the trough. He was a people dog, very domestic and affectionate. He escorted Carl, gently, by his mitt-covered hand, as if he instinctively recognized the tenderness beneath. He sat, ears perked with anticipation when Carl went into the house. Carl would see that he got something.

"Did ya' find enough room for them in — God-a-mighty! What happened to you?" Carl had pulled the scarf off his face with his bandaged hands. Mildred and Helen were in the baby's room just indulging the prodigal mother so Paul hadn't been told yet. There wasn't a mirror in the house other than Mildred's and that was with her. The lamp, as always, was in the window and that didn't do much for its reflective quality.

"You look like hell!" Mildred checked the discolourations on his cheekbones and the exposed areas around his eyes. "That'll peel. You might have some discolouration there depending on how deep the frost went. Let's see your feet and hands." He unwrapped them dutifully. Some of the fingers were swollen. She pinched each of them and he winced every time. "I think you'll be alright here. Let's see your feet.

"I hate to tell you that a few of them don't look good. Did you keep walking on them while you were out, or did you stop for a while?"

"I wasn't about to stop and die but after an hour or so, I ain't really sure what I did. Why?"

"As long as you kept moving and stamping on your feet, chances are you kept the blood flowing and they weren't frozen through. Did you check them when you came in?"

"He was in no shape but I did," Helen explained. "They were still soft and they pinked-up when I pinched them. He couldn't feel a thing. God, I hope he doesn't have to lose any."

"I ain't goin' to; I can take a lot."

"The problem is infection and that can kill you."

"When you touch them, do they feel thick-skinned?" Helen asked.

Carl nodded a yes. "Why do you ask that?"

"I've seen frost injuries a lot in the old country; I know what it feels like. The fingers and toes that return feeling in a few days, are still yours." She pulled off her heavy socks to expose her feet ... three toes on her left and four on her right. "I lost them when I was eight!"

IX

"Scorch-blackened devastation!"

"Gosh, I'm not really sure how to thank you. I don't know what would have happened if you weren't here."

"What I've done for you, anyone could have done. What you did for me is something that nobody else has ever done. I thank God for you!" She hated to leave; she felt a security around Carl that she couldn't really understand, like she had gained back a little bit of something that she'd thought was gone forever.

Mildred bundled Helen into sweaters, scarves, and mitts and Paul rode back to the village with her. The storm had left the landscape extremely treacherous.

Mildred begged Carl's forgiveness for inflicting upon him the responsibility of her son. "Well you told me you were going to make me pay somehow didn't you? And any time you want me to pay again, why you just go right ahead!" Jimmy hung onto his mother with desperate vigour. She had difficulty getting anything done.

"You know, I have to beg your forgiveness on another account." She reached into her large sweater pocket and pulled out the letter. Carl's facial expression was priceless. The letter wasn't very thick and he saw Bertha's neat hand. Though he ached for word from home, his heart sank. Mildred, giggling impishly, reached back into her pocket and pulled out the bundle. She sniffed at the hint of perfume and handed it to him, then took him by his arm and led him to the living room bench and left with a smile of understanding.

Carl hesitated with indecision, then opened Bertha's letter.

Dear Carl:

Papa was so excited when we got your telegraph that he laughed and danced around and cried. He got sick, but he is better now. Arnold wants to throw a few things together and get on the train right now; the place sounds so adventuresome. He said you could build a log cabin to live in real quick, like he read about. Mary didn't sell the place yet. It looks like she's got somebody interested but don't worry because she gave the yard and a few acres to us to live in for keeps for all the years we worked here. She was real sad that the bank treated Papa so bad and wouldn't give him any money to buy the place. She wanted us to have it because she knows how bad we need it. Now you found some land and she wants to give you all of the machinery that you'll need and the horses and cows because she loves them so and wants you to have them and look after them the way you always did, if there is some way you can get them there. She has your address and is going to write to ask you to try.

Max and Papa went to Charles City and it looks like Max might get a job at Hart and Parr to get some more money to help, but he still wants to farm in Canada too. Did you know there is an eating place there named "Bertha's?"

We are all so happy and we just can't wait!

P.S. As if you don't know! There is a really nice girl there named Milly! She asked Papa and Max all about you! She said that we would be hearing lots more about her soon, she hoped. Why didn't you say something about her in your letter? So don't try to be sneaky and lie to me, you!"

"Kissy-kissy!"

Carl laid the letter down, with disbelief, then picked it up again to read the part about the machinery and the horses and cows. He'd have almost everything that people like Paul had to struggle for over many years and they had to be very lucky too. He knew the cattle and teams by name and nature. The machines all carried his mark on them; he did a lot of the repair. It'd be a little bit of home right here, except that here it would be his own. God bless Ivan and Mary Pawlowich, just two of the very few people that Carl took to his heart and knew he could trust no matter what. They'd truly demonstrated their sincerity. He felt light and wonderful.

Carl picked up Milly's enormous letter. He looked at it for a long time, unsure of himself, as was his nature in highly charged emotional situations.

Rather than writing several letters, she explained that she'd decided to put her thoughts and events down almost like a diary and send them as quickly and as often as she could. She explained that she understood the difficulties and the extreme effort he'd have to expend on accomplishing the demands of the homestead. She'd got a copy of the Homestead Act at the library. It was common in Iowa because so many of the homesteaders were American and she'd studied it. She told him to avoid hurting himself because he was too important to everyone. Then she told him of her visit with his father and Max and how proud they all were of him and how they all couldn't wait to get to him.

Milly was surprised that her grandfather knew his family really well. Apparently he'd told her everything he knew about Carl's background, most of all, the admiration, trust and confidence that he had in Carl. "... Told ya'!" had been his response when he'd heard about the homestead. She said that her mother was very impressed with her choice but was worried about her daughter being so far away. Her dad was a whole lot more sceptical, but she'd work on him and after he'd met Carl, she knew he'd have a lot more confidence. Wilbur was even looking to prospects in Canada. She clearly displayed her intent to become a part of Carl's life, when she concluded---

My Very Dearest Carl:

I honestly don't know how you do it, but you inspire confidence and security and faith in people who've hardly met you. I fell in love with you two seconds after I first saw you. You are the only love I'll ever want.

I told you to be careful and patient, but I'm the one who really needs patience; I so want to be with you. I want to be part of your building, your sorrow and joy, your world and everything in it. I want to be there! That's a whole lot more important to me then comfort. Being without you right now sure isn't very comfortable.

Do you know that you are so much a part of my mind, and you might think this is crazy, that I talk to you sometimes and

imagine your answers? I want to know everything that happens to you and your work. I want to know what you need most and how I can help get it for you.

Is there anything that I can get ready for when I get there? You said there weren't any schools there yet and how they're needed. I'm thinking about, maybe, getting some teacher training, but, I'm not just sure where to get it. What do you think?

What worries me so much is that I know we'll need money and I can't earn any of that if I'm in school. Grandpa said he'd help pay for my training, so please, help me decide. Remember always, nobody can love you more than I do.

Write as soon as you can and tell me that you love me too, please! I really need to hear that lots. I wish I could be there to show you how much I love you.

Your Milly.

Carl, too, really needed to hear that. He didn't feel overjoyed or elated, he felt really secure and confident, far more prepared to deal with many of the unforeseen dangers like those he'd already had to face and he wasn't nearly so scared or worried. He knew for certain now, that she was in his corner supporting him and he'd be in her corner supporting her, no matter what happened or what fate threw into their pathway. It was great just knowing that part of his life was secure and predictable.

Paul returned far too quickly, on a horse lathered from a hard run in very difficult conditions. He flew off the animal and left it loose. Frightened, they both met him at the door.

"There's been a fire at the camp. They're all bad hurt and some are already dead. We gotta get there quick! They need sleighs and teams and men to bust a road through and to keep 'em warm until we can get 'em out.

"Early this morning one of 'em stumbled into the village on a horse, near to death, both burned. He's really in bad shape. They'll need to try to get the worst to Doc and the hospital but that's just too far in this weather. There's none of the stuff that burns need. Mildred, you're all we've got!"

Carl stretched a horse blanket tight across the top of the double box and clinched it there with retaining boards. He cleaned the box through to the bare wood, filled in some clean straw and dragged out his spring, mattress and every blanket, quilt and cover Mildred could find. He dug an old grease pail out of the snow beside the granary and quick-manufactured a temporary stove like he'd seen Papa and Ivan do more than once.

Paul had the cow secured, both teams would go for added power. Shovels, axes, even the Mauser were on board. The overly enthusiastic dog was reprimanded to stay at home. In just over an hour, they were off.

Fortunately, Carl's imagination marked accurately the necessary security of the heater. Paul negotiated risks that left Carl and Mildred a bit concerned but his masterful teamsmanship brought them to the frantic village shaken but whole. Wide-eyed Jimmy, sensing the urgency, endured the violent jolting with resignation.

Mildred warned them about the need for determined resolve. "Squeamish stomachs won't save lives!" She'd dealt with fire victims on many occasions both in hospital and on site and knew what human horrors to expect. Some just might not make it and would die painfully and slowly. Some wouldn't appear so bad but would have smoke and heat damage to their lungs. Many wills could fight on to survival, based solely on the stabilizing influence of the caregivers or they could simply surrender to the comfort of death. She told them to expect the horrible stench of scorched flesh and the sounds of pain.

Mildred wasn't overly surprised when Paul told her he'd fought the same fires she'd been at and had dragged, to safety, some of the horrors she'd have treated. "I saw you first!" he smiled.

The villagers needed no warning; fire was distinctly common. They'd lived with it in the old country. There were more than twenty in the camp from this village alone. How many from other villages or neighbouring farms? They'd packed themselves in because there was only the one mill and everybody needed lumber.

Paul changed to the fresh team and followed in the tracks of the others who'd left much earlier. Carl rode the mare, well ahead, to get there in a hurry. A trail had been slaughtered through the heavy, rock-hard drifts. The teams would all be exhausted.

———

Mama'd often spoken to them about the wartime horrors she'd witnessed. Papa's eyes imaged great pain and he'd said nothing. None of that prepared Carl for the shock of actual witness.

The scorch-blackened devastation left not a single building whole. The flames had consumed much of the still-burning saw logs and the sawn lumber and moved on into the surrounding spruce, licking and cracking viciously, despite the snowy deterrent. Some of the early arrivals went at it immediately and had it controlled.

The scene instinctively evoked deep suspicion. Burned flesh and a sooty-paraffiny smell, permeated the air. A torching of this magnitude, despite its late night arrival, must have been of explosive intensity to consume a settlement of this size to this extent with such speed to so entrap its experienced population.

The teams, reacting nervously yet sensing the urgency, fidgeted and screamed but remained transfixed out of an inherent sense of loyalty. Many of their own kind were only horse-shape heaps of blackened, stinking flesh.

Three human figures lay wrapped, beyond the capacity of earthly help. The injured were covered against the cold and drawn as close to the remaining flames as discretion allowed. Some lay inert, others convulsed wildly in absolute agony. Some sat, propped by the supporting arms of family, friend or neighbour, chattering with wildly-waving, blackened arms and grimacing faces in raving delirium or enraged account. Carl was unable to recognize the features of any of them.

The doors had been barred from the outside! The few windows of the primitive shacks had been their only salvation. After the first few got free, they'd managed to free most of the others.

Carl noted Alexsay's huge frame with a pathetic figure in tow and another in his arms, taking them to the sheltering warmth of Paul's sleigh. The vans had already been filled and some were en route to the village.

"Vwada! Pajahlistaw!" (Water! Please!) The blackened, blood streaked arms extended for Carl's compassion.

"Water? You fool!" Carl cursed his own ignorance. He hadn't even thought of it. "Where?" he screamed.

"In the sleigh!" Paul yelled over the crackle. Carl could hardly see him pointing through the smoke.

God, how loud was I? Carl thought, as he raced to meet a returning, soot-blackened Alexsay, who handed him a clay jar.

"Bojay Moy!" (My God!) he croaked pathetically and shook with grief and rage. He'd grown up and worked and played and ate and slept and fought and suffered and laughed with all of these. He'd have been amongst them had he not been to York. He'd thought that in this new world such things could be dropped, if not from memory, then, at least from reality. He was wrong!

Carl clasped the figure and lifted him to pour some of the warm tea down his throat. He responded by grasping into space for the soothing fluid. His bulbous stare was sightless, seared blind by the heat. Carl brought the jar to his cracked and bleeding lips and he drank frantically. The stench was so all-consuming that Carl had to turn and retch. He held and rocked the man, encouraging and praying with him and for him until Mildred and Paul arrived.

She turned down the wrappings to reveal the pathetic remnant of his sleepwear and the cracked and blistered flesh beneath. As she swabbed him where she could, to deaden the pain and disinfect the burns, she looked at Carl with agonized eyes and shook a positive, "No!"

Alexsay returned and touched Paul's shoulder, then said something quietly to him. Paul got down beside Carl and took the weight of support from him. "Some of the horses ain't dead. You'll have to end 'em." There was a man already placed at every remaining team to hold them.

Each deafening report re-echoed in the enclosing, bushy shroud. Carl had never done this before. He had to steel his nerves every time. Somewhere in this wilderness another five terrified and injured animals would perish slowly.

The remaining injured had been placed in the last two vans and Paul's makeshift sleigh. As darkness encircled them, so would the wolves. Someone had to remain to protect the dead and Carl had the gun. He and Alexsay cut a large bundle of boughs and propped most of them against one of the remaining walls for shelter. They dragged around themselves anything of value neglected by the flames. The warped heaters were still in one piece but they and the ashes were still too hot so they built a lively fire near the entrance and kept it going. Sleep would have been, at best, a dereliction of responsibility. Carl's feet and hands ached terribly.

———

Alexsay woke him with a startling roar. The wolves disappeared before Carl could do anything. What Carl heard was far more worrisome then any wolves; the demons had screeched back.

They quickly drew the dead into the sheltering leeward side of the wall and covered them with more boughs. The storm set up a flurry but they were so bushed in that the sound was worse than the fury. They gathered as much dry wood as they could find in the semidarkness and cut and piled many more boughs on their shelter to further deflect the wind and snow, then covered themselves with the smaller boughs and sat to await full daylight.

They scoured the snow-covered remnants of the camp for anything they could use. They carried a cooled heater to their shelter along with a length of yet-whole stovepipe and set it up as best they could in order to warm themselves. The open fire was a hopeless dream in the agitated environment and a real risk to their gaseous, evergreen shelter.

Neither of them had eaten since yesterday morning and they cursed themselves for not having thought to take something. In the urgency of the moment, nobody'd anticipated this degree of unpredictability.

———

Fervent, agonized prayer rose from every set of lips in the village, not for the dead, but rather, for the living. Four more of them were out in the wilderness in this horrible and deadly storm with limited shelter and no food. Two had been sent to York for medical and police assistance and were trapped as well as "Carr-roll and Alyosha.". Any attempt at rescue would be suicidal.

Frightened, Helen walked about the village encouraging everyone that Carl and Alyosha and the others were very strong and clever. If there was a way, they would find it. Then, she hid herself and cried quietly and begged

God for mercy. The men, to Mildred's gratitude, had subdued Paul's insane determination to attempt the trip when the storm first began.

———

Carl and Alexsay scoured the ruins again for anything edible and found only the charred remains of prepared meals in what had been the pantry of the cook shack but everything was scorched brittle. They'd have to find another option. Carl could try to hunt something but neither of them knew the surrounding bush and one would have to remain to protect the dead. Game would be sheltering against the storm and would be all but impossible to locate. It was far too dangerous to venture out too far in this weather despite the sheltering effect of the heavy bush. Walking in these depths was impossible for long. The only option remaining was the scorched-over carcasses of the dead horses.

They endured the next night with no rest or comfort and at daybreak, suppressed their rising gorge and skinned the frozen hide off the hind-quarter of one of the disgusting beasts. The flesh beneath was discoloured a livid greenish-brown and was totally frozen. They employed an axe to free it from the carcass. They'd amassed an assortment of heat-crippled pots and kettles and dropped into the boiling water of one of them a number of smaller chunks of the flesh with the outside colourations shaved away. The immediate response was disgusting as the entrapped blood escaped the frost and clouded the water a bright purple. They allowed it to boil for a long time until they were sure most of the blood leached out, then poured off the water and placed the chunks into a shallower pot with a small amount of water and boiled it to a conclusion.

It was tough and had a peculiar taste of "burned". Carl had never eaten horse before but his and Alexsay's teeth were as powerful as their hunger and they devoured the flesh, then put more on to boil and clear. They cut it finer, then boiled it again into a thick broth and drank and chewed their way through that as well.

Meat, horse, dog or wild game, was not foreign to Doukhobors. They'd been decreed not to but had to eat it many times in the days of tribulation, both here and in the old country when survival and health were para-mount, just as now.

The flesh, though not ideal, did its assigned duty well and both relaxed after the pain of hunger. It had been Alexsay's companion many times in the past but Carl had never experienced anything so terrible. It was ever so much harder to endure than any other kind of pain. He resolved never to be so foolish as to allow it to happen again.

Snow sifted gently through the enclosure and had to be brushed off to prevent melting and wetting their clothing. The wind swirled about but little got through the boughs. They cut off more of the meat and placed it in warm water to leach, then stoked the pathetic heater, checked for contact of the stovepipe and relaxed under a bundle of the boughs. Sleep was risky but a certainty. Both had little in the past forty-eight hours. They hadn't seen a sign of the wolves since the storm began so they felt secure enough to take the risk.

Carl slept through a confused melee of sounds and faces and voices, uncharacteristically stern, abrupt and cruel. He saw Mildred's tearful, pleading face and Paul's agonized features; white with pain and anger. He saw Milly in a pathetic crumpled heap and her explosive reaction when he tried to touch her. He heard distant voices and laughter in the midst of her agony. He jerked into a defensive rage and sat upright, wide-awake. It was dead calm with an extremely bright moon.

The mocking voices were real. They carried long and loud in the dead-cold air. They were laughing viciously, like a sadistic butcher enjoying their victim's agony. Disgusting, filthy words echoed, interspersed with "Doukhobor," time and again.

To Carl's alarm, Alexsay was not in the shelter. Carl crept out anxiously. Alexsay appeared in a distance-consuming trot back toward the shelter, light, silent, and ghostlike for one of such stature. Anticipating Carl's inquisition, his warning finger lay astride his thin, frightful lips, commanding silence. He whirled Carl around as he trotted past and pulled Carl astride. He leaned over and whispered as loud as he dare, only one word, "Assassins!"

Carl was confused. He didn't breathe a word; Alexsay's features told him all he needed to know about the imminent danger. As Carl suspected, the fires hadn't been an accident. The arsonists had returned in the lull to confirm or to complete their devil's handiwork and the shelter was a dead give-away.

They'd be heavily armed so Alexsay whispered again one word and pointed to the shelter. "Bring!" Carl crawled through, grabbed the Mauser and the ammunition then retraced on Alexsay's cold mime to get his parka and mitts. They rushed with the same consuming trot, toward the security of the dense bush some distance from their shelter. The voices were louder as the butchers trotted boldly into the ruins to inspect their handiwork.

Who were they? They certainly weren't the radicals of Alexsay's initial suspicion. The radical sect, which had gained a reputation for their fiery dispersal of all worldly possessions, were certainly misdirected by the very nature of their piety. But they were as peace-loving as all the villagers, lived in their midst, and were their own. The firing of the entire camp was a sadistic and calculated terror tactic.

"Why here?" Carl couldn't believe this was happening and that he had become part of the victimized. Their lives were in deadly danger. Instinctively he wanted to stop and turn and fight, but he bowed to Alexsay's superior tactics. There would be a time to fight but it wasn't now or here.

They gained the heavy tree line and the security of invisibility before they stopped to catch their breath and look back to see what they were up against. They had a major "ace up their sleeve," that was the deadly gun that the pursuers would not anticipate. After all, they were passive Doukhobors; easy, defenseless picking.

Carl counted five in the flickering shadows and moonlight, all rifle armed, all drawn as they entered the ruins. Their intent was clear as they yelled and cursed, then fired the shelter and the bundles covering the dead. They rode, recklessly, through the ruins, looking for hapless survivors, witnesses to their treachery. They'd soon find the trail and would certainly overtake him and Alexsay afoot in this deep snow.

They'd aim for the muzzle flash of his rifle. He and Alexsay moved rapidly to create a maze of tracks and protective shelter, to fire and move and fire again, the advantages of surprise and creativity, of light and dark. They'd have to try to keep their attackers away from the shadow of the heavy undisturbed bush. This would all have to happen very quickly.

"Hey, over here! Ta bastards went this-a-way!"

"Git 'em quick! It's too damn colt and it smells a' dead Doukhobor. I want ta git finished and git back ta where it's warm 'fore somebody comes a' lookin'." The speech style, to Carl's ear, was familiar.

Carl crouched behind his first line. He worried about defenseless Alexsay and threw caution to the wind. He spoke clearly, above the sound of heaving horses and muffled hooves as the rush descended upon him.

Alexsay was gone.

What was the fool going to try? ... No time now! He calmly checked his ammunition for security. He felt only cold determination, absolutely no fear, just as during the fight with the chicken thief. It was only a matter of degree. Papa had taught him well.

He levelled the muzzle at the first of several bright clearings that the onslaught would have to cross, the flurry of snow just before the clearing revealed the rush. The instant the first of the attackers broke into the clear, the sights locked unto him and the rifle bucked and roared. Carl was up and running, the screaming, cursing and the returning fire well behind him. He was at his second line. He stood behind the heavy spruce and drew on the flash of a rifle in the blinding swirl at the tree line. He fired again and ran as the tree erupted splinters, again, well behind him. He wondered what he'd do when he'd run out of new places.

Where was Alexsay?

He crouched at his third line and waited. There was nothing but cursing and muffled confusion. They didn't break cover again; they were running. Carl threw caution to the wind in what he later recognized as a foolish lack of discipline and strategy but he thought nothing now, in the fury of battle. He ran out and after them, firing several times.

He cleared the cover of the bush, back into the camp compound, as a paralyzing, inhuman roar muffled the sound of the retreat. The vaulting shadow of the big man struck the final rider midway and sent horse and all into a crashing heap against one of the few standing walls. The hapless rider smashed on through to the other side.

Carl levelled hastily on the next rider as he turned in the saddle to fire. The heat of Carl's screaming bullet left the rider with little initiative other than retreat and they were gone, the fury of their ride dissipating into the cold distance as Carl cleared the camp. He returned quickly as the riderless horse, flecked with foam and terror, screamed wildly past him and after the retreat.

"Prock-leeyah-tay"! (Dammit!) Alexsay sat amongst the fragments of the shattered wall, cradling an arm, badly distorted, broken by the impact and the fall. He shook off the pain and pointed Carl to the fire still burning over the already charred dead. Carl quickly doused what remained of the smoulder.

"Nyet!" Alexsay remarked, as Carl tried to lead him from the cold to shelter near the remains of the fire, "Coming samore!"

As they headed back, both heard clearly, a flurry of gunfire off in the distance. "Bojay Moy!" They'd run into the rescuing teams from the village ... more death! "Goink!" Alexsay ordered. Carl pumped another shell into the breach and raced out to the clear and the moonlight.

The faint figure, small in the distance, grew rapidly in a determined race for the camp. He was alone and he was armed. The others were nowhere to be seen. Behind him, Carl saw, faintly, a minute dark image and a pillar of rising smoke in the clear, dead-cold, night air ... a van. It had to be the villagers and the racing figure had to be Paul; none of the others carried guns. Carl crouched low in the snow, ready and alert, as the figure approached at a furious pace. He recognized Paul and stood and waved frantically to alert him against shooting.

"What'n hell's been goin' on here? You alright? Where's Alyosha? Who'n hell are those guys? We could hear the shootin' a-way back and we knew something was terribly wrong here. They damn near rode right into us before they saw, then they started shootin'. It's a bloody miracle nobody got hit; they were so wild. They sure stopped short when I shot back. I think one of 'em's the worse for it too. I know I hit one of the horses, but somehow he kept goin'. There was a rider-less horse runnin' with 'em so I imagine you guys did some damage too." Paul could see that Carl was alright, but he was so wrought up that he found it hard to come down.

"That'll make two of 'em. Alexsay got another and I think the first one I shot at is hit bad; he sure did a lot of screamin' and cursin'. They rode right into me, not expecting Doukhobors to have any guns or to fight back. Alexsay's hurt pretty bad. His arm's broke, it looks like, in a couple of places. The one in camp is got to be dead. I've never seen anybody bleed like that. I don't know who they are. They just rode in here a while ago and were ready to kill anything and anybody. I've never heard of anything so mean before. Thank God Alexsay was here; he seemed to sense that they were coming. I can't even think why. They'd have to be after something, because you can't do this to somebody just because you don't like 'em. Maybe we can find something on this guy to tell us."

The vans pulled up and they drove into the camp. One of the horses on the lead van flagged badly and the lantern revealed that the animal had been seriously grazed by one of the wild shots. Paul's mount would have to pull back to the village. The vans, too, had received several hits but miraculously no one inside had been hurt.

Because of the number of injured at the village, only a few of the old men and Paul came back, all afraid for Carl and Alyosha. They'd heard nothing from the two sent to York. A rider had gone out at the same time the vans left — they'd know soon.

There was nothing anyone could do for Alexsay except bind his arm into a sling of sorts, to protect against the rough ride back. The man, steely-hard, was resigned to the necessity of pain but his features revealed untold agony as they moved him into the van and cushioned his arm on a quilt.

The revolting need to collect the dead, burned over the second time, was as close to unbearable as Carl could possibly have come. Paul, whose firefighting experience conditioned him to such disturbing, disagreeable duties, drove the van despite the cold, with the door open.

X

THORLAND DEVELOPERS

It was daybreak when they reached the village and its grieving population. The terror of the old days had returned in the country where they thought safety and freedom to be guaranteed. Much of the youthful manpower of the village had been horribly injured. If they didn't eventually die from their injuries, they would certainly never regain normality.

It was commonly believed that these peaceful people were passive. What Carl saw, as they arrived, was an armed camp on full alert; sentries were concealed at a number of locations and clearance to entry was given only on permission of these sentries. If anyone a sentry failed to recognize attempted entry without permission that unfortunate wouldn't live to regret the attempt.

Alexsay, as strong and tolerant as he was, had difficulty walking into his home and needed Carl's help. He was exhausted beyond endurance. It was his instinctive suspicion and knowledge of the deceitful nature of humankind that kept him awake when Carl slept and it was his instincts that had kept them alive. The butchers would have murdered Carl in his sleep.

Alexsay collapsed once inside his kitchen. Loosha had slept little since he'd gone and sobbed openly at his agony. She helped lift him to the bed that Carl had once slept in and cut the offending sleeves off his arm before Carl pulled the jacket and shirt off him. The horribly swollen and bloodied arm exposed a bone fragment protruding at the lower of the fracture sites. He seemed to lapse into an unusual trance; he was conscious and aware and would answer, yet he seemed to be immune to the agony inflicted by the removal of the garments.

Fractures weren't foreign to the villagers; they'd always dealt with broken arms and legs. Half the village walked on onetime fractures and all of them appeared normal. It was the pain they'd never forget. When the fracture was as difficult and compounded as Alexsay's, Anastas was the authority to be called in. He'd dealt successfully with many but his strength was gone and he'd advise only. Mildred was asleep and no one was allowed to wake her for any reason, not even Paul.

Anastas fed Alexsay some of his sedative mix and regretted that he couldn't offer more but there wasn't much left. He ordered Carl and Paul, with two of the older men, over to do the actual deed. Carl would pull at the elbow to mesh the bone together on the upper fracture, as instructed through Helen.

Alexsay acknowledged Carl's terrified look with a friendly smile and a nod at the moment he was ready. Strong arms held the big man in place. Carl pulled and turned as instructed. Alexsay's eyes rolled wildly but not a sound escaped him. The colour left his face but no more than Carl's. Anastas felt the upper fracture and nodded with approval, then ordered Carl to hold the tension and Paul to grasp the fracture with his broad hands to hold the soft inner bandaging and the wooden splints in place. Anastas wrapped it tightly enough to hold it there.

Carl looked into Alexsay's blank, staring eyes — mercifully, consciousness had left him. The job would be easier.

The lower fracture proved more difficult as Anastas had to make an incision through the flesh and muscle to accommodate the entrance of the bone protrusion back under it; there was no other way. Paul disinfected his hands on the old man's orders and held the splinter in as the old man inserted four very rapid, very precise stitches with material Mildred had in her supply. Carl repeated the pull but with a different turn and Paul held it all together. When both splints were in place, Anastas re-splinted and rewrapped the entire arm to prevent movement at the elbow and a possible loss of fracture alignment. It was done.

Carl shook well beyond a tremble and the old man smiled and patted his head. Loosha hugged and kissed him on the cheek without a single word. Together they pulled off Alexsay's boots and trousers, covered him, adjusted the position of the arm on a gentle cushion and left him to rediscover his pain.

Anastas offered Carl some of the elixir but Carl refused, knowing full well the degree of suffering in all of the neighbouring houses. Loosha knew that he must be starving so she found what she could and fed him. Carl refused to take her bed; she hadn't used it in two days and nights and would need it whether or not she wanted. Some of the women had already fainted with exhaustion and Loosha wasn't far from it. She heaped a quilt and pillow in an obscure corner and Carl covered himself with his parka and remembered little else.

————

The yard was as they left it. The cow, frantic for water, was first to meet her need. The dog was nowhere to be seen. A drifter, he probably went as he had come. Paul approached the snow-covered wooden walk, leading up to the fetal veranda and found the snow, disturbed by his passing, flecked with frozen blood. To his accelerating alarm, he saw the kitchen window smashed and picked out of its frame to allow passage. The door, slightly ajar, was punctuated with two bullet holes. The interior was soot blackened and the kitchen stovepipe was smashed beyond usability. The intruders had lit the stove on the assumption that with the stovepipe gone, it would ignite the house. It had scorched the ceiling, but nothing more.

Smoke damage was everywhere. Mildred's newly sewn living room curtains marked a further attempt to burn the home. They'd proven fire resistant and smouldered themselves out. The bedroom door was kicked through and the bedding that remained was knife-ripped to shreds as were the cushions on Anastas' bench. Jimmy's crib was crushed to splinters.

Paul returned to their bedroom and drew the curtains aside to allow light and a better assessment. He turned back toward the door, which, off-balanced by its injury, had swung closed after he passed through and he witnessed a sight that would haunt his life forever.

One of Mildred's nightgowns was pinned to the back of the door with one of their own kitchen knives. The shocked husband drew the knife free and the garment fell to the floor. He read the business card, pinned through above the nightgown and witnessed a scrawled pencil note that froze his heart.

He buried, as best he could, the pathetic remains of the gentle dog who'd risen in defense of his newfound home. He nailed the door shut from the inside to keep it closed and boarded the window over, then turned and left the remnants of what he had viewed as a happy home and returned where he knew his help was appreciated and needed.

————

The mission to York had been successful. The two familiar, buffalo-robed officers shook Carl awake and led him to the Doughwam. They'd stripped and thoroughly searched the dead attacker, then questioned those who were stable enough to answer. Only Carl and Alexsay remained. Paul hadn't yet returned.

Carl related exactly what he saw of Alexsay's attack on the dead perpetrator, how he'd fired repeatedly at the attackers and what he expected was the result. He was unable to recognize or identify any of the attackers, including the dead one in front of him.

"You're from the Des Moines area aren't you?"

"Maynard really; I don't know much about it. Why do you ask?"

"We found this on him. Ever hear of such?"

The card read,

THORLAND DEVELOPERS
Des Moines Iowa.

Carl's instinct twigged immediately and the officer noticed. "Why? What can you tell us?"

"Never heard of the company but my folks worked for a farmer named Ingmar Thorvaldson for over ten years. When Ingmar died, his son Lars, easy ten years older than me, kicked us off and we moved to Maynard to a farmer there. Lars always was a sneakin', dirty, lazy bastard! 'Thorland?' That sounds like him, even if I never heard of it or him after we left Ingmar's. There's a married older sister but I don't know where she is now, it's been so long. Paul and Mildred, the Karmadys, both lived and worked down there for years. Paul and her were married there and he just brought her back, same time I came. Ask them; they'd have a better chance a' known'. They're somewhere around here right now."

"Yes, we've seen Mrs. Karmady already but she and the Doc are very busy so we haven't bothered her yet. They just lost two more this afternoon. Poor woman is near a nervous wreck. We'll have to look over the four who were burned. I'm sure not lookin' forward to that I'm not afraid to tell ya'." Carl told them about the second burning and the officers paled. "Seen some awful things out here over the years but never anything quite this bad. Judging by what you've seen already, you seem like you can take it ... suppose you can give us a hand? We can't speak the language, only the younger lady could talk to us and she was so upset worrying about everything that she wasn't really much help. Are the two of you together?"

Carl shook a no.

"Seems to think a lot of you though." The officer smiled. "She was sitting beside you, praying, when we came to wake you."

Carl didn't respond to the implied question; pale and shaken, Paul had just walked through the door.

"Oh no! Paul, what happened?"

Paul told them about his place. They produced the card they'd found on the body and asked the question. Paul answered honestly, he really didn't know anything about the company because he'd been out here for over four years. They'd have to ask Mildred. Paul was as afraid of her answer as he knew she would be of the question but he couldn't get to her first and he had to be there to witness and hear her response. She could have shot him through less painfully!

It was getting late when Helen brought very tired Mildred over to the Doughwam. Some of the women told her about the damage to her home and the card they'd shown Paul.

If she'd told him when he came back, frightened over her letter, she would have lost him, she was certain of that. His few letters seemed not to care. She was mad at him for not coming for her long before and she'd honestly believed it was over, that her hopes and dreams were at an absolute, irreversible end. She'd sought solace in the first pair of open arms she could find. She'd written what she considered her final letter but couldn't mail it. When he appeared at her door, worn and nearly broke, ragged and hungry, anxiety and undisguised, pleading love all over his face, she realized at a glance everything that she could possibly want in the man. He'd told her the absolute truth. She saw the premature lines of aging in his sincere, rugged face and her pent-up emotions burst. She threw her emotion to the wind.

He was the love of her life and she didn't want to live it without him. She'd tell him sometime, when things were more secure and he knew her love. Most agonizing was the fact that she couldn't be absolutely certain about Jimmy despite the precautions. They weren't foolproof! Only time, all-consuming faith and appearance could tell her that.

She knew how deeply this would hurt him. She knew that her superior training often crossed Paul's mind but it couldn't have been further from hers. How could she let him know that with absolute certainty, especially now? How could she let him know that he mattered to her more than life? She thought her actions would and the time to tell him would come. She hadn't yet made a real effort to even try, although, at times it showed.

His father was killed when Paul was nine. By the time he was eleven, his sister had died of tuberculosis. His mother also developed the illness, a consequence of caring for her daughter. They had no money to feed themselves let alone pay a doctor. He'd sold papers, emptied spittoons, swept floors and cleaned livery stables. His mother died when he was fifteen and he'd been all alone since.

Paul had given his absolute trust and faith to Mildred and she'd betrayed that. She knew that he couldn't hate her any more than she hated herself. She was certain now, that she was carrying his child and she hadn't yet told him. It would seem like entrapment now and in her own mind she wasn't sure if her motive was totally love, or if there was guilt. She wanted him, she wanted this life and was committed to do everything she had to, to keep him or to die trying. She would have no other chance.

Carl saw, again, Mildred's tearful, terrified, pleading face and Paul's agonized features, white with pain and anger. He, too, was terrified; this was only half of it.

Mildred swallowed her dignity and walked away from the police and around the table toward her husband who backed away from her. She persisted and the police responded, totally oblivious to the personal tragedy. "Mrs. Karmady, we have to ask you these questions!"

"I realize that. I'll answer nothing until I am standing with my husband and though he may never again believe it, the only man I'll ever love." Paul stopped his retreat and waited for her; his reaction was childish anyway. It was better to face it sooner, rather than later. Maybe this wouldn't have happened if he'd come to her sooner. She knew the reason for his anger and she met it head-on, no cringing or crying or pleading for understanding. Her eyes left his, only to glance at the business card and then went immediately back, reaching into his mind.

"I know a great deal about it. I've had a sickening affair with the disgusting perpetrator of that equally disgusting enterprise, just prior to marrying this man, the only man I could possibly ever love, the man who is and will continue to be my reason for living and the man whom I know I've hurt as deeply as any human being can possibly hurt another. I can only ask him to try to forgive me and put this behind us, as best he can, under the circumstance. I've driven him away and I want him back. I offer him all the time he needs to think this through and I don't expect his full trust and his confidence. I don't want it unless I win it all back. I encourage his decision in support of the true relationship that I have so seriously injured." She'd been holding both his hands so strongly that hers began to numb.

The room fell deathly silent. With the exception of the police, Carl, Helen and the two of them, nobody understood the exact words but everybody knew what she meant and nobody more clearly then Paul. Unknowingly, unashamedly, publically, her confession and her honesty would salvage what little there was left of her marriage.

His hard, cold stare melted. "I don't need time. I need our home and our life and our son. I used to be so sure of you, now, hidden and dirty secrets? I have to know, what else? It's going to take me some time to get around this, but I'm afraid it goes far deeper than just me or you. You may have brought this upon lots of innocent people."

He pulled the blood-stained twin to the card the police showed, out of his pocket. "Whoever you chose over me is capable of anything." His words were bitter, displaying the depth of the hurt. "He's butchered our dog, he's smashed up the inside of our home, he tried to burn it down, he's cut our bed to hell, he's smashed our son's cradle to dust, he pinned your nightgown to the bedroom door with our kitchen knife and worst of all, he stuck it through this." He turned the card over to reveal the scrawled writing.

"Found you, Bitch!"

The room swirled, Paul's distraught face blurred, then nothing. She collapsed and he caught her fall, the card dropped to the floor.

"Lars Thorvaldson!" Carl raged. "He ain't after you! He could give a shit about any woman, the vindictive bastard! He's after developed, Doukhobour land, worth big money in the States, to them that's got it and he was here. 'Thorland Developers?' I know it's him! I lived 'round the animal most of my kid life. I hope it's him my bullet went through but if it ain't, I guarantee it will. And if I can't, I know who can, 'cause I know where to start lookin'. He'll run, the yellow bastard, right into a trap. We've got ya, you son of Satan! You won't hurt nobody no more!" He gave the officers the name of Federal Marshal William Brewster and told them where to send the telegraph, then asked to deliver it to York.

Mildred regained consciousness and confirmed Carl's assumption. Doc Holme wrote hastily, a list of the most emergent needs. Carl would return heavily loaded and he carried instructions to take to the hospital, to accommodate the necessary flood of the critical.

———

Heavily wrapped and very cold, Carl rode up to the York station just before daybreak, the horse beyond exhaustion. The word, though grossly under-exaggerated, was already there. The police telegraph went from hand, to wire, to mouth. The stationmaster was sure he'd sold a ticket to a man answering Carl's description late yesterday. To Carl's satisfaction, he had carried a heavily bandaged wound and flatly refused any offer of medical assistance from Ernie, the stationmaster. He was running back to the States and the Marshal's certain trap. "Good!"

Carl didn't have to ride to the hospital; they found him to see how they could help. Doctor Holme was a loved man in the community and nowhere more then on the staff. The panic of the aging, half-frozen, Doukhobour messenger had left them with a fractional knowledge of something unimaginable, Carl confirmed it and worse.

He refused the volunteerism of two well-mounted, capable nurses. Teams with the critical would be in sometime today, they'd have all they could handle here. They'd be desperately short of room and were ordered to find volunteer space in some of the neighbouring homes. Some "burns" would have to be stabilized and sent on to Winnipeg — staff would have to go with them. Working or not, people with any care background and volunteers would be pressed into duty. The train would have to accommodate the burns and would have to be held to do that. They had to convert a car and they'd already begun on the only one available.

A local crowd gathered quickly and would have questioned Carl to death, had not the hospital staff spirited him away to a warm meal and some rest. They were concerned by the appearance of some of his fingers. They'd seen worse stay on but they weren't as sure about a few of his toes.

The livery put up his horse and refused to let him try to ride it back; it was too far gone. They gave him another and would swap back later. He talked to a few of the people who appeared most concerned about the possible need for manpower, especially in the reconstruction of the bush camp. The lumber out of that camp built its way as far as the tumultuous trade of York. Its loss would be a blow to construction. The staff packed the medications tightly into a shoulder pack, to Carl's gratitude, and then he rode.

Alice met him at the door, fully prepared and wouldn't be deterred. She'd go with Al's blessing. How she knew her "Alyosha" was hurt, he didn't ask. Physically overextended, Al wasn't feeling too well but could manage with the twins. Grandma had gone back some time ago but she and Grandpa would be back by Christmas. Alice gave Carl some hot soup, filled two wine skins with tea as hot as they could ply next to themselves, packed a few sandwiches and they were off.

Alice's horsemanship and her mount embarrassed Carl's best effort. Her furious pace would have killed Carl's mount if he hadn't cautioned her to moderation. Her horse seemed hardly phased. She talked constantly with her hands and governed the horse only with knee pressure. Somehow, she'd heard about Max and just couldn't ask enough. Carl knew his brother's future was very suspect. Should he warn Max?

Nah! Let him find out for himself.

They rode into the village, a scant four hours after Carl rode out of York. Two vans with two armed outriders acknowledged them abreast of his place. The doctor was with them. Mildred would be alone again.

God he felt bad for the Karmadys; he loved them like his own family. He'd do whatever he had to, to help them through this. He wanted to free Paul and force them together at every opportunity through this crisis, to show them just how unimportant their petty hurts were. They hurt so much because they cared and loved so much. He didn't think any the less of the fantastic woman. He could see how it could happen and he thought about Milly and the letter he'd written and left at Paul's. He wouldn't let something like that happen to them. He'd run back when he could and clean up the mess and pick it up.

Alice ran to "Alyosha," kissed and hugged him and cried. Alexsay'd spoken constantly about "Crasna Hallawvaya" but Loosha had never met her. There was absolutely no question about who this willful girl was. Alexsay, seriously fevered from the prolonged lack of treatment, fought the infection with everything Mildred and he could throw at it and Carl brought some very powerful reinforcements. His beautiful girl was here now. Alexsay's revival was nothing short of amazing and Loosha desperately needed rest. To the entire village, this dynamic girl would prove a Godsend.

Carl was very glad to see the bond that instinctively developed between Helen and Alice. They became a determined, energetic, hard-nosed team, taking on the worse tasks so necessary in burn cases, stripping the raw and runny wounds, bathing, disinfecting and rebinding. Alice seemed to rouse the very best in the very tired caregivers. She instilled renewed hope in everyone, especially the suffering. Very soon they were asking for "Crasna Hallawvaya." Their pain seemed to disappear when she was around. She displayed an amazing fluency with their language; Alexsay had taught her well.

Helen drew out of her self-inflicted shell and dropped her demure spirit. They went for hours, non-stop. With a bit of Mildred's guidance they soon became very adept at the art of human caregiving.

Two more had died and the bodies were piling up in the doughwam's cold anteroom. Funerals were arranged and the few tired old men left, were overly taxed to build the necessary coffins. They urgently needed help but Carl just couldn't. He hadn't slept since just after they'd brought him and Alexsay in. He crawled into the same obscure corner.

The vans returned near dusk the day after and brought with them a team of two nurses with specialized burn training, equipment, and medication from Winnipeg. They were good! They were very good! Mildred was often openly amazed at the magic they were able to perform on victims that she'd given no hope.

Several more had set up a burn unit at York and with the help of the staff there, the rest of the critical cases could be packed up and sent immediately. Mildred would be the purveyor and Carl did indeed see to it that Paul was the driver. The timely arrival of Alice and the amazing adaptability of Helen and her, gave Mildred the rest and the personal time she needed. She spent all of it with Paul and their son. Carl had spent a large part of the days since his return, helping the beleaguered coffin builders and gravediggers.

A force of six officers and a hastily constructed van, loaded with equipment, stopped at the village and once again grilled those who were now able to explain the situation; Alexsay included. They brought with them their own very proficient interpreter. They'd instructed Carl, with no options, to get himself ready to accompany them back out to the camp. He was the only one capable, who had been there through the second attack.

The village hosted them for the night and cared for their horses. They were trail-ready and carried everything they could possibly need, so accommodation was not necessary but a roof was more than welcome and so was the hot meal.

"Wow! Look at that redhead!"

"And the blond! I didn't think Doukhobors were so good looking!"

The two young officers stalled both duty-bound girls with contrived conversation that was too quiet for Carl to hear. Helen blushed vividly at the advance and Alice said something quietly, alluded to her finger which she cleverly failed to display and nodded toward Carl.

Realizing the inference, Carl blushed as well, as the officers turned and their smiles faded to an expression of disappointed resignation. He nodded with acknowledgment as Alice delivered one of her uniquely expressive winks and a big, clever smile. Helen, with eyebrows raised, delivered only her surprise and perfect smile.

What promised to be an enlightening, educational investigation quickly became a disgusting ordeal that Carl would remember with misgiving and distrust.

"Well, what did you see when you first came into the camp? Where'd you come from? How many of the buildings were on fire? Where'd it first start? What did you do? Were the doors really barred? Did you see anything suspicious or unusual?" Carl explained that he'd never been at the camp before. He didn't know where the doors were.

"Well why are you here if you don't know anything?"

"Because you made me come and because I'm the only one left whole enough to be able to come." Carl had an uneasy feeling that something was wrong and he was in no mood to cater to the whims of the officer who was his junior and was feeling the influence of his new uniform. The contemptuous attitude of "ignorant Doukhobor!" oozed out of the recruit.

The charred hinges and door handles easily revealed the location of the doors. Beside the ashes of what once was the doors, they found the charred remains of partially consumed heavy planks or metal lining bars. "What does that tell you?"

"You said some must have got out through the windows, how do you know?"

"If the doors were barred, how else...?"

"How'd the fires start?"

"You could smell the kerosene."

"Where'd they start?"

"Look at the walls still standing, do you see any of the windows still in 'em? They must have thrown burning kerosene through 'em."

They sifted through the snow and ashes of what had been the inside and found bits of molten glass.

"You said some got through the windows but how many?"

"We never found a one inside. If the doors were barred, how else? Maybe a few got out and helped the others ... You think the attackers changed their minds?"

"How many were there?"

"There were at least twenty from our village alone — how many from elsewhere, I don't know."

"No, no, how many attackers?"

"Did you ask me that?"

"Don't get smart with me!"

"Then don't ask stupid questions!"

"That's enough Corporal! Here! Go sieve somethin'!" The senior officer reprimanded the youthful recruit and sent him packing.

"There had to be a lot more than the five I saw. How else would they trap and fire so many healthy, strong men and buildings so quickly and completely? They were big, they were mean, and they weren't afraid of much. They left a trail a blind man could follow and you fellas ain't on it."

They sifted the camp for three days, two of them wasted, while the trails grew colder and the leads got longer.

"Why? Why do you think they'd leave so much to follow? Why'd so many carry Thorland cards on 'em?" Carl grew impatient. The investigation was thinly veiled and leading nowhere. The attackers were guaranteed gone.

"We telegraphed all the border crossings and we're watching all the railway stations, yet, there's no crossings."

"Well, ya' know, now, that's peculiar; I found one the first time I asked. They could still be around, I don't know. I've heard and seen enough to know that there are lots around who'd like to grab Doukhobor-developed land. It's worth lots to them not to have to swing an axe or walk a plough and there are those in the States and here too, who'd pay plenty for it, if the Doukhobors could be scared off." Other than that, Carl stayed tight-lipped with a gut-wrenching suspicion, partially twigged by Papa's warnings and conversations with Alexsay about corrupt authorities and political opportunists. The Lars Thorvaldsons could be here only to do the dirty work. This investigation was a sham.

"I'm new here, I don't know the country or the people. I don't know anything about tracking and you're too damn late for that anyway; they've all disappeared by this time. I told you everything I know and you've checked me out six ways from Sunday and found I ain't lyin'. My friends and neighbours are suffering and dying and being buried and you kept me from them. Happy 'wild goose chasin'; I'm goin' home where I'm needed for more than just an excuse. You can't arrest me and you can't keep me. This is a joke!"

Carl rode back. They packed up to leave too, their mission seemingly accomplished.

———

The ominous calm of finality shrouded the village. Only morning and evening showed signs of life and then it was mostly the older men and younger women. They appeared in the street with faces covered, not against the cold as much as the possibility of someone looking into their tortured souls or against looking into someone else's. Inconsolable grief is a very private emotion.

Behind the drawn blinds, the fathers, the mothers the wives and sisters, the brothers, and the sons and daughters were trying to come to terms with the realization that life in the new world no more held the promise they'd so anxiously anticipated.

Carl had been gone for four days. Alexsay was up and around and the police went at him just as they had Carl and got nothing. He and Anastas were not surprised; it was the same old story on either side of the ocean. They didn't expect any positive conclusion.

Carl went to Paul's that evening to do what he could. He nursed the door back to closure using whatever he could adapt. He separated the stovepipes, pounded them straight, re-clinched them and got the kitchen stove back into service. The letter he'd written to Milly was nowhere to be seen. The girls had likely picked it up, he'd ask them about it tomorrow.

He found what he could and prepared himself something hot, the first in many days and ate it, without taste, in the terrible solitude of himself; there was too much and it was too painful. He'd never, in his poverty-stricken childhood even imagined the horrors and the tribulations he'd lived through in the last two weeks. He thought of the song Mama often sang to him and the kids and he dreamed of the security of "Canaan's Happy Land". He cried long and hard and loud, he wasn't ashamed, he didn't remember ever doing that, even as a child. He wanted to be warm and safe and home with Papa and the kids and he wanted Milly there with him. He wrote late into the night on whatever paper he could find and emptied his heart. It might worry her but he had to.

His bed was gone so he slept under his mackinaw on the ruins of Paul and Mildred's, with hope against the other terrible premonition.

He spent most of the morning washing the walls and trying to get the smell out of the place. Only new paint could right this mess. Jimmy's cradle was smashed beyond repair. That was the most hurtful of all, right up there with an outright attack on the child. Carl could kill for that! There was nothing Carl could do to fix Paul and Mildred's bed and there was no possibility of getting any help out of the village now; they were crippled far worse and were in desperate need themselves.

XI

"I always keep my promise!"

"Oh God no, I've got to warn her!"

Helen handed him the ragged remains of his heartfelt letter. She'd found it crumpled and torn in a corner near the table he'd written it on, thrown there with contempt. The envelope with Milly's name and address, and his name and return address, was gone. The vindictive animal knew.

Alice's "Lightning" was bred to the task. He rode up to the station at York in under three hours. The telegraphs were brief and marked "Urgent," to Milly or anyone of her family and to the Marshal.

Before he was able to send, Ernie handed him an "urgent."

> **"THORVALDSON DEAD.**
> **WILBUR CRITICAL.**
> **EMILY BADLY HURT.**
> **COME IF POSSIBLE.**
> **WM. BREWSTER".**

He saw, again, Milly doubled in pain.

In cold, cruel anguish, he rushed to the hospital but Paul and Mildred had already gone. All the necessary transfers were done so their return would not be hurried. Carl rode, frantically, back to the McPhersons and caught them there.

His money was at Paul's with his packs. He hadn't much on him and the trip back to get more would take another day. Paul had even less and Mildred's was still somewhere in banker's limbo. Al would take him in tomorrow and loan him what was necessary. Carl didn't know what to expect or how long he'd be gone. He didn't even have a change of clothes so he'd have to buy some. It took them most of the long evening to talk the blood back into his pallid features.

Mildred lapsed into a state of near incoherence, very near the edge of physical and emotional break. She reasoned that her terrible indiscretion had reached into and disrupted the lives of everyone and everything she'd touched. Paul could see that his emotional state was minor by comparison and he was getting really worried about her.

Al got Carl on the train the next afternoon and his return began; not at all triumphant as he'd imagined but shattered by the horrors of an old reality that had dogged him for his entire youth, always just beyond his realm or reach. Nothing good ever lasted very long. The girl he loved had been seriously injured by filth from his depressing past. *How is she? What about her family? What will they think of me now? I'm the kind of luck that nobody wants inflicted on anything or anybody dear to them.* He saw again Milly's violent reaction when he reached out to touch her.

Everything was so ominous, so black! He couldn't eat or sleep or think logically and the journey taking him back was an agonizing blur; thought-filled and painful. Just like every other time in his depressing life, he'd lose out again.

———

The dismal relic rolled noisily into Charles City at an equally dismal hour. Three people met him, Milly's Bertha, welcoming Max, and the pain-ridden Marshal.

"God, you look tired! When'd you eat or sleep last?" Max, thirteen months Carl's junior, stood taller than Carl but was built slighter. They clasped each other in their traditional way, both hands clasping both forearms. The fact that they were brothers was clearly evident in their eyes and facial bone structure. Max's appearance was how Milly had been able to recognize him and Papa as Carl's family.

"Come on! We'll get ya' somethin' to eat and then some sleep." Bertha delivered a tearful kiss. "Thank God you're alright! Marshal told us what was goin' on up there and who and what seemed to be behind it. You must've had a hell of a time."

"Not as bad as most. He was up there to kill Doukhobors and he was mad at Mildred. He didn't know she was up there until after he got there so he went after her too ... goin' to kill two birds with one stone! ... didn't know about me either until then. We weren't home so he wrecked the place then found my letter with Milly's address on it. That'd be his twisted way of gettin' back at me for God knows what; it was so long ago. How is she? When can I see her?" He looked pleadingly at the distraught, worn face of the grandfather.

"She's gone...!"

The words hit like a hammer! Carl's legs buckled, Max alone kept him standing and the startled Marshal realized what he'd said. "No! No! Not that way! God, I'm sorry I put it that way! What I meant to finish is that she ain't here; they took her to Des Moines to care for her."

Carl groaned audibly. "Oh Lord! How bad is it? What did that animal do to her?"

"It ain't the body hurt that's so bad anymore; time and rest'll take care a' that but he hurt her in about as bad a way as any man can." The Marshal's voice shook with emotion and broke part way through.

"She begged us not to tell ya'," Bertha sobbed. "She figured you suffered enough and you didn't need this, yet she's always cryin' and won't talk to us anymore and seems not to hear and keeps talkin' to you as if you were there and beggin' you to forgive her. God man, she sure needs ya' now. It's worse yet and we're real scared for her. Wilbur died this mornin' in Rochester. She ain't been told yet and we don't know how. The folks were with Wilbur and they ain't back yet. They and we are hopin' that maybe you bein' around'll help."

"It's bad enough to lose one but he's gone now and I can accept that. Seein' her alive and breathin' yet dead to everything around her is a-way worse. We know you mean everything to her. She talked about ya' all the time and even cried 'cause she's so lonesome for ya'. It's even hard for us and her folks to watch. Please love her like she needs to be loved right now. What happened to her is hurtful to any man but I'm countin' on your understanding and ability to talk to her and her folks. I know you can help!

Her looks will come back, I ain't sure of her soul. You'll have to be it 'cause we can't seem to." The Marshal clasped both Carl's hands in urgent appeal.

Carl reached to hold the sorrowing grandfather and Max stopped him rudely. "Don't!" he warned. The Marshal moved with great difficulty. "Put a bullet into him and he's hurt pretty bad. He just walked out of the hospital this evening, to be here. You'd best rest while you're still able to walk. You ain't too far from falling down yourself right now. Come on, we're staying over Bertha's."

The walk was as hard as the walk to Paul's before the pneumonia. "We'll catch the train in the morning. You'll get to see her tomorrow. You've got to sleep and eat something."

"What on earth happened to you there, son? Look at your face!"

Bertha's hadn't yet returned to normal and Carl asked.

"Here's where it happened ... gave us the slip at the station. He wound up here; maybe to get somethin' to eat, we ain't sure. Bertha figures she'd seen him in, a long while before. Milly was here gettin' ready for the breakfast ... her turn to open, otherwise it would a' been Bertha. It was pure chance so don't blame yourself. I don't think he knew who she was. Max was workin' nights so she was the only one there ... first we realized was we heard the shootin'. Wilbur'd walked in to warn 'er and caught him at it ... animal shot the kid four times and Milly saw it. I came in like a damned fool; I should 'a' known better but these were my grandkids ... bastard hit me before I could level on him. Max came in from the back while he was after finishin' me and put an end to him ... broke his lousy neck!"

Bertha'd stood with the Marshal and her very best friend when they were young and got married. She'd watched their children and grandchildren grow up. They'd eaten her ice cream and drank her soda pop. Now one of their grandchildren was dead and the other was badly hurt, right under her sheltering, loving nose, when it should have been her in that bed, or that grave; her life was spent. "What kind of God could allow that to happen or such low bastards to walk the face a' the earth?" She held on to Carl hard and long, crying bitterly, then fed him and put him to bed. "She's been bad hurt but you're about the only hope we've got for her. She just stares off when the family or I try to talk to her. If you're what I think, you'll help. She kept talkin' to you and beggin' you to forgive her as if she'd done somethin' wrong. God I'm sure glad of you; I know she'll be alright now."

She kissed him goodnight, just like she would the child of her own, that she'd never had; the love of her life had married her best friend so she nurtured their family like they were her own.

True to form, the train was late and they didn't arrive in Des Moines until it was nearly dark. "Bertha's" stayed closed and she was with Carl and the Marshal. Max had to work, there was nothing more he could do anyway.

Two forlorn figures met them on the platform, eyes sunken, shoulders stooped. Carl recognized the devastated mother and assumed accurately. Milly's father looked weary and old. He stood taller than all of them and was a bit overweight, stern, but good-hearted looking.

When Carl stepped off the train, the man had him in his long grasp; he knew exactly who Carl was. Carl centered the parents of the girl he loved, both hung on, crying uncontrollably. Nobody said much; they didn't have to. Then they led to the carriage and to the hospital.

———

"You're Carl? She wanted so badly to stay awake for you, but she's very weak. You can go in if you want and I'm sure you do. She's asleep now. We had to give her a sedative a while ago and it got the better of her. I wish I could tell you what to expect but a lot of that depends on you. You mean an awful lot to her and that's the critically important thing right now. Physically, she's a lot better now than she was when they brought her in. She was badly beaten, you're lucky to have her alive. Talk to her quietly, maybe she'll wake up and recognize you. God, I hope she does!" The white clad figure led Carl down the long antiseptic hallway and stopped at the door of the single room. "I'll be at the desk just down the hall if you need me." The rest stayed in the waiting room and prayed.

Although his heart pounded, Carl stayed very calm and determined; this was critically important. Neither nerves nor fears would resolve any part of what would happen here.

Her head was heavily bandaged and a stitched, disinfectant-stained scar ran diagonally from the bridge of her nose, under her discoloured, right eye and down her cheek. Her bottom lip protruded into stitching, so the kiss he wanted to deliver, was out. Despite the bit of discolouration and swelling, this was the prettiest sight Carl could recall. He picked up the small hand towel and gently dabbed the tear that ran its slow way down her cheek. She stirred quietly, but seemingly, stayed asleep. She knew, that's all he needed to know. His terrible fear banished, he pulled up the chair and sat beside her, holding her reddened, knuckle-bruised hand.

———

The smiling nurse beckoned the anxious parents, quietly, to the partially opened door. Carl, head down, leaned heavily against the bed, asleep. Milly's free hand slowly stroked his head. They walked back to their near-by hotel free of half of the most painful burden that any parent could carry. At least one of their children would be alright.

———

She stirred and Carl sat up. Her puffed eyelids fluttered and opened, her frightened eyes stared over into his; they were just as beautiful as he remembered.

"Hi you!" he whispered.

"You did come!" Her eyes welled up and she sobbed piteously. "I'm so ashamed!"

"Of me?" He draped his hands down over his rustic dress and he smiled broadly in sham ignorance.

"Oh Carl, can you find it in your heart to forgive me?"

"For what? You did everything right! What's even better, you saved the girl I love and I love you even more for doing that. Maybe I can't kiss your lips but I can sure kiss your cheek." He turned her head and kissed the perfect cheek, "and I can hold you." He gently lifted her head and shoulders, watching for signs of pain. He saw none and sat diagonally on the bed beside her, then leaned back against her pillow, cradling her against him and held her as tightly as he dared. "That's not hurting you is it?"

"No!" she muffled, her swollen lip still interrupting and she cried quietly and trembled.

"Easy; easy, it's alright! Get rid of it if you can and take as long as you need. I'm stayin' right here and you're goin' to have an awful time gettin' rid of me." He reached down her left side and fondled her free hand while he held her right closely against his waist. She rolled her head slowly on his shoulder to look up into his face and his smiling, gentle eyes, then snuggled into his comforting, warm nest and the tears stopped. Their fears and insecurities were foolish and needless. It didn't matter what they felt or looked like; the torture and the real pain were gone, only the physical hurt remained.

The reflection from the dimmed hallway barely lighted the room. Relaxed and secure, they both slept again.

———

The nurse looked in several times, smiling broadly when she saw the arrangement. It was totally against hospital policy but it was magical medicine. When the suffering parents appeared before daybreak, she showed them just as she had earlier and whispered a grateful "Thank God! I wouldn't have given a plug nickel for her mental state."

They stood long and held each other, knowing full well that they would be losing their, now, only child, to this strange and entirely pleasing young man and the new world that was his. It hurt in a wonderful way. The life that they'd given her was hers, she'd have to live it for as long as she had it. It was a miracle that it too was not taken from her and from them; he'd helped to bring it back. They'd lost one in her defense and now they would gain another. It is said that, "God never closes a door, without first opening a window." They returned to the hotel to sleep back some of the strength they'd need for the ordeal to come.

———

"Honestly, I feel so helpless and foolish expecting you to do this but my hand's so shaky and gosh, I'm so hungry, I'd slop all over the bed." She pulled heavily on the straw; her severely lacerated lip wouldn't allow her to drink any other way. Nurse Krantz told Carl that she hadn't taken much fluid and had eaten next to nothing since she got here. It was becoming a very dangerous concern.

He fed her the entire bowl of fluid oatmeal and dipped the toast into the coffee, then fed that to her to avoid scratching her very tender lip. He was spooning the marmalade to her as her parents walked in. "Don't worry, if my kind of luck holds the way it's been the last couple of months, I'll more than likely be callin' on your help, in kind, an awful lot."

"I was wondering what happened to your face, but didn't like to ask."

"Well, to spell it out as fast as I can, I've had a good crack on the head."

"I noticed the scar last night."

"I've had a bout of pneumonia, and damn near froze but you were there." Milly'd puzzle over that. "My fingers and toes are still botherin' me. Oh. Hi!" He turned to acknowledge the parents who stood behind him and just watched and listened. Milly hadn't noticed them either; she was so enthralled by the look of him.

"And from what Dad's been telling us, you got involved in what seems to be a major incident in your country." Chris Hallvarson produced a copy of the newest Des Moines weekly, headlined.

"MASS MURDER OF SECTARIAN DOUKHOBORS IN CANADA HAS DES MOINES-MAYNARD CONNECTION."

Phyllis walked over to the bed to embrace her rejuvenated daughter and the first anxious question was, "How is Wilbur?" They hadn't realized that Carl hadn't yet told her and the pain reflected on their faces revealed the truth. Milly slumped back onto her pillow; Carl had her sitting for the first time. She whimpered pathetically and both parents were at her side. Carl was going to leave them to their grief but Milly demanded his return.

"He was so horribly hurt! The doctors told us that there wasn't much chance and he had the very best; there was nothing they could do. He never regained consciousness."

"Dad told us that both he and you knew the animal."

"Yes, we unfortunately did!" Anticipating the worst, Carl told them the exact circumstance, including the recent events that led to his hurried arrival. Their response was stunned silence. They knew about Carl's belated attempt at warning because the Marshal had shown them the telegraph. There was nobody at Charles to receive the one he'd sent to them, until the station master, hearing the crisis, delivered the Marshal's to the hospital. Chris produced it and showed it to Milly.

"You mean he knew our address too?"

"Yes! It was on the letter I hadn't yet mailed to you because of the fire at the camp. He knew, then, that I was there too and I was afraid he'd come after you out of spite. He must have been suspicious that somebody was waitin' because he left the train and wound up at Bertha's, knowing he could get somethin' to eat and to hide. He didn't expect you to be there when he smashed in. He couldn't have known who you were and he wouldn't give a damn anyway. The Marshal jailed him several times for bothering women."

Milly stared straight ahead, unsure what to think. Carl drew the tattered, smoke-stained letter from his shirt pocket and nervously handed it to her, along with the neater, most recent. She noted his emotion and smiled, more to herself then at him. She read the tattered remnant slowly and her injured lip quivered. "You realize what you've asked with this letter?" She handed it to her confused mother. Carl was afraid of what he thought was coming.

"Right off, I want you to know that he beat me so badly because I fought him with my very life. Wilbur died because he's a lot like me; he attacked. He'd rather die than allow that — Grandpa too. I saw what Max did and I know that he saved Grandpa's life and mine. He'd have saved Wilbur's too if he could. I knew Wilbur wouldn't make it; I saw what happened to him. I didn't care if I lived or died either but I couldn't forget about you; I couldn't leave you. I need you more than I realized but you seem to know that, this letter tells me that. I'm answering you now, in the presence of my parents whom I love dearly, that I want to spend the rest of my life, for as long as it is, with you. Now, you have your answer whether you wanted it now or not and I want all of you to come hold me because I want to cry, if you don't mind."

That afternoon, the grieving parents had to leave their only daughter, to go home and bury their only son. There was no way Milly would be able to travel to Charles; she had great difficulty balancing when she sat up with Carl's help. She had several cracked ribs, lacerations and a skull fracture that still worried the doctor. She'd lost a lot of blood and it would take time to build that back but at least she was eating again.

The Marshal asked Doc Halfred to check his wound because it was extremely painful and Halfred warned him to get back into bed, preferably in the Des Moines hospital. He refused and would travel back to attend the services so Halfred treated him and prescribed powerful pain medication, and he left with Bertha. Carl and Milly were left to deal with the grief as best they could.

Carl stayed with her the entire day of the funeral and kept her out of her depression by wheeling her around the hospital and wrapping her, with permission, and pushing her out into the fresh, crisp air to look at some of the near-by displays. Christmas was just around the corner.

Carl telegraphed Paul and Mildred to let them know and mailed a letter telling them what he was likely to do. Within a matter of days, Carl and Milly received a congratulatory telegraph from "ALL YOUR FRIENDS" at York long before Carl's letter could have arrived there.

The Marshal told Carl not to worry about money because he was more than able to help but Carl didn't want to do that. The hospital put a cot in Milly's room and Carl agreed to help with maintenance and patient care wherever his strength was needed and they paid him, better than he'd ever been paid before, for the extent of his efforts. He was more than grateful and Milly was very happy with the circumstance. Her speedy recovery was amazing.

Milly made it absolutely clear that she meant to attend some teacher training as soon as she was able; she'd already made some arrangements. She'd be extremely lonesome and miss him desperately but she expected him to return to "...our land and help with the rebuilding." It was clear to her that their home would never be built if the lumber camp wasn't restored. She took a keen interest in the people and wished she could be there to help, "...but all in good time, first things first!" This time he wouldn't leave a lovesick young girl; he'd leave a lonesome young wife. It was positive, it was determined, it was final and "You'd better get used to the idea." He didn't really know how to broach the possibility. Typically, she, again said what he was thinking.

A half-dozen paper people descended upon the hospital. They'd heard that someone from Canada, who had been in the battle and knew accurately, the Des Moines connection, was in the city and they were hungry for the story — the more sensational the better. Carl would again become the unwilling center, this time with a picture of himself and his, "... ailing fiancée" with the story on front-page billing. He told it simply and accurately and typically didn't mince with the truth as he saw it. They'd know the reality of the story instead of the distorted myth.

The hospital staff issued a special invitation to their Christmas worship and banquet. They considered Milly's revival nothing short of miraculous and were delighted with the result. They simply demanded to know when and where the marriage was to take place and they made it clear that they all planned to contribute and some of them planned to attend. Carl was very familiar with one of their former, very much appreciated staff members who'd married that "Karmady fella" and moved to Canada with him.

Carl gave them an address. He'd told some of the more intimate of Mildred's friends about what had happened and how much the couple needed encouragement and support. They would surely get it.

———

Milly walked haltingly, with Carl's help, out of the hospital to catch the train home. She really wasn't strong enough but she was very stable and was mending in every way at a marvellous pace. Doctor Halfred and Nurse Krantz told Carl what to expect and instructed him what to do, in case something happened but they didn't anticipate anything. "Just bein' careful, that's all!" The Charles hospital knew she'd be coming and would check her just to be certain. Besides, with all that had happened, the funeral expense and all, the huge medical bill would be very hard to pay.

She travelled well and an experienced nurse, along with her parents, Grandpa, Bertha, and Max met the train. The story had reached the Charles paper and many well-wishers, friends, curiosity seekers and sensationalists were there as well. The family and close friends who understood, were polite but firm and again Max took things in hand with an abrupt, "No!

Not right now!" They knew who he was and what he'd done and they weren't about to push it.

The nurse, a friend of the family, went to the Hallvarsons' home with them, got Milly right into bed and checked her injuries and vitals thoroughly. Carl, without question, remained responsible for her secure arrival to the safety of her bed. The parents were confident and relaxed with the responsible attitude of this handsome young man.

Mrs. Hallvarson took some supper up to her; the stairs were too difficult for Milly. Carl offered to carry her down but both she and her mother insisted and Carl knew they wanted to talk. He kissed Milly on the forehead and turned to leave when she pulled him back and kissed him ever so gently on his lips while her mother watched. "I've wanted to do that ever since the night you came. God I missed you!" Carl squeezed her hands and smiled. When he turned to leave, Mother's eyes were filled with tears. Carl hugged her and kissed her forehead as well.

"I ain't got too much to offer her yet, but you can be sure that I love her and I'll see to it that she's cared for the way you'd want."

"I know that!" she smiled. "You'll have to forgive my mother's heart. I know you'll be good to her and for her. Lord knows, what happened here is about as hard as it can get." She returned the kiss and Carl left. He hadn't met or seen Wilbur in life or death. All he'd seen was a picture and that was several years old. He'd be Arnold's age.

———

Carl, Max, and Milly's father, Chris Hallvarson met the train, the same one Carl had taken four months before. Papa, tall, ramrod straight, white haired and thinner, stepped off like someone half his age. He wasn't a man to show his emotion; a lifetime of cruelty and abuse had turned his emotion inward yet he couldn't contain himself or his pride. His eyes were wet with admiration for his first born as he clasped Carl in a hug. He'd never done that before. Carl had achieved what no other Buechler had, as far back as Papa's history knew. He'd made them landowners. He'd opened the door and let them in. He was extremely proud of Carl, of all of them. They'd grown up hard and straight and strong and honest and now Carl would bring a new, beautiful and courageous young lady into his family and he was proud of her too; she was made of the right stuff; a determined fighter, capable of withstanding anything. She fought to win.

"Mine Godt, Frieda, you vas right!"

As they circled each other in a family hug and drew Chris in, the stooped, grey-haired, tiny woman, took Carl totally by surprise. She threw her arms around him and kissed him on the cheek, just as she had before he left.

"God it's good to see you again! What on earth have you done to yourself? You're thin and ... your face?"

"Mrs. Pawlowich!"

"I hope you can forgive me; I just had to come and see my boy. Is it true?" Carl nodded an adamant yes. The Buechler children had grown up under her watchful eye and she loved them all dearly. "And the young lady who captured you? I just have to meet her. I've heard a lot about her. Bertha tells me everything. Thank God you're alright; you sure had us all worried from all of what we'd been hearing from Bill."

At their age, they were changing fast; they seemed to have grown and matured. With the events of the last month, they just worshipped the ground their two older brothers walked on. They'd bragged them up to all their friends and anyone who'd listen. They couldn't ask all of their questions fast enough but they got few answers; there were just too many things happening.

August was the quiet one, the thoughtful one. Almost inconspicuous, he was natured like his mother. He could enter a room full of people without being noticed and with eyes and ears, leave it shortly after with more knowledge than any there and do it without uttering a word. His school records topped both his class and his siblings. He'd stand, watch, smile, speak when necessary and no more than necessary. Like Max, nothing escaped his notice.

Bertha had the fair features of her mother with even more emphatic eyes and the bone structure of a potential beauty, complete with naturally blond hair, now closely curled. Mary had taken her in hand and saw to it that the thoroughly excitable and spontaneous girl was dressed to look like a proper young lady, combed, curled, pressed and under a flowered bonnet. If Carl had seen her from a distance on the street, he'd have difficulty recognizing her. She was no longer the little girl but she couldn't lose it all. She ran up and gave Carl her usual girlish kiss, then looked around frantically.

"Well, where is she?" She'd heard so much about Milly that she expected to recognize her right off. She just knew she'd love her! This was the biggest event of her childhood; her big brother had a girl and Max and Papa said she was really pretty but she'd been too sick to be at the funeral.

"She's at home yet," Chris Hallvarson told her. "We're taking you to Bertha's to get ready, then after the church, we'll all meet there, for the meal. There are lots of people who want to meet you folks. Did I ever tell you that you're about the prettiest girl I've ever seen?" Of course, several times. Bertha just loved this flattering big man and would willingly soak up all the admiration and praise he had to offer. Milly was sure lucky to have such a wonderful father.

Chris saw, in this family, a close bond that he'd lacked in his youth. His father had been a good provider but he was an untouchable man. He seemed always at a distance. Like so many during that turbulent national war, he'd seen and suffered terrible things. Like so many, after the war, he talked little and seemed lost in a world of his own. Chris knew his daughter would not suffer the fate of his mother; these people loved her. She was just as impulsive, daring and outgoing. She'd be comfortable. He was very grateful for that.

Carl was a bit surprised at the ease and obvious familiarity he observed between his family and the Hallvarsons. Carl felt almost like the stranger here; the Hallvarsons were more familiar with Papa and Max then they were with him. Milly had seen to it that her family met Papa and Max when they first came. They spoke with common knowledge of events that were unfamiliar to Carl, yet he'd been gone only a few months. They'd met young Bertha and the other boys for the first time at the funeral and kept Bertha for the night. Papa and the boys stayed with Max, over the restaurant. At one time, Bertha had it filled with roomers but age and circumstances had forced her to give that up until Max came. He helped when his shift at the plant was done, or when he was off.

———

"How do you do it? You seem to know exactly what to do and you've got it done while I'm still thinking about it. I didn't have to tell the family about us, they've taken the two of us as an absolute."

"Are you disappointed? Am I being too pushy? I don't mean to be, but I get carried away with things when it comes to you and me. I'm sorry if I do."

"You can be as pushy as you want when it comes to me. I know that you think I'm a bit shy and I guess when it comes to things like this, I am. I know you realize that I want exactly the same things as you when it comes to us. Things can't happen soon enough for me; I got so lonesome for you. I've seen what that country can do to a couple when there's nothing and life is so hard." He'd told her about what happened to the McPhersons and how time and distance had hurt Paul and Mildred. "I wouldn't have let that happen to us."

"How easy do you think it's been here when you were gone? This isn't me! This isn't my life! You are, and everything that you have to do. I don't care if we have to live in a cave until we get something. You've got a lot going for you. It'll take a while for me to get over this, then I'll get some training and get up there as soon as I can. I know what Mrs. Pawlowich asked of you and that will be a real help if you can find a place to keep the stock. You'll surely need the horses and some machinery in a few months to get started." The girl had a lot mapped out in her mind.

"Did I tell you just how nice you look? You're getting back to the real you. I'd love you regardless of what happened, I want you to know that. Maybe this was all meant to be." The bulky head bandage was gone and she wore a beautifully flowered bonnet to cover the injury. It would be a while before her fantastic hair could fully grow back and her chest was still very tender. The stitching under her eye was gone and the scar, still evident, would heal very well. Mother had cleverly covered it with her make-up. Her lip, carrying a hint of lip rouge, though still very tender, had rediscovered its beautiful form.

The carriage rolled them up to the steps of the church and several cameras of the local news hounds. They asked only for a pose. Although Milly was walking strongly, Carl was helping her up the steps when the door flew open to beautiful young Bertha. Milly could have recognized those eyes anywhere; the Buechler children had all inherited their mother's eyes. Besides, Papa had shown her the family picture.

Bertha stopped short, stared with no inhibition, liked what she saw, squealed with girlish glee, threw up her arms and without invitation, planted a horrendous kiss on Milly's good cheek and hung on. Milly had passed Bertha's discriminating approval. Carl shuddered; it must have hurt, but all Milly did was flinch a bit.

"Take it easy, she's got cracked ribs!"

"Oh gosh, I'm so sorry!" Bertha stepped back with alarm. Milly responded with a corresponding hug of her own, though somewhat less aggressive.

"Bertha, you're just as pretty as Carl said you are."

"And so are you. For once in his silly life my big brother knows what he's talking about. Did you know, he's so shy that he didn't tell me about you? Papa did. How'd you do it? Did you know that the silly is scared of girls?"

"You could have fooled me! All I did was this." She turned on startled Carl and administered the boldest kiss she'd been able to muster yet. He blushed wildly at this impromptu act in front of all these people, much to the delight of both Berthas, the family, and friends.

Despite her recent injuries, Milly looked fantastic in her full length, lilac gown and loose fitting cardigan of similar colour, but of darker hue. Few in the assemblage had ever seen Carl and certainly had never seen him looking like this. The rumour mills ground out fantastic stories about this guy, his brother and his family and curiosity had taken on a life of its own. The Marshal, still in obvious pain, led Carl to the conspicuous pew at the head of the assemblage.

Young Bertha was puzzled. "What's going on? Why's he sitting way over there instead of with us? Where'd Milly go? Why ain't she with him?" Both Carl and Milly shied away from the publicity and sensationalism attached to their circumstance. Things could get out of hand so they wanted everything kept low key. Few, other than the immediate families and closest friends, even realized that this was more than a worship service. Young Bertha couldn't keep quiet about anything so she hadn't been told. She didn't even question why Mrs. Pawlowich had taken such pains to see to it that she was looking extra good. Time didn't allow for all of the formalities and neither Carl nor Milly held much stock in formality. The press, equally unaware, treated it as a photo opportunity. Carl and Milly realized that wouldn't last long.

The pastor walked quietly down the aisle to where young Bertha sat and motioned her to him. Very puzzled, she followed. Carl could hear her squeal in the little back antechamber where Milly waited. Milly'd told him she was going to get Bertha into the wedding party but she hadn't told him everything.

Max came up to join Carl who had assumed that he'd stand alone, winked slyly and sat beside him. Carl was puzzled but didn't ask, in fact, he was getting just a bit nervous and emotional. The pastor returned to the pulpit dressed in nothing more than an informal suit.

"Just a few weeks ago, many of you sat in these pews to grieve with the Hallvarsons over the tragic loss of their son, brother, and grandson; a courageous young man, who sacrificed himself so that others of his family might live. The account is very well known to all of you. For the benefit of those who do not already know or suspect, this afternoon we gather for a very different reason. We gather to honour the sister, the brave young lady who fought her attacker and survived very beautifully. She will this day be united in marriage with the young man that you've read so much about recently and now you see seated before you." A single clapping in the assemblage erupted into a general reaction of approval that ran on for some time before it settled.

"Many of you, no doubt, have asked yourself, why I, pastor of this assembly, am not garbed in my usual robe. The answer is very simple. I am not conducting this marriage. I surrender my accustomed role to one who is, in reality, far more qualified then I ... a man of the law, very well known to all of us, who saw the bride, since her birth, through many of her joys and sorrows; a man, who in his many years of public service, was called into many roles. This is one of many for which he was notarized. Welcome with me the bride's grandfather, Federal Marshal William Thomas Brewster."

The respect with which the community held the Marshal was more than apparent. "It might be of some interest to you to note that the Marshal was also very familiar with the groom and his family throughout their childhood. Marshal Brewster."

He walked in slowly and carefully, favouring his right leg, dressed in the black robe of the Justice. He shook, first Max's hand, then Carl's. "Ready son?"

Carl nodded.

The gentle old instrument, at the obviously qualified hand of its mistress, eased into the bridal announcement and the procession began.

Completely unabashed by the sudden role inflicted upon her, smiling young Bertha marched out with the vigour of emotional familiarity, smiling from beam to beam over the large, full bouquet and coming behind her, the bridal maid, carrying a full head of beautifully done, shocking, red hair. Carl looked questioningly at Max who flushed his characteristic Buechler embarrassment. Carl had sadly underestimated her determined resolve. Alice delivered her usual, suggestive, side wink as she approached. Max assumed the wink was delivered to him and flushed brightly.

Milly now wore a full length, trailing veil of gown-light lilac that Carl didn't know about. How she'd done all of this in such a short time, confused him. Despite the slight hint of bruising, she'd refused to wear the matching lace face-veil. She wanted everyone to see her as she was, and now especially, after some of the vicious rumours that were circulating.

Carl felt suddenly weak; he'd met this girl only once, just a few months before, for only a few hours and now she was minutes away from becoming his life-long partner in marriage. This was something beyond his anticipation and very much faster then he'd imagined. He looked over at Papa's smiling, composed face and renewed his confidence. He looked at Milly and was surprised by the same impish, playful wink that he'd seen from Alice. Obviously they'd communicated prior to this and he wondered, humorously, just to what extent. Their eyes and confident, secure smiles locked and stayed the course until Milly stood directly across from him.

With confidence, Chris Hallvarson handed his only daughter and now his only child, over to this very appealing young man. He couldn't hide the little tear that she saw in the corner of his eye. Before she took Carl's hand, she reached up and kissed her father, securely, on his grateful cheek.

"Family, friends, neighbours, ladies, and gentlemen, for over forty years I've enforced the laws of the country and this state and I can say that during that time there have been many things that have given me much joy and pleasure. In nearly all of those, either one of these two young people have been directly involved. The bride is my only granddaughter and I have had the pleasure of serving the groom and his family on several occasions over the years. I have recently had the concerns of a grandfather when I again met this young man and realized, that in the strange way of things, he would become a permanent part of my small family and I would have the pleasure of the two of them together. Most of you also know of the fact that if it hadn't been for the groom's brother, neither I, nor my granddaughter would now have life. I want to thank Fred Buechler for raising such a fine family and I want to say that nothing in my entire life gives me as much pleasure as conducting the marriage of these two young people. I will forever be grateful for that privilege and I thank you Emily.

"My wound and age tell me it is time to surrender my duties to the country and I can promise these two that I will soon have lots of time to devote to the interests of my future great-grandchildren. Judging by what I've been told and what we read in the papers, somebody's got to keep these two young fellas in line." He reached over and gave both Milly and Alice a conspicuous nudge. For the first time Carl saw Alice actually blush. Carl wondered how she'd done this much.

Carl answered the questions as the Marshal asked them and so did Milly. This is what they were supposed to do; this is what was meant to be.

"Now by the authority vested in me by the state of Iowa and in the eyes of God Almighty and the family and friends here assembled, I pronounce you man and wife. You may kiss the bride." This was really the first thing that either of them remembered clearly and they obeyed the instruction expertly, oblivious to the cheer that went up from the assembly. They moved toward the table that the pastor had set for the signature, opposite the ancient, well-preserved organ and now came into clear view of its mistress. This time the obviously prearranged wink came from the strained, yet smiling face of the next surprise — it was Mildred.

"Ladies and gentlemen, I present to you Mr. and Mrs. Carl and Emily Buechler."

It was real! It had happened! The pretty stranger that the lonesome, backward, country boy had met for the first time by an accident of fate, was now his wife and the circumstances had given both of them a bit of celebrity status in the quiet, uneventful, little, mid-western city.

They had little time to notice each other's response to the gauntlet of well-wishing and cheek kissing and hugging and hand shaking and shoulder slapping that afflicted their path back up the aisle; the place was packed. Only the stern lead of the Marshal and little sister Bertha, preserved their way from total blockage. Very concerned about Milly's ability to withstand the onslaught, Carl held her as firmly as he dared, but she stayed the course.

The media, at the entrance, had multiplied at least tenfold and again Max allowed only photographs. He promised talk later. The loving kiss was by far the most popular. Max was a bit unnerved and Alice smiled at the opportunity when the photographers demanded, with some prompting from sister Bertha, no less from the bridal maid and groomsman. Strangely, to the amusement of Carl and his young sister, it took very little persuasion. Max was embarrassed but it was clear to all and especially to the anticipating Alice that he really wanted to. The event superseded Carl and Milly's performance many-fold, due to the firm nature of the lip-lock and it was difficult to believe that it had not been well rehearsed. Carl knew that it was a totally novel experience to both of them and he was delighted. Everyone liked this open and uninhibited redhead.

A decorative four-placer, for the ride to the reception, replaced the carriage that had brought Carl and Milly. It was only three blocks, easily walkable, but Carl was still glad because Milly didn't have the strength and it would have meant running a gauntlet of inquisitors. Carl's meagre childhood had taught him a social place and the attention he'd received over the past weeks, still unnerved him a bit. Milly was naturally curious but the emotion in someone else, directed at her and Carl was a bit annoying. Of the much appreciated gifting from the Des Moines staff, this standoutish carriage was, without their knowledge, the only breath of cold in the warmth of the intent. They remained polite and told Max to leave the curtain open, while they smiled falsely.

Bertha was already there and the Marshal rushed to her side as the carriage drew up. The church-front media, already there, stood in wait. "You'll get out of their road and leave 'em alone right now! I ain't done yet and I'd be only too glad ta lock you up until they're ready ta talk to you, if ever. I will talk to ya' only when I'm good and ready." Max's abrupt vault from the carriage and the long, lean, grey-haired, older man, consuming the distance with a rapid, military gait and thunder on his brow, told them they'd be in serious trouble if they didn't.

As quickly as the storm gathered, it dispersed. Family, true friends, and well-wishers, all who knew the miracle of Carl in Milly's life, lined the walk and the gauntlet repeated itself to the door. Sister Bertha, accompanied by tiny, grey-haired Mary showered the couple with baskets of flower petals they'd hand-plucked off the blossoms and wet-eyed Mary kissed Milly. "Welcome to our lives you beautiful girl! Our Carl is surely one lucky boy."

They were nobodies from nowhere and expected a simple family marriage, yet were receiving such heartfelt recognition from so many that it was hard for them to understand. Never in their young lives had either of them imagined the extent of their innocent reach. After the dirt, filth and pain of the recent past, life held renewed hope and promise.

His school-bag-come-lunch-bag sat on the bench, exactly where he'd left it, months before, with its top gapping wide. The top-most pillar of a marbled wedding cake projected through.

"God, you look nice! How'd you do it in so little time? That colour isn't like anything I've seen a bride in before. It's just perfect!"

She leaned over and whispered back into in his ear as the attention focused away from them. "It was easy really. You see, I knew this was going to happen. I bought it about a month after you left." She nibbled, invitingly on his ear lobe and growled quietly, "You lucky boy!" Carl looked around nervously to see if anyone had noticed as she delivered him another of those suggestive come-hither winks, then laid her head on his shoulder to observe the Alice spectacle.

She was an unknown and she was certainly spectacular. Carl really enjoyed Max's predicament and Alice's charmed embarrassment. He learned that she'd got their home address and simply started to write to Max. Because she knew about Milly, she wrote to her as well, Carl didn't want to know just what. Somehow, she'd been able to negotiate the rest. This really looked promising; they were so well matched. Both stood a head above others of their genders. The family and friends just simply looked, liked, and encouraged.

The warm breath, near his other ear, alerted Carl as the seductive voice whispered into it. "You lucky boy!" growled a familiar chord, then blew gently on his cheek and giggled. She'd been directly behind him on her blessings approach when the opportunity arose and Mildred wouldn't pass it up. Milly heard and lifted her head so that Carl could turn into the big wide inquisitive eyes of Jimmy.

"Well hi-ya pal!" He lifted the happy little smile onto his lap and turned to kiss Mother on her cheek as she delivered him a huge hug.

"I should say, 'you lucky girl!' I've seen him without anything on too!" Mildred stopped with Carl's shocked reaction and Milly's open-mouth inability to respond. She paused quite deliberately, waggling her questioning finger between the two of them with feigned surprise. "You mean to tell me that the two of you haven't ...? Well! I never!" and exploded into her familiar laughter. She sounded like the old Mildred as the two fumbled for a response. She threw her arms around both of them and pulled them to her with affection. "I know, I know!"

Milly noted Carl's discomfort with the revelation. She took his hand. "That's one of the things I really love about you; your emotions are so obvious. Mildred, Alice, and I met last night when you were off talking to Grandpa, and we talked a long time about you and your life out there. They told me everything. I'm prepared to let them love you like they do on three counts. You've got to keep loving me like you do and let me love you like I do and you have to be prepared to share me with this guy." She pulled the squirming boy off Carl's lap and onto hers in response to his welcoming reach. It took Carl a while to translate what Milly had just said. She was going to be fun too.

Carl's smile straightened as he asked, "And Paul?"

"He's fine. There's a large crew at the camp and he's there most of the time now. He's a lot stronger then I've been. With the pressure of all the burned and the horrid mess at home, I was starting to come apart. He knows how I feel about him — I'm the one who's having the problems."

"She told us about it," Milly whispered.

"God bless that man; I love him so and I had to treat both of us so dirty." Her voice wavered and tears broke.

Carl stood up and held her. "How's he reacting to you?"

"He's fine!" she whispered. "I think I was near to a mental collapse and he was very worried about me, God bless him!" she repeated. "I love him so! He made me come here because he was gone most of the time and he knew the support all you wonderful people would give me. All my old friends have done wonders and the two of you'll never know just how good you've made me feel. I have to be needed. That part of my life will never be pure but at least you've all made me feel clean and good about myself again. I haven't told him about the baby yet because I want him to want me, not to feel trapped. He's done that and the girls gave me a complete going-over. Things will be just fine if I back off. I can tell him when we get back that he's going to be Daddy." Carl didn't know.

"He is Daddy!" Milly insisted.

"You silly woman, look at him!" Carl pointed to Jimmy. "He is Paul!"

"Oh God, I know you're right and I sure am glad for your assurance because it seems everything's been so unsure." She wept quietly on Carl's shoulder as Milly, with Jimmy, rose and put an arm around her.

"What happened?" The concerned guardian Max approached quickly when he noticed.

Sensing the nature of the discussion, Alice whispered, "I'll tell you later."

"Let's eat!" Old Bertha's big voice called. The marriage party sat at the table of honour and were being served. The rest filed past the large loaded tables, helped themselves, and sat where they could. There were so many. It was to be friends and family only and it was.

Trusty, experienced Old Bertha knew the ropes well. They couldn't all find room to sit yet there would be leftovers for days to come. Papa and the Marshal sat together, their stern exteriors melting with joy, pride and admiration. Carl saw Papa lift his eyes and knew he was talking to Mama.

Mary Pawlowich, with a lifetime of big crew experience, insisted on running the kitchen like a little drill sergeant and Bertha oversaw the entire battle. Mildred and the younger Bertha were banished from its interior. Dishes clattered through and shone back on the table, thanks largely to the willing Des Moines hospital staff.

Alice dominated both Jimmy and Max and never left either of them for any reason. Everyone there, sooner or later made it a point to talk to this girl just to get a closer look at her, to see if it was real.

Cutlery clinked, laughter roared, the din was deafening. Communication degenerated to hand-cupped ear-shouting. Carl and Milly didn't have a second to themselves. Carl hoped she wasn't getting too tired; she certainly looked whole and happy. He wasn't accustomed to all the attention but he surely needed the fellowship and laughter after the stress of the last while.

The old piano beat a simple, emphatic chord, repeatedly until the hubbub died. "If I can get your attention please!" Mildred's request sounded more like an order and the room fell silent. "The bride has something to say."

"Not all that long ago, a miracle walked through that door and into my life and sat at that very same table. Even now I know he doesn't realize what he's done to me. I don't think I'd be whole enough to be talking to you or anyone if he hadn't appeared at my hospital bed that night. I know that the rest of my life wouldn't be worth living without him. Those of you who know him realize that he has a way of getting into your mind and your heart and you just can't get him out. He can walk into a hopeless situation and help you feel good again, about the very few good things left. The beauty of this wonderful person is that he doesn't even know he's doing it. My love and my life, this is yours." She sat at the well-cared-for piano, with no music, shut her eyes and poured her heart onto the keyboard.

Carl didn't know what it was; that didn't really matter. No one could fail to recognize the depth and emotion. It wasn't a love that needed understanding; it just was. Carl had never heard her play before and he'd certainly never heard anyone play like this and all for him. He rose silently and walked to her, placed both his hands on her shoulders as she leaned her head against his arm, the music flowed without interruption until she had finished and Carl wasn't sure if she'd finished or just quit. He could feel her begin to tremble with the emotion.

"Thank-you my darling; you can't imagine how great this makes me feel. Nobody's ever made me feel this way. God how I love you!" She stood and kissed him longer and harder than ever.

"Whattid he say? Whattid he say?"

"Never mind, just look at 'em!"

"Well!" Mildred broke the impasse as she wiped her eyes. She moved onto the bench and erupted into a merry waltzing rhythm as the table and chairs scraped away to make room for the couple. Carl hadn't danced much but Mama'd taught him some and he caught on very quickly. He was ever worried about Milly and holding her carefully, he moved slowly, looking all the while, into her eyes. She tired easily and they sat down, holding each other as the room broke into song and Mildred's powerful clear voice led the lot as the coffee flowed.

Their joined hands made the first cut into the cake and old Bertha took over; there were so many that she had to cut very small.

Mildred led the couple back to the head table, knowing Milly would be getting tired and the couple would have to leave soon. The group singing stopped. Mildred asked Papa and the Hallvarsons to join their children.

"In honour of the mother who couldn't be here and the father and family who feel, so nearly, her presence with them." Gertrude Krantz, the white-clad figure, who'd first led Carl to Milly's bedside, was of Austrian extraction and knew well the traditional wedding song. They'd learned from Max that it was sung at Mama and Papa's wedding. It was also famil-iar in the Scandinavian countries and was well known to the Hallvarsons. They'd requested it at Carl and Milly's marriage. The Buechler children had often heard it sung at weddings they'd attended.

The duet was totally unaccompanied voice and the two were more than qualified. It was a song of joy and the promise that, until now, had so eluded Papa. He just beamed and held up his hands to touch Mama's. The Buechler children had never seen their father this emotional. Mama was here with him at the marriage of their first-born just as surely as if she filled the chair beside him. Carl and Milly moved to either side of him and held the happy old man who'd seen so little joy in his difficult life.

"Ve, me undt my children, tank-you! Me undt Mama tank-you! You make us very happy dis day. I tank my boy who brings land undt a beautiful new gairule to dis family. You make dis auld man very happy. Tank-you, tank-you, tank-you every one!"

The colour was beginning to drain from Milly's face and Carl could see she was very tired. They'd have to leave the gathering soon. Carl walked over to Max and Alice and told them to look after any presentations. Carl informed the Hallvarsons who went over to Milly and spoke quietly to her and Max rose to inform the assembly that regrettably, the couple had to leave and wished the revelry to continue for as long as they wanted.

They ran again, the gauntlet of well-wishers, said their good-byes and walked alone, out into the cold clear night, to the waiting carriage and the beautiful suite in the Grand Hotel, a gift from the City, for the best human-interest story to hit their fair streets in a decade.

"I'm sorry Mr. Buechler, I'm going to have to refuse your offer to carry me over the threshold; I ache all over and you look tired enough to fall asleep while you're doing it." She threw her arms around him in the open doorway and whispered apologetically," I'm so sorry I can't give you the wedding night I and you have dreamed about. You're so darn understand-ing that it's criminal!"

"Well, Mrs. Buechler, I've already got more on my wedding night then I've ever imagined I'd have. Not very long ago I was a lonesome, homesick boy, not even thinking about any girl, let alone a wife so beautiful that it still confuses me and I find myself hoping this isn't just a dream."

"Let's dream it together so that when we wake up, we're both still here. I can hardly believe it myself. In case you haven't noticed, I'm a very pas-sionate girl and I intend to reward you for your patience, with interest and I intend for us to be very full and happy. Chew on that while I get ready for the beautiful man I fully intend to share my bed with tonight, under the same covers this time. I want to know if I'm as lucky as Alice and Mildred say I am; I'm so darn jealous. Don't disappoint me now!" Carl helped her off with her coat, unpinned the veil and followed both into the closet with his own. She disappeared into the adjoining room with a swish of the beautiful gown and the sly wink that, to now, had escaped any consequence.

The door knocked and Carl, somewhat annoyed, made for It. "You'd think after all that happened today, the least they could do is leave us alone tonight!" He jerked the door open, fully intending to be rude to the inter-loper and startled a pretty, young lady with a bottle of wine, a bucket of ice, two glasses and a beautiful, welcoming, congratulatory card. "Oh gosh! I'm sorry if I startled you."

"That's alright ... compliments of the manager." She handed Carl the silver tray, lined with lace. She hesitated.

"Yes?" Carl asked.

"Can I say my congratulations too? Emily's sure a lucky girl. You're every bit as good-looking as everybody says you are. Say 'Hi!' to her from

Sally. We went to school together. You sure look nice together; we saw you in your carriage right after church. God bless both of you with a long and happy life. Bye!" and she was gone before Carl could even thank her.

"You're not readyyy!" Milly teased through the crack in the door. "I'm just going to have to come out there and give you a hand. Who gave us that?"

"Compliments of the manager and Sally said 'hi!' and that I was good-looking and left her congratulations."

"She always did have a keen sense of beauty but I saw you first. Besides, she's not as good looking as this!"

XII
"To saw and build anew!"

A week after their wedding, Milly's strength had improved so markedly that Carl travelled with her back to Des Moines for her to investigate the training program she'd enquired about.

The headmaster, a very discriminating judge of character, struck a favourable chord with the young couple. He'd read the papers and already knew a great deal about both of them. Being of Russian ancestry and knowing the enterprising nature of the press and their free-play with the truth, he grilled Carl for at least an hour about the Doukhobor circumstance and the reality of everything he'd read or heard. He came away much informed and impressed with the fact that his initial suspicions were very close to the reality.

He questioned Carl about the attitude of the pioneer Canadian community, acknowledging that he and many of his teachers had grown up and began their careers in such a circumstance. He assured Milly that he would gear her program to meet such a need and added that, "It won't be by the book." Rural America still suffered a chronic shortage and the formal institutions were falling far short of meeting the numbers or equipping the practitioners. He'd place her directly into a classroom under the directorship of an experienced teacher certified for the purpose. Because of the time factor, it would be intensive. "It won't be easy but you will be ready. From what I know about you already, you're the determined kind we need but I want you whole and healthy first."

Since the death of Milly's grandmother, the Marshal had lived like a virtual miser and had laid away a substantial guarantee. He had a small retirement pension that would keep him very nicely. Phyllis and Chris were secure and his only concern now, was his one remaining grandchild. He admired her new husband's independence yet told him that it would eventually go to Milly anyway so what better time than when they most needed it to get a start? Carl wouldn't have to worry about her security and well-being.

Whenever the Marshal was in Des Moines for any length of time, he lived in an upstairs room with a family he knew well. Milly would have been happy with that but Carl worried about the constant stairs. She was recovering rapidly but her strength would take a long time to rebuild. Her father's work, in the burgeoning petroleum industry, took him to Des Moines several times a month. Neither her parents nor Carl wanted her to be alone for too long. She just wasn't an alone person and now she'd have a special reason to feel very lonely and the room was a bit cramped. Carl and Milly found a neat three-roomer on the ground floor, at a reasonable price, a lot closer to the school to which she'd been assigned.

Carl and Milly quietly dreaded the day he would have to leave. His future and now hers would be in a new, primitive world, far from the urban life to which she'd been born. She was personally thrilled and would get ready to do all that she possibly could to make it a better place for them. She teased Carl that he might just as well realize that she looked as much to the adventure as she did to being with him and she was naturally very impatient. "I can't think of a more interesting place to spend the rest of my life with you."

They travelled to Maynard because there was no way Papa or Mary would tolerate Carl's departure without he and Milly coming to the home and community of his childhood. Papa adored his new daughter-in-law. He'd have dominated her time entirely if Mary had let him. Milly could draw out of him, things from the darkness of his mind that had burdened him for most of his difficult life and he felt light and free again. He took her to all the places he liked to go and to meet all the friends he so valued. Carl often found them talking and laughing and was very pleased with the secure bond that had instinctively developed between them. In the warmth of the big, familiar bed, Milly told Carl things about his father that he never imagined behind the stern, disciplined exterior. She'd brought magic into all of their lives.

Papa looked with anxiety toward the sudden relationship between Max and the unusually "Vunderful gairule," Alice. She was spellbinding and Papa couldn't talk enough about her. He was concerned that something would happen and he'd told Max, in no uncertain terms, that he expected Max to bring this "goodt ting" into the family. Papa knew she'd be going back with Carl and Mildred and he wanted Carl to make sure that nothing would spoil it. "I loog for you, Milly. You looging Alice for Max." That sounded more like an order then a request. "Mama undt me, ve vant dis ting!"

Carl was overjoyed when Mary asked him to take Dan and Ben with him. She was well aware of the desperate need and he loved the matched pair of powerful black Percherons. He arranged to ship them. There'd be more than enough feed now that so many of the horses had been lost.

Carl was evasive when they tried to pin him down to an exact date. Milly's face revealed her emotion on the matter. It really hurt. Carl had been here over a month. He'd have to make the decision soon.

That night, again in the comfort of the warm bed, he and Milly decided that postponing it longer wouldn't make it any easier and they decided that next week, likely Thursday, would be as painful as any.

Mary, Papa, and the kids arranged a small gathering at the larger Pawlowich home for Milly to meet some of Carl's old friends and neighbours. Papa and the boys would look to getting the team on the right train.

———

Max informed Carl, as soon as they stepped off the train, that there was a letter from York. Work at the bush camp had come to an end. The weather was unusually stormy and cold and the steamer just couldn't function, they couldn't wait for warmer. To rebuild, they had to have lumber, lots of it. They'd have to do something else and they asked Carl to look into the possibility of finding a gasoline-powered engine large enough to operate the mill.

Max was on it immediately and before the day was out, had found their answer. Hart and Parr had developed an engine large enough to run the power plant of a fair-sized town. They'd built an even larger twin cylinder model and were testing it for performance and durability. What better way to work it then to put it out under those rough conditions? They'd have the engine mounted on a separator carriage with wide wheels to avoid its bogging down in the soft conditions of the bush. The company would have preferred a location closer to the plant to be able to deal with any problem that might arise, but the harsh conditions Carl described and Max's emphasis on the emergent nature of the circumstance convinced the company engineers; they read the papers too. Their engines would have to function under the worst of conditions.

Max had the engine. Carl sent the telegram immediately.

––––––

In the strange way of the world, the anxiety that Max and Alice were suffering was lifted. She and Max had been inseparable and she made it clear that she didn't like leaving Max one little bit. The Canadian West was a vast new potential market and a durable, proven engine was the best marketing tool. Who better to send out with the engine and stir up new sales, then an alert, enterprising young man, with an interest in the country? Max would be it.

Alice screamed with joy when she heard. They'd consume all of Max's time preparing him for the task but she didn't care; Bertha'd keep her busy in the restaurant. Carl too, was delighted; his brother would be out there with him.

Alice begged to be allowed to wait and come with Max when the engine was ready in a week or so and she was hard to deny. Mildred and Carl would travel back without her and do their level best to explain to the McPhersons that their little girl was in love and they'd have to recognize that she'd found that life of her own that Al had worried about. She'd come back a few days later, with her Buechler.

Wednesday evening was particularly depressing for Carl and Milly. Very little in their recent marriage was as it should have been. Yet, if it hadn't been for the horrible beating, it was unlikely that Carl would have returned and they wouldn't now be married. At least now, they had hope and each other. The separation would be only for a little while and it would make their lives ever so much better when they were back together, yet it would seem very long.

They went out for a private supper away from everyone and everything. They spoke very little and they walked slowly and thoughtfully back to the Hallvarsons'. Chris and Phyllis had disappeared conspicuously and left the house to them. Phyllis had spoken to her daughter, more like a friend than a mother. She knew how much it hurt.

They just stood and held each other until the "All Aboard!" Then he kissed her and she assured him, come-what-may, she'd be there with him sometime next summer, teacher's certificate or not. Then she said, "As silly as this sounds after what happened to me, you be careful!" and he was gone again.

———

As the latitude climbed so did the snow, and the temperature fell. Carl got to see a little of the Lake District. He liked this kind of country but it was particularly dreary this time of the year. Snow mounds often surpassed the window levels, glimpses of the countryside were incidental at best. The tiny lake settlements were winter-desolate yet their people were as warm and as friendly as summer sunshine. Isolation brought people a lot closer.

Carl was grateful for the fact that tight-fisted economics had given way to common-sense reality. The old, congested "wheezer" had either died, or been retired. A new puller with far more vitality and a conscientious crew rolled them through the tunnel of freezing vapours at an impressive rate, without a hitch but the Passenger stayed the same. It had been chilly last October and now, at this rate of speed, it was damn cold. The unfortunates like Carl, Milly, and little Jim, who had no choice or who didn't know better, made up the entire passenger load. They crowded the roaring potbelly.

Milly saw to it that Carl's assumed lunch bag was as full of tasty novelties as she could fill it but it was all cold and hot was the demand. Every stop saw a total exodus to whatever and the pots were soon drained. Sleep, an ideal escape, was an erratic unreality. Somebody was always up and at the potbelly. The clang of the shovel or the clash of the door was like a thunderclap. The rolling roadbed was far less forgiving and had become a bone-jarring rock. Hardware could withstand the temperature and it had to catch up with humanity so there was only the one Passenger but the freighters stretched back to the caboose. The Livestockers, including Carl's team, were closed tighter then last fall, so the horses, their sole occupants, were comfortable. Carl watered and fed every chance he got; they had to be ready.

When they rolled into Winnipeg, the bottom had dropped out of the thermometer. Carl couldn't ever remember feeling such deathly temperatures. How in God's name could anyone work in this at the bush camp, with no decent shelter? He'd wrapped his face with Mildred's scarf, his own wrapped around the loose parka hood to draw it in and deflect the wind. Exposure meant certain frostbite in minutes.

The horses roared and snorted, threw their heads and tended to walk over Carl in a desperate rush for the shelter of the next car. With all the freight, the ordeal consumed the better part of two torturous hours. By the time it was done, Carl lacked the initiative to volunteer for the coal detail. There were quite a few there and they exchanged at frequent intervals.

After the rush of last autumn, humanity was now a scarcity around the large station. Carl and Mildred had to walk a roaring hell with a wrapped and angry Jimmy, to a cafe a block away and it took them a full half hour to teach the blood back through their hands and feet. Carl's were still very sensitive.

The sandwich offering at Portage was gone; there were no takers. The only living inhabitant of the station was the master but the stove was warm and the restaurant in the hotel, a short distance away, was open.

The night was awfully long and Jimmy wasn't the only one who was irritable. The Passenger was as empty as the American but the car was warmer, with at least a pretence of winterization. Archie and Hank weren't piloting this one.

It was, all told, a thoroughly dismal trip; Carl's heart and mind were with Milly. Mildred was often so lost in thought that Carl had to repeat things to get her attention and she grew more distracted as the train approached York. Carl had to assure her, several times that Paul would be alright but it wasn't a guarantee. She wondered how he would react to the news of her already advanced pregnancy. Would he be upset because she hadn't told him earlier? How would he have taken it if she had? Carl was sure he would understand but she should certainly tell him why. The baby would come at a better time, after the rush of spring seeding. At least that was in her favour.

The train rolled up to the familiar station in the late afternoon as the sky was beginning to darken. The solitary figure on the platform, wrapped in his own vapour, was Paul. There was no team that looked like his so he must have stabled them. Carl took the sleeping child as they stepped off the train into the frigid, thankfully quiet air. Paul was at the very bottom of the step. He didn't have to guess which car they were in; it was the only one. He wrapped Mildred before she reached the platform, lifted her off the step, and kissed her.

"Talk about mistakes, I didn't make one when I married you and neither did you. Now you just forget about it right now because I'm not going to let you keep beating yourself over what you did to me — you haven't done anything to me, just to my pride. I think I'm over that because I was awfully thoughtless too. Everything I did was so damned important and just had to be done first. I'm really sorry for that and I hope you can forgive me too." He didn't wait for her response.

"Here he is!" He lifted Jimmy out of Carl's arms and rocked him lovingly. "Congratulations!" He extended a freed arm to Carl. "Let's get you out of the cold and we'll get the luggage." He took Mildred and Jimmy into the station as Carl turned and carried as much as he could to the platform. By the time he'd returned with the rest, Paul had the first load gone. "Is that all?"

"Not quite!" Carl led to the Livestocker and Ben and Dan. The team had grown antsy in the confines of the car for so long and charged out with such enthusiasm that Paul had to jump to get clear.

"Oooh they're beauties! God they're big! We sure in hell can use them!" Paul smiled broadly at the unexpected windfall. They tied the team to the hitching rail and went to one of the freighters to get the harnesses. They too were of very good quality.

Paul reacted to the description of the engine like a boy anticipating a new bicycle. They'd have to raise some money but the deal was based on a lengthy, trial testing period, under these adverse conditions. "Thank God for the Buechler boys!" He clasped his hands heavenward in good-humoured response.

"It'll be heavier'n hell!" Carl warned. "It's on a thresher carriage and I just ain't sure how we're goin' to get it to the village, let alone the camp. We'll have to build some kind of sleigh and it'll take two or three teams to pull it. We'll have to bring some of them from the camp."

"We're all back now. We had to shut things down until it warms up a bit ... just too cold and to much frostbite. Mildred'll have more work cut out for her. I sure wish that somebody could take some of the load off her, as delicate as she is. A lot of the burns are havin' a real bugger with their lungs and there's lot's of pneumonia. A couple died in Winnipeg and three more in the hospital here. It raised absolute hell in our village and all the others. You can just see the "beat" in their faces.

"The old fellas, who should be takin' it easy are workin' like two men. We'll be losin' some a' them if we don't slack off. Al needs his boys; there's a lot on his place and Al just hasn't been feeling too well lately. Grandpa is still fairly good but he's in about the same shape as the old fellas in the village. He'd do it but they won't let him. We can sure use him on some of the blacksmithing. A few of the other settlers are pitching in but they got herds of their own and it's pretty hard on their women and kids and you were right, some'a the others just laugh and say dirty things about the Doukhobors. ... Ain't no doubt about what they're thinkin', the dirty bastards! They'd sell their mother for a nickel. This whole country was built on that mill. I'll show you last week's *Winnipeg Press*. I guarantee, it'll make you mad. Some say the 'Bones' paper is sayin' the same thing. Some helluvan investigation that was! The first two fellas who came, got a few good leads and were suddenly transferred as far ta hell out'a here as they could send 'em.

"We'll barn the team, then get somethin' decent to eat; I can just imagine what kind of a ride that was." He smiled, "I notice Alice ain't with you. Grandma is in a bit of a fidget over Al lettin' her go, so you're goin' to have to do some explaining; he's your brother."

"God I hope it warms up a bit so we can get the engine there."

They had to wake Mildred when they got back but she was more than willing to get a good meal. Carl was a bit worried about the strain of the tiring trip on her but she seemed alright.

The van was a blessing of ingenuity. By the time they got Paul's team hitched, with Carl's in tow and drove up to the station, the tiny heater had the interior at coat-stripping temperature.

It was pitch black when they drove up to the hospital to pick up more much needed medication. The drive out to Al's was rough and un-nerving, but again, Paul treated it as a matter-of-fact event. The snow level had easily doubled. Paul said that this was working up to be the worst winter since he'd come.

"Where's Alice?" Carl heard as Mildred entered the house. He was glad she was there to answer. He knew Grandma's high-strung nature.

The boys came out to help with the barn packing. "Man's that a team! Where'd you get 'em? Man, can we use 'em!" They tied a few cows, three to a stall, unharnessed and fed everything, including the cows and went to the house. The thermometer near the door read forty-six degrees. Carl'd already lost all doubt that he and Milly were going to get all the challenge their adventurous spirits could stand.

Grandma fretted and grumbled about her granddaughter living in sin. Grandpa smiled, "Now Mother, I ain't surprised. You saw the letters before she hid them. What did you think? I ain't forgot how your folks acted toward me. Have you forgot what we did?" That shut her up. They didn't throw anything more at her about the past.

Knowing Alice, Carl suspected that she and Max had not been occupying one of the separate beds in separate rooms that Bertha had given them. He'd often seen the way they smiled and touched each other as if they had a special secret. "Let me put it this way, I ain't goin' to give you an absolute guarantee but I'm almost certain that when they get here in a week or so, they'll be thinking 'wedding' and I'd be thinkin' it too!" Grandma still wasn't comfortable with the idea. She wouldn't be until she met Max.

Al handed Carl the latest copy of the *Winnipeg Press*, front page up. The attack had been front-page news for the last month as it was now. During all of that time, Paul told him, they'd been very careful to avoid the truth. The fact that some had returned to assess their handiwork and would surely have killed Carl and Alexsay, wasn't ever mentioned as it was in the American press and to Paul's knowledge only the *Bones* paper ever made any reference to the Thorland connection. Carl stared back at the headline.

SECTARIAN DOUKHOBORS AUTHORS
OF BUSH CAMP MURDERS?

**"Police investigators have, to date, turned up few
clues to any outside involvement in the recent
attack on the sawmill bush camp that resulted in
the tragic death of fourteen, and serious injury
to, at least, twenty-six others!" Police spokesmen
stated yesterday. "Investigators have reason to
believe and have, in fact, spoken to many, in the
surrounding community, who suspect that this was
the handiwork of the radical religious sect who
have a history of fanaticism against worldliness
and have, on occasions, been known to behave
erratically in their acts of redemption and puri-
fication. Investigators, who have explored this
likelihood, have encountered a conspiracy of tight-
lipped silence, doubtless an attempt by the sect to
protect its own. The investigation is on-going, yet
without a break, Police are likely to achieve little."**

It disgusted Carl more then it angered him. His sense of the nature
of the investigation indicated that this was the likely direction the police
would go. He hadn't understood how blatant the lie could be. Even jour-
nalists in the States had picked up on the American connection and hit
close to the truth. Despite the fact that their knowledge was founded on
hearsay and they'd never come close to the site, they'd managed to twig
unto the most likely scenario ... land, politics, corruption, and greed in
high places. **"This can be nothing more than a deliberate attempt
to drive Doukhobors off their land."**

Grandpa was as tall and raw-boned as his son but he looked healthy
and vibrant. Hard, heavy work at the forges showed in his tanned leather
skin but he was a totally positive man. "With hard work and good sense
you can get most things done without hurtin' yourself! You ain't been usin'
good sense! Ask yourself, do you really need all of this and maybe lose
your health?" He'd reprimanded Al many times, when, after a separation of
several years, he'd once again seen his work-worn son.

Of course, Grandma had to feed everyone and they ate again to be polite. How the McPhersons did it Carl wasn't sure; their place had become a regular roadhouse on the trip to York and Al wouldn't have it any other way. The villagers never once stopped there without contributing in some way to the McPherson larder. Summers, it was warm and even then the round trip was just too much for man and beast if there was any amount of business to get done. Now it was an attempt at suicide. The Hotel was hard-pressed, at times, to keep the rail traffic housed and fed. Even now, it was always close to full, because of the heavy construction and work crews.

Most had little beyond their basic necessities. There was absolutely no question; there was a need and Al had the means. Al and the kids had an awful job keeping up with the workload but they managed a fair-sized garden that surely wouldn't be enough. The Doukhobors grew well beyond their ability to consume so there was always plenty and when they saw a need, they were always there.

Al joked that at times, his root cellar could have been bigger, and so could his living room. The floor stayed shiny from all the horse blanket beds that frequented its surface and the dish cupboard could have served two threshing crews. The kids loved it because it broke the monotony of winter and they were becoming adept at wrapping their tongues around the Russian language.

The next morning proved worse. The thermometer's message stayed where it was and a "Nor'wester" roared wildly. Travel was out. The torching frost required complete coverage of the entire face. Even the exposed eyes burned and could function only through narrow slits. The boys and Carl were up and out at the barn before the rest moved. They fed and cleaned, and milked the four cows. The cows were near to calving and the milking had been restricted now to once daily. Even that didn't have to happen but tradition demanded plenty of cream and things like cottage cheese. The flock of spoiled chickens laid better with its fortification. The pigs had become pork so they were out of the road. The herd of beef animals were well sheltered but the attempt at feeding them had to wait until daybreak. Watering all of these would be a joy, especially the spoiled, soft animals in the barn but that was for later.

A light went on in the house and they could see Grandpa at the stove through the frosted window before they came in. They strained the milk into the usual containers and sat to coffee when Grandma came out and started the oatmeal and eggs to boil. "I sure am sorry for you young folks having to live apart so long. That's something we never had to go through. It must be awful hard. Al told us what happened to Paul and Mildred. Maybe it's better than what happened to Al's and him having to raise the kids without a mother. This is a good country in the summertime but it's pure hell in the winter. The house is built good but you just can't warm it up and I get sick of walking around all day wrapped up like a bloomin' mummy." She launched into the subject of Alice again and wanted to know everything she could about Max. By the time Carl finished his account she felt a lot more secure but wouldn't be content until she got to see and grill Max about himself.

The oatmeal and eggs were a thing of the past before Al came out and wondered what the event was because there didn't seem to be a hurry to get anywhere. They'd have all day, by the looks of it, to do nothing but the chores and keep warm. Grandma had a second batch finished when Paul came out looking like somebody had lifted a big stone off him. Carl couldn't help but smile.

Talk drifted to the heavy engine and how to get it to the bush. Grandpa laughed at the complex visions the youngsters around him concocted. "Spend all the time and work building a heavy toboggan and how are ya' goin' to pull it? Put it on two sleighs chained together and you're goin' to be a mile wide and nothing will trail. You've got fifty miles to go down a narrow single trail that's rougher 'n hell now. Ya' tip that thing and it's next spring before you'll upright it. I've done lots of thinkin' about lots of heavy problems. We had to winter-move a smaller locomotive up into the bush to a mine years ago and we made it. This is small compared to that. You'll build a set of skids under each of the wheels and then chain 'em so they got some free play and can flex so the damn thing don't tip and they don't come around with the wheel in a sharp dip. Then you hook onto it like it is. You'll need lots of chain to hook teams in tandem and we might have to re-enforce the hitch. Chances are, if it's as big as you say, it'll be as heavy as a separator. We can do most of that right here, startin' this mornin', after the chores." He sat down and drew a picture of what he meant. It was ridiculously simple and sheltering under a four-foot snowdrift, they had material to build the skids.

By suppertime, the creative old man had them build a set of four skids by spiking ten-ply of heavy, ten-inch, eight-foot planking together for each. They gouged out a seat in each as wide as they dared, because they weren't sure of the width of the wheels or the curve.

Grandpa cut pieces long enough, off a three-quarter inch rod, forge-heated and flattened a head on each, then threaded the other end. He didn't have a bit long enough so he measured and drilled the skids from both sides, then burned the rest of the way by driving a red hot rod through what thickness was left ... three to a skid ... twelve in all, almost as fast as the boys had them cut and nailed and then torqued them together. He cut and drilled a couple of heavy plates for each end-binding bolt.

Grandpa was very pleased. He could still prove himself very useful in this young man's world. All they could do now was wait for civilized temperatures, have a heck of a good visit, razz Carl about newlyweds and Paul and Mildred about pointers that they could give him on the art of procreation.

Next morning it had warmed up quite a bit and true to form, it started to snow hard. Carl decided that a trip back to York wouldn't be too dangerous. He wanted to get word to Milly that he was back and safe. He'd written but that would take a week so he'd telegraph as briefly as he could. Mildred had to restock and they'd need paint and repairs. They'd have to guess what and how much, so she, Paul, Carl, and the cabin-bound boys hitched the confined and frustrated Ben and Dan to the village van to work out some of their cramps. The grateful team enjoyed it at a brisk pace but the passengers were a bit shaken up. Grandpa and Jimmy had become fast friends so he stayed behind in case the weather did become violent again.

They picked up some salvage flats pulled off an old bridge. They were heavier then they needed to be for the skid bottoms but Al's big forge would heat them for bending. They were too long and heavy for the van so somebody'd have to hitch the sleigh and bring them. They couldn't find any countersink bolts long enough but Grandpa would solve that in a hurry with some more rod.

They got back with the van packed, not a bit too soon. They hadn't wasted a second yet it was dark and the growling wind ripped the snow into a fury. The last mile was pretty testy but the powerful blacks took it in stride. They were work-experienced and hardened and they'd do anything for Carl. He was their pet.

It howled through the night and into the next day and again the endless sitting and waiting.

Two days later, the wind was gone but the cold was back. Paul had to get to the village to let them know of the impending need for teams and manpower. Grudgingly, Mildred let discretion overrule her desire. With Jimmy and in her condition it would be a foolish risk. Grandma said she'd tie her up if she tried; she really enjoyed Mildred's company. Loaded with firewood and grub, Paul left before daybreak the next morning.

If it stayed this way, they'd get the engine as far as Al's and let it sit until the weather broke. Al, Grandpa McPherson and Carl, wrapped and padded, sleighed in, got the plates, and picked up the telegraph; the engine was on its way. It would be here in a few days.

"How do I do it? Easy! I just take the shape of the skid into my eye, then bend the iron around it." Carl was amazed at the skill of the old man who jokingly responded to Carl's questioning. He'd heated the flat to a white-hot jelly faster than Carl could have a fire in a forge and anviled it to the perfect angle the first try. He clinched the toe and heel of it then cooled and slipped it over the skid perfectly.

As if Carl doubted his skill, he repeated the exact procedure on all four tries. Al drilled half-inch holes at two-foot intervals along the flat and angle, and countersank each with a bigger bit. Carl cut the half-inch rod to the required length, then heated one end to a white heat. The old man clamped it vertically into the heavy leg vise, dropped one of the skid plates over it with the countersink up and about half an inch of heated rod projecting, pounded it down into the hole into a perfect countersunk bolt head, then filed the excess to a smooth surface. He repeated the same with every hole while Al threaded the bolts.

Carl slipped each skid plate over, centered it because it was a lot narrower than the skid itself and punch marked each hole, then drilled through tolerably for each bolt, just to impress the teasing old man, and the skids were ready to fit to the wheels. The forge kept the large granary working warm but a bit on the smoky side. The forty-degree temperatures didn't bother them a bit.

Now they'd have to wait again. Rather than that, Al built a light wooden frame to fit his sleigh box and Carl tack-covered it with some tin and two old canvass horse blankets while Grandpa manufactured a small stove, not too much different than Carl's. The village van was gone and they'd need some protection on the road; Alice wouldn't be able to stand such temperatures on the ride out. Neither could they. They pulled a load of straw close up across the mouth of the open calf shed and packed more under and over the load to block the opening from the wind. There'd be more teams and the barn and cattle shelter were full. Nothing could survive without any shelter in this freeze. They were ready.

Al and Carl sleighed in, the morning of the expected arrival, only to learn that there'd been a delay, a breakdown due to the adverse conditions. The Winnipeg train would be on time but they hadn't made the connection. They wouldn't be here until tomorrow. Carl and Al waited and it was, indeed worth it to both of them.

Carl received a letter from his wife. It was marked with her Des Moines address, just a week ago, so she was enrolled in training and in action, and he loved her determination and drive. He missed her terribly yet was glad because there was nothing she could do here but, like Mildred, sit and wait. His letter would miss her but she'd have it as soon as her folks passed it on. She indicated that:

"There is an interesting turn of events that won't really surprise you! There'll be another wedding sometime this spring or summer in the Buechler family, so the Buechlers, who are, or will soon be there and the McPhersons, might just as well get started with the planning. Beg, borrow or steal, I don't care, finished or not, I'm not going to miss that one. See you then."

He showed that portion to Al who looked at it long, without a word, handed it back to Carl with a smile and said, "Ain't surprised, in fact, I expected it. I know my little girl; she's a lot like her mother ... same kind of personality. God how I'll always love that woman! I see her in Alice every day. I see myself, when I was younger, in you, and if your brother is anything like you, I'll see my hopes and dreams all over again. Maybe this time they'll come true. I was real worried 'bout her when I sent her but she was with Mildred and you were already there so I knew no harm would come to her. Since we moved out here, she'd never been past York. How could I say no? It would have torn her heart out. I knew how much she wanted to be at your wedding and the letters she left layin' around told me all about Max.

"I ain't domineering but I'm mother and father wrapped into one. She can't talk to me like she could her mother, but at least she talks to me, maybe a lot more about most things girls don't want to tell their fathers. I love her and respect her judgment, although at times it's hard to follow. I know what she's goin' to do and just between you and me, I expect to be a grandfather in a shorter period of time then most fathers hope to be and I'm happy over it. For Christ sake, don't tell Mother! She'll meet Max and like him just like she attached to you, then she'll be alright. She'll want to dominate the wedding but Pa will hold her down there ... tell the truth, this makes me happier'n I've been in a very long time."

They went to the hotel, had a hot coffee and a fresh baked raisin bun and went home in anticipation of tomorrow. Mildred would be the only one they'd tell tonight.

It took all of them to manhandle the skids into the sleigh box and the boys were very long-faced when they were told that there wouldn't be enough room in the sleigh now, with Alice and Max, for the ride back. They didn't care about Alice and they were only curious about Max but what they really wanted was to see it. Just imagine, an engine so advanced that it didn't need steam to run on. It would run on a weird-smelling stuff called gasoline that burned real hard. The teacher at York had told them about it once. They had to see it to be able to brag about it to some of the know-it-alls.

They were early and the train was late, so they barned the teams. Ben and Dan trailed along behind because they weren't sure one team could haul the heavy machine off the flat. The train rolled in, an hour and a half late, with Hank and Archie both waving wildly on the way by when they recognized Carl. They brought the strange engine to their usual pinpoint, then switched it back until the loaded flat paralleled the dock. The yard

engine wasn't worth the manpower and effort in these vicious temperatures. Carl would talk to them a bit later but first there was Max and Alice.

Both of them climbed off wearing mile-wide smiles because they
had wonderful news. That done and the congratulations and smiles and
engagement ring viewing out of the way, Carl went on board to rescue the
luggage with Max and to administer the usual Buechler brotherly jibes.

Alice would have been abandoned for the machine had she not wrapped
herself against the biting and tagged along. She was more than just a bit
curious too.

It was clearly visible in its beautiful black and red paint but a lot of its
vitals were hidden behind wooden boxing to keep the snow out. Carl lined
Ben and Dan over from the stable as Al and Max loosed the restricting
cables and pried the floor stops free. They'd forgotten another double-tree,
so Al hitched his team and brought the sleigh. Now Alice could sit out of
the wind.

The engine rolled off easily and down the incline, restricted by the
powerful beasts, then out into the vacant yard, where it would stay until
they could muster the manpower and the weather to make the trip.

"Ta 'ell ya' say! Ya' were there? Ya' sure get around don'tcha, and married
too? Well fer the love a' Pete! ... got ta stop and ask more. Just wait 'til we
tell folks up and down the line ya'll be famous. Sorry we can't visit more
but the master's wavin' us out. Bye, nice seein' ya." Filled with hot soup,
Archie was gone.

Max checked with Ernie about security. There'd been no money
involved yet and it was Max's responsibility. It was getting dark, the wind
was picking up, and Alice was nearly sleepwalking. It was pitch black when
the houselights sparkled through the soupy atmosphere.

"Damn, I didn't think it could get so cold!"

"Cover your face! Here!" She wrapped her scarf around before Max led
the nuzzling blacks into their stall. Max was their pet too. Carl and the boys
fed the works again as Al, Grandpa, and Max went in.

By the time Carl walked in, the flushed grandmother had just given
Max her second hug and kiss and went back to Alice's hand to look at the
ring again. She hadn't expected this. She was readying a stern lecture about
honour and integrity and here they'd stolen all of her momentum by doing

just what she was going to tell them was the right thing. She'd instantly fallen as much in love with this fella as her granddaughter did.

The meal was well under way, when a very tired Paul drove in. Carl and the boys dressed quickly and rushed the exhausted team into the barn, watered, and fed them. The team trembled violently, despite the blankets that covered them and they breathed heavily. They were nearly asleep, standing up, as the warmth and security filtered out the hellish afternoon.

"Damn, what a ride! There was a time I was sure we weren't going to make it. It was fairly good when I left this morning, but it sure cut-up, the closer I got ... places I had to shovel the team through ... much worse than when I went. Sure glad I didn't try to take the two of you along." Jim hung to his dad with wondering eyes on his tired, whisker-covered face. "It's the worst winter I've seen since I've been out here, really, the worst I've ever seen!" Al couldn't remember another one like it either.

"Well I'll be darned!" He looked at Alice's ringed finger. "You Buechler boys sure have a way around the ladies. You're goin' to drive your dad broke just marryin' you off. Welcome to the clan fella! I hope your engine works as fast as you do."

Alice hadn't slept much. The trip had dragged her right down and Max was all-in too. They said their good nights as Grandma showed Max to the boy's room, as far away from Alice's as she could get him. She didn't notice their sly humorous smiles. It was a bit cramped but the young fellows were flattered. They could brag that they'd slept in the same room with the heroes of the bush camp and Charles City.

The next day found the cold as intense but the wind was better, so Carl, Max, Al, and the boys went in to see if they could get the engine up onto the skids. Al took two teams and Carl wrapped up and barebacked in on Dan, with Ben in tow. If they got it on, they'd try to secure it and see how it pulled. Paul was worn out; he hadn't slept much for the last three days and Grandpa wanted to stick around in case a storm blew up inside the house.

Al had a railroad jack and they got another from the station freight shed. They jacked and blocked and jacked again until the skids slid under freely. Then they dropped each of the front wheels into the precut seat and jacked and cut and dropped again until they had both front wheels fit securely.

Then they did the back. By one o'clock, the engine sat up on all four and they began the process of trying to secure it. They didn't have enough chains, so Al, who was well known, did a bit of scrounging and borrowing and came up with a few more. By four they had it secured and ready ... some hot soup at The Hotel and they were off to try their luck.

Al's experience had taught him so he saw to it that the skids sat on two-by-fours to keep the weight from freezing them down. When Ben and Dan heaved into it, it broke free easily and they walked away but they had to strain. It'd need two teams on the road so they got another longer chain from station agent Ernie and hitched the second team ahead of the first. With lots of inquisition and even some scornful derision behind the muffled, hand-hidden, "Doukhobors," they pulled out of York with an hour of daylight ahead of them.

It was very dark and very cold when the McPherson yard awoke to the abnormal squeal of heavy metal against hard-packed snow, the blowing whinny of horses and the gleeful laughter of success as the miracle of advanced engineering slid in. They'd accomplished much more in these adverse conditions then they ever imagined they would. They were very cold, but happy. The teams were put in and fed, the machine had been pulled up again on to planks and every one had a little bit of faith restored in themselves and their initiative. The entire household was light and jovial. It felt good!

Late next afternoon, a van pulled in with two teams in tow. Alexsay, always the risk taker, climbed out alone. His arm, now unsplinted but heavily wrapped, hung from a sling. He could move it only at the shoulder and made it a point to feed himself with it to get it functional again. He explained that things were awfully hard at the village and able manpower had to be stretched. Five men had vanned back out to the camp to try to finish a log bunkhouse. The rest had established a relay system toward York in known, friendly, farmyards and crews would be out to prepare the trail in advance. They utilized, fully, every resource they could find.

Alexsay was amazed that the engine was already at Al's but it was not to move any farther until the trail had been prepared and the weather was a bit more favourable. They couldn't wait too long. They'd have to tough it out a bit; they needed lumber. When the trail crew got here, it was a go. Be ready!

Accommodations were a bit tight and somebody would have to floor it. Alice demanded that Alexsay be given something comfortable to sleep in. Always the imp, she was closer to reality then Grandma realized when she suggested openly, that she could resolve the problem. She got the anticipated reaction. She'd have floored it if she had to.

She introduced Max as her "new" love. Alexsay laughed with joy when he heard the news and he immediately went to work on Max's grasp of English according to "Alyosha" because they'd most certainly have to communicate. There was no way the village was going to let "Crasna Hallawvaya" escape a grand event. Her mutual adoration of big "Alyosha" and the admiration she gained with her devotion to the grieving and the burned had endeared her to the entire population.

The weather turned even more vicious. The thermometer hit a new low and then dropped some more. The despised "Norther" howled its deathly grasp. Even getting the chores done was an ordeal of intense proportion; totally covered still netted dangerous frostbite if the men attempted to push their exposure time. Carl's toes started to act up again. Al just couldn't stand it. He'd fight for hours to get warmed up. Paul, Max, the boys, and their "hard as nails" Grandpa, braved the elements with little or no apparent consequences; the livestock needed extra care. To keep them watered in these temperatures was unrealistically difficult. It was very hard to maintain a favourable positive image of this country through this.

Just sitting around was terribly burdensome. Riding to York to see if he could pick something up was as impractical as it was dangerous. Alice had some paper so Carl wrote a lot, always to Milly, and his message wasn't always as cheerful as he'd like. The last thing he wanted to do was give her an extra burden. He buried himself in peeling potatoes, washing dishes and the floors, carrying in water and wood, carrying water to the barn-locked livestock, carrying out the manure and competing with everyone else for the privilege of doing any one of these things. In reality, they couldn't do a lot but wait.

It seemed to bother everyone but Alice. She was in love and she and Max had all kinds of time to be together in the chaperone of everyone else.

Their once fly-by-night relationship was turning out to be ideal. Everyone, including Grandma, was beginning to take the couple for granted and as far as the two of them cared, that was just fine. For the past several nights, Carl noticed that Max was absent from the bed roll for extended bathroom breaks that lasted most of the night. The stairs were very well made; virtually creakless. If anyone else noticed, they didn't say anything. Carl found that humorous but he was a bit resentful too. It was almost six weeks since their marriage and he and Milly had been together for little more than two of it. He still sat at Al's, hostage to this horrible environment.

When the blow finally stopped they had to shovel for an hour to free the engine. The yard was hardly recognizable and entrance and exit were impossible without many more hours of intense shovel work. Everything around the place demanded an extreme effort that was almost a blessing after their prolonged lethargy. It would make moving the engine a much greater challenge and could put lumber production into crisis. It was pushing through February and a couple of weeks would put them on the threshold of the spring breakup.

Carl, Max, and Paul sleighed out to see what the road was like. Clear open areas were fine but bushed-in areas would require great man and animal power and the route would require some re-adjustment to avoid the worst places. They'd have to shovel their way through as they went. Advance preparation was useless with the weather as unpredictable as this. Every inch gained would put them that much closer. They sleighed through to the Carlsons', the first relay yard and were welcomed with much enthusiasm. They were very cold and they ate, rested and headed back with hopes of enough daylight.

By the next afternoon, it was a radically different world. The sun beat the snow into a wet slush and the roof ran merrily. A southeaster blew steadily with the warmth of spring, renewing hope and enthusiasm. The decision was a go! The teams, with Ben and Dan the anchors, again, were hitched and the engine moved, with intense effort, up the ragged shovel-tunnel, out to the trail. Paul, the clear master of multiple-hitch and an unpredictable road, a skill gained as chief teamster with the Des Moines Fire Department, was at the reins and Max rode the engine. Carl, on Alice's

Lightning, rode point and determined the route. Alexsay vanned up the rear with the two replacement teams and a load of everything that could possibly be necessary. Al rode ahead to the next relay to see to it that all was ready there and to meet with the relay teams for the next stage. They'd been mapping and developing the next relay. Hopefully it would be better than this portion. The boys, in a light, homemade cutter "goferred" with enthusiasm. Within four hours, the engine had advanced more than half the distance to the Carlson's. They'd stopped twice to shovel a guarantee rather than lose a gamble.

Before exhausting the teams, they switched and the first two rested to an easy walk behind Alexsay as the next pulled with new vigour. They fed the teams and ate what the boys brought, as warm as they could keep it and pulled away by one o'clock. They afternooned in a lot more difficulty as the remaining miles proved a lot more obstinate. By sunset, they slid into the yard. The trail crew was waiting and ready for next morning. The boys ferried them back to Al's for the night because the Carlson house wasn't big enough for both crews.

Just after daybreak, they were back and caught up to the already road-bound second relay. The bolts, the chains, and the securing wires, all had to be tightened. The edges of the skids were clear-showing wear but the skid plates at the center were their salvation.

Somebody at the village had switched on his thinking lights and during the evil weather had gone to work and devised a giant snow scoop that, with some manpower, good teams, and compassion for the road crew could move huge gulps of snow out of the bound areas. It was a blessed time saver and it was highly effective.

They'd clevised additional chains to the carriage frame of the engine and hitched on two mounted outriders to produce additional pull power when it was needed, increasing the speed. In the narrow stretches, they'd drop off and hook on again when they could. Yet, what they multiplied in pull-power, they lost in time as the snow burden grew and it took more to clear. They completed the second phase, a mile or two longer then the first, after dark. Paul vanned it back to Al's that night because Mildred was desperately needed. Another burn victim had passed away because of respiratory failure and all necessary medication had long been consumed. Carl, Al, and the boys had brought covers with them and simply settled into the soft deep hayloft for the night. A few nights ago, they'd have frozen to death.

The last stage to the village was the longest and the most difficult but the manpower and the horsepower doubled. With more chains, enhanced horse and shovel power, they slid past Carl's after sunset and into the village. It was the first sign of enthusiasm and welcome Carl had seen since the infamy; the lights shone again. Mildred and Paul had passed the cavalcade in the afternoon and Carl already saw the signs of her handiwork hobbling out with pain in check, to greet them. They were back home, thank God!

Max wandered in after dark and somebody escorted him to the welcome gathering at the doughwam and a big supper. He'd climbed off at the Buechler homestead, to be the second of his creed to walk upon its wonder. Like Carl, he too was very emotional and stood a long time, waist deep, in the midst of the future yard. He'd file on his own as close as he could and as soon as he could.

He was welcomed as heartily as if he was a long lost member of the community. After all, was he not "Car-roll's" brother, the future man in "Crasna Hallawvaya's" life, the man who brought with him the mechanical salvation of their lumber business? Now they'd saw and build anew like they'd done so many times in their troubled past. With warmer weather they could revive the steamer and run the planer to produce fine, finished lumber at the same time.

At daybreak, they were out at the engine. They'd run it here, to be sure nothing in its torturous journey had wronged it. They pulled off the defending boxes and the packing out of the air intakes and carburetion unit. The spark magneto had been well protected to keep snow or moisture out of it but Max was sure it would be fouled enough by the humidity of the warm weather to cause condensation. He'd been trained to dismantle it, clean it and reassemble the unit. They brought enough gasoline with them to test run it and to run it on the mill. They'd have to get more shipped into York but, other than delivery to the camp, Chris Hallvarson's guarantee was good.

To warm the engine for starting they'd simply heat water, take out the drainage plug at the bottom of the cooling chamber and run the hot water through into a washtub that would hold all of it, start the warmed engine, then poured the water back once it was running. It was so warm during this spell that they didn't really have to do this but they thought it safer; the engine wasn't really theirs.

The entire village gathered and many outside teams appeared. This was the first gasoline-powered engine that anyone out here had ever seen, though all had heard so much about them. All work had stopped by the time Max poured a few drops of gasoline through the open petcocks into the large combustion chambers. Carl turned the long starting handle on the ratcheted sprocket mounted on the left of the two large, heavy flywheels and slowly brought the engine up to full compression on one of the two pistons. The right side flywheel carried the large belt pulley that would run the sawmill. At the signal from Max, he violently swung the flywheel through the combustion stroke and the engine barked and wheezed a violent blast of exhaust and fire out the exhaust port and petcock hole. The other cylinder, driven by the force of the first explosion, responded in kind as Carl jerked the heavy handle off the machine and the wheels whirled with ease. Max slammed the petcocks shut and the cylinders, up to full vacuum, drew in the air-gasoline mixture from the carburetor and compressed it on the following stroke, as the timed spark ignited the mixture to the next explosions in each cylinder in succession. Max slammed the flat of his mitt-covered hand over the air intake to draw less air and more gasoline into the chambers. The engine barked again and continued to bark rapidly and steadily up to speed as Max governed its intake, until it settled to an erratic explosion pattern, determined by the engine speed. The fuel-air intake valve was governed to open only when the speed reduced to the point where another explosion was required to bring it back to speed. They poured the tubbed water back in to cool the combustion chambers.

The unstable fire-pattern led to concern from the millers who knew it would require steady, uniform power to run the saw. Max explained that when under load, the engine would fire steadily and uniformly, to eliminate that problem.

Whether they lived together collectively or lived together separately didn't matter. It was as much the need to communicate as it was the engine that had brought them here and it was to be expected. They'd watched the progress of the engine and the grapevine seemed to take on a life of its own; everyone knew when and where. It was an elixir, it was part of the healing. Life had to go on as it had since the beginning of time.

Since Carl had arrived, there had never been a gathering of such a multitude. Everybody seemed to know him, Mildred and Max. Everyone had heard the story and wanted to see and to meet. "Where is she? When'll she be here? Next year maybe?" Somehow, they'd heard that one of these guys was bringing a teacher in here soon. They'd have a teacher for their kids and they couldn't wait.

"Who's marryin' the McPherson girl? You know, the redhead from down York way, who'd been here to help after the fire? You are? An' you're her dad?"

Nobody came empty handed. They didn't have lots, but everybody brought something and collectively, there was far more than necessary. The fellowship went on until after dark. The chores would be neglected: "They'll do just fine 'til we git back."

"I'll come help all I can."

" I'm okay fer lumber right now but he needs a granary," or "a better barn," or "an addition," or "my brother's comin' out," or "I can't just now, but I'll need lots next year." They'd be as good as their word, as difficult as that would be. If they said they'd be, they'd be!

Carl and Max rode out to the bush the next day, to see what they were up against. The bush crew had been through the day after the weather warmed so there was a trail.

Crossing the river'd be something else. The direct crossing would cut off several miles but it was dangerously steep. The bridge would be easier but neither Carl nor Max felt sure of it. It had been built to carry light loads and it was an old structure. They scouted the banks for a mile on either side and found nothing safer. They'd have to try the ford.

The trail from the river to the camp was extremely heavy. As the bush approached the snow grew deeper, the open areas were fewer and farther between, and the uphill slope constant. They'd need at least three teams full-time.

The road crew started out sometime after them. By the time they got back to the river, the crew was there and were clearing the bank at the fording. Because they were very afraid of storms, they weren't waiting. The engine had left some time ago and would get as far as it would that night. It was below freezing again but still warm enough to be safe. They'd van-out overnight. The engine pulled up to the river that night so Max and Carl left it guarded and went back to the village.

The next morning, Carl brought his team on a logging sleigh and Max brought another. The road crew, joined by the five from the camp, had the bank cleared and were busy with shovels, scraping every vestige of snow away down to the bare dirt to prevent the tobogganing of the engine. It wouldn't slide on bare dirt or at least they hoped it wouldn't. There was no way they could hook a team behind unless it was backwards and then they would risk the well-being of much needed horses.

Almost every team from the entire neighbourhood returned on every conveyance they had, with the entire healthy population crammed into every corner with every rope and chain available. It would be a daylong event. The few that stayed with the engine had things ready, with a big fire going. Borsch, bread and hard-boiled eggs, warmed quickly and fed everybody.

The chains and ropes were tied to the rear axle and solid, smooth wooden bars were tied through at frequent intervals to provide a secure handhold, just the same as they'd used several years before when horse power was scarce and human power turned the first furrows for the first gardens and crops. The entire population grabbed hold and Ben and Dan, the heaviest team, were the only ones out front. If the machine gave way, one team could stay ahead of it, pushed by the pole and the neck yoke. A second team, not having anything to drive their pace, would hinder the escape of the team behind. They'd pile up and there'd be a heavy engine smashing through from behind.

The huge beasts lunged into the harness and Alexsay's voice roared, "Nyet!" as the populace instinctively leaned back against it. The engine moved and toppled forward over the brink, and the speed increased perceptibly. The neck yoke grew taut as the team instinctively backed against it and held. Alexsay roared again and the ropes and chains snapped tight. The neck yoke slacked back down and the team began the gentle push to the bottom. It all stopped at the river edge with Paul's "Whoa!"

The river ice was secure. Choppers had proven that. Though it would be slippery, resistance would be considerably reduced. Now the reverse began. The chains and ropes were tied at every angle and every horse and human was harnessed to the pull back up to the top. Alexsay roared again and the pull was united and overwhelming. The engine vaulted forward and the pace accelerated, over the ice, to a near run.

They hit the incline with tremendous momentum that faded quickly into desperate, determination, and ultimate exertion. The load climbed as the hooves and feet struggled for foundation. It slowed to a crawl and maintained a steady creep toward the top. It seemed forever, as the teamsters roared, the horses heaved and whinnied, and the populace groaned and cursed.

The front ranks were over the ledge and the speed picked up as the traction multiplied. It was over and pulled away. The only audible sound was the struggle for breath. Their exertion had been supreme but successful. They sat and chuckled, then cheered. Although dinner hadn't been over much more than an hour, now there was tea, gallons of it and lots of bread and it was very welcome. Mouths were parched, as much from the psychological as from the physical.

People returned to their homes. Paul, Carl, Max, and two others remained and the struggle toward the bush would continue until some of the other teams returned with vans for the night. By the time it grew dark, they'd advanced another four miles. With any luck they'd be at the camp tomorrow.

The thermometer was beginning to fall again and they prayed that liveable temperatures would hold a couple of days longer. They led the teams back to the river for water. It would be warmer for them under the bank so one of the vans went with them and would stay the night. The other, well endowed with firewood, stayed with the engine as did Carl and Max, armed with the Mauser and Paul's Winchester. Riders had been seen in the distance late that afternoon and they weren't coming to help.

It was cloudy and very dark. They heard what they took to be horses, several times, but none approached too closely so they weren't part of the crew. The night was long, sleepless, unnerving, and uneventful.

Shortly after daybreak, the teams returned and the engine got under way. Paul and Al scouted out and found the tracks of a couple riders who'd come to within a quarter mile of the engine and then turned and retreated. They decided to send one rider out to follow the trail and anticipate its source or direction. It had to be locals who knew the location of the engine or someone who'd followed with deliberation and motive.

Noon saw them within sight of the bush camp, they'd be there by dark. The bunkhouse crew came out with two well-rested teams to take over from the blacks. By lantern-light, they lined the engine up as best they could, fed the teams and had melted snow for the horses and themselves. It was still warm enough for the horses to safely overnight outside.

The crew had put together a crude shelter from some of the burned remains, and had covered it with spruce boughs. It was leaky but draft resistant and the sad stove functioned admirably. They ate what there was and crawled under their blankets stretched over spruce boughs. Sleep came easily. Two of the camp crew always stood watch.

Before noon a huge contingent, fully equipped, from the villages and the district appeared to behold the wonder in action. Carl had water heating and Max had the mag dry and sure.

Tightening the belt would be a perpetual problem. They'd have to team-draw the engine, or hand bar it, then drive steel pegs into the frozen ground to hold it after it was running. A spring-loaded idler pulley, just off the saw pulley, would have to be drawn tight against the belt with everything flying at full force. It was a doable nuisance but extremely dangerous. Max would telegraph Hart-Parr for a clutch-operated engagement pulley to solve the problem but for now, this would have to do.

The saw was serviced and everything had been thoroughly checked. The attackers had somehow failed to notice it or didn't find the time. Logs were pulled onto the level log-deck and the first was canted onto the saw bed and the pikes driven home to secure it. Max and Carl repeated the start-up procedure but it took several attempts before the engine coughed to life and stayed functional. Max let it warm up for full power, then several of the experienced mill men carefully slipped the belt over the whirling pulley and held it on with a flat board as the engine was barred back and the pegs driven in to retain its position. The springed tightener brought the belt up to tension.

Max turned the fuel feed up and the engine barked up to operating speed. The sawyer threw the feed-lever and the log jerked into the screaming blade. The engine cracked deafeningly and settled into a burdensome, rapping beat. Max adjusted the fuel needle again and the starving engine snapped back. The cheer echoed above the roar. Within ten seconds, the log had cleared the blade and the sawyer smiled broadly as he reversed the lever. It jerked back to start position. He pumped the cross feed lever and the log moved over, board width with one notch and plank width with two. He slammed the feed lever ahead harder and the log vaulted into the saw much more aggressively. It screamed louder and the engine knuckled down with even more determination. Flames erupted from the exhaust ports and the log tore through easily at twice the speed. The cheer became a roar. This machine could nearly double their daily production. Within minutes, the twenty-inch, sixteen-foot log lay piled crudely, as clear, white planking.

They had enough fuel for the rest of the day. They didn't stop.

XIII
"Snake-belly low!"

The McPherson twins pulled into the camp the next afternoon with three barrels of gasoline, an hour after Max had shut the engine down for lack of it. What they lacked in knowledge they balanced with youth and agility. They had the engine refuelled before Max could finish servicing it. Nothing encouraged their will like praise and they got that in abundance.

The saw screamed by the light of many lanterns, well into the night, long after the cutters and haulers were driven back by the darkness. The capacity was now there. They'd started logging as soon as the harvest was finished and now had to start all over again with severely depleted manpower in the deepest snow any of them could remember. They left the mill with a skeleton crew and concentrated on getting the trail into shape to be able to carry the sleighs. The logs would have to be skidded out to a load site, necessitating even more construction and manpower. There was no other way.

Hot food was a problem so the women from the villages cooked volumes and ran a daily shuttle until the cook shack could be finished. Two men had been assigned to its construction and within a few days it was enclosed. They'd stripped a good stove, tables, and benches out of somewhere and they were installed and pushed smoke and hot food a day after the windows were in. Home-stuffed mattressing and quilting nightly covered the floor until the same two men could get the much larger bunkhouse ready. The weather held mercifully steady.

Because of concern about Mildred, Paul came and went often. Every time he went, he took a load of lumber with him to the village. York, constantly putting a strain on the mill's capacity, consumed as much as the boys could deliver and demanded more. On their third trip the boys appeared in separate sleighs, the other had been furnished by one of the builders solely to supply his needs. He told the boys he'd send more if he could get as much lumber as he needed for the summer. He told them that a scalper had bought up other sources, moved in and was trying to gouge prices in anticipation of the inability of the camp to meet the need or the competition. The vipers were beginning to raise their ugly heads.

The boys reported that on their last return trip, they'd been followed by two riders who'd made their presence known, clearly an act of intimidation. The next trip found Al and his irate father on the sleighs, both armed and angry. Grandpa had taken the time to make of his grandsons reasonably good marksmen. The stalkers didn't reappear.

Despite the difficult conditions, the mill produced an impressive volume, largely because the gasoline power could function in the cold. It required less manpower and several crewmen became familiar with its nature and felt comfortable with its function. Confident in their ability, Max found that he had more free time, which he devoted to helping with the construction of the bunkhouse. He'd soon have to head back to York, telegraph Charles City with the results, and receive instructions for his next move.

Though the engine performed well, Max told Carl there were many areas where improvements would be necessary. He'd already consumed most of his supply of spare parts and he'd need more. The next models would take these cold weather conditions into account. Even some of the replacement parts would be an improvement; keeping the magneto dry was almost a daily ritual. Another problem was the burdensome need to clean the air intake every few minutes, because of the constant, fine sawdust produced by the mill. Max had devised a length of pipe to put the intake well above the dust level but it was makeshift and kept falling off. As soon as time allowed, they'd build around the engine to protect it from the dust and weather.

The bunkhouse was semi-finished, the grateful crew, now wrapped in warmth and on the crude beds, found considerably more comfort. The intense labour and the horrendous hours were so telling that some of the older men had to go back to the village to rest. Yet, to a man, they always returned within a few days and renewed their efforts. There were the usual injuries but fortunately, nothing major.

Carl stayed the course. He, Ben, and Dan slugged loads of logs non-stop and the mill experienced only minor delays. The boys ferried his and Milly's letters back and forth regularly. They thought it humorous that the couple could find so much to write about.

Early March turned warmer but the weather was much more unsettled. The winds and storms made travel back and forth unpredictable and dangerous for the twins. Either Al or Grandpa tried to be with them but it wasn't always possible. They'd established a series of dependable relay stops at the same farmyards so that their progress was always monitored. Each trip the boys brought fuel with them and the supply outstripped the immediate need, so that was no longer a problem.

The real difficulty would be the condition of the trails. They decided to shut the Mill down once again and concentrate on getting logs to the site and the cut lumber out to the village before the river broke or they lost their snow cover.

By the end of the first week, snow conditions in the bush were still fine. Carl could hardly notice the difference but the trek to the village was fraught with growing patches of bare ground and the loads were reduced. The ford was covered in early melt water and the ice would be getting rotten. The boys came alone for what they thought would be their last load with the sleighs. They'd have to stop until things dried off enough for wagons, but then there'd be the problem of the bridge. They'd have to light-load stockpile the village and the boys could load heavier to York.

Still the anxious market screamed for more. The boys were pushing their endurance to the limit. Loaded, they'd reached the village with great difficulty and Alexsay wanted them to stay. They rested their teams for the night and headed out before daybreak, while the frost gave them an advantage. Alexsay saw them off with much concern.

By late afternoon, Alexsay's concern had given way to a gnawing anxiety. Indulging his anxiety, he climbed onto one of the few horses left at the village and followed in their tracks. The temperature had dropped ominously and it was starting to snow.

Alice, on her light, fast horse headed out into the threatening murk. Al followed with the light cutter. It was dark and the wind whirled huge flakes when Alice and Alexsay met on the usual trail ... no boys, no teams, no lumber and no sleighs. They must have tried an alternate route because of the reduced snow cover and must have bogged down or worse. That scared everybody.

———

Max returned from York, elated. He'd telegraphed Charles City about his next option and was instructed to encourage interest in the gasoline engines as a power source for the production of electricity. Max had given them the first-market initiative in the Canadian west and they'd appointed him soul distributor with the hope that this energetic, young man would be up to the task.

On his first presentation, he made the same offer that they'd given the lumber camp. The Council of York instructed him to bring a unit in with the promise of more if the first performed up to their expectations. They'd been looking at the electronic potential for some time and the ground-breaking offer of Hart-Parr, through Max, was an unforeseen windfall. As a further promotion, the company offered to send in electronics technicians to help the town with its program of electrification and to encourage sales through that example.

When he stepped through the door, his joy, like the weather, deteriorated. Grandma, the only one left at home, was frantic. Al and Alice should have been back. Grandpa had saddled one of the inexperienced young horses and gone out with the hope of finding them. Nobody had seen or heard of the twins. They should have been back long before now. Everybody was out in this, looking for them. For Max to go out was pointless and would only compound the problem. That entire night would agonize Max and leave Grandma an exhausted nervous wreck. The breath of hell roared outside, and nobody had returned.

Nobody!

———

All work in the camp came to a halt with the wild weather. The wind in the bush didn't bother as much as the heavy snowfall. They'd laid up a fair pile of saw logs in the last several days and planned to start the saw again the next morning. Carl, glad of the volume advantage, was anxious to get back to Paul's for a day or so. He hadn't been there since before he'd left for Des Moines and Milly. His clothes were rotting off his back and he found himself difficult to tolerate.

When the weather demons descended, like Alexsay, his ominous instinct kicked in; something wasn't right. A quick trip to the open told him that any attempt in this whirl could be extremely risky.

Late next morning, when the blow had diminished, Helen rode into the camp on an exhausted horse. Alice had ridden into the village through the storm last night. The McPherson boys had not made Al's or York. All of those capable, from the village, were out before daybreak when the wind diminished and barely ten miles south, well off the beaten track, they'd come across one of the sleighs; heavily damaged, with its load scattered on seemingly level snow. Clearly the team had been running wild. In the early light they'd dug through the rubble and found lots of blood. Tracks of any kind were snow-covered and difficult. John McPherson had ridden in several hours after Alice, barely able to stay in the saddle, badly frostbitten. Mildred was treating him now. Nobody knew where Al and Alexsay were.

———

By the time Carl reached the village, the heavy Percherons laboured franti-cally for air. Al's light cutter sat in front of Alexsay's house; the team, steam-ing and rasping heavily from an urgent, inhumane driving. Carl flew off Dan and ran into the tearful, prayer-filled room. Alexsay, frost burned and shaken, sat on the bench near the blanket-covered doorway to the familiar bedroom. Carl rushed in to find Mildred and Loosha working frantically on convulsing Michael.

Mildred tried desperately to stabilize his erratic heartbeat. She instructed Carl to hold the boy's nose, to pry and hold open the stubborn jaw-set, to place his mouth over the boy's and blow into his lungs in a specific way and to count out the spaces between blows, mentally, until she told him to stop. She kept a steady, forceful, downward pulsing-push with the combined balls of her hand palms on the area of his heart to mimic its beat. Michael'd bled extremely heavily and only the cold had prevented his death on that account.

The beat went on and on. Loosha wrapped heavy towels, soaked in heated water, around the boy's body to try to bring his temperature back up. He coughed suddenly and retched violently, almost before Carl could withdraw. Mildred grabbed his shoulders and rolled him to his side to prevent the vomit from being drawn into his lungs. He coughed again to clear them. Loosha wiped him clean and rolled him back. His breath came in gulps but he was breathing.

Mildred tested his pulse and directed her attention to the rest of him. His parka and heavy pants, scattered at random in the hasty bid to get at him, seemed to be soaked more from the outside then from within. He had a vicious tear through the flesh of his right thigh, the skin had been ripped away into a loose flap from the bone of the same leg, just below the knee. The splintered surface of the bone had endured a tremendous force and only its youth prevented a complete fracture. He showed no sign of consciousness.

Mildred was very much afraid but refused to say so as she stitched the flap back and pried open the upper wound to check its interior for infectious material before she cleansed, disinfected and closed it. The expression on her face showed alarm. Something driven at high speed entered, glanced off the bone and tore the flesh loose in the wake of its passage. "Only a bullet could have done this!" Carl checked the bloodied underwear and the pants and found all the evidence that he needed.

"Where'd you find him?" Carl demanded!

With some difficulty, Alexsay explained that he'd followed an erratic snow-covered disturbance of the surface and found the snow-covered boy several miles off the intended trail. He'd apparently tried to hang on to the terrified team or had mounted to try to ride to safety and had fallen off because of his injuries.

Al had taken Alexsay's horse and had ridden off to search in another direction from the Carlson place at daybreak. Alexsay didn't know where he was. More importantly, where were Mitch and the other team?

———

Alice rode back out to the site to try anything to find the boy; there was nothing she could do for the one already found. He was still alive, that's all that mattered! She'd trust Mildred to keep him that way. She wasn't as hopeful for the other one.

When Max and Carl found her and the small exhausted search party, it was nearly dark. Max left his horse and hers and took the van to get her home. She was past the ability to ride. Carl rode away to find Al as the wind churned up again; Mitchell was in the hospital, at York.

Early that morning, through the whirling haze, frosted over, incoherent and completely unaware of his location, he'd ridden into a farmyard. The barking dog alerted the farm family and their timely action stabilized him, warmed him and rushed him to York. They had no idea who he was or where from. The staff knew the McPhersons and sent someone out to inform Max and to stay with the terrified grandmother. At that point, neither she nor Max knew anything about any of the others. Max had to ride all the way back to the village to find out.

———

Al had found Mitchell's sleigh, several miles off the trail and well away from any area of settlement. The gouge, through the heavy snow, tracked his desperate flight and the roiled flight path indicated the passage of many pursuit horses. Did they have Mitchell or did he unhitch and run earlier? He had the 30-30 and Al found several spent cartridges on the load. He knew his boys as well as he knew himself. Mitch would hang on to the load for as long as he could with the hope of salvaging it. Only necessity could make him drop it if they hadn't already caught him. Al was certain he was too smart to let that happen. "Where's Mike? Why weren't they together?"

———

Carl saw the smoke from some distance and headed for it to find the despairing father, dowsing the smoldering load. The pursuers had attempted to set it on fire. Carl knew that Michael was hanging feebly to life. He trusted Mildred's ability and the wealth of experience in the hands of people like Anastas. Alice was with Max and would be home by now. Grandpa was frostbitten and seething, only the villagers held him in check so he was alright. The only one they knew nothing about was Mitch. They rode hard for York through a heavy swirl but the temperature had moderated and the late night ride under the clear, moonlit sky, was well within the range of endurance.

———

Mitch had regained consciousness for a short time but the only thing the staff could get out of him was, "Where's Mike? How is he?" They assured him, falsely, that Mike was alright, to calm him. Mitch wasn't in any immediate danger; they had his body temperature back to normal. They were trying everything they knew to teach the circulation back into his frostbound hands and toes. His face was a vivid red and his nose and cheekbones displayed grotesque frost damage.

Michael was in far more danger. He'd been on the ground all night before Alexsay found him and Carl knew he'd have to be brought here if there was to be any hope. He avoided any mention of his concern to Al but spoke separately to a nurse who assured him that if they couldn't move him yet, Doc. Holme would go out in the morning, weather permitting. They found Carl and Al something to eat; neither'd had anything since yesterday and only now did its effect begin to sap their endurance.

Al would stay at the hospital with Mitch until tomorrow, then head for the village and Mike. Carl told Al he'd go back to the farm to see how Alice and Grandma were but headed out directly to the village. He met the van a mile or two north of Al's. Mildred and Anastas held the boy to life but just barely. In a frantic bid they decided to make the dangerous, late night gamble, to get the boy to the hospital.

Carl rode back hard. Doctor Holme and the staff were ready for them when they arrived. Al had fallen into exhaustion and Doc. Holme had sedated him to sleep. They warned Carl to get some rest or he'd be next. They put Mildred into a bed, immediately and would treat and observe her because she'd begun to bleed and was dangerously close to miscarrying. Paul stayed at the hospital with Mildred and Carl made Al's as the sun split the horizon.

———

Shortly before noon, the worried contractor who awaited the lumber delivery, rode out to Al's. A good and decent family man, he'd dispatched a rider, the previous morning, to investigate the whereabouts of the load and found only Grandma at home. She relayed the problem as best she could in her state of mind so the rider, heading north toward the village, came across Alice, the small search group and the damaged sleigh. He returned to tell the contractor who immediately went to the two officers at the small York detachment and received a cold, "Ah Christ! Them damned Doukhobors again!" and nothing more. To his knowledge, the officers had made no attempt to leave their barracks.

With several men, the contractor went to the interloping, lumber-shark, promised him dire consequences if his tactics continued and left there with the lowlife bloodied and on the floor. The two officers appeared at his door and attempted to charge him with assault when a half dozen witnesses threatened to disclose the truth and brought their own lawyer with them. The contractor was a well-respected and influential member of the community and the York Council.

The wheels of wrath had been set into motion. Carl told Mayor Alpert about the previous encounter he'd had with the police and the result. The council had heard only the selected version and was incensed that the entire body had been misinformed. The mayor would see to it that the matter would be looked at immediately; things were getting out of hand. They'd have to establish their own authority. Carl wired the Marshal.

That evening, Carl returned to the hospital to learn two very horrible facts. Michael had passed away. They'd tried everything they could to keep his heart beating but he'd lost too much blood. His hands and feet were frozen beyond medical salvage and he'd likely suffer some severe brain damage. Doc Holme said there was no possibility of survival. The damage was just too severe. The second horrible consequence was the fact that Mildred lost her baby. She was near emotional collapse and now where would this leave her?

Al seemed to be in control and concentrated, now, on the badly injured Mitchell.

Paul had witnessed Mildred's terrible roller coaster over the past several months and wasn't overly shocked at the consequence. His greatest fear was that this latest affliction could push her over the edge.

———

That afternoon, one of Michael's horses wandered into Sean Murphy's yard, exhausted and starving, dragging the neck yoke and the remnants of a torn hayme strap. Sean found the other horse on the back-track, dead of a bullet wound. He'd run until he collapsed and died. The other, bound to him, had dragged his dead companion nearly a mile until the very strong strap finally broke and freed him.

———

Word spread quickly through the close town and a large crowd gathered at the hall. The Town Council, under advisement from the contractor, met quickly that afternoon and decided to call the public meeting. They listened intently to the series of events as Carl had seen them and quickly realized that they'd have to take matters in hand. The word that Michael McPherson had just died, inflamed the already smoldering anger.

Carl informed the assembly that he'd wired an old and experienced law officer, from Iowa, whom he knew very well, to act as a private investigator and advisor to the Doukhobor Community. Federal Marshal William Brewster, now retired, would arrive within the week. To avoid a conflict, Carl told them exactly what his relationship was. It didn't matter to the assembly.

A nurse rushed in to inform the assembly that Al McPherson, father of the dead boy, had just been arrested and hauled off to the jail. Paul Karmady, who'd been there at his wife's bedside, had tried to intervene and had been clubbed unconscious by one of the officers and was jailed as well, despite the doctor's warning that he had a likely concussion.

Al was a respected member of the community and Mildred and Paul's dedicated care of the burn victims was well known and admired. Before the assembly adjourned, they passed a motion to place their town and community under their own legal enforcement and they voted that individual to be William Brewster.

The mayor and council, with Carl and the same lawyer who had the contractor freed, marched up to the barracks and demanded to see the prisoners, to know the charges and to have Paul Karmady returned to the hospital to receive treatment. The officers refused them entry, claimed that they'd treated Mr. Karmady and that Mr. McPherson was charged with actions that had endangered the lives of minors and resulted in the death of his son.

The lawyer informed the officers that he had spoken to the hospital staff and the doctor hadn't been allowed to check, let alone treat Mr. Karmady. "Do you claim to be able to diagnose and treat as well? The staff who witnessed your action state that you used excessive force. As a matter-of-fact, without saying a single word, you struck Mr. Karmady simply because he asked for an explanation of your action against Mr. McPherson. When the doctor intervened to check Mr. Karmady's injury, you seized and cuffed him to a heating pipe and left him there until someone filed him free. The charges against Mr. McPherson can only be acted upon following an investigation and a judgment to that effect. You haven't done either of those and you are acting outside the law and are liable to charges. The council is well within their right to demand the release of both men immediately or they will have to take whatever reasonable actions are necessary to protect the rights of the injured man, the man wrongfully detained, and the interests of their community."

Paul was still unconscious and was, in fact, feverish. Learning this, the councillors announced to the two very disturbed young officers that their irresponsible actions had endangered too many people in the community, that the council and the burgesses had decided to assume the legal responsibility for their town and community and that both of them were to stand down until such time as a senior officer was present to answer for their actions. The officers' attempt at protecting their authority met with closure behind cell doors.

Carl and the contractor returned to the station and again telegraphed the Marshal of the recent events and urged his hurried arrival. Ernie, not at the meeting, heard what had transpired and informed them that the officers had submitted a lengthy telegraph to the detachment at Regina, requesting direction in the current circumstance and within the hour had received an answer. Ernie knew what the telegraphs said but could be held liable because his duties were sworn to secrecy. He told them what the written statements the officers gave him to send, looked like, then advised that they return to the barracks immediately and have a bit of a look around.

They located both documents after a brief search and handed both to the lawyer, who was pleased with their revealing content.

Al, shaken by Michael's death and now the humiliation he'd been subjected to, was very emotionally hurt. He personally felt some responsibility for Michael's death. He should have been there with them. He'd checked their route, informed all of the favourable farmers along the way and had their promise and cooperation in the event of any problem. The boys were accomplished horsemen, responsible, alert, and duty bound. Al didn't know what more he could have done and wouldn't know until Mitchell was sound enough to tell him.

Doc. Holme kept Mitch sedated until he knew the boy was out of danger; he was very concerned about the frost damage to his hands and feet. The boy's face would blister and scar some but it would heal. There didn't appear to be any lung damage from the cold; he'd been on the warm horse all of the time and that was his salvation.

Mildred had been asleep when the officers dragged Paul off. The hospital avoided telling her anything until Carl came and told her. She was weak but in no danger and she was an exceptionally good nurse so they put Paul in the room with her, for observation, and watched her reaction. She seemed to collect herself, push her emotions aside and concentrate on him. Paul was now conscious but had a severe headache.

One of the nurses offered to go with Carl; they'd heard that Alice and Grandpa had some frost injury. They knew Grandma would be inconsolable.

Carl took over the care of the livestock. Grandma went in and stayed with Mitchell throughout his pain-filled reawakening while Al made all the necessary arrangements and then came home.

Alice had Max to console her and he had a full time job. She managed to function normally around the house but broke into fits of self-reproach for her failure to do more. She'd ridden, that night, within a half mile of Michael and could have been his salvation had she only known.

John McPherson cursed himself for not being with the boys as he had on so many other trips. They'd set up a series of watches and stops yet it wasn't enough; the low-life were watching for this very opportunity. He'd just come back late in the afternoon after slipping away without anyone's knowledge, to the attack site and searching most of the day for anything that could tell him "Who?" He'd promised himself that the last act of his long and difficult life would be to get the bastards who did this to his grandsons, into his gun sights. Both he and Carl had difficulty waiting for the Marshal's arrival.

———

In the presence of Hugh, the young lawyer, Mayor Alpert, Al, Carl, and Doc Holme, Mitchell, with some difficulty, told everything he knew or could remember.

Because of the exposed ground the boys had decided to leave the trail and head across the fields, if the snow wasn't too difficult, to the less-used trail a mile west. The going was extremely difficult and they'd stopped to rest the teams and discuss the logic of what they were trying to do.

They heard the horsemen before they saw them and when the horde rounded the bush, hardly a half mile back, the boys knew they weren't after observation or harassment. They were coming hard and yelling. Mitch, who carried the rifle, told Michael to run south until he was out of sight behind the bush, then head back for the original trail and try to get to the Murphy place. Mitchell would run as far as the team could, in the direction he was going and try to hold them with his fire until Mike got to some help. Mitch drew their attention with several hasty shots from the running sleigh and they returned fire.

By the time Mike disappeared, Mitch's team was near exhaustion so he stopped them and took careful aim. The attackers' fire from the saddle was wild and scattered — his was steady and telling. He was certain he'd hit several times, even at that great distance. They turned and retreated to the east, then followed the bush line south, out of Mitch's effective range, clearly after Michael. Mitch, reading their intent, tore the traces off, split the team, mounted one and rode in that direction. He could hear the gunfire but couldn't see. He hoped Mike was out of range.

They again rounded the bush and came at him. He had no alternative but to run as hard as he could, to the west, into the gathering storm. His lead was too great and the weather covered his escape but he was in strange country.

―――――

Carl, Max, and Mayor Alpert met the train and the hard-faced Marshal William Brewster. The Marshal blocked their attempt at turning, in surprise, to greet the very familiar figure stepping off the train some distance behind him. "You don't know him, you've never seen him and he sure ain't your brother! I'll tell you later." August walked, conscious of, but oblivious to their stares, toward The Hotel. His naive look was ideal. He carried unusually stern features.

―――――

For most of his difficult life, Papa'd seen and often lived as a victim of brutality and abuse — now his boys were suffering the same in kind. He'd have come himself but he realized that he was no longer capable and his three youngest needed him at home, so August was it. Now there'd be three Buechler boys there and he had absolute faith in their abilities. He'd taught them well and now with the Marshal, they'd be hard to beat.

―――――

They went directly to the small town-office meeting room where the Council and the surrounding rural body had assembled to administer the brief signing and oath of office and the Marshal became the "Law" in York and district. Then their collective knowledge briefed the Marshal up to the latest and Hugh Everett, the young Lawyer, briefed him on the local by-laws and the territorial statutes that gave them the right and him the authority to do what he had to.

―――――

Mitch was asleep. The Marshal stood long and looked at the battered features, red with the rage of the elements, the hands and feet wrapped in gauze bandaging. He was old beyond his years, driven by necessity to a responsibility that took him from imaginative play into a battle of swinish greed and mad-dog commercialism.

"There's no way that filth didn't know who was on the sleighs. They had ta be watchin' and waitin' for the time when Al and John weren't there. They certainly didn't expect the fiery reaction they got from the kid."

"That may well have been the fuse that resulted in the vicious degree of the attack."

Knowing the extent of the attack on the bush camp, the Marshal doubted that it would have made a difference. "Seen a lot in my years, but never such snake-belly low, crawlin' sons-a-bitches. There's more'n local brains 'n purpose behind this. I want to talk to the couple a' babies ya' got locked up before 'Big Daddy' gets at 'em. Any idea when they're likely to be comin'?"

"Well, you know, dogonit, we've been just so darn busy with everything that's happened here since all of this started, that I didn't have a chance to get a telegraph away until this morning. They won't be showing up until sometime tomorrow at the earliest." Hugh smiled. The Marshal liked this guy already and he'd just met him.

"Don't want you in there with me when I go at these roosters. That way ya' got reason to know nothin' if some hothead defense attorney goes at ya'. They're a couple of real tough guys alright, in them nice uniforms, but they're scared shitless and I ain't goin' to be too nice to 'em. I want you fellas to stand in the window so they can see ya'. They won't be able ta claim I beat anything out of 'em, or intimidated 'em in any way. Hear all that ya' can, but hear nothin', ya understand?"

He walked in abruptly, slamming the door behind him. He whirled the chair around backward and slammed it to the floor, then planted himself into it, the backrest under his arms. His speech was abrupt and forceful and his eyes flashed. Carl could hear little of what was said, only when the Marshal raised his voice. He grilled the recruits for over an hour and they grew steadily more agitated and vocal.

In terms of legal ethics, Hugh knew that much of what the Marshal said and did was not at all acceptable, but then, he didn't know a thing about it; he couldn't hear a word. All he'd need were the facts that the Marshal got out of them.

"Ain't tellin' ya' nothin' ya' don't have to know, that way ya' won't have to lie about it, and the wrong people won't hear a slip of the tongue. Only me and him need to know." He acknowledged Hugh. "In all my days, I ain't seen anybody so bald-faced and open. Bastards don't seem to give a damn, they're so sure of themselves. They think everybody is deaf and blind or so damn stupid or scared of 'em that they won't say nothin'. Somebody in the Force is awful twisted. So when they come, one of two things is goin' to happen and I want to warn ya' fellas. If the guy is straight, he's goin' to question the two and come talk to you and the council to get the straight poop. If he ain't, he's goin' to tear into the two, right proper, in front of anybody who'll care to listen, then he'll promise some kind of punishment that'll never happen and then he'll come after Al and Paul on the charges that the young two started with. He'll try to find some way around the statutes to beat you guys and to try to pin somethin' on them or maybe the Doukhobors. His orders are either comin' from higher up or he's got some private deal with the snakes that'll net him a helluva profit. You can bet we'll have a time tryin' to find out who or what. It ain't all from the States neither, though Thorvaldson was into this up to his filthy, busted neck and you can bet some of these guys are still carryin' his cards. Those two greenies told me more'n they know and the telegraphs you've got are a real gold mine. Let 'em call a hearing; we've already got more'n I've had to work with in most cases. Who's the snake that's been double-dealin' in the lumber?"

"We'll point him out to you. He's usually big-mouthing it at the cafe about this time ... far as we know he brings the lumber in from somewhere east. We ain't had time to go after the railroad records to find out. I don't think we can get ahold of them without legal authority," Hugh advised.

"That's the hard, slow way, if ever. Usually they'll stall and throw up all kinds of roadblocks, real or imagined. By the time we get around 'em, we'll all be dead and buried. We've got to trace it through the people that bring the loads. Somehow we've got to connect with some of them."

"That is no problem. I know a couple already that'll tell me," Carl Advised.

"Hot damn!" the Marshal smiled.

They followed the mayor to the hotel and sat at a large table at the back, near the window, down two seats and across the aisle from the totally oblivious August. The Marshal had to smile; "These Buechler boys are something else! ... damndest actors I've ever seen. Nobody knows anybody." They ordered coffee and the popular raisin bun as a large, puffy, brusque man, sporting a heavy blue welt to his right cheekbone, boomed his way in to dominate the setting.

He acknowledged the mayor with a look that spoke daggers then plunked himself down in the booth behind August. The Marshal delivered August a slight nod in the man's direction. August turned himself sideways and lazily leaned against the wall side of his booth, leisurely extending his left leg toward the aisle side of his seat, casually observed the massive profile diagonally opposite, then delivered a casual wink with his off-eye.

Clothes bleached and colour blind, patched and stitched by accident not design, unwashed, unshaved, and uncombed, hungry for anything, anyway, homeless, hopeless, hateful and meaner than a starving dog, the ideal match to the purpose at hand; within the hour August was employed. They'd have to find a way of feeding him what they needed him to know and he'd have to inform them somehow.

"That's easy!" the mayor stated. "That cute young waitress doesn't know it yet, but she's going to take a shine to the young fella. She'll tell him and he'll tell her, then she'll tell us while their shining up to each other. Now, what could be more natural and innocent? I know she'll do it and we can trust her; she's my niece and she's the right kind."

"Hope August knows it. He ain't too friendly around girls."

"That ain't what we've seen from the Buechler boys."

August answered the knock on the door of the cheapest room in the establishment and encountered the vision of loveliness he'd watched with interest down in the cafe. To his tongue-tied anticipation, she walked right in without invitation, closed and locked the door behind her and announced that she was Carol and that he'd best get used to seeing her around because they were going to indulge in a whirlwind romance whether he knew or not, even if it was not.

August wasn't sure if he'd died and gone to heaven until she finished her good humoured laugh at his reaction and told him why she was there and what they were expected to do. Then he felt better. That was something in his brief indoctrination into the world of undercover policing that the Marshal failed to mention. Then she threw him again when she asked him if he liked kissing girls because he was going to have to do that to her once in a while, where everybody could see, just to throw them off and maybe because he might learn to like it too. Then she spoiled that again by telling him that he wasn't supposed to get any funny ideas because she had a boyfriend whom she was serious about. August had better be ready to explain the circumstance to him if he found out because she didn't really want to lose him.

———

Carl took the Marshal out to Al's because he wanted to meet them, to see if he could bring back some assurance and security into their lives again. He'd had a long visit with Alice at Carl and Milly's wedding and had learned a great deal about her family. He liked her open, personable nature.

He warned them about the reaction they might get from the investigating police and if things got sticky they were supposed to let him, Carl, or Max know immediately. There was no way they were going to try to come after Al again. He told them to go ahead with the funeral and to try to keep people around the place with all their eyes open to every move or stranger they saw anywhere near. He wanted to know every move before it happened. "The galling roosters are so cock-sure of themselves and so mean and hateful that they're liable to try anything." The family was openly grateful for the knowledge that something positive was going to happen, especially Grandpa. He spoke long into the evening with the Marshal and unloaded much of his hatred.

"When ya' get them bastards all lined up, let me have the gun. I'll save everybody lots a' time and money. Then they can do what ta hell ever they want with me, I don't really care!"

———

The Presbyterian Church couldn't begin to hold the public reaction to this tragic funeral. There wasn't a child growing up amongst them who hadn't been required, in this rough environment, to take responsibility for labours that should have been well beyond their years. They were all guilty and they all knew it; there just weren't enough hands. If it didn't get done either you and yours or your dependent livestock starved or froze or crawled back like beaten dogs.

The much larger town hall filled to overflow out into the street and the doors stayed open to expel some of the words. They'd asked Carl to deliver the eulogy but he graciously acknowledged one of the boys who'd been a hard and fast friend to the twins throughout childhood. Carl coached his remarks with an exceptionally emotional result.

Mildred managed the service with some discomfort; she wept uncontrollably. Alice sat with Max and her father; her scarred features hard as etched stone. She never shed a tear but Max held her to control her visible shaking.

Anastas offered a brief statement in prayer, in which he outlined the value of human life, especially in one so young, so violently taken and the pointless inhumanity of it. "'The wealth of the entire world is not worth the life of a single child!' Yet, God allows nothing without a greater plan and Michael's role was beyond the understanding of the living. It is to us to accept that fact, to grieve for his loss but to glorify his heavenly calling and to anticipate the wonderful day when, once again, he will stand to greet us."

Helen's interpretation was halting and very emotional but completely clear. He'd be about her brother's age when she'd last seen him. Carl, Max, Alexsay, Ivan, Sven, and Sean carried the hardwood casket to is final rest next to his mother, up against the peaceful, wooded bluff, and the lonesome, white, wooden cross now had a reluctant companion.

———

The next morning, Carl and the Marshal rode out to the village to learn everything he could from them about the background that he may not have learned from Carl or Max. They spent the afternoon out at the site to recreate the attack on the boys in their own minds. Many of the searchers, including Alexsay, went with them. The Marshal was very much impressed by the degree of their sincerity and their stoic sense of reality. They followed, as accurately as they could, the course of events relayed by Mitchell. They searched the area for as long as light allowed. It had warmed quite a bit but there hadn't been much of a thaw since, so things such as expended rifle cartridges wouldn't be visible until that happened. The lifetime of experience gave the Marshal vision for things that most would not see or would take for granted. He saw things that verified Mitch's account with absolute certainty. His fire had been telling; there were hits and wounds that would be exceptionally hard to hide or disguise.

"Ta hell with 'em! I ain't goin' ta worry about 'em until I get back. Let 'em try! Hugh will know what to do and Alpert and the council will deal with whatever they're foolish enough to try if any of 'em do. I've locked up more'n one of my own kind, even seen one of 'em get the business end of a rope. They don't worry me a damn bit."

Next morning, they went out to the mill and Carl walked the Marshal through everything he knew about events there, including what had happened to him and Alexsay. He was interested to know if the firefight site involving Carl had been disturbed. He'd come back to hunt for spent cartridges and match them with the returning fire on Mitch. The pile of saw logs had grown enormously, because the mill had sat since the attack on the boys. Most of the sawn lumber had been hauled to the village so there wasn't any reason for any delay. Yet "The wealth of the entire world was not worth the life of a single child!"

The Marshal spoke to the two scouts who'd followed the mysterious horsemen who had intimidated the boys and had spied on the engine the night Carl and Max had heard their late night approach. They said a lot to confirm his suspicion. "They're the same two ya' had locked up for the last while, ya know! They were ordered by some biggy to keep an eye on the Doukhobors and nail 'em on any excuse they could find. Instead of policin' they had 'em spyin' on honest folks to see if they could find or trump up a charge. They charged Al with contributing to his son's death under the same trump. Telegraph ordered 'em to do that. It'll take a judge to knock 'em off that road. As far as I've been able to gather, I doubt that they've ever been out to where the boys were hit. Best have somebody keep an eye on it. We'll need everything we can find out there. If there's ever goin' to be anybody who'll find the actual butchers, I'm afraid it'll have to be us. We may never get right to the source but we can sure in hell knock 'em off our backs! We got to find where they dumped the first two police you said acted on the fire. I'm sure they're straight. If we run into any kind of judge at all, I'll find out where they are."

The lane entrance into Paul's yard was impossible to negotiate with the horses. Carl and the Marshal swam their way through. As far as either of them could tell, nothing had been touched there. Carl's packs were still as he had left them in the newly constructed storage-granary. Paul's oats were still as Carl first saw them last fall. As soon as the trails dried he'd have to latch on to a wagon and help Paul get some of it in. He had to be out of money. Carl's was safe so he gathered all of it and would pay Al back and bank the rest. The window was back in but the inside, though it was considerably cleaner, was still as forlorn and empty. It'd take all the love Carl was sure they could find, to bring it back. How many hits could two people take and still pull together? Carl knew just how much this baby meant to both of them.

There was nothing fit to eat left there anymore so they headed back to the village that night to talk more to the people there.

The Marshal was completely thorough. He insisted on crawling through the snow to the site of Carl's future yard. He wanted to know everything he could; this was where his only living grandchild was going to spend the rest of her life and he felt as much a part of it as if it was his decision. He wanted Carl to build as soon and as well as he could. "Ya know, it really hurts me to see how you young folks have to struggle for every nickel and grab at every chance to make a life for yourselves. She's all we got left to carry our hopes into the future. I lived on nothin' since her Grandma died, to sock away some security for 'em. Now Wilbur's dead and she's all there is so don't take no short cuts! I sure hate to see you apart this way. Ya' know, I'd give everything I've got if I could see and talk to her Grandma again. I suppose I will soon but not in this world. My money don't mean a damn to me! You and her do! I can see what's takin' shape out here and I'll roll over any bastard, just like McPherson said, or I'll die tryin'. I don't care what happens to me neither!" Carl could tell the wound was still bothering him quite a bit.

———

York was in an uproar. A force of five officers had rolled in and attempted to override the authority of the council as the Marshal had predicted. Hugh had telegraphed the Winnipeg detachment with information regarding the events at York and demanded a full investigation. He'd contacted colleagues in Winnipeg to get them to pressure the Force and he'd asked advice from his old instructors. The York detachment, though not at all pleased, had been telegraphed an order to stand down to the local enforcement officer. There would be a full investigation. The local officers and the new arrivals, who made their feelings clear, were ordered to remain at York until it was complete.

———

Part of August's menial chores as an ignorant, young underling, was to sweep and clean the small office nightly; a fateful decision for his employer. Hadn't he anticipated this bumpkin's ability to read? All correspondence was by mail, and nothing more than the main door was locked. August had the key, the broom and the ability! In a week, August had achieved amazing results.

The Marshal was right; they were extremely arrogant and careless. Carol indicated that they were totally oblivious to the swirl that was shaping up around them. They were dealing with ignorant Doukhobors and were morally obligated to get them out of the road of unrestricted commerce, using any tactic they could. August had given Carol names, some of them enlightening, and told her about plans in the works, to coordinate the simultaneous firing of the lumber that they knew was in store at the village and the camp, then try to pin it on the Doukhobor radicals. "The local authorities will see to it that any problems will be dealt with!" The action was to take place as soon as it dried off a bit but they didn't say when.

August saw documents that tied them to Thorland and the accounts there. He took none of them but he had a fantastic memory. He wrote down everything he was afraid he'd forget but only when he got back to his room and then he gave it to Carol.

Defiant and spirited, Carol never carried anything openly. Everything, in or out, travelled securely tucked inside her bra and she took great pleasure in letting the completely puzzled uncle-Mayor, Max and Carl know it.

Hugh had taken action to access accounts in and out of the York bank based on these records but that would take time and a judge's approval. He even had that virtually guaranteed. Justice McArthur, one of Hugh's law school instructors, since elevated to the bench, had been placed in the judicial district that included York.

"By Gad, that boy's good!"

"And lucky too!"

Within two days of Hugh's telegraph, two commanding officers from the Winnipeg detachment appeared at York and immediately contacted the Marshal, Hugh, and the council. The meeting was brief and cordial. Hugh outlined the action the council had taken and placed the evidence, with special emphasis on the telegraph. The Marshal, Carl, and Paul presented statements under Hugh's careful direction. The officers asked surprisingly few questions. The written reports they'd received about the situation at York were considerably different than what they'd heard from Carl, Paul, and Alexsay and only one of these guys was a much reviled Doukhobor.

There would be a full investigation of all of the events leading up to the current situation. The commanding officer at Regina was pulled from active service and the first two officers to investigate the bush camp attack would be called back and were to testify before the inquiry.

The Marshal met privately with the senior Winnipeg officers to develop a working relationship with the force and he shared, selectively, some of the material coming out of his investigation to this point, including the incriminating knowledge of another possible attack on the lumber supply. The officers appeared very much concerned about the safety of the people who could be injured if such an incident took place yet agreed that little could be done, legally, until it happened because it was only rumoured. The Marshal said nothing of August and the rest of his findings.

The dates of the inquiry wouldn't be set for some time and the Marshal wanted to play out his options to their full. Like Carl, he was very concerned about the possibility of political implications beneath the surface and he wasn't totally sure of the Force. He didn't trust anybody. If any action occurred immediately, he'd be as suspicious as if it didn't occur at all. He warned August to be especially careful because they might well be investigating "the leak" and because he was new, he'd be the one to watch. "Keep your eyes and ears open but leave the papers alone. We'll get all of 'em whenever we need 'em, unless somebody tips 'em off first. We'll watch for that too and step in if we have to. You've seen the officers here, watch for any contact between your people and the Force. If that happens, get to me right away."

Carl, Max, and the Marshal rode back out to the village and warned them about what they'd learned. They didn't know, with the way events were shaping up, when, if ever, the attack would come. They rode to the camp and issued the same warning, to establish a watch and a rapid system of communication when the word came down. Riders were immediately dispatched to all the other villages and the guard was up. They'd know soon.

The Marshal recruited the safe farmers on Al's advice and set up an alarm watch, day or night, along the route. Then, all they could do was wait. "Surely ta God, with all the police runnin' around York the last little while, they wouldn't be stupid enough to try any time soon but ya never know. After all, ain't 'the local authorities' supposed to look after everything?"

The hospital was prepared to release Paul. Mildred had stayed right with him. It was long past the time for them to get at nursing their lives back. The Marshal rode back alone and Max went to the camp. Carl nighted over with Anastas. The next day, he and Helen rode to Paul's to get some heat and life back into the place for the family's return. Jimmy had been isolated too much, of late, from his parents. Carl immediately got at the lane into the yard and by noon had it barely passable again. Helen had both stoves going and by that afternoon the place began to feel a lot better. He shovelled the place clear and opened the woodpile and the clothesline. Helen pulled out and washed the soot off the dishes and cupboards, then swept the place again, from end to end.

She'd brought with her a kind of deodorant-disinfectant that smelled like pine boughs and placed some on each of the stoves, then mixed it with the wash-water and went at the floors and walls of the kitchen first. It performed miracles against the soot and the smell. There wouldn't be time to do everything today but she'd come back and help Mildred as soon as she got here. Helen, Mildred, and Alice had grown very close.

Paul and Mildred's bed sported one of the same mattresses that had been stuffed for the camp and somebody got a good quilt for them. Someone had thrown together a miniature bed for Jimmy. It reflected Alexsay's idea of a child's ability to adapt to a bed as soon as he was able to walk. The bed that Carl used was still at the village. Carl hadn't seen it since the night of the fires.

Helen was a bit more receptive to Carl's circumstance after they'd eaten and rested from their labours. She was very interested in Milly and she wanted to see a picture. Mildred told her about everything that had happened, how Carl reacted, how Milly looked, what a beautiful couple they made and how happy they seemed to be. Helen understood but it really highlighted the emptiness in her own life. Carl was so much like something she so desperately needed and she'd hoped so hopelessly. Her life was so terrifyingly full yet so personally empty ... everything for everybody else and nothing for her. She'd lived with it for so long. Without a family, her consuming desire was for one of her own.

Carl didn't want to tell Helen about August; the more people who knew, the more it would endanger him. He couldn't imagine it but he wasn't just too sure about the romance of convenience.

The mill was cutting again but Carl would stick around until Paul and Mildred got back and he knew they were secure. Paul's injury could still be a problem and Mildred was physically strong but emotionally weak; she continued to blame herself for everything. Paul would have to take the rest of the time until spring seeding to rest and heal — they'd both have to.

Carl didn't want to let the fires die out and have the house cool off again. In light of what had happened already, he wouldn't let Helen ride back alone. He saw her back and then returned to Paul's by bright, beautiful and warm moonlight.

Funny how warm moonlight can make you think about somebody you love. He dug out the writing paper and wrote everything to her.

In the still dark of early morning, Carl could hear it and feel it; the warmth and the sounds of dripping water. He opened the door to comfortable humidity. It would be a glorious spring day. March was very nearly gone and it was more than welcome. There wasn't anyone in the entire country who didn't carry a scar or two of the hellish winter.

XIV
"They'd defend their own!"

Sunshine and warmth meant a future worth anticipating. God would grant them another opportunity and they'd heal. The people who'd suffered such loss and pain felt hope and smiled and greeted and visited on the street and invited one another in for no other reason than to invite and to drink tea. Carl could hear laughter again.

Those carrying the distortions of fire appeared in the street to hobble their way to the doughwam or to the stables or to the neighbours or to the sloppy, wet, gurgling countryside that they'd thought they'd never again see. They didn't hate and they forgot their hurt in the searching joy of life and the moment. Their smiles were wonderful. They wanted to work, to do, to build, to live again. They pulled off their wrappings and felt the healing elixir of the sun's magic on their raw exteriors.

The sombre little face broke into a wide, welcoming smile and his arms shot up to the embrace. Somehow, he knew his world would right itself again. He hadn't seen his mom and dad in a long time, but then, he'd almost gotten used to them disappearing and reappearing so fast. There were sick people all over and they had to help, he knew that somehow. But why didn't they come back? These ladies were nice to him but he didn't belong here. Now Carl was here and things would be better; Carl meant they'd be back and together soon.

They dined Carl and packed him and Helen and the beautiful boy off in Al's light cutter while there was still enough snow to get it back. They'd go to York and bring back "Pavlowa" and beloved "Mill-der." There were so many in this village who saw and felt this beautiful day because of what those two had done for them. The debt was more than they could repay, but they'd try.

About the same time Carl left, so did several of the village women, for Paul's and the necessary restoration of those wonderfully kind people and their damaged lives. They had her paint and they'd risk Mildred's favour with their choice of a colour scheme.

The morning was so absolutely perfect. Carl spoke to Helen of his plans, as they drove past his place and she seemed so very pleased that he placed such confidence in her feminine assessment of what Milly might think, yet she was clearly misty eyed. Carl noticed and smiled and assured her that her time would come, maybe sooner then she anticipated.

Carl looked forward to getting an update from the Marshal; so much could happen out here in such a few days. On the ride down, his Mauser lay behind the seat and both he and Helen nervously scoured the horizons on every side.

Travel was slow and careful so the trip to Al's took nearly four hours, but they made it to a large dinner ... very silent and very painful. Bad news had once again broached the tranquility of the sorrowing household. Some of Mitchell's fingers and toes had been amputated and the boy was still in intense physical and emotional pain. Michael was as much a part of him as living and breathing.

Carl and Helen left the cutter and took the van that Al had brought out from York and would bring Paul and Mildred out to Al's again for the night. They'd get home tomorrow to a bit of peace and quiet, or so everyone hoped.

Jimmy squealed with joy and rushed to his tearful mother and upset father. Paul's head was still lightly bandaged and his eyes dark-shadowed the consequence of the blow. One headache was gone with another now imminent. Apparently the disagreement had been going on for some time because Paul was clearly growing frustrated and angry. Mildred's sunken eyes told them that she'd been in a lengthy cry. Jimmy was puzzled; this was a happy reunion for him. Why were Mommy and Daddy so angry and sad?

"Please, will you try to reason with her? I've tried and tried to talk her down to reality. It's because she loves me so much that she has to leave, otherwise she's bound that her actions are going to destroy both of us. I've told her a thousand times that I've forgiven her and that I love her and want her with me always but I can't seem to get her to believe me."

"I want to believe you! Oh God, how I want to believe you! How can I? I can't even believe myself. I did this, not you, not any of you! I'll live with it! I can't expect you to. Every morning for the rest of our lives, I'd look at you and know that you will never think of me or trust me like you did when we first met."

"Dammit woman, you want everything like when we first met? Well, they're not and they never will be! I can't make them the same and neither can you. We're not the same. Do I hate what you did? Yes, because it hurt me and us really bad. This wouldn't be happening now if it didn't. Do I hate you for it? No more then I hated getting my skull cracked. Do I hate my skull? It'll heal and I'll get over it, just like we'll get over it. It'll take time. You lost the baby? Well you're not the first. Did that hurt us? Yes it surely did. We can do something about that but we've got to want to. We're alive and we're a family for as long as you want us to be. I may hate what you did, so do you. I can say that it doesn't change how I feel about you but it surely seems to have changed the way you feel about me and yourself. You didn't burn or shoot or hit anybody. You did everything that you could and more then you should have. How many people wouldn't be alive today if you didn't do what you did? Now, are we a family and do we have a home and do we start again or not?"

"No! I mean yes! Oh God, I don't know what I mean, Paul!"

"Well go then, damn you, and rot in some nuthouse somewhere raving about what could have been because you're too stubborn or dumb or twisted to see what you're destroying! I've been alone most of my life and you're leaving to make things better for me? Well ta hell with you, then, go! You're not destroying me and I'm not lettin' you destroy our son's life along with yours! You're not fit to raise him the way you are now! We've still got a home even if you haven't and we're goin' there right now whether you're comin' or not. I've put up with as much as I'm going to!" He seized the startled, very disturbed, Jimmy and distorted with anger, turned and strode rapidly toward the waiting team.

"No Paul! Oh God, no! Don't!" She felt her legs doubling under her. Helen jerked her roughly back onto her feet. Carl was speechless and terribly confused by the spectacle that he never once imagined could happen. He didn't know what to do.

"You crazy woman!" Helen, her fair features flushed with anger, shook Mildred, fully four inches taller and forty pounds heavier, like a rag doll and pinned her forcefully against the large maple that backed her. "I saw my father beaten to his death when I was barely old enough to remember, I saw my mother raped in front of my eyes and I was powerless to stop it! I saw her give birth to my little bastard half-brother as a result, less than a year after they butchered my father! I saw fire and death and I have never seen any of my family again. I ran, I starved, I froze and I hid with all the others before I was ten years old. You lost a baby and it's beaten you? I've seen hundreds lost and helped deliver some of them. Anastas had a wife and four children. He was privileged to witness, with his own eyes, every one of their deaths. Have you seen the hand-drawn picture he made to keep them in his memory? He takes it out and talks to them and prays for them every night and waits for the time when he can again join them and you want to leave?

"Paul has difficulty writing his own name because he, like I, was not privileged with the right to education. He saw his little sister and then his mother perish slowly and painfully from tuberculosis and he scorched himself in the hell of fires until he found some hope for a future and a family, again, out here. I saw how he hurt and yearned over the love of you, while you, you spoiled, privileged brat, would abuse and defile his trust? Now you are prepared to throw away, that which so many of us would give our lives to have? Either you go to him and try to make things right, or I can promise you, I will! I saw how overjoyed he was when your son was born and I helped to write every word he said to you and now you want to take his son away? If you don't love him, I do, as a friend and a very good and courageous man. I will not see him alone again!"

She released a shaken and trembling Mildred, turned and walked quickly away toward The Hotel cafe. Carl walked to the van before he followed Helen.

"Go to her! She needs you! Now!" His look and the words warned Paul not to argue. "We'll be at the cafe — don't worry about us. Take her home and don't just tell her how you really feel about her; show her. We'll get to Al's."

Paul cradled the gently weeping little boy as he walked back to the forlorn, despairing woman who he would always love. He could see how badly she felt and he was ashamed that he'd lost his temper but what could he do?

"I'd still fall off a horse for you."

"And I'll always pick you up, even if you don't want me to. Now, you're comin' to the home I spent all those years building for us, where you belong. If I'm being too rough, that's really too bad. You leave me little choice. Get in!"

They went home. Everybody else would have to look after themselves. It was time to deal with their family.

———

Helen disregarded the disgusting snort and the contemptuous "Pee yoo! Smell 'at? ... smells like Doukhobor!" clear enough for the silenced room to hear, as she sat down at the only vacant table. She was badly shaken and crying. The room was nearly full and everybody couldn't help but notice.

"Think you've got somethin' to bawl about bitchy-girl? Just you wait 'til I get done wipin' the scum 'a ya' off the face of the earth, then ya'll ...!" The Hotel keeper's hand dropped below the counter as the inflated frame hoisted himself up out of the seat.

The man's bulk rocked violently and crashed to the floor as a blood-spout erupted from his mouth and nose. Carl, consumed by rage, yanked his bulk to its gelatinous legs and prepared to finish the disgusting chore when powerful arms encircled him and he let the garbage collapse back to the litter where it belonged.

"Take 'er easy boy! Want ta kill 'im an' then what? Drag that bag 'a shit ta hell out'a my place and git the Marshal!" The Hotel keeper roared. "We got too much at stake now an' we can't lose it; we're sa close." He knew something that Carl didn't.

"You alright ma'am?" The question came from an anxious, unkempt face with a clear set of Buechler eyes under all the hair. Helen's anxious expression blended into confusion.

"I'm fine thank you!" she stuttered and then he was gone to help drag the scum out of the place and Carl, shaken and more frightened now then angry, came and sat down. She'd learned over a lifetime to disregard such attempted confrontations, so Carl's reaction shocked her. The man was huge, at least twice Carl's weight yet Carl had dispatched him with such ease as to make it seem effortless. What frightened her and Carl both was the fact that in that moment, Carl had lost all sight of logic and reason. Carl couldn't recall a time when he'd come so close to killing another human being out of sheer hatred and what concerned him was the fact that he'd actually taken pleasure in doing it. All in the room knew what the disgusting creature had done to so many people.

"B'fore ya' start hollerin' an' lecturin', I'm here ta tell ya', that if he didn't, I would' a'. I was fer throwin' him out anyway and if he'd a' made one step to the lady, I'm tellin' ya' here an' now, I'd a' blowed his ga'damned head ta' hell of a' his shoulders!" The Hotel keeper pulled the cocked and loaded double sawed-off from under the till counter to emphasize his point.

"Dammit man! Drop the hammers, easy now! An' take the shells out before ya' blow half of us ta blazes!" the Marshal ordered. "What happened?"

Carl didn't have to explain. Everybody tried to speak at once.

"Sure hope you didn't hurt him too much; I'd hate to have that takin' up hospital space when ya got a perfectly good undertaker in town!" Everybody laughed nervously, even Carl and Helen. "Don't blame ya', but be careful a' your temper; that could a' cost us," the Marshal reprimanded Carl quietly.

"You must be Helen? Everybody I've met talks about you and none of 'em done any justice. Take it from an old man who's seen almost everything and none of it near as close to good lookin' as you are." Helen dropped into her vivid, beautiful blush as the atmosphere lightened again. The Marshal surely knew how to relax a tensed situation. "Bring this girl and fella a good supper on me," he ordered.

"Ta hell ya' will I say! It's on the house! First damn good piece a' action I seen against that domineering sunuvagun since he first come in here. Ya' can be damned sure he ain't comin' in agin!" The entire room seemed to take on a sense of relief and riddance and the chatter elevated freely, to good humour.

"Who was that guy who asked me how I was?" Helen asked quietly.

"I don't know; I didn't notice." But Carl knew it had to be August.

"Ah come on! He was the closest thing to you since I saw you when I dragged you in out of the storm; kind of scrubby looking. He actually looked a bit like you and Max.

"Really?"

"Don't fiddle with me!" she frowned. "Now, come on, who is he? I know you've got other brothers. Is he one of them? What's going on? How come he helped drag out the dirty-mouthed guy?"

"Better tell her before she 'lets the cat out of the bag' without knowin' it!"

Hardly above a whisper, "He's my brother, August, but don't you breathe a word to anybody, at any time, even if it kills you. Promise now, because it can sure kill him."

In similar fashion, the Marshal explained the role fully and Helen was shocked. She'd never heard of such goings on. Most of the time when things like this happened to her and her Doukhobors, they simply took the blows and fled as hard and as far as they could. These people were actually doing something about righting a gross wrong and they were very close and very good.

———

"Follow me!" the attractive waitress ordered Helen. "I'll show you to your room." Helen followed, with encouragement from Carl and the Marshal.

"What room?" she asked, as she and the waitress climbed the stairs.

"I'm Carol," the waitress said as she closed the door behind them and extended her hand in acquaintance. "I understand the Marshal told you and now you're into our dangerous little game over your pretty neck. I hope it doesn't scare you."

"Scare me? I can assure you, nothing much scares me."

Carol told her about their intriguing scheme and romance. "The room's for you for the night. Carl's with the Marshal; we're going to meet later tonight, so stay put and rest a bit." She turned in afterthought. "Oh, by the way, I'm already taken and the romance is just play-acting so he's all yours if you want him. He's really cute too, when he's all cleaned up and shaved.

He's acting right now but it won't be long ...!" she emphasized suggestively and smiled as she left.

Was this what Carl meant when he'd said what he did as they went past his place? Her heart gave her a little skip of anticipation but she put it to rest. She'd seen nothing but disappointments. Yet he was handsome, Carl's brother! "Maybe?" she smiled. "If he's anything like Carl ...!" She looked forward to finding out.

————

"We're takin' a heck of a chance meetin' like this," Hugh warned, "but we almost have to. August's been hearing so many funny things, so I think they might be suspicious and are spreadin' all kinds of false rumours."

"They pulled most of their men out a' here, one or two at a time, so we wouldn't notice. August said he was told to ride west about ten miles to be sure nobody's seen him and then head north to the reserve land and then back east to the post north of the village. That's maybe where their gatherin'," Carol advised.

"What I'm thinkin' is that they're likely to split up and hit several places at once, hopin' that we expect them to hit the lumber at the village," the Marshal warned. "They must suspect that we're watchin' after the attack on the boys."

"We may have eyes for 'em in our bunch too," Alpert cautioned. "That's why we're meetin' with only the few of us. I ain't even sure about the council, so they ain't gettin' the whole shot from me."

"Carl, you an' Helen are headin' back first thing in the mornin' and warn 'em up there," the Marshal ordered. "Then you an' Max ride to the post and see what ya' can see. Maybe try to get there near dark and watch out for eyes. Come from some backward way so they don't expect — maybe from the north. Get back to me as quick as ya can. Al's talked to a few of the farmers he knows he can trust and they're all ready to do what they have to. After the attack on the boys, most of 'em know nobody's safe an' they're madder'n hell!"

"The hearing is comin' next week," Hugh advised. "It's my guess that's their window 'cause we'll all be tied up, even the police. I wired the judge this afternoon. He'll be here when he should and show himself openly.

We'll cancel at the last minute on some trumped up excuse, so they won't be able to get the word out. I've got a guarantee of whatever search and seizure measures we need and we could move on the files right now if we had to; the papers are all drawn up and signed. They're legal the minute his pen left the paper ... got their office watched, so the Marshal can move instantly if they try to skip out with the documents. August says, as far as he knows, everything we need's still there. He's seen most of it. We're in ideal legal shape!"

Carl worried about August. "Maybe we should pull him out? Once he's gone, we've got no way to reach him. He ain't just too sure where every-body else is told to go. It could be a test to see what we do."

"Get back for the inquiry," the Marshal ordered. "We'll get back out late that night and we'll ride hell-bent-for-leather. I keep worryin' 'bout what they meant by the 'authorities lookin' after everything'. We'd better have folks ready up there ... think you can do that? ... Got ta figure some way a' gettin' August out of it. An' for God sake keep your eyes open on the road. Bastards know who ya' are an' they could be layin' for ya'. Get word back somehow, somebody they don't know about. Good luck and be careful!"

———

Carl and Helen rode out on two livery horses with full harness. Carl thought he might be able to pick Paul's wagon up at Al's and get it back, but there was still too much snow in places, so they left the livery team at Al's and would take the same cutter back to the village, with one of Al's teams.

———

Grandpa was gone again; ... out at the attack sites. He just couldn't get the hatred out of his spirit or the blood out of his eye; he had to find some-thing. He'd come from visiting Mitchell yesterday and he'd raved all night. They didn't even try to stop him early this morning. Grandma was very worried, so Carl told her he'd keep an eye out for him, maybe even take him with them.

Grandpa had proven himself in many a pinch and he was hard as nails. In his younger days, before the responsibility of family, he'd ridden in a traveling show as a trick shooter, and shelved many prizes for his marksmanship. Few could match his speed and accuracy with a lever-action from the saddle.

He wasn't at either of the attack sites, but the evidence of his being was everywhere. He'd scoured the site and left, trailing north along the rough disturbance that told him of the attacker's retreat. He was trailing an instinct that nobody'd yet had time for.

It was late afternoon by the time they entered the village. The bawnyah pumped smoke gleefully and one of the first people they met was a newly washed Mildred, her eyes shone and her cheeks smiled.

"I want to thank you for what you did for me, for the three of us. I don't know how I could have been so foolish. You were so right. Gosh these people are so good to us!"

"To you?" Helen countered. "How can those who still have their lives, or their father's, or brother's, or son's, or husband's, because of what you did for them, be otherwise? Their goodness pales by comparison!"

"The house was warm and clean and so very freshly painted. I felt so foolish, low and hateful of myself when we got home last night. This place sure is beautiful in the warmth of spring. I woke up this morning, in my own bed again, with the husband I very nearly drove away lying next to me and our little boy yelling for something dry and something to eat and the sun and the birds and the gurgling water and I'm glad to be home again. I made Paul bring me here this afternoon to thank them and found myself useful and needed again. Anastas came down with a bad cough and a cold so I've got to check on him and maybe give him something for it. I'll need a few more things for the burns that I was in no shape to even anticipate before I left, so if anybody's heading back to York soon, let me know." Mildred had come to terms with her reality.

Helen rushed with Mildred to Anastas and Carl helped himself to the warmth of the steam and the fellowship within. He was becoming intolerable, even to himself; everyone else was just being polite.

———

When John McPherson rode in to Alexsay's, tired and very hungry, it was nearly dark. He wore a wicked smile of satisfaction. "Boys sure in hell left their mark! Followed what seemed like a trail back up north ... run across a dead, half-eaten horse and a couple a' fresh graves just outside a' the post. Nobody up there knew me or figured anything –sure a hellish bunch a' mean lookers gatherin' up there, one of 'em carryin' a bad wound, just loafin' round. They're up to somethin'. Rode up to the Indian village and they told me plenty. The dead buggers ... dead a couple weeks, a few days after what they done to the boys. They must a' died a' gunshot 'cause everybody sure wanted to keep their mouths shut. They'd come up onto the reserve lookin' for women and some 'a the boys up there drove 'em off, nearly killed a couple! Sure hate 'em! More than willing to watch an' help an' tell us what they're up to. Dug around the sleigh a while and found some interesting shell casings. Marshal 'll sure be interested!"

They met that night, at the doughwam; the entire village, old, young, burned or whole, to listen to what Carl, Helen, and John knew and had to say; to hear and to decide what they were going to do to meet what was to befall them. This time it would be no surprise. Emotions ran high. Mothers, wives, children of the dead, sat in disbelief. Were those who had killed their loved ones once again going to fall upon them for more? "Nyet!" Not this time. This time they'd defend their own with every fibre of their beings and their friends and neighbours would stand with them.

Carl and John rode out to the mill next morning and late that afternoon, with Max, headed north to the reserve settlement to cement the alliance. The elders displayed intense hatred for what they'd suffered over many years from these authorities and their cruel henchmen. They were prepared to throw everything they could against their tormentors. They knew when, they knew where, and they knew who. History'd taught them to keep their mouths shut and their noses clean until the evil turned against them. Now it had done that. Two of their women had been abused and badly hurt — only a miracle had saved the perpetrators. They found a commonality with the Doukhobors in their mutual distrust of authority. They were excellent trackers and observers. They'd be the eyes, ears, and the early warning system. They were ghosts in the night.

Carl and John sat long and watched the bustle at the post and counted twenty-three. With others they knew were still coming, they were very suspicious of a split assault. It would be very hard to defend. The natives said they would give plenty of warning because they knew the attackers had absolutely no idea that their intentions were known. "Surprise will be ours!"

———

The trails were becoming slop. Neither sleigh nor wagon could travel. John McPherson went back home; they'd be worried and he had to see the Marshal to reveal his findings and inform him of the alliance they'd accomplished with the natives. Carl and Max went back to the mill to help with what logs were still unsawn and to stack the lumber away from the mill. The two construction men were working on a hasty enclosure around the engine, to protect it from the weather and, perhaps, to reduce some of the problems they were having with the dust and constant moisture build-up in the magneto.

The logs were sawn in a couple days and the mill shut down until conditions dried. The older men went back to the village, supposedly to rest, and the youngsters, including Carl, stayed to secure everything and to build in earnest. In a few more days, they had the basics of several more bunkhouses and a large stable, framed and standing.

Carl and Max would have to return to York for the inquiry and they both grew progressively more nervous and apprehensive. The night before their departure, they again warned the crew to be on the alert. Sentries had been placed every night since the attack on the McPherson boys and now they'd be doubly alert and well armed.

As Carl and Max headed north again toward the post and the reserve, to see and confirm, they met a single Indian coming hard and quiet, like a ghost, out of the trees where he'd concealed his ride. "Come soon! Maybe tomorrow, maybe next ... many mans, many horse, many gun ... brings can for burn! Crazy-drunk! ... bad! ... go now! We come. No run! We catch!" He turned and disappeared, almost instantly, into the trees. They turned and rode hard for the village.

Helen ran out in tears to meet them. Anastas had Alice's lathered and exhausted horse at the trough. "Oh God Carl, August's been shot! ...

Murphy's know! Sean will have a fresh horse! Go!" She handed Carl a tightly wrapped loaf of bread and he rode, wild with fear.

There was no horse ready. Carl, panicking and angry, stormed toward the house as Sean casually walked out. "What in the name a' hell ya' doin?" he raged.

"Visiting with my guest." Sean said, almost callously. "Come in fer somethin' ta eat."

"What the hell man? August could be dead!"

"Don't think so! Why don't you come in and ask 'im?"

There he sat, clean shaven, hair cut, neatly clothed, well rested and smiling. "What the hell kind of an idea for a joke is this? Should give ya' a damned good lickin'!"

"Well, the Marshal had to get me out didn't he? Carol caught me foolin' around with another woman the other night and she got mad and shot me. They rushed me to the hospital but I didn't make it. They put poor Carol in jail and then buried an empty box with me in it this afternoon. You're too late for my funeral."

"Damn! You'd think they'd find some way to let us know."

"We sent Alice! Gather she didn't tell you."

"She knows? I didn't get to see Alice. Helen said you were shot and I lit out right then."

"Damned few knew until they told Alice and sent her out to tell you guys so you wouldn't come ridin' in like fools, tippin' everybody off. She wasn't supposed to tell anyone else. Get something to eat, because you and Max got to ride to York tonight. You got to be seen plenty in the morning. He'll be here in a little while 'cause Alice'll tell 'im. I want you guys to think about me resting and all comfy while you're sweatin' it out chasin' bad guys."

"That's what ta' hell you might think! This ain't no free-lunch hotel ya' know! Got six cows need milkin' an' mother ain't goin' to feed no free-loader for nothin'," Sean joked. "Might be a busy day after tamarra, chasin' the same bad guys. Sure hope none 'a us get hurt!"

Carl ate.

"Who's Helen?"

"Why man, she's the lady that you got shot over. The one you asked in the cafe, remember?"

Max rode in, nearly as disturbed as Carl about the shocking deception. He too was just a bit upset but how else could it be done?

They rode into York late and made as big a spectacle as discretion and the hour would allow. "There's lots stirrin' at the post but the natives figure they ain't movin' until tomorrow night. It'll be then, they're sure!"

"That may well be but we got a few strange ones in town tonight." The Marshal added. "They may be part of the inquiry but I doubt it. I and some of the locals are goin' to have to keep an eye on things here. Police will be here in the morning. The word's out, is it ready up north? One thing we ain't thought about and it's awful simple, the only way across the river now, is at the bridge and there's only one a' them. Near as I know, nobody's watchin' that. You fellas can't leave until late tomorrow 'cause you have to appear. I got to set somebody to watchin' it."

"If they burn that, we can't cross either and the camp's wide open. All they have to do is that and they'd cut the lumber off until we can get another built. But they're after more than that with all the people they've got and Hugh says we've got to catch 'em red-handed," Alpert concluded.

The Marshal, the mayor, and the entire council met the train next morning and presented as much welcome and fanfare as the judge and his staff would tolerate and attention would allow. When that service had been performed and the judge met with the council to discuss the set up for the inquiry, the Marshal received a telegraph informing him that the police, paramount to the inquiry, were unavoidably detained. The inquiry would have to be on hold to allow them the time. That shocking revelation wasn't common knowledge until that afternoon, to the disgust of many of the participants. The justice and his crew were put up at The Hotel and frequented the cafe and the street for most of the afternoon and evening.

Carl and Max drifted out, separately, midafternoon and joined up at Al's before the intense ride to the village. Al and his father had ridden north early that morning, filled with a blood lust that terrified both Alice and her grandmother. A neighbour would come in and help with evening chores. The Marshal wouldn't follow until late evening, with a gruelling ride that would put him on the line at the village after midnight.

———

The village was as peaceful and tranquil as ever. People frequented the street and visited cheerily with eyes and ears glued to the northern horizon. Closer observation would have revealed that they were all women, all ferrying pots and pans to the very well-lit doughwam. There was no unusual number of horses around. The trails leading to the village had been empty most of the evening, yet by midnight, the barns bulged.

The huge piles of lumber, all cross-stacked to promote better drying, lay south of the barns and the villagers had recently taken to leaving their sleighs, wagons, vans, and racks in the same railed-in enclosure. Piles of straw had recently been placed in the intervening space but far enough away from the barns to prevent an accidental firing. To the south, the tight line of conveyance — to the north, the line of very flammable straw and then the barns, to the west, a series of closely spaced granaries, to the east, a barbed wire fence with a gate that was left tauntingly open. Any attempt at the lumber would have to pass through this gate into the lethal enclosure.

He was amongst them before any knew; as silent as a stalking cat. He'd picked out Carl and Max; the same ghost they'd met several days before. "Coming!" he stated in a whisper. In the bare light, he held up two fingers and pointed to the bridge and to the camp. Then he held up one and pointed west toward Paul's, held up the fingers on both hands and then again on one to imply a number, then pointed down to indicate here.

"Oh Lord, Paul and Mildred again!" Carl vaulted to his feet as the Indian grabbed him and pulled him back. He placed his flat hand at a low level, cupped his hands to his chest at breast level and then levelled higher up for Paul. He pointed to himself, pointed north and made the shape of an inverted "V" to indicate they'd been taken to the native settlement so they'd be safe.

All anyone could do now was sit and wait. The doughwam was doing a good job of distraction as the sounds of loud laughter, talk, and clattering dishes echoed clear to the enclosure. Singing, somewhat imbalanced feminine, filled the pallid void for some time, then died away and the clatter wound down as the figures hurried back home. The lights gradually flickered and died and only the stars, the pale, low, but promising moon, and the frog song took up the darkness and the silence.

Carl began to worry about the Marshal. He should have been there long ago. He likely saw the west group because they had to come out of the strangers at York. He'd be trying something. Carl hadn't seen Al or his dad. He hoped their anger hadn't driven them into a personal, independent, vendetta.

They heard the blowing and heaving before the hoof beat, up from the south and Sven Carlson flew into the village street in a flat-out run and skidded to a violent stop. "They're after the camp agin!" he roared carelessly. "They're skirtin' to the south a' here for the bridge. They'll cross and fire it, then hit the camp! Git over there real quick!"

The Indian clamped his hand over Carl's mouth as he saw the order on Carl's lips. "No, he bad!" He pointed toward the west. "See there!"

"Get the horses!" Carl yelled, as he raced round the stack and barn toward Sven, then dropped him with a single blow to the side of his head.

"What ta' hell ya' doin'?" The others were puzzled.

"Get back and stay! They know we're here waitin' and they're tryin' to draw us away. Alyosha, get as many of the women as can ride a horse, quick, and head 'em out to the east. The rest of ya, stay put. He's part of 'em."

A dozen horses carrying broom-wielding matrons crowned in fur caps, clattered noisily out of the village and into the darkness, only to draw to a halt a mile east and wait quietly.

"Christ man, they got Helga an' the kids! They got men at Al's an' Sean's an' Paul's too! They'll hurt 'em if we don't. They'll be waitin' at the bridge for the fellas ya sent too. They mean blood!" Sven argued frantically, straining at his bonds.

"Gag 'im. We can't risk it!" Carl couldn't question the point; there wasn't time. In the dead still immediate, they could hear the echoes of hard-ridden horses to the west and then the faint, distant clatter of gunfire from the bridge. Carl had no certain knowledge who was there; more than likely the two McPhersons. The gunfire erupted into a shuddering roll then, as suddenly, fell silent. The Indian pointed at himself several times then pointed toward the bridge and the camp. They were there waiting.

The rush drew to a sudden halt vaguely visible in the pale moonlight. Carl's hasty count turned up a possible dozen or more as the Indian had indicated. They each held a thin, pillared object aloft as a single, lurid flame fanned into a multitude across the line of pillars and the darkness shattered into violent light. The cans of kerosene clearly reflected, as they jerked them free of their saddle restraints and resumed the advance. Carl's mind convulsed instinctively. He looked at Alexsay and saw the same fear.

"They're after the houses!" Carl roared and they were all up and running for the street. "Stay under cover if you can!" Carl screamed as the stillness exploded around him.

The horsemen had nearly reached the first houses as the withering gunfire erupted. There were eighteen armed defenders and their initial fire was running and ineffectual but the shock of its magnitude took the attackers by total surprise. Torches and cans flew in every direction, igniting instantly around the riders, silhouetting and scorching them simultaneously. Before they knew the source of the gunfire and attempted a return, the second, scattered volley, more carefully delivered, all but annihilated their rank. The returning fire was wild and delivered in the throes of violent retreat. A third round was even more accurately delivered and left only three in the saddle racing out of the ring of firelight and into obscurity.

Before Carl could gain a field of better vision beyond the flames, more rapid gunfire dispelled any hope of their escape. John McPherson, hatless and wild, rode violently into the circle of light and fired two more rapid shots into two of the downed, who had cleared the flames afoot and tried to fire back.

It was over in minutes. The defenders pulled anything that survived the gunfire clear of the flames, amidst the screams of just agony, then attacked the flames before they could spread to the nearest houses.

"Out and around the buildings, look for footers!," Carl ordered. "There were supposed to be fifteen but I could only count twelve. Keep low, dark, and quiet and for God sake be careful of who you shoot at; there's women and kids hidin' out there somewhere! Sing out a warning but don't leave yourself open when ya do! Even if they answer, don't show yourself until you see 'em good. Be awful careful of the women or the bridge men comin' back in. Some of these boys are goin' to talk and if they don't, I guarantee, they'll scream!"

Riders were coming back and the sentry warning received an immediate female response. Shortly after, Al McPherson met the same encounter and gained admission. The bridge was secure but he knew nothing about the camp. He'd heard no shooting or action of any kind. Al was at the bridge himself when they came. He'd made contact with the Indian defenders so he knew they were there but he didn't know where, or how many.

When the attackers came, they rode up as casually as if there was no concern, expecting to set up their own ambush. "Thought we were too damn dumb to think of the only bridge in this whole country. I sure as hell caught 'em off guard! Even now I ain't sure how many there were but I can guarantee there ain't many now. When the Indians cut loose, I don't think it lasted more'n a few seconds. What they did to 'em I don't know and I sure don't give a damn! There was an awful lot of screamin' and hollerin'. One of the Indians came up and told me I could go; they'd finish up there. I didn't ask what he meant. We'll find out quick; it'll be daybreak soon and we'd best get back to the camp to see if anything's left there."

Carl handed the interrogation of the few remaining attackers to John McPherson and Alexsay. "Strip 'em if you have to and get every bit of information you can out of their stuff. Ask 'em nicely only once, then make it hurt as much as you have to. If they don't, there's still some kerosene left. Tie 'em to those posts before the Marshal gets here. You got any matches?" Carl made his instruction abundantly clear, within earshot of the bound and guarded prisoners. "Ain't anybody goin' to know that the fire didn't finish 'em!"

———

The bridge scene was as tranquil as nature made it. There was not a shred of evidence that a fight had taken place here a couple of hours before — no natives or horses or wounded or dead, as if nothing had happened. "Just try and prove anything!" Al was confused; he didn't know much either.

They rode up to the camp in full light, so they were visible from a great distance. With the firepower set up there, Carl was glad it was full light. Everyone was tense and excited and talked at once. They'd heard the gunfire at the bridge very clearly but couldn't hear the village encounter. There were horses swirling around much of the night and a lot of scream-ing and yelling but nothing hit the camp. They never saw a soul and were extremely worried about some surprise tactic. They'd watched the bush behind them, expecting something from there but it never came. Carl told them about the native vigilance and the fact that they'd been watching the camp all night. What had happened was anyone's guess. They'd just been preparing to send out a rider to investigate the area, to get some idea, when the three rode up.

Carl and Max went out with them and found the remaining snow swirled with insane turmoil and there was blood flecked out into it at several locations; once again, no wounded or dead.

––––––

The post swarmed. A half-dozen uniformed officers led, dragged, or carried the decrepit and wounded to the wagons; all of them cuffed or chained. No doubt they saw the party watching but none came out to question or challenge. The party skirted the post and went into the native settlement as peacefully and passively as on any normal day and drew no more attention than a few friendly waves and smiles from some of the kids.

The ghost of the previous night, walked past Carl with no hint of recognition and shoved a tight package into his pocket so neatly that only the brush of a sensation told him it had happened. All the elders would say was that all was well with the world and the gods had looked to the just deserts of everyone. They smiled, dismissed and then invited their guests to take tea with them and discuss future cooperation. The police had ridden in earlier, to ask anyone if they'd seen or heard or knew anything about the attack at the village and, of course, they could justly say they didn't. As far as any knew, nothing had happened at the bridge or the camp. Carl noted several neatly gauze-bandaged and stitched injuries. One of the elders approached Carl and asked him to thank 'her' for them, then handed him a heavy package, tightly wrapped in store-bought paper and asked him to give it to, "One Who Heals All."

––––––

Carl learned that he owed Sven Carlson an apology. Sven had been forced into his attempted ploy, because he thought they held his family and they had, but not for long. Sven's oldest, a healthy, physical specimen of fifteen years, slipped unseen, out of her bedroom window, corral-caught a horse and rode like a demon into McPherson's only minutes after the Marshal had stopped there, totally foiling the hostage attempt by his presence, before it even happened.

The Marshal didn't arrive at the village as he'd determined, because he'd encountered priorities both at York and at Sven's. The hostage attempt on the Murphy family ended a dismal and painful failure for the taker, as a consequence of action by their skilled and dangerous guest.

The Marshal, when he arrived, told Carl that the corrupt lumber tycoon had been shot dead in the street last evening, with pinpoint accuracy. People heard the shot but there were no witnesses and the Marshal smiled as he stated that he wasn't going to expend much effort on such a futile investigation.

The two officers at the village had interrogated almost everybody they could find but always under the watchful eye of the suspicious Marshal. He was clearly satisfied that these two were the genuine article. Grandpa McPherson was never singled out or questioned; he was just an angry, grandfatherly, insignificant, old man. He and Al whispered quietly off to one side and seemed to satisfy each other.

In his private discussion with the Marshal, Carl reached into his pocket to retrieve the tight little parcel the ghost had placed there and he folded back its blood-encrusted wrappings. Neither had imagined that such tactics were employed anymore. It concealed a tuft of dark hair with a bit of skin attached to it. It was a human scalp.

Justice McArthur and his former protégé buggied out that afternoon to witness the circumstance first hand. There was no inquiry to worry about because the police did indeed have a priority and McArthur wanted to see what it was. Hugh and the Marshal'd told him what was likely to happen and he'd, off the record, became a co-conspirator. "No hot-shot lawyer's going to weasel and wiggle the murdering bastards out of this one!"

He wanted to see if the Doukhobors were as primitive and uncivilized as some would have him believe and he wanted to put the York situation to bed once and for all. For now, he, Hugh, and August, were being dined as special guests at the doughwam and they were thoroughly engrossed in a conversation with Paul, Anastas, August, and Alexsay, courtesy of the prettiest translator the justice could remember.

"For backward people, some of them are sure good lookin' or haven't you noticed?" August was all eyes.

The justice and Hugh remained for the night, experienced the pleasure of a steam bath, and went back the next morning. The inquiry into the conduct of the commanding officer, out of Regina, was to go ahead as soon as possible but had to be postponed because of these actions. The judge's time was far too scheduled. He couldn't stay any longer. The Marshal had seized and locked away all the papers from the small lumber office and he and Hugh would look through the stack before anything could be disclosed. Much of it would be used in prosecuting the attackers and the rest would be used in further investigation to counter the legal "step dancing."

They all anticipated an end to the hell of the past winter. They couldn't endure much more.

XV

Co-operation and Community

He tore the wrapping off the parcel like a kid under a Christmas tree. What he really wanted to see was the picture she'd put right on top. Her beautiful hair had fully grown back and it was perfect. Just a hint of a scar showed along her cheek and it seemed to add to her genuineness. Carl knew it was there but those who didn't wouldn't even notice. She held the third finger of her left hand to emphasize her wedding band and she smiled with a love that brought tears to his eyes. "Can I have really married someone so absolutely perfect?"

They'd been asking her about terrible things happening "up there!" and she could honestly tell them very little. She lived with constant anxiety and begged Carl for any information. His telegraph, followed by the letter, would give her some assurance. He asked her to get word, as quickly as she was able, to Papa and the kids and tell them that they were all safe.

Despite her busy schedule, she'd taken a part-time job on weekends, when they needed her, at a mail order company, filling orders and modeling the clothes for the artistry and photography department. She got to wear all of the latest, finest, and most elaborate fashions and she promised to send him a copy of the catalogue with lots of her in it. She said it was a dream world but it helped fill her time and her mind and it would be something to add to their memories. She liked the extra money so she wouldn't have to take so much from her folks and Grandpa. They were having enough trouble paying the huge medical bills.

She looked prim, she looked modest, and she looked professional with her staff and her class yet she looked very far away from him. He loved the pictures but he loved her more and because he did, he'd willingly give her all the time and space that she needed or they'd both always wonder what could have been.

In spite of all she had to do, she found time particularly lonely. Her folks came down to see her every chance they got; they were finding life awfully lonely too. She was filled with hopes, dreams, plans, and the anxiety of not being there with him to get on with some of them. She'd drawn a house design and asked him about the possibilities of it, in their given circumstance. "Papa," she'd taken to calling him that too, dropped in to see her and bring her anything he could and talk to her. He too wished that he could be out "there."

"Did you know that he has already instructed me to provide him with as many grandchildren as I possibly can? He has been here with that wonderful Mary Pawlowich. She just takes over like a mother and we get along so very well. I can't help but love both of them! She told me she would just love to come out and see that big new country of ours."

Now, with Max and Alice getting married, she was doubly determined to get to him, regardless of what happened at her school or to her training. She felt an overwhelming gratitude for the degree of his understanding but she didn't say much more because she thought it would make him feel worse. He determined to keep himself busy or he'd be useless to himself and everyone else if he spent his time thinking too much.

Tucked in amongst everything else was Bertha's letter from home. Papa and Mary were going to send Carl and the boys one of the ploughs and a disk. They'd send some of the cows to help them get a start but it looked like they'd have to seed Mary's again this year. The second deal to sell seemed like it was going to fall through. The banker wasn't any kinder to anyone else then he was to Papa. He seemed to distrust anybody, old or young, without a substantial bankroll, never questioning the fact that anyone in that circumstance wouldn't need a banker at all.

They would have a great deal of difficulty putting in the crop if they sent another team, so for the time being, Carl and the boys would have to try to work around it somehow or maybe make some kind of a deal to buy another team. Papa'd need the wagons too, so that would be something else they'd have to work around.

"Let us know when Max and Alice are planning for, in plenty of time, so we can try to get there. Papa would just die and so would I if we couldn't make it. I just wish we could find a little bit more money!"

That brought tears to his eyes when he read it. He'd have to try to help them. He still had most of what he'd brought but he'd need seed and he'd have to build somehow. He knew that August had nothing, Max would need everything he had or could earn, and they all simply refused to borrow. Maybe he could hang on to a little because Milly'd need some. They needed so much to be together. He hated being dependent on her family for so many things. Despite the Marshal's assurances and willingness he wanted to stand on his own feet. In his entire life, both he and his family had never taken anything without giving in return. He felt that way towards his family too.

———

Carl had some time to spend looking and asking around for leads to another good team and a wagon. He'd need another set of harness too. A new set would be ideal but they were extremely expensive so that was out. Nothing was more irritating when there was so much work to do and old harnesses kept breaking. The livery also ran the local delivery dray around York and he was constantly dabbling in things like teams and wagons and harness. Because he was in the business to make a profit he wasn't likely to put Carl onto a good deal without capitalizing on it some way himself. Carl couldn't depend too much on anything this guy said.

Max hadn't been around long enough to gain many leads on good used stuff but he was in the best position, simply because he was the Hart Parr distributor to Western Canada. Carl turned to him to keep his eyes and ears open for all of the things that he and August would need. Other than that, there was little Carl could do but keep alert and talk to people wherever he could.

The Marshal and Hugh were busy with preparations for the hearing and he'd have to wait a bit for the trails to dry before he went back. He found the sudden lull hard to take after the furious events of the recent past and he wasn't, in the least, a relaxed person. He'd become somewhat known around York, so he had no problem striking up conversations or friendships. He met Hank and Archie again, so he asked them to keep their eyes open too. They rolled past many plots filled with new and used and they'd ask around. They assured him that they'd let him know and that for shovelling a bit of coal and time at the controls, they could get him almost anywhere in the west, for nothing more than the food he ate. He was very tempted, but again, the spirit of the land was in him and that's where he'd have to be soon.

Construction slowed to the buildings that had been started before the thaw; lumber was impossible to get from the camp. The contractor-councillor would have taken him on but the land would be ready by then and he'd need to be there. Max would have welcomed his company because he had to get out and push engines. Max's fare would be looked after but his wouldn't, so that wouldn't be making any money. He'd already picked up a few dollars shovelling coal into the tenders when the trains came in and he'd delivered a number of loads for the livery dray.

When the engine-generator rolled in, Carl helped Max drag it off the flat onto a heavy wagon and out to the prepared site. A concrete base had been poured during a warm spell. He helped set up the unit for a couple of days, learning and earning at the same time.

Instructions, sent with the engine, told them what to do to get ready for the electronic technician so Carl was again employed at unloading and digging in posts to run the lines. The ground, a foot below the surfaced, was still largely frostbound so the effort was labour intensive and time consuming.

Within a week, with the sizeable crew, the building around the engine was up, the posts down the main street were in, the engine and generator were firmly mounted and Max had started and run the engine with just about the entire town and much of the surrounding country gathered to witness and to cheer. The technician would be in within a few days and the huge, heavy, rolls of wire were lying on the station dock, waiting to be unrolled and hoisted up the poles. They could have had that done too but they weren't sure which went where. If they made a mistake, it would be awfully hard to roll it back up again and they surely didn't want to cut it if they didn't have to.

John McPherson had experienced the difficulty of handling heavy rolls of wire and had devised a reel system that he'd mounted to a wagon. He'd been working on it since the problem had presented itself, and the town provided him the material. His aptitude had gained him some notoriety and he found himself overly employed with many of the technical problems.

The town would need a way to lift the heavy wire up the poles, to be able to tighten it and provide a platform for the manpower when it was suspended. John devise a crane with a winch and a platform mounted to it, on the same wagon as the reel. The entire job could be done in one operation. Time was his enemy, so he was given as much manpower and shop equipment as he needed. The fabrication and engineering were no problem to him because he'd been party to building similar devices many years before for telegraph linesmen and he'd learned what worked and what didn't. When the technician arrived, so did McPherson's mechanical wonder and they were ready.

Alice had already begun her wifely duty to her future family's enterprise. She'd used her innate artistic ability that few, even in her own family, realized she had and she'd produced a number of special invitations that she'd mailed to the officials in the surrounding communities to attend a special event which she displayed as:

"York Enlightenment!
Turning on the lights!"

Electric lighting was paramount to the agendas of many of the mid-sized urban areas of the west. She'd gone to the council with her idea and received enthusiastic support, then she suggested that a committee of townsfolk be chosen to organize it rather than her. She'd accomplish her purpose by getting the electro-enthusiasts there to witness the event and put them in contact with her soon-to-be husband and his machinery enterprise.

Carl got Al to contact his recent father-in-law in Charles City and his oil company connections to establish a fuel and oil outlet at York that would go hand-in-hand with the coming of gasoline power. Mitch's disabilities would make the rigours of farming unlikely for him and here was an opportunity too good to pass up. Al would find himself in much the same position as Max. He was in on the ground floor and he'd have to carry the burden until Mitch was of age and capable. The boy's depend-ability, in the past, made of him a virtual guarantee for the enterprise.

Carl would very much have liked to stick around for the electronics involved because he'd like to learn a bit about it but the call of his land drew him and he had to leave. He wired all of the money he'd earned the last two weeks to Papa and Milly.

The old, dependable gang-plough sporting a new set of shears and the seven-foot disk rolled up behind the equally dependable Hank and Archie one afternoon, along with a live cargo of four very pregnant, young and healthy, heifers. Carl had taught these same, to pail feed as newborns.

Hank told Carl that he'd become somewhat "arse twisted!" with his counterparts and let them know in selective terms that common decency would have seen to it that the basic needs of the living cargo were, at least, tentatively cared for during their passage up. He'd found Carl's animals wildly hungry and nearly dropping of dehydration. Hank and Archie looked to the need immediately and the animals, somewhat revived, still showed signs of their ordeal. Carl anticipated miscarriages but fortunately the youthful animals withstood the deprivation very well.

Papa and the boys had the animals all rope-trained and they were tied, along with some equally deprived horses, all the way up, so it was a simple endeavour to rope-lead them slowly, with Alice's help, out to Al's to rest and feed-up. Carl took Paul's naked wagon back in and with Al's help and a few others, they loaded the disk aboard an improvised frame of poplar logs and chained the plough behind.

During a coal stop, Archie'd banked the fire and walked over to a wagon with a "For Sale" on it. This one was more than just a little bit better than the others he'd investigated so he'd offered the owner a ten-dollar retainer until he got the okay from Carl. Trusting his judgment, Carl gave him back his ten plus the other twenty-two required and they promised to bring it up next trip. Carl would be back soon because August wanted to file on a homestead and the York Council would be throwing on the lights by then. Carl wanted very much to be a part of that event.

———

The trip back was an all-day determination. The plough made the load considerably heavier and by the time the village appeared over the rise, it was near dusk. Both Carl and the team were wishing they'd eaten more before they left.

The villagers pulled the steamer, along with the planer-shaper, from the camp and Carl heard the high-pitched scream long before the village appeared. It was a high-energy job and August had both the youth and the energy.

Carl's arrival signalled the shutdown and supper. They hadn't seen Carl for weeks and they began to wonder what had happened to him.

Alexsay's kitchen was too small but the evening was warm, so Alexsay hung a lantern outside his door and accumulated chairs and benches for an impromptu gathering to catch up on the latest. Nobody had left the village for the last while.

The women, in particular, were very pleased with the news of Alice and Max's decision. They'd begin, almost immediately, to make plans for the event and they knew that Carl's wife and the rest of his family would be coming. There was a very great welcome to prepare.

Carl's pictures brought smiles and anticipation to many of them. Carl hadn't realized the depth of their gratitude. He had laid his life on the line for them and they'd love everything that he loved. They'd do whatever was necessary to see to it that he and his wife and the rest of his family had all of the necessities.

Carl learned, much to his satisfaction, that August and Helen were often seen, in the evening, walking together and talking for hours. Everyone quietly left them alone to allow the troubled young lady to develop her relationship with this good-looking young man of her national origin.

They spent hours with Anastas, to the joy of the old man. They'd become his hope and his closest earthly family. August's grasp of the Russian language, after so brief a stay, had surpassed Carl's by a wide margin. He was definitely serious.

Unloading the disk proved more of a challenge than driving up beside a platform and pulling it straight off. They had to build a ramp out of the heaviest planks they had, for security. One can't drop a disk from a four-foot height and expect to get away without major damage. It was noon before it sat securely on the ground. Carl would leave it at the village until he'd need it. He wanted to check it for problems before he left the village repair shop. That afternoon, he pulled the plough to his, then took the wagon and the team back to Paul's.

———

The sun had beamed gloriously for several weeks without a single swirl or flurry and the island-like yard projected out of a shallow lake. The soothing murmur of running water was a constant. In the high-bushed encircle-ment, not a single patch of wintery residual remained. It was completely dry and was already becoming a scene of greenery. Birds found its warmth a comfortable refuge from the raw spring winds and expressed their grati-tude with irrepressible harmony and a flurry of nest cleaning and building. The setting, filled with life and tranquility, pacified the frayed nerves. Paul had chosen well.

The powerful little voice echoed cheerily and barely preceded its source in a collective dash across the yard to greet his favourite chum. Jimmy had developed a distance-consuming run that put him beside the wagon as quickly as Carl rolled up to the barn. The teams and even the cow, by way of greeting, echoed a raucous disharmony and a plump fur-ball with ears, awoken from its puppy-nap, yapped its way across the yard to nose-test the interloper, then planted determinedly in Carl's path to demand his imme-diate attention.

The greeting over, Jim perched high up on Carl's shoulders, head buried to the eyes into Carl's cap and hands knotted into Carl's hair when Paul came out of the barn with two pails of oats for the livestock. "Well hello stranger. Where the heck ya' been? We thought you'd lost patience and gone back to the States. What's new? Pull the wagon over to the posts so we can throw the box back on." He didn't wait for Carl's answer. They'd talk things over later.

The home was a home again and the family was a family. Carl could sense the old familiar ease and he was relieved and glad. They were among the nicest people and the most trustworthy friends he'd ever known and he loved them dearly.

"Well, it seems the Buechler boys are snapping up the eligible girls of the community! Helen's suddenly a changed and happy girl. I don't know how you guys manage to do that to us but you surely do."

"I'm glad they're getting along so well."

"I think it's just a bit more than that. They walked over here, a day or so ago, just for somewhere to go. I tell you, if I've ever seen a young couple with their heads screwed on, they're it! It's almost embarrassing when I think about how scatterbrained I've been. It's almost like they've always been together. They're looking after each other and everybody else, just like some of the old folks. It's nice to see. … Won't be any whirlwind romance here like the rest of us. They're lettin' it grow and take its time. Would you believe that I saw them walking back with their arms around each other and her leaning her head against his shoulder? With them being together all of the time, I'll bet you, if you give them another month, he'll even kiss her!" Mildred smiled.

If anything, the house looked better. Carl liked the brighter colours. Mildred had redone the living room curtains, using what she could salvage from the old and simply adding to them, they looked just fine.

Mildred's nest egg had to be severely strained with the horribly large medical bill because Paul didn't have much left at all. There was more healthcare work in the district then she cared to mention but there was little in it because everybody was about as well off as they were. "How do you say 'no' to somebody who's sick or hurt?"

"I can tell you that I'm awfully darn lucky to have people like the Pawlowiches behind me! I'm even luckier to have the family I've got. Now there's three of us here and three more at home. I really shouldn't say that because here's home now. The luckiest and the best thing to ever happen to me is Milly. I look at this and I just have to cry! I still can't see how somebody like her can just walk up one day and smile at me and make all of this happen."

"Well now, there you go again, selling yourself short. Just because you see yourself every day in the trough water doesn't mean that everybody else sees you the same way. We're girls and we see things differently. Take it from me, you guys are the best looking things we've ever seen and I think we're the lucky ones. We're funny that way."

Carl produced the package of pictures that would be Paul's first good look at Milly. He'd only seen her fleetingly at the cafe in Charles when they passed through last fall. "Wow, have you got a good eye!"

"There ya' go! She is good looking but she's even nicer when you get to know her. Say hello to your teacher." She showed the picture to the curious boy.

"I started to say, before I got off on Milly again, that I've come back with a gang-plough and a good disk but what's more important, I've got four healthy heifers, all of 'em in calf, ready to drop in a month or so and no place to put 'em until I can get a pasture fence up. I'd ask the villagers but their cattle have all dropped calves and their corrals are crowded already. They pasture everything, except the milk cows, some distance away and with mine still carryin', I'd hate to ship them off where I can't keep an eye on 'em."

Paul wouldn't wait for Carl to finish his request. "You most certainly can! I've got pasture one heck of a lot bigger then I need yet and with mine being gone most of the time, I've got all kinds of feed. If we're short, the village has always got more than they use.

"How are things goin' with the Marshal and Hugh? I suppose you'll be hauled up on the stand. Wonder if they'll have the sense or the decency to get it over before seeding, or will they be draggin' you off the plough? Offer the judge a job, at real workin' man's wages, if he does."

Carl told him everything he knew or had heard in the two weeks he was around York but it wasn't much. Both of them were interested in the events leading up to the "Turning on of lights" but electricity and lights were nothing new to Paul or Mildred. Des Moines'd had them for some time. "Only the hicks considered kerosene a miracle of modern technology yet it's what fed and clothed Milly throughout her childhood."

Paul asked Carl to stay over to give him a hand getting the box on the wagon in the morning. Mildred had the squeaky old couch back upstairs all ready for Carl. They were expecting him back and she wouldn't have it any other way. He'd helped instil a sense of security and confidence in everyone. It didn't matter how bad things got, he always seemed to find some way to turn things around in it.

Carl was impressed when the early morning chorus woke him. The air filled with the sounds of living and the smells of fresh, revitalized, earth and the hissing, gentle, gurgle of moving water. Only all-consuming exhaustion could inspire sleep on a morning such as this. Carl heard a rooster crow and that amazed him. He'd been gone for several weeks — things changed quickly around here.

"Dada! Dada!" The little figure pulled himself to his feet on the door-frame and charged to Carl's bed. The concept of "Dad" hadn't yet associated itself with father; it just referred to a friendly man and Carl was one.

"Is he up there?"

"Yep! I guess he learned to climb stairs."

"He's learning too much. I've got to keep an eye on him twenty-five hours a day, the last little while. It scares me to think what's next."

"I guess it's all part of his heredity."

"Well don't let him try to come down on his own." She said something else he didn't hear.

"What?"

"I said I hope you have six in about five years."

They had a glorious discussion under the warming blanket. Jimmy had a distinct advantage, because he understood more of Carl then Carl did of him but Carl didn't care. When the coffee smells wafted upstairs, Carl called a halt, dressed and they made their way back down. Mildred didn't know it but Carl instructed his companion to negotiate the downward trend, backward, on hands and knees. If he was going to do it, he was going to do it as safely as he could. Carl recalled the bitter experience August had on his first try. It had taken months for him to heal. Carl kidded him about not being the same ever since.

Getting the box onto the wagon was always more of a challenge then getting it onto the sleigh. It was simply a matter of down or up. This time it was up. A large part of quality is determined by weight and the double box, built to haul grain, was of very good quality. They pulled the sleigh and box under the posted winch and hoisted the front up, crowbarred it back until the rear touched the ground, then pulled the sleigh out from under it. That was the easy part.

They lifted the front up as high as the rope block and tackle would allow, then tried to back the wagon under it with the team. They finally had to settle for close. Then they wheel-rolled it back more accurately and barred the ground end of the box over to line it, then let the front end down onto the rear wagon bunk.

Though the front was heavier, it was still a long way from teetering. When they tried to lift the back with a bar, the earthly resistance was gone and the fragile human initiative failed to keep it from backsliding down the bunk, tearing the bar out of their human grasp, nearly pinning them, until it found the earth again.

Seeing the predicament through the window, Mildred came out to show them both up and simply suggested they hook the winch to the wagon tongue and the other end to the elevated front of the box and use the mechanical advantage to pull the box down and on to the wagon.

When it worked and the box remained only to be pried on a bit farther, Mildred walked smugly back to the house and to their embarrassment said something that sounded like, "Using brain instead of back." Most of the morning had been consumed by the simplicity. She gave them an awfully good dinner though; she was her old self again.

———

Carl went back to the bush camp for a re-acquaintance with his team that afternoon, and by noon the next day, had them back. He tried dropping the plough into the ground and found frost still predominant so that wasn't an option yet. He took them back to Paul's and left them in the corral, picked up his double bit, and went back to cut a few fence posts if he could find some suitable willow stands in the low spots. Willows outlasted everything else many times.

His own didn't have that many but the parcel immediately south of his was fraught with many clumps and by the time of the late robin, he'd successfully cut, by his sketchy count, over sixty posts and he was thoroughly pleased with the hasty accomplishment. ·

He wasn't too interested in getting Paul involved in heavy labour just yet but the wagon came in handy the next morning. Both Carl and Mildred warned Paul that he wasn't going to get away with the jar of the swinging axe so he promised to load only as long as his head stayed clear. He'd still been getting frequent headaches and needed to take things with a grain of sense.

The lumber pile at the village was nearly planed through and they told Carl and Paul to haul the posts there. They'd hook the steamer to the wood saw and sharpen their posts and Carl's with much less "ax-ertion," as August put it.

Carl and Paul chose the easy way at first. They drove around the sloughs that were free enough from snow or clear of the excessive waters and cut what was within easy reach. By sundown that evening, they'd cut, loaded and hauled over two hundred, a successful day's work with little sign to the willows that anyone had even been there. Paul would likely need a couple of hundred replacements and he wanted to extend his fences around the yard to keep livestock away from the garden and the house front yard. Carl had no idea how many he'd need. He'd cut as many as he could before seeding and all the other things that took immediacy over posts. He needed to fence in the yard and have enough to pasture the cattle and horses for the summer. To make the countryside cattle-proof, it took time, money, and patience, all of which were in scarce supply.

By the time Paul and Carl had cut and hauled six-hundred posts, the planer sat forsaken and the wood saw regained celebrity. August had already finished the village post supply and started on Paul and Carl's. By the time they rolled in with their last load, he was halfway through their pile. As soon as they threw off the last one, they began loading those already sharpened.

August had become reasonably adept at hitting the blade at the right angle and soon gained a reputation as a sawyer with no mean dexterity. Most of the men were older, so their macho spirit and youthful vigour were a thing of the past. They were content to let August prove himself.

They weren't the only patrons of the enterprise. Almost the entire neighbourhood recognized and appreciated the ease and labour-saving nature of the saw, and thousands of posts passed through August's hands within the week. It would be some time before individuals accumulated the financial wherewithal to set up sawing equipment of their own. Until then, "cooperation" and "community" were the pass-codes of the time.

———

A neighbour to the north of Paul, who had successfully negotiated a small, double-box load of grain into York, indicated that the road was soft but passable. They greased the wagon wheels and Carl levelled Paul's box with oats, the first that Paul had been able to deliver since he'd harvested it.

Paul, Carl, and August had talked over the land options available and August would file on the quarter a half-mile to the south of Paul's and a mile west of Carl's so the three left as early as chores would allow, with Dan and Ben in tow. Maybe, by now, Hank and Archie had brought up the wagon and they could haul with two teams. Carl hoped the wagon was as good as Archie thought; there really wasn't time now for too many repairs.

They found the road still dangerously soft and the trip was so telling on the team that they hooked Carl's on for the last leg. It was well into the afternoon before they rolled up to the recently constructed scale, siding the rails at York, to weigh the load.

Even this was an improvement. Prior to this, all the grain had to be bagged in equal volumes to estimate the bushel weight. Getting it into the car was still a matter of, "the might of arms." Carl made short work of it and then Paul weighed the empty wagon to accurately determine the bushels.

Elevators to receive, weigh, and lift the grain to a height that allowed it to run by the force of gravity, either directly into a car, or into storage bins, were known in the eastern grain producing areas but they were just beginning to appear in the west. The weigh scale at York was only the first step in the construction of this one.

Max had already inked a deal for an engine to run this one and he was out and dealing on a number of others. The "Turning on of the Lights" event at York would bring lots of interest in the gasoline engines. Charles City was already shipping Max reams of advertising booklets and fliers to flood the Canadian west. The mechanical revolution was exploding upon them much more quickly then they'd expected and they were pressured to keep up. The plant was extremely pleased with the "first place" initiative that Max gave them in the new and vastly undeveloped Canadian prairie. As far as Max knew, there were none yet producing in Canada.

Max would soon be a frequent passenger to points further west. Within short order, he would be looking to find additional distributers and dealers because he wouldn't be able to handle it all. The country was just too big to cover alone. Carl saw him sitting on a gold mine; a wealthy Buechler. "Maybe some of it'll rub off?" he joked.

Ernie, the stationmaster, knew of no wagon yet, so Ben and Dan pulled them home. Although they were powerful, they weren't speedsters so it was well after nine when they drove into Paul's yard.

It seemed that they'd just crawled in when the birds, the rooster, and then the pup, who responded vocally to the first crow, woke them at daybreak. Carl was up and found the kettle still warm because the fire hadn't really had time to die.

Because they'd pulled the wagon up to the barn bin last night, Carl had another light load on by half-past six. It was beautifully warm and bright and he hardly felt the rapid exertion. By the time Paul was out and had the team harnessed, Carl was done.

Carl thought this country an absolute prize but Paul warned him that both the winter and the spring were very unusual and he shouldn't base any assumptions on what he'd seen so far; Paul hadn't seen anything like it either. He'd seen plenty of the normal that he cursed almost as much as the horrible.

They ate hurriedly and took a rapidly assembled lunch and a two-quarter of boiling hot tea. The Percherons, obviously a stronger team, rolled them onto the scales again, by noon. There was still no wagon; the train wouldn't be in until later that afternoon. They watered and fed the team and decided to wait a bit before heading back.

The two loads in, hardly quartered the barn bin. There were the granaries chock-full yet because it was a really good crop. The price wasn't all that good but there was lots of it. That was Paul's salvation.

The Marshal insisted they come over to the cafe and bought them a fresh coffee and Carol's favoured raisin buns. He and Hugh were more than ready for the inquiry but nothing as far as a date and time had been revealed so they were bound to York for the "when" and they were growing impatient. None of them had seen Max in a week and they didn't really know where he was. He was clearly living a sales man's dream.

The train rumbled in when they were about half way through and before they could finish, Hank walked in to announce that Carl's prize was aboard, grabbed a rapid lunch to go for the two of them and was off; they were running late. Carl suspected that he should have stopped at Al's to get the other team but the effort would have been wasted if the wagon wasn't there. They'd chain it behind until they got to Al's. It wouldn't pull any heavier than a load but they didn't want to tire the team more than they had to.

The wagon was in an excellent state of repair and it had recently been repainted a vivid green. It was altogether better for the price then Carl expected. Hank and Archie were as good as their word.

They were at Al's by half-past three and hooked Paul's team to Carl's wagon. They felt guilty about not greasing the wheels but they looked and sounded alright. Paul left with it immediately, to get home in better time. Carl waited for his team to rest, water, and feed. He followed an hour later.

Loading the next morning was doubly as exerting and Carl had to put a lot more into it. He had both filled by seven-thirty, before he ate. Paul had been bound to try it himself last night but Mildred had threatened to crack him up the other side of his head and finish him quick, without as much suffering, if he tried. His exhaustion, as much as her persuasion, altered his intent rather quickly.

The trail was drying a lot so they could load heavier but decided against it; the teams would wear too much. They needed their strength for seeding. They'd lay off a day or two to rest them before they made the next trips. They'd night over at Al's to ease up on them. Mildred had determined that she was perfectly capable of looking after what there was without their observance and she wasn't afraid of the dark anymore. The pup was proving to be an alert, extremely loud alarm and she knew how to "...handle the Winchester very well, thank-you."

———

The McPherson "wonder machine" hoisted wire and manpower off in the distance on a side street. The posts on Front, propped up rickety, homebuilt ladders, with equally rickety occupants attempting to bolt light holders to the tops with one hand, while holding desperately to the post with the other. They were clearly successful because most of the brackets were up. The wiring of the Main Street lights was just about complete and the guaranteed date of the "Turn on" would be on the 29th. The word was out and the event would, hopefully, prove a success.

Flighty and scatterbrained Alice was surprising everyone. She did all the advertising and her home-drawn stack of pamphlets went to all of the right places. She opened, with admiration, the eyes of the council and the organizing committee. Red hair fronted for a lot more than a mischievous girl.

Max rolled in on the eastbound. He'd been gone a long time and returned victorious, with an amazing battery of sales. Engines of every size, for a multitude of purposes, fell in waves before his determined advance. The pamphlets and brochures were preceding him to all the councils and grain handling cooperatives springing up all over the countryside. Alice and Max had spent the time wisely and had arranged a schedule of stops on his way to the up-and-coming center on the South Saskatchewan River.

He returned with a welcome surprise for both Carl and August; two teams of Clydesdales, young, strong, and harness-broken, as much alike as peas in a pod, complete with harnesses of moderate quality.

"Where'd you find these beauties?"

"Auction market, Bridge Town, it was right up near the tracks, so there's no way I could miss it. Teams were there by the dozens. These two were so nicely colour-matched that I couldn't help but bid on 'em. Came from some poor bugger who got killed last winter in a horse accident. Raised and broke horses for this very thing and I guess he met his match. Sure hope they ain't these. Kind of disappointed in the harnesses but they're in such demand out there, I was lucky to get these ... damn near paid as much for 'em as I had to pay for the teams.

"Had a real good time there, passing out dozens of information packages ... place was overloaded with folks, both town and country, almost like one heck of a big party. There'll be a bunch of 'em down for the 'Light Up' so I'm sure there'll be more sales then. Too bad we ain't got a running elevator set up here with an engine; I'd sell a lot more. Have to send the order in and maybe wire 'em to warn 'em they'd better get a move on! I've never in my life imagined it was possible to throw together so much in such a hurry. I'll more'n pay for these teams just at that one stop alone. Most of the towns and villages along the way had the packages Alice mailed, so they were waitin' and sure showed me a time. Need threshing and cutting equipment more'n anything, even steamers are way short. Some of 'em have to stack thresh most of the winter and everybody's so anxious about it, even the town folk. Damn, I'm tired! Seen Alice at all? Catch a ride out with you? Where's August?"

"He's back up at the village, maybe out at his place, clearing."

"He's filed? Where? Damn, I don't know what to do! I'm so much a farmer but now I'm into this line and doin' so darn well, I hate to quit. I think I'll wait a while and see what happens."

"If we can get places built, with both Papa and the boys, we could get another three together and with patents and stuff, maybe we can put together more than enough but we'll have to act quick. We're sure goin' to need machinery because it's goin' to take a lot. You're goin' to have your hands so darn full that you'll need help and maybe in some of the off months we can give you a hand there but we don't want to smear too thin. You've got all kinds of connections already and you'll have a dealership network set up, as long as the company plays fair with you but you can't trust nobody. I ain't tellin' you but I'm agreein', you are best to stay put for the time being and watch what happens. If we can pull it off, we'll have more'n enough for the near future. Then, maybe, if we have to and can put things together, we can buy more. Papa will be tickled but we know he ain't goin' to be able to take the hit for too long. We don't know yet about Bertha either. Just because she's a girl don't mean she ain't goin' to get a family and need land. We'll see what they say when they get here for your wedding."

"It'll be more then nice for the boys and Bertha. Papa's been halfway 'round the world in his life but they ain't seen nothin' yet. I'll put together a few dollars and give 'em some help too. They'll have to get back because of Mary's. We sure can't let her down after everything she's been. You know, I don't know what you think, but it seems that her and Papa are gettin' along really well and I'm just startin' to wonder. I don't know what her girl thinks but she's so far away that Mary doesn't see her much and they move around a lot. I know what Mama meant to him and nobody'll replace her in his heart but I'd like to see him with somebody in his later years. What do you think?"

"I sure ain't goin' to stand in his way. Milly thought the same as you but they'll have to decide. Maybe they ain't even thinkin'. I know where Papa is goin' to want to be but what about her? After all the suffering and work he's done, finally, toward the end of his life, I know he's goin' to want some land with just his name on it. It won't matter to him how long, just as long as it happens his dream will come true. We'll all have families of our own to center on and that'll leave him feeling out of place, I know him ... as independent as he is."

They thought of hitching one of each of the young teams with one of the old, experienced, horses but they knew that could result in confusion and probably wouldn't teach the youngsters anything but confusion. Horses, in an accustomed hitch, became creatures of habit and often reacted adversely, for a time, with a new partner and neither Paul nor Carl could afford a fight with the teams or a damaged wagon. They tied the youngsters behind as far as Al's to see how they reacted. 'A guarantee from a stranger was as good as no guarantee at all, until you checked things out.' They could fool with them at home whenever they found time with less valuable loads.

They trailed passively out to Al's, giving the boys a bit of confidence. They seemed a bit confused by their surroundings and possibly subdued because of a bit of fear and uncertainty. Handling with patience, understanding, and some hard work would take care of excessive spiritedness. Clydes, by their very nature, were not prone to hyperactivity. Like the Percherons, they were pullers not speedsters.

Carl and Paul left in good time the next morning, with the teams in tow, as passive as lambs. They rolled in to Paul's just after ten. Carl's pulled his wagon and, because of the newcomers, Paul's two-trip team stayed at Al's for a rest-over. They'd bring them next trip. Carl would have to get something fenced in a hurry because Paul's capacity would be strained with more of the Buechler livestock than the Karmady. Carl would have to pick up a bunch of barbed next trip.

He walked over to explore August's quarter and was pleased that it was at least as good as his own though it would be more difficult to break. There was a larger portion covered with bush, although it looked like all higher, water-free land.

He crossed the quarter between, to his and realized that Paul's assessment and his initial choice were both good. There were only two water-filled low spots and the run across, below his yard site, also drained from these. The dip at the roadway crossing was rather abrupt and Carl visualized its potential as a deep, water-storage basin if a dam-come-road allowance blocked the water's passage. He could build a control gate to relieve the spring rush and to prevent the potential of road damage if such a rush washed over it. He didn't want the flood held too far back unto his arable land either and a floodgate could accomplish both. Possession of the quarter to the west of his home would suit his circumstance quite well and would become a must to reduce the potential of conflict if another should acquire it and dispute his plan for water control.

He cut another fifty willow posts and piled them near their fall for pickup, then walked over to the village that evening for a brief visit. Helen, with confirmation from August, simply informed him that it was their intention, to eventually make him her brother through marriage but that they'd wait until things were settled for the family. They were together and not hundreds of miles apart like Carl and Milly, so there was no need for such desperate opportunism. They told him that they both knew that they belonged together and that was that. Just their appearance in each other's presence told him that — they didn't have to.

Carl wrote Milly again, telling her as much as he could in the limited context of a letter. He told her about August and Helen's attraction but not about their, already plans. He knew how she would hurt. Her two brothers-in-law were there with their girls and circumstance was keeping her away from the most important human being in the most important place in her life.

XVI

"York Enlightenment!"

A raw, sour wind out of the southeast blew them home. It wasn't the deathly cold of the January type yet it prodded and pushed its way around and under and through the parka and chilled to the bone. Carl and Paul both crawled off the makeshift seats and down into the semi-shelter of the four-footer boxes but it swept down and around and through almost as badly. They were very glad when the teams, sensing the impending and anticipating the warmth of barn and feed, jangled them into the yard at an impressive rate, just at sundown.

Paul found it difficult to lift himself back over the side and crawl down the wheel. Carl was a lot better and ordered him in. Barning and caring for the teams brought Carl some warmth and mobility. He decided it would be verging on insanity for him to attempt to load the last of the barned oats. They'd left that morning at daybreak. "Long enough, there's always tomorrow."

———

"Ah shoot!"

Carl woke to the sickening, all too familiar screech and the shuddering vibration of the house to the assault of the nor'wester. He stumbled down the darkened stairs to the kitchen window, once again a wall of white. He was stoking the stove when Paul and Mildred, wrapped in a Hudson Bay, stumbled in sleepily, to see what was happening.

Paul smiled at the length of the winter-weary faces. It was childish and foolish and they knew it, but it was something predictable that they had looked forward to instead of the dread each day brought for most of the winter. They all needed, desperately, to get a bit of relaxation. They hadn't laughed in months and now this. "Dammit!"

"Might just as well get used to it; it happens every year and it ain't happened this year yet. Indians say they saw the 'fighting moon, red as blood' ... a battle between winter and summer. Summer's goin' to win and winter's fightin' a losing battle but it'll put up one devil of a fight. Don't worry; spring was taken by surprise and it'll fight its way back just as quick." Paul was concerned about the animals but there was no way he was going out to barn them. It wasn't terribly cold, they'd just have to get into the shelter of the building and tough it through.

Going back to bed was useless because they were too wide awake, so Carl pulled on his smock against the cool of the warming house and cracked a half dozen eggs into the fry-pan, while Paul and Mildred went back to dress. It was futile to expect the alert little boy to sleep through the fury. By the time his parents came out again, he'd dragged himself and his blanket out and planted in Carl's lap beside the friendly stove.

Paul was right. By the time breakfast was over and the room spread with early light, the screamer had dropped to a sullen grumble and Carl could easily see the barn and the animals huddled in its lee. No longer ripped apart by the violent wind, huge, water-heavy flakes dropped hypnotically onto the ground and soon smothered it.

By noon it had stopped and the penetrating wind occasionally swirled it up. When Carl came out after a silent, brooding lunch, his spirits buoyed with the warming sun. He hitched one of the young teams to Paul's manure slide and dragged through the sloppy depths to his place, to try to accomplish something and take his mind off his ugly mood.

He paced off his yard-site to determine a more accurate location for his house and axed a bundle of light poplar pegs. He chose a corner to start from and attempted to lay out and square the house dimensions as best he could, by himself, according to Milly's plan. He'd try to give her what she wanted. With as little as he had, he surely wasn't going to restrict her imagination.

Somebody at the village must have seen him mucking around because Alexsay, with his arm wrapped against the cold, hauled both August and Anastas out with him to see what was going on. Carl welcomed their company as much as the warming tea against the frustration of his futile attempts.

Both Carl and August, fancying themselves reasonably versed in the art of construction, were absolutely amazed at the simplicity of the operation and the technical expertise of these presumably, backward people ... amazing! Three down one side, four up the other and five diagonally across made a perfectly square corner. Even a cord with five equally spaced knots would do the trick. Within a couple of hours the pattern was laid out, pegged, and twined around, ready for some spade work.

The glorious sun on the clearing horizon dropped into a spectacular sunset such as Carl and August had never seen. At this latitude, the sun angled through a far denser atmosphere and reflected its colours off the few clouds deserted by the fleeing storm. The more it passed through, the more it amplified. When this country displayed its favour, it was hard to deny. Despite the cruelty it could inflict, the beholder had to love it.

The slide tobogganed, light as a feather, over the watery remnant as the energetic young team, inspired by the afternoon's boredom, vented their frustrations in a muscle-flexing dash for Paul's and a good drink and warm feed. Carl was surrounded by beauty and anticipation, his depression totally gone. He knew Milly was happy too; he could feel it and she was thinking about him. She'd be here in July — that she'd guaranteed. Still, it was too long and it was too hard to wait. He could understand Mildred's emotion after three long, disappointment-filled years and he could understand Paul's hurt.

Carl woke from his reverie to prevent his momentum-driven propulsion into the slop, in front of the barn, by the heeling, stiff-legged, stop. He and August had more or less decided to attempt the trip into York, just for fun for a change. They were certain they'd have no trouble filling the wagon with willing passengers. The sizeable feeder that he and Paul had nailed together was heaped and he knew the Karmadys had decided the same. Nobody'd have to stay back to look to the valuable animals and miss the events at York. Water wasn't a problem; it was everywhere and filled everything. He felt good again, like he hadn't since the burdens of knowledge and adulthood had clouded childhood reason.

———

It was early and it was cool. Mildred and Paul perched on the makeshift seat with her hand on the reins of the youthful Clydes. Teams stretched ahead and behind and good-natured banter flew between. Carl and his wide-eyed little companion sat on the lower bench he'd dropped in just before they left. There was lots of room; only the back half of the box was piled high with hay. August and Helen had planned to ride along but their persuasion had enticed Anastas to come along. After Michael's funeral, he had confined himself to the village and needed some contact with the reality of the outside. They'd taken the village four-seater team-buggy and were riding somewhere up ahead.

Alexsay's arm was a constant pain, especially in the cool dampness, he and Loosha stayed back. They were no less curious but Alexsay was tortured by an astute political sensibility. Many in high places detested the Brotherhood and the Doukhobor way of life was under assault. He had found the nearly frozen, dying boy. "Why was he there?" He loathed the prospect of facing the smiling, deceitful hypocrites.

As they pulled past Carl's yard-site, the sun split the eastern horizon with an inversion of the spectacle of last evening and the bird chorus turned on well above the jangle of the trace chains and the grinding crush of the wheels. Paul's yard was an enclosed sanctuary in a storm but it restricted the spectacular sun-works and the sight amazed Mildred. She pulled the team to a stand just to view it. The teams behind drew to a silent halt and those ahead had pulled away so she clicked her chargers to a trot to close the gap. She loved it here … ever so grateful that she hadn't persisted in her stupidity and for the strength of the man she loved.

The warmth, radiating against the exposed cheek, soon banished the chill. Jimmy, once excited by the initial promise of adventure and curiosities, now lulled by the tedium of the wheels, wormed further into Carl's parka and drifted off. Rather than separate the child from his security, Carl crawled onto the hay and kept the boy sheltered. The trip held few novelties for him. The exertion of the past days, the gentle drone of the wheels, and the couple's quiet, personal conversation, lulled him as effectively.

The enormous pressure on his chest and the abrupt "Roolf!" of the ever-vigilant Duke, woke Carl. Jim woke earlier and crawled himself free. He couldn't quite negotiate the upper edge of the box, so he climbed onto Carl's exposed chest to grab the edge and survey the McPherson yard-scape. The rest of the teams rolled on by but Grandma'd left Paul with orders to stop. She knew that she and Alice would likely be grass-widowed and would need a ride, so here they were, as near to kin as Grandma could find in this country.

Carl had successfully slept his way there and felt wonderful ... no work or business or life and death urgency as every other time — he'd just relaxed. His premonition told him of a wonderful day to come instead of its usual detriment.

They'd eaten in the early morning darkness so Grandma's biscuits and bacon and jam were welcome and hurried. When they'd done and Carl and Paul finished the dishes, it was just ten o'clock.

Grandma readied herself and Alice needed Mildred's confident hair styling to finish her "look." The brash young girl whom Carl had first met, in his naked splendour, through the shower room door, was a wonder to behold. She walked up boldly and planted a huge kiss on his cheek.

"Thank you, thank you, thank you!"

"For what?"

"For walking into my life one day and changing it forever. You led me to Max, and Max to this, and I'm so happy I could bust. I just love what's happened to me because of you and your family." She'd primped and polished and stitched and sewed her way to perfection. It was, in large part, her initiative and imagination that had been the catalyst to this day's events. She and Max would be seated on the platform with all the other officials and she was absolutely thrilled and proud.

Max, who'd been gone for days, had come last night and left early this morning with Al and Mitch. He knew that Hart-Parr would be sending a delegation to the event but only yesterday had he learned that he'd be the official spokesman and he rushed back, a bundle of nerves, to put something together. Carl remembered how stage fright had consumed Max almost every time at the "Maynard School Christmas Pageant." Grandma laughed at the degree of childlike nerves that consumed the robust young man. He and Alice wrote and rewrote and scratched and changed and agonized and practiced late into the night to get it just right and even then his voice shook with the passion.

They hadn't seen Grandpa in days. He was doing what he'd done his entire life and he loved it. His instinctive problem-solutions had become an absolute necessity and his mind and knowledge had been stretched to capacity. The lights would go on — that was an absolute, in large part due to the determined direction of the experienced old man.

———

The town was abuzz! Ambassadors appeared from every home and hamlet for a hundred miles to fill every nook and cranny that could support a bed or a blanket. Carrying the visual and emotional scars of a winter of seclusion, strange, familiar faces appeared again, to re-acquaint themselves with humanity. And they were hungry; as much for the sight of a friendly face as for the taste of an apple or an orange or a sugar-sweet peppermint that they hadn't known all winter. They were obvious and out of place and laughed at the wrong times or spoke out of turn and were aware of their own awkwardness and turned or blushed shyly; their mannerisms more akin to the animals who'd been their sole companions for the past five or six months.

York had seen only a slight sprinkle of snow so tents, both real and makeshift-horse-blanket, filled the station and town plots and wherever else the railroad or the town would allow. The livery plot hosted scores of stark, skeletal wagons beside their overturned bodies. Some even supported the projecting end of a thin stovepipe and a few had emulated Carl's interim ambulance creation. Their inhabitants scurried about the necessities, self-conscious of the lingering horse aroma but it was so familiar that nobody gave a damn; they were there to enjoy themselves. Nobody had much money and didn't really care what anyone smelled like. Those who did, soon found themselves alone.

Enterprisers, those with foresight and those with claptrap opportunism, set up shop with enthusiasm to capitalize on an opportunity. The local businessmen were swamped beyond their capacity. Family, friends, and acquaintances, from the cradle to the crutch, were pressed into the fray and just couldn't meet the demand. There were thousands to feed and accommodate, the hungry and roofless were grateful for the enterprise. There wasn't an empty building or bunk or chair or table; both private and public. People opened their homes for company, for compassion, for principle and for profit. Several trains, throughout the past days, rolled in from either direction. The publicity had spread from letter to word.

The Marshal was as flustered as Carl had ever seen. In two days, his charge had magnified an explosive ten-fold, and he lacked the bodies to patrol the masses or answer the questions. Almost as soon as Carl and Paul had crawled off the wagon and tied the team to the rear wheel, he pressed them into service and gave them hasty authority "to put the pinch" on any malcontents they might happen across.

Shysters, conmen, and crap-artists, straight as a corkscrew, set up shop right alongside the impromptu food vendors and attempted to lure people to their easy, "get rich quick" schemes. The Marshal allowed only so much. Good, clean fun was one thing but fraudulent gambling was beyond his tolerance. Several of these enterprises met with a short lifespan and his invitation to leave as quickly as they came or "... decorate the inside of our jail!" He'd already found accommodation for an out of town enterpriser with a bevy of "beauteous ladies." The ladies were given an option to join their pimp or wash off the "war-paint" and wait tables or cook or sweep for a decent day's wages. "An' if that bastard tries to hurt ya', he'll wish ta' hell he'd never come!" Carl was impressed by the fact that without all the gaudy paint, they appeared to be decent, fair-looking girls and actually appeared to be grateful for the rescue.

Carl was unaccustomed to notoriety. Word of his actions in the events of the past winter gained him considerably more notice than he relished. When he appeared, he drew stares and whispers to nearbys. Some, most of whom Carl had no recollection, changed course to step directly into his path, call him, with familiarity, by name and extend a hand of greeting. A few displayed their antipathy by stepping out of his way with looks of intense hatred. The Marshal had warned both him and Paul to be very careful. "There's rats in the best a' places! They know both a' ya'. Keep a sharp eye out! There's no tellin' what hotheads are around. Ya' can't always tell by their looks."

The Marshal left August alone. Spruced and polished, nobody recognized him and that was a lot safer. One thing the criminal mind detested, above all else, was deceit. Despite the fact that it was essential to their stock and trade, they didn't like when it was employed against them. August was guilty of that.

Helen was out of her element. She'd long learned, from bitter experience, that obscurity was security. She'd modeled her clothing for this long anticipated occasion on a more conventional design. This was the closest thing to a real date that she and August ever had. Besides, she knew how August would react in her defense and she wanted to avoid that at all costs. The only evidence of her Doukhobor heritage was the embroidery on the shawl that she wore, instead, over her shoulders, displaying her beautiful hair and perfect features. Her skirt and blouse were of Doukhobor-weave but snug fitting instead of the traditional loose and yardy. Nobody took her for what she was and she was grateful.

Yet obscurity was a dream. Her exceptional good looks drew both smiles and stares from passers-by. Some of the older, pleasant women complimented her on her appearance and motivated her glowing blush. She was flattered and grateful, yet loathing; she hated the distinction. Because she now looked Anglo-Saxon in design, she was a beautiful young woman and drew their admiration. For most of her life, in her accustomed dress, she'd been a contemptible "Doukie," despised for her association rather than admired for her beauty.

Max had known that Hart-Parr would give him all the support that he'd need to capitalize on this opportunity. He didn't realize the extent until they appeared yesterday, eighteen of them, with railcar accommodations. Technicians and experts, real and rushed like Max, prepared to answer all of the questions that prospective buyers could throw at them; all equipped with leaflets, brochures and brag sheets. A large, brightly coloured tent, with pennants aflutter, appeared south of the tracks, and engines barked and sputtered in a multitude of tempos and whirled out the mechanical whine of generators and pumps and mills.

Max was acknowledged as the local authority and all were instructed to recognize his universal expertise. Carl marvelled at his calm, authoritative character and nobody noted his inexperience. Alice, with him everywhere, was cool, collected, calm and totally out of character. Clearly, Hart-Parr was impressed by what he'd done for the company in so short a time and he was their "man" out here. Carl knew it scared Max silly yet he and August were proud of him.

Most prominent was the massive, prototype, gasoline-powered, traction engine; one of the first they'd displayed, certainly in this country. Two cavernous cylinders barked out as much explosive power as some of the biggest steamers. It and the plough that followed, crowded, fully, one half of the flat. Max knew they were at it but he'd no idea of the intensive day and night marathon to get it off the drawing board and onto its wheels and into the field.

They'd harnessed to it a plough, such as none here had ever seen or imagined — eight bottoms, each shearing sixteen inches of ground, over ten feet rolled at a single pass, four passes on the half mile every hour. "That's over forty feet; a half mile long. How many teams and men would it take to do that?" This could all be done with only five or six men, no horses, no harnesses, no feed and no exhausted, aching muscles. It not only stole the show, it was the show and the talk of the entire event. It would perform this afternoon.

The town had built a good, strong, covered stage between the town office and the community hall, like they intended it to be there for a long time. They'd filled the plot with benches and all the chairs they could find and there was still lots of standing room. Light-bearing posts surrounded the entire area and tables by the dozens were stacked off to one side to make room for the chairs. Fired pits sizzled and sputtered their aromatic burdens. This was where the official ceremony was to take place that evening.

The carefully rehearsed speeching and congratulating would be done by sundown, when it was getting fairly close to dark, to make the "lighting-up" more dramatic. The hall, also wired with lights, would serve as the fallback if the weather turned bad. The local "Music Makers" as they called themselves, most of them old-folk experienced musicians, had built a platform right into the double doors of the hall main entrance. It would serve both inside and out in the event that either or both were necessary. They'd voluntarily offered to play far into the well-lit night for the dancing and barbecuing and merry-making.

The Marshal ordered Carl to the station to meet the train, greet the newcomers and "Keep an eye out." He made it sound ominous. "Besides, ya never know who ya'll meet there. Might be surprisin'."

Carl was on the platform when the monster roared past and ground to its usual screaming halt.

"Best listen, know who that is?"

"Yeah, I seen what he done ta that big, ugly bastard, up ta The Hotel last winter — one who was dirty-mouthin' that young Doukie girl."

"Quit yer damn shovin'! I sure ain't interested in makin' him mad!"

Carl was surprised and a bit hurt that his justifiable, well-intentioned actions of the past winter had generated such trepidation in the minds of so many people. He didn't think himself so threatening but they stopped and they listened to his orders so it wasn't all bad.

"Carl! Oh Heavens! Carl!"

He knew the beautiful voice before he turned, he thought he was dreaming, his heart skipped. She covered the distance before he could regain his composure and react. "Milly! Oh my goodness! M-m-m!" Her lips muffled the word and her crushing embrace nearly winded him. He laughed in the midst of the prolonged kiss and had to push himself away to get a breath. "But how...?"

"Never mind that! Just let me kiss you until I've had enough." She ran her hands up the back of his head and through his hair, knocking his hat to the platform. The hubbub diminished to universal giggle. Carl was aware that the horde brushed past, taking advantage of his indisposition.

"I know what you're about! Behave, 'cause I'm still watchin'!"

"What?" Milly asked, as if she was somehow being admonished.

"Not you, them! The Marshal made me a deputy to control this mob. God, is this really you?" He ran his hands up and down her back as if to convince himself. "How on earth did you manage this big a surprise?"

She drew her head back and stared at him in disbelief. "You mean you didn't get my telegraph? I sent it last week. Grandpa knew 'cause Dad wired him." She paused in thought. "Why, that old bugger, he picked up my telegraph and didn't tell you, did he?" She had such a beautiful smile and he'd missed it so much.

"Now I know why he sent me here and what he meant when he said that I might see somebody I know. This is, without doubt, the nicest surprise he could have pulled and I could kiss him too." He enveloped her in one massive hug and then apologized for being so rough. He waved to

Chris Hallvarson who struggled into view with a mass of luggage. "Gosh, I'd best give him a hand. Go on, git! Not you! Them! She's my wife and I ain't seen her in months."

"Ah!"

Carl had known they wouldn't be happy until they knew.

"How'd you get away?"

"Al McPherson wired Dad for some help to establish a fuel business out here. Is he Alice's Dad? Dad took it to the company and they decided to send him and Mom out to get a better picture of what was likely to happen."

"Is she here too?"

"No! When they came down and told me about it, she said I looked so down-hearted that she said I was to go instead. I tell you, I'm not a selfish brat but I'd have really been hurt if they were both here with you and I wasn't. I guess I am, a bit, when it comes to you." She leaned up and kissed him again as they walked toward Chris and the mound of luggage. "My supervising teacher and the headmaster both said I should go. I'm afraid I talk an awful lot about you all the time and I think they understood more then I realized. School is out for a week anyway and I could be back in two, to finish up and get the rest of the stuff. But I'll be back in July," she reassured, "and then you'll never get rid of me 'cause that'll be my final move boy. You'll have me forever!"

"Well, you can believe I'm sure glad you're here now. Gosh, how'm I goin' to do my job now?" he moaned. "When are you goin' back?"

"Don't worry about your job. Grandpa cooked up this surprise so he doesn't, for one minute, expect you to leave me to chase bad guys. We'll be here for only a few days, until Dad can take advantage of what's happening here now and help Al McPherson get things into place. It's goin' to be awfully short and we've got a lot of time to make up for. Are you sure you're up to it?" Carl blushed and he didn't know why. She giggled in her fashion. "Besides, there's a lot here that I want to see and know; you talk about such interesting people. Will I get to see Mildred and her man? Paul, is it? I know I'll see Alice because she's always writing me and telling me about Max and you. Will I get to meet this Helen of August's that you keep talking about? Is she really as pretty as all that?"

"Judge for yourself!" Carl nodded the handsome couple who beat them to her father and were shaking by way of introduction and re-acquaintance.

"Oooh golly, is she ever! Now I can see why your letters had me worried. She's real wow! Alice told me that she thought the girl had a crush on you," she teased. "But then, so did Alice and she said so."

"You do the nicest and most thoughtful things. I know you'd like to hear more from me but this last winter has been pure hell for everybody, especially the Doukhobors and the McPhersons. That's Al comin' up to your dad right now."

"I can see where Alice gets her build."

"Well I'll be dog-goned!" said Al. "You've got to be the new Mrs. Buechler. Carl is one heck of a guy! Why didn't he tell us you were comin'?" He wrapped her in his three-foot arms. "You're sure welcome here. I don't want to tattle but ya' know Carl's talkin' about ya' so much that even if I didn't see the pictures that he's always showin', I think I'd know you." To Chris-"I sure thank you for comin' up and giving us a start but even more, thank you for bringin' this grand young lady with you. You're sure a grand lookin' couple."

Both Milly and Carl flushed with the flattery.

August mimicked Al's performance. "Well hello! This is sure a surprise. Now we won't have to see Carl's long face all the time." Carl was always a bit uncomfortable with teasing, and his entire family took great pleasure in the art of inflicting him.

"And you have got to be Helen!" Milly reached out. "Carl wrote so much about you. Come here and let me give you a great big hug; I fully believe you're goin' to become the sister I've never had and I surely hope that's going to happen soon. It'll be nice having somebody close in the family that I can talk girl-talk to."

Helen smiled. "You're even nicer than Carl's pictures. You'll never really know just how much your words mean to me. I lost my family when I was a child and now your brother-in-law is making me a part of one, I'm so happy you're a part of it too. I've always dreamed of somebody like you and Alice. Oh gosh!" her hands went up to her cheeks and she held her flushed face in tearful disbelief. "Can this be really happening to me?"

"I know, I find it hard to believe too; everything's happening so fast. We can thank the Buechler boys for it. I think they're just as surprised as we are."

For the first time in public, bashful August kissed his equally modest girl. Both apologized and blushed fiercely, to the amusement of the family. "This is really nice, all of us together for the first time like this. We'll have to find Max and Alice and the Marshal. Where's Anastas?" Carl asked.

"Mitch took him off to see the plant and the switching house. The boy surprises me. I knew Alyosha did a lot to teach Alice but I didn't realize Mitch could speak Russian so well. I think they've even got Dad with them to explain everything," Al added.

Carl delivered a handshake to his recent father-in-law. He didn't have an opportunity until he made one. "Well this is sure one heck of a nice surprise; I sure missed her an awful lot."

"You may have just done me the biggest favour of my life; this is a huge new country with all kinds of opportunity and a big market. This is a real break! You've got some idea of how we both feel about Emily being so far away. You've given us a reason to be glad because business will bring us here often. This market is my responsibility now and Al will be my first Canadian agency. We should be able to get up to see our grandchildren once in a while. No reason for us to stay down there now; nobody there but the two of us." His remark was too sincere to be an attempt at humour.

"Where on earth are we going to night-over in all of this rush? Sure seems to be a lot of action around a place that's so new and unprepared. It looks like most of the buildings were put up in the last year or so."

"They have; people have been settled here for more than twenty years. I've been here for a good fifteen and I'm the second on my place. This ain't the first town site either. Actually, I was a mile closer to the old place. Sure made things harder for folks havin' to tear down and rebuild here. Wouldn't 'a cost the road anymore to drive through there. Big minds think in straight lines, I guess. There's my place just five miles north. Ain't enough beds for everybody but we can double-up and I've got lots a blankets and a few extra mattresses. Mother's a natural born hostess and the floors are clean, we'd sure be disappointed if nobody used 'em!" Al smiled.

"Marshal saw to it that there was a room booked. We've got a couple of young folks here who haven't seen each other since New Year's and aren't exactly anxious to host a crowd for the night." Now Chris was ribbing them and he meant this too.

"Where can we get something to eat? Wasn't much open early this morning and we didn't think to bring much. A guy's got to learn a few things about travelling into strange territory."

"The Hotel's booked for guests and so's the restaurant — you're guests, ain't ya'? So, let's go!"

They carried all of the luggage and boxes to the freight shed until they knew where to put them. Milly'd brought lots of stuff that would stay here with Carl until she returned in July with the rest of it. Carl would see to it that there was a place for it and there were walls around them; he'd promised her that.

"Well fer I'll be go ta blazes! Are you who I think ya' are?" Bill smiled. "Why ya' sure are! I reconize ya' from the pitures he's been showin' all o'er the place. That man a' yours sure done a lots a braggin' 'boutcha' an' I can see he ain't said half a' it and what he said ain't wrong. Marshal said ya' was comin'. Why didn't ya tell us b'fore?"

"He didn't tell you because he didn't know." Milly laughed and kissed Carl's cheek for all to see and the place laughed and clapped. "Gee, does everybody know who I am? I thank all of you for making me feel so welcome. I think I'm going to like it here, because I like you all already." They laughed and clapped again and then sensing that it was over, went right back to their eating and chatter.

"Hi, I'm Carol! Golly, it's a good thing you're here, because I and all the girls around, had one heck of a crush on your man. Now that I see you, I'm goin' to give up on that and I'm looking to be your friend if you'll let me. I understand you're a piano player and I'm only half of one so I'd like a few pointers from you any chance we get. Besides, I like to sing and I ain't half bad if I've got the right company."

"Why, I sure will, now that you're giving up on my man."

Carol laughed. "I'm about as engaged as anyone can get, to a wonderful fella, in case you've misunderstood. I'm really full of wind. Most people can tell but you've got to be sure over things like that. I had to explain it to Helen." She smiled at her firm and bashful friend. "I don't think she was just too sure about me and August. I have to thank August too; he encouraged Hal to put this on my finger." She displayed the thin band. "So I'm glad it happened the way it did. Got your room all ready; the Marshal booked it. So he's your grandfather and this has got to be your dad? I can see the similarity ... knew he was coming too, so that helps. Ooh! There's a big table free and it's yours. You're our responsibility now. Booked a lot of space for supper too, like for a family gathering and I can see why, so don't fill yourselves now. Is he your dad or your father-in-law?" She didn't let Chris answer. "Our raisin buns are fresh out of the oven. With this many people around, they're always fresh, so I'll recommend that. You'll have to be fed by seven because that's when the evening starts. The light-up is after eight, near dark and most of you are a part of that. We'll have you ready. Sure hope he knows how to dance!" she wondered out loud, as if to herself and delivered Carl a painful pinch on the popular cheek. She was gone as quickly as she reappeared with coffee and raisin buns, without waiting for a "yes" or a "no" on the order. Carol wasn't a grass-grower. The words came so fast that Milly hadn't a chance to respond to any of it. She didn't have to; Carol knew what Milly'd say.

"I didn't realize that frontier folks were so fun-loving. It's hard to believe that all the things you went through really happened in a place like this."

Al answered. "Oh it all happened alright and smilin' snakes are still crawlin' everywhere, otherwise the Marshal'd be here with us. He knows what to look for and believe me, he's lookin'. Man's got eyes in the back a' his head. Hearings are yet to come and Carl'll be one of the witnesses. He needs eyes in the back of his head too and so do you. You've heard about my boy Mike and even Mitch'll be carryin' it the rest a' his life. I heard about your brother and Alice told me he didn't do you too much good neither. Marshal's still havin' some trouble with the wound he's carryin', so be real careful, please! And...!" His voice began to waver and then trailed off. "Oh God, I'm sorry! I shouldn't be talkin' this now." Al smeared the tears away from his pain-filled eyes with the balls of both his hands

Milly swallowed hard for control and Chris's eyes choked back. The noise-filled room fell strangely silent; everybody'd heard and saw and knew. The sore still ran red in the close community. When a few conspicuous sneerers rose to pay their bill, the proprietor told them that they could leave his place and never return or they'd meet the business end of his shotgun.

When John McPherson walked in with his labouring grandson and Anastas, a large part of the room bowed a sharp, quick, acknowledgement, a universal sign of respect. The country knew them on sight. Milly's eyes met those of the thin, stooped, strangely dressed old man and held him. She sensed something unusual.

"Bojay moy!" He began to tremble and his eyes filled.

Helen rose quickly, went to him and spoke quietly to discover his strange affliction. He'd heard nothing about Milly's arrival so he had no opportunity to reason the connection.

Realizing her involvement, Milly rose and led Anastas to a seat beside her. His strange look never once left her face, even as he sat. He trembled visibly. "What's wrong? What have I done?"

Helen had difficulty getting a response from the old man and when she did, it was halting and interspersed with emotional tremor and hard swallowing, as if the pill was too big. His trembling hand reached into an inner shirt pocket and drew out a worn and carefully wrapped envelope. Helen drew from it a large, folded piece of paper with a precise, hand drawing of a woman in strange dress and four children of varying size. His trembling finger pointed to the smallest, a girl of no more than eight or nine. Helen's feature responded with a look of wonder and amazement.

"This is all he has left of his family. He drew it himself from his memory. He lost all of them during the tribulation. He has never shown this to anyone before. I knew of it because I'd often seen him praying for them at night when he thought I was asleep and he talks to the picture as he would to them in life." She reached the picture across the old man to Milly's hand — he made no attempt to stop them. When Milly held the drawing, he pointed to the little girl.

Here, suddenly, was this strange young woman that so strongly resembled what "Anastasia" might look like at Milly's age, had she been so fortunate as to survive. She had died in his arms, at the age of ten; the last living and the youngest of his children, beside a feeble fire in the cold and hungry Kavkaz. (Caucasian wilderness) She lies buried somewhere on Mokray Gori (Wet Mountain) hundreds of kilometers from the nearest of her brothers or sister. Nobody, not even he, now would be able to locate a one of the burial sites. That was the story of so many of his people who had survived to this shore.

After Helen's riveting account, Anastas, the first to regain himself, reached over with a neatly hemmed piece of simple cloth cut to serve as a handkerchief, for Milly to wipe her eyes. He told her and all of them, in words obscure to all but Helen and Mitchell, that this coincidence was not to be tearful but rather joy-filled. He was very glad that "Carr-roll" had come into his life and brought her to him; she was his memory renewed, come to bless his final years until he was reunited with his own. That was the most that he could wish for and far more than he'd expected, in what yet remained of this life.

———

It was a beautiful afternoon for the technological wonder. Max was a flurry of activity so Alice latched herself to Milly and Helen, to stay out of the way. The other Buechlers were in the thick of the action; they'd be part of the plough crew. The Marshal had ordered a rope barrier put up to keep human curiosity in check and everyone knew the consequence of crossing the line.

Every human being, including those from padlocked businesses in this bursting town, was there, to be among the first to behold this mechanical spectacle. Nobody had seen anything like it, even with steam power.

A large, very strong man whirled the crank over on compression and the monster took on life. A thunderous blast of fire-acrid, fume-heavy smoke, followed by a second, even more emphatic and the machine shook from stem to stern. The blasting concussions smoothed out into a regular steady dance, until it ran up to a satisfactory speed, then dropped off into intermittent fire to retain its momentum just as was the habit of the mill engine. They allowed it to bark on erratically for some time to be sure it was up in temperature to meet the coming challenge.

It cracked viciously and jumped to the command of the large clutching lever, as Max drove it forcefully forward to guarantee a solid lock and the huge drivers dug into the prairie meadow and rolled up to travel speed. Max whirled the ship-large wheel into a turn and the beast responded quickly, away from the crowd-line, toward the flag that marked the starting point. The co-operator turned open more fuel to meet the coming load. At the signal, the crew levered their plough, easily, into the spring-mellowed sod and it instantly disappeared under a smooth ribbon of rich, black, root-infested, virgin soil. By the time the shears were all in, the engine hammered a burdensome beat and the huge drive-lugs tore into the sod, ripping up a trail in their wake. The exhaust smoke, blackened with the initial exertion, drifted to a white as the technician adjusted the fuel flow to meet the requirement of the load and the beat picked up and smoothed out. The machine seemed to gain more vigour as the temperature and fuel mixtures coordinated.

Before Carl realized it, the crowds diminished in the distance and the order to set out came. Max whirled the wheel into the return flag and without stopping, the plough crew set in again. When Max whirled into the next turn, the response of the huge crowd was clearly audible over the roar of the drive gears and the engine.

They didn't stop. It took just over an hour for the large measured field to lay black and beautiful, a feat of unimaginable proportion. It would have taken eight heavy horses and four strong men several days of killing exertion to match that. It was miraculous!

———

The generator engine barked irregularly in the distance, muffled by the closure of the building. The sun went down and the visible fringes told Carl that it was nearly a match to last evening's. The greetings and the flowery speechifying was at an end. Despite the fact that everyone there had eaten less than three hours before, the aroma from the large, burdened, barbecue spits tantalized the most disciplined pallets.

Like the huge engine, Max began his words very erratically. Both Carl and August, knowing his foible, were very anxious. As he warmed up, he too smoothed out and picked up speed. The huge assembly, still in awe of the sheer power of technology, glued to his words; he was the superman of the day. He wisely didn't make a sales pitch but rather talked about the wondrous land and the promise of the future with people of such will and determination. Without that the best of technology and intentions would make any attempt to mechanize, totally useless.

"The reason that anything is built is to make our work easier. All progress is meaningless if there is no people-driven purpose behind it. Everything we do, we do to make life better. This is for you!" He waved his arm in a grandiose, stagey fashion and his finger came to a point on Mayor Alpert with his hand on the heavy, lever-like, master switch.

The engine barked angrily as it accelerated the huge generator up to speed. The technician gave the signal and the Mayor dropped the handle to the contacts. Instantly the square erupted into blinding, unaccustomed light. A prolonged "Ooooh!" exploded into a mighty cheer as the crowd roared its approval. Most of them had never seen light so vivid from the wicks of the best keroseners.

The windows of the hall erupted with the same, as the next switch fell and then the greatest miracle of all! Street by street, the dogs, the childish hide-and-seekers and the young couples, stealing a kiss in the shadows, were revealed in their compromise. Life in York would never again be as discreet. The villain could no longer conceal his intent in shadow and the innocent could now walk in safety, knowing that stealth was exposed.

By the time the huge barbeque was winding down, Milly and Mildred had circled the old town hall piano with a ring of vocal merry makers. Carol hadn't been kidding when she said she wasn't half bad. She and her Hal had been rehearsing several pieces for presentation that evening; both had gained experience and some renown with the Presbyterian church choir. The civil elements within the rugged frontier-pioneer society sang away many of the long winter evenings for enjoyment and it showed in the instant harmony.

Mildred was a clear master of the art of choral arrangement. Within fifteen minutes, she'd put together several challenging numbers to add to the merriment. Carl could carry a tune, but singing was a long way from his strong suit. He, August, and Max didn't know most of the words, but the girls made them stand in anyway and at least try or they threatened to call, publically, for their trio to sing "Three Blind Mice" as a round. None of them knew what a "round" was.

Paul, Al, and Chris contributed, as best they could, to the bass parts. Helen had a beautiful voice but her English repertoire was as lacking as the boys so she teamed with Anastas in a Russian vocal elegy that they'd often sung together publically. It meant a great deal to the old man and he put his heart and his power into it. Their harmony, from long practice, was perfection.

Chris was aware of the fact that the Marshal was a better than average tenor and with Alice and her grandparents, he pushed the Marshal into a powerful and voluminous rendition that rattled the windows. The stern-faced lawman seemed to love it and so did everyone else.

Hundreds ate and sang along and laughed and joked like they hadn't for many years, at least since they found themselves in this huge and empty country. Terror and tension, trial and tribulation fell by the way and smiles and joy prevailed.

The music makers wound themselves up as their elderly cohorts wound down. Anastas had never been part of such an event; he'd never been so accepted into the fold. They'd cheered and congratulated him on his vocal ability. Few had ever shown him anything but scorn so he came away with a refreshed view but come away he must; his age and the early morning demanded it. The McPhersons were as depleted as he so they headed home, as did most of the seniors. They hated to but they had to. Chris and the Marshal disappeared as well and a crew of the Marshal's recruits assumed the responsibility for the well-lit night.

Carl held his wife for the first time since they'd parted and pretended to dance. She didn't care as she rested her head on his shoulder, as long as he held her like she'd so often dreamed over the past months. They moved slowly, rhythmically, without really hearing anything. Carol didn't get her dance; she and her Hal were undergoing a similar emotion and were inseparable.

Helen and August were strangers to the aesthetic activity and were embarrassed until Mildred and Paul took upon their enlightenment. Paul was little more than a pretence but he pretended well. They forced the couple very closely together, like they wanted to for some time but lacked a logical, explainable reason; there were always people watching. Mildred embarrassed them further when she said they'd better get to know what each other felt like or their wedding night could be very confusing.

Carl and Milly excused themselves to the accusing smiles and left for their room. Paul, Mildred, August and Helen left for the McPhersons' and the promise of a light in the window and accommodation befitting the degree of their exhaustion, with the encouragement to be reasonably quiet.

It had been a wonderful, joy-filled day like few could remember, a necessary redemption for the flagging human spirit.

XVII

"God is with you!"

"It's so big and empty and green, I've never seen the sky so dark with ducks and geese. There must be a hundred million of 'em. It's even better then you told me. How can anything this open and natural be as miserable as you told me it was this winter?"

"Winter was cold and wild but that's to be expected. What we didn't expect was the human filth that stormed in. Hope we've seen the last of that kind!"

"And you were just lucky enough to hit it right on," Paul added. "Every other winter since I came was so damned boring, I darn near went silly. If I didn't have the village, so close, to walk over to a couple of nights a week, or the bush camp to work at, I would have. I tell you, the worst person to live alone with is yourself. But I can tell you, I'll be only too glad to be bored again. I don't want to see any more of the hell I saw this past winter for as long as I live."

They crested the rise and the outside few houses, skirting the covering bush of the village, came into view, pushing chimney smoke straight up into the dead-still, early evening air. The rest, obscured from this location, supported similar pillars, revealing its size.

The bird chorus, led by dozens of exalting robins, drowned the wheel-crunch. Milly'd heard them before but never in such a noise vacuum. She'd spent very little time anywhere but in Charles or Des Moines and the bird chorus certainly didn't flourish there.

"Oh gosh, is it always this peaceful and beautiful out here?" She winced at the stupidity of her own question.

"Hardly, so enjoy it while it's here and you have the time. Most times you're so darn busy you haven't got time."

"As close as I came? I think I'll always make time. Where's our place? Why are we turning? Are we going to the Karmady's? When will I get to see ours?" Nobody responded, they just smiled and it frustrated her.

They rounded the small, obscuring, poplar bluff and: "Well I'll be darned!" The pegs and the twined borders were replaced by huge piles of freshly dug earth, the consequence of a substantial effort.

"Joan Emily Buechler, met the makings of our new home! Neighbours must have done this the last couple of days. I was telling you about squaring it up." Carl helped her off the wagon and the questions came in a flurry as they walked the perimeter of the neatly dug foundation. Everything was so fresh that the warmed earth still steamed into the cooling evening. They'd missed the crew by a few minutes.

"Now you're standing in the living room, now the kitchen, now somewhere between the two bedrooms."

"But...?" She recognized her plan and it didn't provide for two bedrooms on the main floor.

"Well, I altered it a bit. You've seen how handy Al's washroom is, so I figure to put something in like it. Besides, you don't always want to be running up and down stairs to quiet a crying baby do you?" Milly blushed; she knew both Paul and Mildred heard.

The sky colour, flirting through the budding leaves, told Carl the light display would be short in coming. It wouldn't be as spectacular as the other evening because there weren't so many deflecting clouds but it would be better than average. He led her clear of the bush to an open view of the skyline and the exploding crimsons as the sun dropped below the horizon. "Welcome home!"

———

"Don't be too surprised at the reception you get. These folks are really looking forward to meeting you. They'll know you're here by now and they'll give you a big welcome. Some of them are horribly hurt, not at all very nice to look at. They'll need your encouragement."

August, Helen and Anastas rolled in just before dinner and caught the labouring people off guard. Several were over at Carl's and the rest were at their gardens and the machinery. This was important; this was "Carr-roll's" "Mee-lee", not just any girl — one, too, who'd felt the wrath of the demon as they had and survived. The preparations began.

There was a kinship here. There was a bond that tribulation had wrought and it was steely-hard and would last forever. The maimed, the crippled, the disfigured — they were one with her. They knew of her amazing likeness to Anastas and the wonder she had brought since yesterday. Who was this miracle? Was she a Godsend? Was she a reincarnation of little Anastasia?

"There she is, look upon her! She is such a beauty, a miracle to behold! She was badly injured by that beast, yet look how fine she is!" Their pent-up emotion went beyond anticipation. They couldn't wait for the wagon, especially those who were mobile enough. They hobbled out to meet her, as scarred, doubled, and wretched as they were. She was new, she was life, she was hope! She gave them courage because she'd fought the same impossible odds and won. She could show them how to love life again. Without hope, death was preferable.

Milly seemed innocently delighted. "They're the ones who survived, just as you did. It's you they want!" They surrounded the wagon, holding their scarred, discoloured features in their equally disfigured hands, tears streaming, all speaking emotionally, hardly audibly. "Mee-lee! Mee-lee!" Others reached up to take Milly's extended hand and kiss it.

"What should I do?" she whispered; this was completely unexpected.

Paul called upon his basic understanding of the language but they were so excited and spoke so quickly. "They consider you their salvation. Mildred healed their body, now you're here to heal their spirits. They've been talkin' to Anastas from what I gather. To them, you're a miracle come to give them renewed hope in their hour of darkness. You survived the same evil that hurt them and now they look to you for hope. They're referring to you as their redeemer. They want you to come down and walk amongst them so they can touch you and especially, so you can touch and heal them."

"But I can't understand a word. How can I show them hope?"

"That doesn't matter, just speak to them. They'll understand more than you think. You seem to have found new life and joy. They want to know how?"

"This is your doing more than mine. Without you, none of this would be happening." Before Carl could react, she was off the wagon with a dozen hands to help and he followed. They handed Mildred and "Jee-mee" down too, to walk amongst them. Paul climbed off and led the team in. Life would be good and right for them again! They knew, they'd been waiting and hoping!

The urgent preparations stopped only briefly. They had to come, they had to see, they had to greet, to touch, to hug, to kiss. They greeted Carl as warmly and thanked him repeatedly for bringing her amongst them.

The chimney over the bawnyah smoked cheerily. She'd come a long hard way, that's the least they could do for a special guest. "You're going to love this!" Carl whispered as they led her and Mildred toward it. "Better take a change of clothes."

"What?" she asked suspiciously, unsure of what was happening.

———

"That was wonderful but not as good as this morning!" she whispered warmly into Carl's ear. "Do you suppose they'd let just the two of us in there together some evening?" she teased.

"I don't see why not! They believe in love as much as we do."

August blushed and Helen couldn't suppress her humorous chuckle; they were walking close enough to overhear. Mildred, just dying to know what they'd said, was walking farther back but she was too polite to ask.

Jimmy, freshly washed, ran well ahead. Mildred wasn't sure how he'd gotten that way. Somebody'd tubbed him while she was steaming. He'd become a welcome obligation to the suffering village and the delightful little boy had grown accustomed to the universal care. Anastas took Jimmy's hand and the two gentlemanly walked to their place between his parents and the honoured guest.

Somehow, somebody had gotten a hold of the large picture Milly had sent Carl and pinned it over her seat at the guest table. Below it, a white paper covered Anastas' drawing with a square hole cut in it to expose only that portion of the hand portrait that revealed Anastasia, whose adult likeness now stood before them. Milly looked at it for a long time. Her eyes displayed her emotion.

The doughwam bulged, the room rippled with anticipation and the places at the tables filled quickly. Many weren't Doukhobor. Somebody'd ridden out and told. This time of the year was extremely busy but they'd stopped. Paul said that many of them came back and forth to visit once in a while but they'd never really gathered like this, to his recollection.

A tiny, ribboned, dark-haired girl, scrubbed and curly, wormed her way between Carl and Milly and pulled on the skirt. "You goin' be mine teacher?"

That told both of them why the entire neighbourhood was here. Milly crouched into a child-high hug. "Well I guess I am! And who are you?"

"Me Samanfa Murphy. Dats mine Mommy 'n Daddy 'n dats Jimmy, mine bruver 'n them's mine ssisers, Suzy 'n Emmy!"

"Well did you know that my name's Emily too and that lady's little boy over there, he's Jimmy?"

"Oh!" and she was off in his direction, her interest diverted to the potential of a new playmate.

Because of the crowd, the format would change. There was more than enough food; nobody came gratis. The tables were loaded with the traditional Doukhobor fare plus the interestingly new contributions of the multinational gathering. Anastas offered a prayer of thanksgiving and Carlie Carlson offered a Norwegian blessing while Sven and Helen translated for the gathering.

Milly began the meal. Guests, newcomers, and children always ate first; there wasn't enough room for all in one sitting. Before, during, or after, everyone ate the simple, solid and filling food, the fruits of their own labours.

The members of the choir ate with the first and readied themselves. Their male members, now sadly depleted, buried their painful mutations under beaming smiles and shuffled into their accustomed places. One apologized for their seeming disarray; they hadn't rehearsed as a group since before that terrible day and had only this afternoon prepared a brief presentation. They'd lost a little but they'd certainly not forgotten. They sang again of the wonders of life and the beauties of nature and friendship and love. The once powerful bass wavered and faded with the effort but stood the course and received a hearty acknowledgement for their determination.

Milly noted immediately, the reaction of gratitude from the gathering to Mildred's very emotional "Lord's Prayer." The rest of the neighbourhood hadn't heard her and even Milly was amazed by the depth of the powerful voice. The Doukhobors worshipped this ministering angel. Lives had been altered and more importantly, saved by her skilled and healing hands. Yet, like them, she was very fallible. God knew the tribulation was going to happen. He'd sent her to be their salvation.

"Now, those many gravely injured, who still breathe and struggle with their crippled lives and emotional pain, are to be given another salvation, a saviour who knows the agony they suffer because, she suffered it with them. God is good! God is just! Yet, he can take only so many into the peace and warmth of his presence, the rest he has to leave to the cold, hard cruelty of their mortality. Even here his hand of mercy prevails; he's sent Paul and Carl and Max and August to lead into the battle against the fiend and to prepare the way for these angels and now they are here. Most of the physical pain is gone and now the emotional pain will go too. The second miracle is afoot and amongst us." Their smiling faces told, already, how much less it hurt; she'd show them how.

The translation puzzled Milly; they were talking about her! She had no redeeming qualities. She didn't have any knowledge of how to help people with their emotional problems. She'd nearly lost her life and only the miracle of very good doctors, very close, had kept her from bleeding to death or dying of infection and only Carl drew her back from the brink of an emotional abyss.

"I didn't either! All I did was walk up to your bed and touch you and talk to you and fall asleep. You did the rest and I don't know what I did for you or how it happened. I know my being there helped you fight your way back. That's all they expect from you. Don't worry or think about it. Just be there and touch them and talk to them and then fall asleep peacefully and it will work. They want to see you normal because they too want to be normal. Be yourself, that's all you have to be. You too have power that you don't know about. Did you notice how they stare at your face and touch the side where you were stitched? You're beautiful again! The way they want to be!" He caressed her cheek gently, with the back off his fingers as the room watched in silence. "Tell them how you feel, just like you told me."

She did, haltingly, emotionally and quietly. She was in a totally new circumstance. It would take her a while to get used to the status they inflicted upon her and she was uneasy with it and said so.

"Do not being. Vwe knowing dat Hristos even not knowing forst vwhat could he doing. Bohu (God) giwing what to do! He syendying you! He giwing you! You giwing here awready!" He waved his gnarled, purple hand around to indicate the entire assembly. "Looking dyetty! (children) You knowing! You tyeeching! You helping awready!" The same woman who helped the shell of a once robust, middle-aged man, onto his shaky legs, now helped him slump back into his seat. He smiled as the tears rolled down his cheeks and hers.

Milly looked to Carl with an unspoken, questioning, "How?"

Helen responded before Carl could. "He's right! All these people and their culture are new to you. They rescued and raised me. I've seen them every day of my life since I was a child. Believe me when I tell you that you, all of you, have brought a very great difference into our lives; you've performed miracles! Where would we be now if none of you were here this terrible winter? From where did the burned get back their lives? From where will they get back their hope and inspiration? Where would the children of this entire community be from now on, without someone to guide and teach them? Very few people here, Doukhobor or not, can read or write. How will they prepare their children for the trials of the future without you?"

"But they have to know that I haven't got any idea what it is that they expect me to do for them. I can't perform miracles like they seem to think. I can maybe teach their kids and I can play a piano pretty well but I've never really grown a carrot or a potato by myself. How can I heal their beaten spirits? I've never really done anything without someone's help or guidance."

"And so you already have it. God is with you! We are all with you! How do you think it is that you so hurriedly met and married this man who fought so fiercely for us and now brings you to the place where you are so desperately needed at such a critical time? Did you know that just over a week ago the very same man who spoke to you, tried to take his life because it was now so useless and painful for him? Only the promise of your arrival prevented his achieving that desire and God sent you here earlier than we expected for a reason. I have never in all my years heard that man say a word in public. I didn't think he knew a word of English yet we all heard him and know what he says is the truth. Look at him now, the way he looks at you. He knows that only a miracle of circumstances saved you to be with us here today. You don't have to know or think what to do. You will be shown and you will know all when you have to."

Milly rose from her seat and made her way through the throng to the homebuilt wheel chair, enveloped the anticipating man in a warming hug, stroked his head, and lightly kissed his scar-blistered forehead. She knew exactly what to do.

The man stared with wonder, stroked her scarred cheek several times, then took both her hands in his and kissed them. Neither of them said a word as the woman, equally speechless, rose and returned Milly's hug with great enthusiasm and the brightest smile. She knew she would never have to fear for her man again. He was back, filled with life and renewed hope.

Milly returned, as bright and smiling and warm as Carl could ever hope to see. He knew that she understood and knew what her role would be. She was very important to this entire community and she was very grateful. She informed them that she would have to return to finish her training and to get all her necessities but she would be back in a few months with the rest of Carl's family for the marriage of Max and "Crasna Hallawvaya."

They already knew — that was why her presence here now was so valuable and so miraculous. It had to be divinely inspired because it was not part of the anticipated human plan. Milly had often thought that the strange series of circumstances that had brought her and Carl together so solidly and so quickly were more than just a blind quirk of chance. Was there indeed a divine destiny at work in their lives? She kissed Carl with gratitude as she sat down to a resounding cheer and yet another song of welcome.

Before the night was over, absolutely everyone would have to speak to and take the hand of this girl and none more enthusiastically than the children who would become her charges in the next few years. The Doukhobors trusted very few with the destiny of their children.

"So, what's on the agenda for tomorrow?" she asked, snuggling into the depths of the softest bed she'd ever rested in. Carl's cot at the Karmadys' was too small and sway-backed, so the Buechlers found themselves in the smothering depths of Loosha's mastery. Carl had always loved this bed and Loosha knew it. What better place to put this special couple?

"Well, first thing I'm going to do is check the disk, then we're going home and you're going to get some guidance in the art of planting those potatoes and carrots that you talked about. Love's great but we still can't live on it. Something tells me we're going to have a few mouths to feed this summer and winter too — we'd better have plenty. Now, tell me truthfully, what do you think of the place this foolish man brought you to?"

———

The hardened steel blades whispered quietly in the heavy humus rather than singing metallically as Carl was accustomed to in the work-hardened soils. Dan and Ben walked away with an ease uncommon to either of them. "This land is fantastic!"

This was his! Since God-all-mighty, he was the first to put seeds into it. Since only that same God could remember, he was the first to do this on land with only the Buechler name on it. Within the hour, Carl had an area sufficient to feed a small village double-worked and ready for their first seeds in this frontier world. It smelled so vital, fresh, and new.

Alexsay's root cellar kept them rock hard and nearly as fresh as the day they came out of the soil. Carl felt guilty about taking so many until he'd crawled down the confined space to get them and saw the huge volume that Alexsay would have to carry out come potato-harvest time. "No nyeedying!" Carl had fed their pigs and chickens several times and they surely didn't need any either.

By the time Milly had the seed packs separated and sorted and the hoes and shovels and rakes unpacked, Carl had the potatoes split with at least two good "eyes" per portion. Milly hadn't done much of it but she was anything but naive to the art of gardening. This was different; this was hers, totally and independently. She told Carl, in no uncertain terms, that the garden was to be her domain. She knew very well what to do and Carl's anticipated instruction was unnecessary. "I said I'd never done this without somebody and now I've got you. We had to eat back home too ya' know!"

He unhitched the disk and hooked to the plough. "How're we going to plant potatoes with that?" she asked.

"It's easier to show you then explain." He set the plough into the soft, fresh, soil. The Percherons pulled it easily and laid open a furrow the full length of the worked strip, starting along one side.

She walked down the row dropping potatoes at precise intervals, flat down and eyes up for faster germination. By the time he got back to the start end, she'd dropped the entire row and turned to see what his next move would be. Carl dropped the plough and governed its depth with the foot pedal. The experienced team paced along at the appropriate width to roll the first mouldboard soil over on to the planted row, covering them neatly and entirely.

"Hey! That's slick!"

He returned, holding the plough out with the foot-lift. Only his strength and youth permitted that; it was extremely heavy. Most would have levered it out. Milly waited for him at the start end. She wasn't sure what next but suspected a second pass to allow row spacing and she was absolutely right. As soon as he returned and dropped in, the team walked away and she began dropping again. By the time he returned and got more of the split potatoes carried to the start for her, she'd finished the second row

"Back home, Papa always ran the plough and we dropped 'em in. I feel guilty. You're doin' all the work." She walked over and kissed him, then smudged a dirty finger under his nose, pulled his overall's bib away and dropped a potato well down into its confines, laughing gleefully at his contorted efforts to retrieve it.

"The only problem I can see with spreading it over such a large space is that there's so much more to hoe."

"The village has a horse cultivator. It's kind of homemade but it works just fine. Paul used it all the time. I think they'll let us use it too. It takes no time at all." They stood hand in hand surveying the degree of their handiwork. ... neat, clean, big, and beautiful. The villagers had offered to roll in and do the job in short order but Milly told them that theirs too, was important and this was her first garden. She wanted to pull her own weight so she asked them to allow her that privilege. She'd be gone back in a few days and wouldn't be back until July, long after the weeds would take over. Carl would need help then, with everything else he had to do.

"What on earth are we going to do with all of these potatoes? Our postage stamp patch, back home, fed all four of us for the year."

"We haven't got 'em yet and if something should happen there's no store handy or money around to buy more because everybody here will be in the same boat. When that no-good, Lars, kicked us off, Mama lost the garden and we'd have starved if the Pawlowiches hadn't taken us in. Since then we always planted way more then we needed because there's always some poor soul goin' to need it. Back there we could always sell what was left. We did that for years. Out here, after last winter, I've come to expect the unexpected."

She kissed him again, this time without the smudge or the potato. "Got to be somebody in the family with a bit of sense. Be patient! I'm a city girl but I promise, I won't be for long."

Carl had a fire going to heat the water for tea with some extra to wash. Prim and proper or grim and grimy, it was absolutely impossible for her to be anything but beautiful. They'd laboured nonstop for three hours and Carl rode most of that yet she'd insisted on finishing the huge potato patch first. "Don't be silly! I was made for this! I love it and you! It's for 'us' now, not for 'me' anymore. I think I'm about the only newlywed who doesn't have a mad on for her in-laws. Mind you, I don't plan to live with them for the rest of our lives but I sure like them because they've shown me that they think I'm alright."

By the time Carl had the team unhitched and looked to, Milly'd found two lengthy pieces of the discarded twine and tied it together to peg-out and furrow several rows for the peas she'd poured into an old syrup tin. In a pinch Carl found syrup tins really handy. They'd often served as a cooking pot for many prairie bachelors and hard-up families in their lean days. He'd brought as many as they could spare from home.

"What's this small tin with the little holes punched in the top for? Surely it's not an emergency salt shaker!"

"No, it's for the smaller seed. They're so small that you can't spread 'em by hand so we put 'em in the shaker and shake 'em out down the row just like they were salt. You can just barely see 'em so you can tell if they're not on too heavy. It's alright to do 'em now but you can't when the wind's up or they'll just blow away. Don't make the row too deep, just so you can see some moisture."

Carl covered the last of the peas and Milly had another row ready. "Mrs. Pawlowich taught us a trick that even Papa didn't know. Seed one row of carrots and then plant one of onions and keep doing that. She said it keeps the onion maggots away and, by golly, it sure works, though I can't imagine onion maggots in this new land." They didn't have any set onions with them so they did every second row until they had enough carrots and then used the same shaker for the later seed onions in some of the inter-rows. The village had lots of small sets that they could have so they'd plant the rest after they got them.

They planted the root crops, turnips, beets and parsnips with difficulty, because the shaker holes were too small for the larger seed but Carl had nothing to make one with larger holes and he didn't want to spoil this one.

Both Helen and Loosha warned them to wait with the beans, cucumbers and corn until later when they were sure of no more frost; up here the climate was a lot different. The lessons of another's experiences in new territory were, wisely, well heeded and saved a lot of unnecessary work or disastrous losses. They were well into the planting season back in Iowa but out here, with the recent late snowstorm, they knew they were pushing their luck. Milly was desperate to do her part and Helen had promised Carl that they'd help replant if anything happened so go ahead. Helen had the foresight to start an unusually large number of tomato plants because she expected Carl would need some.

They surveyed their enormous job with pride and sat for the hot tea. The sun was beginning to drop and they hadn't stopped once. It was a long day and Milly'd been on her feet for all of it. He remembered well what had happened to him last fall when he pushed beyond common sense. Just five months ago, she lay clinging to life and Carl felt ashamed and worried. She flexed her muscles in a feigned show of stamina and laughed as she groaned her way down to an uncomfortable perch on one of the flatter stumps and pulled Carl down onto his knees beside her, with her one arm around his shoulders and the other attached to the large cup of tea. "I've felt worse after a day of absolute foolery. I can feel it but it doesn't bother me. A good wash and feed and a night's sleep and I won't even know it happened."

They were both getting hungry but they'd do a bit more. Milly went to the bush and broke off a large bundle of dry branches to mark the extremities of the garden rows in case something obliterated them or volunteer grass crept in to the new soil and had to be exterminated before the vegetables displayed themselves. Carl hooked back up to the disk and the team, idly bored most of the afternoon, leaned into it with renewed vigour.

August would be wandering past soon with one of the experienced village teams. He'd been pulling Paul's walker most of the day to try to get some of his own turned and some crop in. It was still seasonally early but Carl wanted his seeded as soon as he could, then he'd give August a hand. Max couldn't help because he was so pressed with the machinery. Besides, Al with all his acres and now only his dad to help, would need any available free time Max could find. Paul was a brute for work but his machinery was inadequate and his recent injury left him with some difficulty. He too could use some help. The village manpower was severely depleted yet Carl knew they'd do all they could. Carl wondered how all the work would get done.

The setting sun began its light show so Carl turned on the seat to wave Milly's attention to it and was alarmed by what he saw. She stood, stock still, frozen with fear! The huge, ugly beast stood not a hundred feet from her, at the skirt of the bush, as stock as she, and the two stared at each other but with very different emotions. It was the very same animal Carl had encountered in very nearly the same place last fall. He knew the animal meant her no harm but she didn't. He could well imagine her fear and he prayed she wouldn't do something to frighten the moose and prompt a hostile reaction.

Without further thought, Carl turned Dan and Ben to ease his way back and possibly drive the animal off. The creature crossed the team's line of vision and they reacted with a clamber that startled everyone. The creature caught this action and uttered an air-splitting snort that motivated all three into a desperate, fear-filled, sprint for safety, in very different directions. Carl caught Milly's blithe form flying over the rough soil in his direction as he sawed on the reins to control the normally passive team's attempt to escape the apparition. Carl wasn't sure just how he stopped them but he almost instantly became the center of salvation as they and Milly turned upon him for their defense. He couldn't tell which of the three trembled the most. He didn't see where the moose went but he must have done it just as quickly because when everybody looked over with anxious anticipation, the creature had vanished.

Milly's trembling as he held her and the teams whinnying and fearful nasal blowing subsided into wonder and question. "Is that what I think it is? It's huge! I had no idea they were so big! Where did it come from? Why is it here? Is it as dangerous as it looks?" Carl was sure the team was asking exactly the same. Milly, like Carl, had only seen pictures. The team hadn't even seen that.

"It was!" Carl responded. He didn't want to be too flippant because she was really frightened and he couldn't blame her. He was just as anxious when he'd first seen the creature. "That's the biggest moose anybody in these parts has ever seen. He's real smart and real old. I was standing just about where you were when I saw him last fall. He was heading in the opposite direction for the wintering bush, now I guess he's heading back for better summer grazing territory wherever that is. Paul tracked him all of these years and has never seen him. Here, both of us, the very first day either of us is out here and we both see him. Not too many in the village have seen him either. I guess our place is right on his path. Want to bet we see him again?"

"No I don't want to bet! I'd like to see him again but from a whole lot farther away. Cripes he scared me! I just can't stop shaking! Boy am I glad you're here! I'd have died if I was alone! Are they dangerous?"

"I don't think you were any more afraid of him then he was of you. If you had him trapped in a corner or if you looked threatening or made a move that he thought would hurt him, he'd probably attack. What you did was just about as right as you could get. He'd look at you for a while because he was curious, then he'd keep on his way. I don't know what he'd do if you were right in it. If he's anything like a buffalo, he'd like to travel in a straight line. Don't ask me why but they all seem to."

"I did what I did because I was so darned scared not because it was right. Let's go, that's enough for today. It'll take me the rest of the evening to stop shaking. Man, I don't feel tired anymore. Am I ever glad I got this chance to be a real part of our start. I'm hungry, let's go." She led his hand as he led the team off the worked land.

Alexsay had returned some time ago and was getting a bit worried about them. His arm was extremely painful this evening so Anastas had given him some of his elixir to help. After the supper and clean-up he excused himself and went to bed. The others went outside to sit the warm evening.

Within short order, many of the villagers walked over to ask how their day had been, about their plans, how they could help and all about Milly's home and family. They'd certainly love to meet her dad and hoped he'd find the time to get out and see her new home in the making. They were fascinated by this new arrival and used any excuse to be near her and get her attention; especially the children

XVIII
"Any one of ya' sons-a-bitches!"

"Where is he?"

Too much had happened to too many in her troubled life and anxiety pervaded her spirit. She'd walked clear of the village to get a better view in the direction of his place. After an hour's patient watching, she was preparing to walk over in the gathering darkness whether Carl would come with her or not, when another of the concerned watchers ran back and told her that a team and wagon was on its way out from the Karmadys'. It appeared that Paul rode alone.

"Oh Lord no! Oh Lord no! Oh Lord no!" Stumbling and flailing, her eyes streaming, instinctively, she ran to meet the wagon.

"Easy girl! Easy! He'll be alright!" Paul sawed frantically on the reins to regain control of the startled team.

August lay in the wagon box, battered and bandaged, on the old quilt. Helen threw herself, frantically, over the low tailgate, ripping her blouse and barking her forearm on the rough and splintery wood in a hasty bid to get to him.

"Oh thank God! Oh thank God! I knew something bad had happened!" she responded to August's surprise. He cradled his right arm in a hurried sling. His swollen face was blotched with bruising and a large cut ran down the side of his right cheek, the perimeter caked with dried blood and iodine.

Carl, too, scrambled over the tailgate; he'd seen Helen's reaction when he was some distance away and he ran, sick with fear. "What in God's name happened?"

"Not really sure! Unhitched the plough and was walkin' the team back. Just southeast of Paul's, the team went nuts. I heard one hellish racket, some kind 'a howling and they ran wild! Didn't want to lose them; they weren't mine. Don't know for sure what happened ... must've got tangled ... woke when Mildred was patchin' me ... hurt to beat blazes!"

"Mildred was goin' in to clean Jim up and get some supper on the go. The dog roared fit to deafen 'er and the team tore into the yard, almost crazy and draggin' August. I could see 'im workin' all day from where I was and I saw 'im goin' around the bush back to the village. A bit later Mildred came flyin out to get my help. He was out cold, all bloodied and banged up ... didn't know how serious until Mildred checked 'im. Everything moves but that's a pure miracle. Tore half his clothes off when he hit the gatepost and I don't know why he ain't dead. That was a new, heavy post and he snapped it like a matchstick! May have fractured some ribs ... sure are swollen and black and blue. Mildered'll tell better in a few days when the swelling goes down. He only just came 'round a while ago. I was goin' to leave 'im and come tell you but he wouldn't hear of it; wanted to be back here."

Carl and Paul limped August into Anastas's and got him into bed with painful difficulty. Mildred had given him something so he was practically oblivious by this time and went to sleep immediately.

Helen couldn't let go! It took them some time to convince her that her tragic past was not going to repeat itself. Anastas hauled out a stuffed mattress, then insisted she drink some of his mixture. Secure in the knowledge that August was in no real danger, Carl left while Milly bandaged Helen's arm and talked her to sleep.

Paul had returned immediately to help Mildred because one of the horses carried a serious wound that she was trying to care for as well as an upset little boy. "Wounded how? With what?" Carl went back and told Milly of his intention, shouldered the Mauser and despite his tiring day, walked over to Paul's to be certain.

The wound looked like the horse had been the one to hit the gatepost; a loose piece of skin hung from a gapping tear in the animal's left flank.

Carl returned late, after a calming talk with the Karmadys and told Milly, who sat up with Loosha, that he was reasonably sure that their encounter with the moose had been re-enacted with a much less stable team.

———

Morning brought a raw, cool drizzle. The delay irritated Milly so she buried her disappointment in good cheer. August needed some, everybody did.

"What's goin' to become of it?" he lamented. "I hoped to get at least a few acres in. Now, I can hardly move. Things were goin' so darn good too … bet I got near two acres done yesterday and now this? Dammit! How could somethin' this crazy happen? Been around horses all my life … had more than one runaway and never so much as messed up my hair. Played a game with those butchers that could have got me killed and again, not so much as a scratch. Now, when it's so darned important to me? Why?" His eyes filled with angry tears.

"Take it easy! You're young and alive. You'll heal fast. There's lots of people to help and it's still early, you'll get a lot in. Besides, I just know you'll be up and around in no time." Milly touched his forehead and felt a fever that worried her but she said nothing. She'd ask Mildred about it later. He felt better with her assurance and it gave Helen a bit of confidence. "Besides, something like this really brought Carl and me closer together and I believe it'll do the same for the two of you," she teased. "This'll give you a perfect excuse to spend the whole day together. Just do whatever you want. You'll be surprised what can happen. You guys belong together so get to it!"

Milly did what she knew the people would like and she enjoyed it too. She went from door to door looking in on as many of the injured as she could, just to ask them how they felt and what bothered them and encourage their efforts to push their limits. They were more interested in asking about her then reliving their experiences. They had to be drawn out of their pain, back into the world and others around them and Milly discovered her ability to do that. With the help of his joy-filled wife, she helped Fedya out of his wheelchair and took him for his first supported walk down the village street for all to see and greet. They were all going to miss her terribly until her return.

———

The Moose had apparently been taken as much by surprise as Milly. His enormous weight left a clear imprint of his abrupt stop and hurried retreat in the soft earth of the light brush prairie. For years he'd left the cover of the heavy bush-swamp, mosquito-live torture for the open grazing of the light-bush prairie, without a care or worry. Now, these strange, vicious, little creatures so throttled his domain that life was a constant ordeal and his aging temperament was likely growing unstable. Two such encounters in so short a time and distance, where none had been the season before, could have angered him to the point where he reacted with unnatural hostility.

Alexsay was a superior tracker. Carl shouldn't have been surprised; he'd found Michael, covered in snow, when nobody else could. Alexsay told Carl that back in the old country, he'd learned the art quickly and painfully and had suffered many near misses that so many of his family and friends had not survived. He carried the scars to prove it. It paid, many times over, to be very careful and vigilant. Obvious solutions were not always correct solutions and the experience of the winter past left him extremely suspicious. He, more than Carl, insisted on the investigation and he wanted the security of Carl's determined attitude and weapon.

After the encounter, the animal had instinctively skirted Carl's yard-site under the cover of the light scrub, then continued on a south-westerly course toward the rougher, yet unpeopled, predator-free country that would allow him some security and seclusion. They tracked his course well south of and several miles beyond August's encounter site. He'd been nowhere near. His stride was constant, until for no explainable reason, he stopped several times as if to listen or observe. Each stop held a north-westerly attention and after each stop, his gait lengthened with an apparent need to clear the area as quickly as possible. Carl's assumption had been wrong.

What, then, had startled so experienced a team to such a degree? They walked the three miles back up to Paul's for some rest and warmth, then to back-track the flight path. The heavy cloud cover was starting to crack yet the light drizzle made them cold and miserable.

They found several shreds of August's clothing, along the flight path and the marks were evident through the light brush, fortunately nothing heavier. August had been dragged for a good half-mile but what did it and from where?

The team had reacted with lightning speed. Deep gouge marks displayed the urgency of their reaction. Something must have threatened from the bush less than fifty yards away. Horses are far more alert to danger than that. Why didn't they sense something long before they were so taken? Were they familiar with the nature of whatever it was until its response terrified them?

Carl and Alexsay circled out from the site and soon discovered that August had been very fortunate. The team's flight angled up steeply toward Paul's yard and the pursuers diagonalled across to close the gap rapidly. Alexsay found there were horsemen with many lighter creatures that didn't break the surface of the sod. As the rip marks in the grass told him, Alexsay said they had clawed feet; he was sure they were large dogs. He couldn't tell how many. He'd seen the tactic in the old country used in the cruel act of human pursuit. He too had heard the dogs but in this country, thought nothing of it.

Why would they attack August and the team? Did they know who he was and what he'd done? Maybe they didn't know the country and didn't realize there was a yard so close until the large pup broke the cover of the surrounding bush with a deafening torrent of canine abuse. Why would so large a pack be intimidated by one unruly pup? Were they afraid of discovery? Hopefully the dogs had broken away and the hunters were pursuing to call them off.

They warned the Karmadys and returned to the village for horses to track the hunters and to warn other settlers.

————

Their contempt for the intelligence of these homesteaders was beyond Carl's comprehension. The retreat trailed toward the maligned post and was consumed by the traffic around it. There were only four or five horses in the corral but there wasn't time to watch right now. They circled to observe all that they could, then rode to warn the native settlement.

There they learned of a rather large number of very noisy dogs. After the attempted attack on the village, the natives watched the post constantly and refused to allow any of its frequenters anywhere near the reservation. They indicated that the horsemen and dogs had left the post several days ago, heading in a southwesterly direction and other riders had left toward the southeast between the village and the bush camp at the same time. Native scouts followed but weren't back yet.

Determined and very angry, Carl and Alexsay rode into the post compound, now half filled with sweat-flecked, saddled horses. The racket from an isolated shed told them of the dogs. Cradling the Mauser, Carl walked into the post-come-saloon to ask the direct questions of the motley proprietor and the room now filled with whiskeyed stench.

With the clash of the heavy bolt, the derision stopped and the room fell silent. Firearms propped the tables, chairs and walls but the stench froze. Carl's eyes flamed and his lip curled. "Come on, any one of ya sons-a'-bitches! I've seen this tear a hole through a railroad tie! Want to see what it'll do to you? Or maybe you'd like to have a go at him?" He acknowledged Alexsay's mass framed in the doorway with one of their kerosene cans in hand. The screaming of the attack hounds and the flicker in the darkening sky told them what he'd been about. "Or me?" Carl dropped the stock of the heavy weapon and brought his right hand over his head with such blinding speed and force that it even surprised him, then down through the crudely built table that exploded into shatter. "Come around with your guns and horses and kerosene and dogs and hurt anyone else and I can promise you that what we done to you already will seem like a Sunday picnic!"

The silence shattered with the deafening report. Glass shards and splintered wood tore out of the crude counter that served as a bar and the whiskey barrel behind it exploded its contents onto the proprietor and the nearbys. When the stench again found the courage to crawl out, the two were gone. They were scrambling for their weapons when the rifle thundered several more times and the heavy plank door splintered inward with each report.

They lost all interest in pursuit when the partially consumed kerosene can came crashing through the window. "Chorty! (devils) You vwant make borning? I giwing you borning!" To their horror, caught by the lesson taught of their own treachery, they found the remnant of the door immovable — barred from the outside.

A kerosene-soaked torch followed the can. The other window was equally dangerous with that cannon somewhere out there, so rather than burn, they busied themselves with fighting the flames while Carl and Alexsay rode securely into the darkness, away from the flames and the agonizing yelps of the perishing attack hounds. They rode without a word, each wrestling with his fear and anger. None of their actions had been studied.

The clocks read well after midnight when they rode into its anxious relief, and found the village fully alert. Hidden sentries challenged their intent to enter. The Marshal, Chris, and Max were preparing to ride out to look for them.

The riders and dogs had been heavily occupied for the last several nights. Their apparent intent was to hit hard when it hurt most. They knew who and they knew where. The Carlsons had been hit the night before last and the Murphys early yesterday morning. Both yards had been fired and the livestock driven off. Some of the outbuildings were burned but the houses were still there when the Marshal, Chris, and Max rode in. Sean Murphy was suffering serious burns and there were reports of other injuries but the Marshal didn't have time to detail. Mildred and Paul were at Murphy's now, caring for Sean.

Near as anyone knew, the attackers moved under cover; nobody'd seen or heard them until they attacked. Whether they crossed paths with August by accident or design was debatable. Paul's could have been next and then, likely the village.

"We heard nothin' until Carlson came rushin' in with his girl badly hurt. Anybody know anything about the lumber camp? What did you fellas find out? There had to be lots more. Where in hell were the rest of 'em?" the Marshal asked.

Several men were out at the camp to shut things down until after seeding and they'd just come back last night. Nothing was touched there yet and they'd seen a small group of natives that they thought were hunting. They didn't talk to any of them because they were already past the camp trail, moving slowly to the southeast, as if they were tracking something. Carl related the events of their encounter and what they'd learned from the Indians.

"Ya didn't kill any of 'em did ya?" the Marshal asked anxiously.

"Don't think so ... sure scared the blazes out of 'em though. Alexsay took good care of the dogs, roasted 'em up real good, near as I could tell and should have smoked the post pretty well too."

"Now, look, ya damned fools! Ya' never go off half-cocked like that with so many! How in hell do you know how many there were who weren't in the post? You knew from the Indians that the place was crawlin' with 'em."

Alexsay shook his head with an emphatic, "Nyet! Zasnool!" (asleep) He held up three fingers, then drove his massive fist into the palm of his injured hand to indicate just how they came by their unexpected sleep. On the prowl, the giant could be as silent as a panther yet as deadly as a raging bear.

All of the houses were well-lit yet Carl hadn't seen Milly. He knew her well enough to know that wild horses couldn't keep her anxious nature and curiosity in check. "Fella from the reserve, the one ya' call 'Ghost', came in around dark to warn 'em somethin' was up and to tell where the two of you were. All the injured and the kids are out of the village an' hidin' ... had no idea what was comin'. I ain't sure just where they are but we got the place well covered now. They'll be wet and cold and damned tired. Best find 'em and bring 'em back in. I don't think there'll be any more than what ya 'saw at the post so they should be okay tonight."

———

"Call! Call!" The little voice of recognition escaped the attempt to stifle it.

"Jimmy? Are you there, Milly?"

"Oh thank God!" she shuddered. "You alright? What in blazes is going on?"

He was nearly on top of them and didn't see a thing. It was dead black and they were well hidden; the barn lantern was feeble at best. She came out of the heavy willow scrub, well wrapped, as were they all. "We could hear lots of shooting a while ago and now, look." She pointed to the dull red glow on the underside of the heavily overcast northern sky; the post was in flames. It was too far away for them to hear his shooting. He smiled but said nothing.

Jimmy, torn once again from a peaceful sleep by the urgent plea for his parents' help, was alert enough and experienced enough to know that he was once again on the verge of his terrifying insecurity. He'd seen

Carl's image in the faint lantern glow and threw instinct to the wind. He'd squirmed himself free and dashed to the security and trust and hung to him, whimpering pathetically.

August crawled himself out of the bush, aching and extremely angry. Helen stayed with him. Anastas refused to leave his home but insisted that they go.

Gradually, the word spread and all of the others gathered around Carl, asking what Milly was the first to want to know. "Are we safe or can we expect more of last winter?" It took Carl some time and difficulty to convince them that there was no immediate danger and they could go back to their homes to rest. If the miserable creatures were after revenge, it would certainly be far from their minds now. Carl skirted Milly's question of what he meant and she was far too tired to push it.

He appeared like a bloodied apparition on the circled edge of the weak light. Carl noticed him immediately but the rest were startled. "Medicine Lady, bring! Horts bad!" The frantic man, alone and on foot, carried large, bloody wounds to the entire right side of his head, his right eyelid was torn open and the eye, not only swollen shut, was caked thick with congealed blood. Bloody scratches through his torn garments covered both his hands and arms. It took some time for the man to realize that Mildred wasn't here either. He'd already been at the Karmadys'. Carl would come now with whomever he could get to help.

The food was cold but Milly and Helen warmed it again on Anastas's stove and fed them while the others gathered what they might need. Carl and Alexsay hadn't eaten since that morning and Max, Chris and the Marshal weren't too far behind.

The Indian was extremely upset. He was suffering great pain but wouldn't allow anyone but Mildred to treat his wounds. He ate desperately, like a starving man. They'd trailed for several days with nothing but what they could find on the trail. They hadn't even gotten back to their camp when they ran into this.

———

After Carl and Alexsay had cleared the post, the horde, with their whiskeyed lustre, gave the flames the upper hand. With their blood up, they roared off toward the village, consumed by their fickle rage and bent on revenge.

The returning natives watched with misgiving. Exhausted, very hungry, and poorly armed, they had no contact with anyone from their camp or the village and wanted to avoid an encounter. Yet, knowing the consequences of inaction, in the darkness, they began a running battle with the much larger group and with their superior night ability and knowledge of the terrain, succeeded in scattering them.

Most of them were hurt but he didn't know how badly. His horse had gone down, dumping him into the tangle and then disappeared. He couldn't risk a fight, in the dark, on foot, and injured as he was, so he'd run for help. He asked for as many lanterns as they could spare. "Come suns, mans go die!"

Alexsay and several others hitched their teams to carry the injured. Anastas and Loosha would do all they could. Milly wanted desperately to come but realized that Jimmy and the terrified villagers needed her and Helen to help set up for the wounded. Both Carl and Chris didn't want her anywhere near the post; none of them knew what to expect. The Marshal would go with them while Max and Chris would stay at the village and help August set up some kind of a defense. There'd be no rest this night.

The mounted riders carried lanterns in advance of the wagons to avoid accident in the darkness. The trail-less, scrub prairie could be treacherous even in the daylight but they were inviting a bullet. Nobody knew how many rogues were scattered, half-drunken and scared deadly.

The encounter took place less than four miles from the village. The native action had indeed saved their hide and the village would do whatever they could to help them now. It was too far back to the reservation camp so they agreed to get the wounded back to the village as quickly as possible. Facilities there were a lot better for such things.

The Indian, now mounted, stopped and waved the others to do the same. They listened intently to the breathing of the horses in the deathly silence. He spoke loudly in his own language and received only the click of a rifle bolt in the near-silence. The Mauser vaulted to Carl's shoulder but the Indian pulled its muzzle down, then dismounted and broke with the circle of light for several minutes. When he returned, he half-carried one of his badly wounded partners, then waved Carl and the Marshal, with lantern in hand, to follow him to two more; one so badly wounded he couldn't move and another with a badly injured leg, likely broken, who sat with him, trying to help and protect.

Carl could hear the agonized breathing of great pain. Some distance beyond he found the dying horse. He couldn't risk dispatching it because he didn't know who was where. The stench had to be somewhere.

He sensed, more than heard, the approach and doused the light, then moved away as quietly as he could and waited. It took some time but it closed with him. He crouched with his weapon ready. He felt himself begin to tremble and he didn't know why. It was strange to him; he didn't react to fear this way but he'd never been in such an encounter in such blackness. He felt conspicuous, with absolutely no idea who or what this superior specter was. Then, except for the muffled conversation around the wounded some distance away — absolute silence. He was sure his heart was pounding loud enough to alarm the entire world. He remained in limbo for several minutes, not sure what to do, afraid that any move could well be his last.

The Indian spoke sharply from the lighted huddle and the rustle resumed around and past him, toward the light. They were from the native camp and weren't quite sure of his intent so they stopped and waited for him to show his hand. They knew exactly where he was.

Relief brought with it a strange weakness. His legs hardly lifted him, then nearly buckled again when the Ghost spoke to him from no more than several feet away. Carl smiled at the terror the stench must have felt at this encounter. He'd certainly waste no more time searching for their wounded. He hoped they'd all "go die" if the devil would have them.

"Horse bad! Me do. No bullet! You do?" The pain-wracked creature was beginning to cry out in agony.

There'd been six natives in the party and only four were accounted for. If the others were still alive, they'd be sure to be absolutely silent because they too didn't know who was where. The camp party split in the two most likely directions. If the two were hurt and could move, they'd try to get back to their camp. Carl and the Marshal each went with one of the groups; not many of the Indians were armed.

Carl was amazed at the instincts of these people in the silence and darkness. Within a matter of minutes, his group found one of the missing, unconscious, but still alive. They weren't yet out of sight of the lights as the wagons moved the others toward the village. They stayed with him while Carl went back for a wagon and lantern. Within the hour he returned with both, although the light wasn't necessary as it had dawned enough that Carl could see clearly.

The Marshal's group had a much longer, tiring ordeal. They trekked all the way back to the smouldering post and found nobody. He returned, in daylight, having learned that the one unaccounted native rode back into their camp during the night, with only a minor wound. The encampment had already dispatched trackers to hunt down the marauders and said they would take care of it if they found any.

The Marshal took pleasure in a pretence of deafness. He didn't really care; he knew their deserving destiny. The hellhole was a heap of rubble and he'd do his best to see that it stayed that way. When his horse walked him into the village, he was asleep in the saddle. In forty-odd years of law enforcement, that had never happened to him. He'd actually thought it was impossible.

Mildred and Paul were back and with the village's help, were caring for the wounded. Mildred had some difficulty convincing the Ghost that the one who refused to regain consciousness had to be taken to the hospital at York. Carl assured him that the man would die if they didn't and assured him of good treatment or he would personally deal with anyone who tried otherwise. The Marshal guaranteed it and that seemed to satisfy him. They wagoned the rest back to the native camp and Mildred promised to be back there in a few days to check and re-treat them.

Everyone was exhausted beyond rationality yet the community had to be warned. Without the post, the rogues had no refuge and could be extremely dangerous. They'd run, but they couldn't have cleared the area yet. They had to have injuries, they had to be exhausted, and they had to leave a trail.

"The Indians are takin' care of that. I gave 'em all the 30-30 shells I had on me."

Like the Marshal, Carl didn't really care.

———

"Carl!" Milly shook him and he was instantly awake. The shallow slant of sun under the window blind told him it was afternoon. "Could be more trouble. Grandpa told me to wake you."

"He go!" the Ghost spread-eagled his fingers. In their desperation, the marauders had scattered and left the tracking natives with a bit of a dilemma. "Where mans go? No find! ... horts, hungry, scare! Very bad! Hide farm place maybe horts people. Go Heals Lady place." He held up three fingers. "What can do?" He looked to the Marshal and Carl for confident enlightenment.

"Oh my good Lord!" Milly's voice trembled with shock and panic. "The Karmadys just went home."

Carl's reaction was instinctive, he whirled toward the nearest horse.

"Hold 'er boy! ... go barrel-assin' in there and you'll kill 'em sure and maybe yourself too! If they got 'em, they'll keep 'em for as long as they're protection. They can't see us comin' or they will. You know the yard and the country, how can we get close without 'em seein'?"

"The yard's all bushed in but they can still be watchin' this way. I can get up from the south, from August's ... have to go along the south edge of mine and there can't be more than a few of us either. There's lots of light scrub but it's still pretty open and they can still see ... might have to wait until dark for a lot of us to get there. Where are your fellas?"

The Ghost shrugged. They'd spread out too, to warn as many as they could in the country but the country was huge. He'd come back to warn the Karmadys and the village to stay alert but he was too late. "Go now!" He grabbed Carl's arm and indicated Alexsay. "Bring gun!" He was armed with a museum piece but nobody had any ammunition for it.

"Be awfully careful!" Her wet-stained eyes and tremulous voice told him of her fear. "And bring them back okay." He kissed Milly and trotted after the other two, already disappearing around the infringing bush south of the hay yard.

———

There wasn't a sound from the yard. Where was the alert pup? The amorous young animal had become the joy of the family. He and Jim were inseparable. The cow and the calf were wandering aimlessly away from the accustomed company of the teams and out of the pasture fence.

Carl bush-crawled in from the west where there was heavily budding foliage and the only vantage from the house was the little window in between the kitchen cupboard shelves. The toilet, the newly constructed storage shed and the woodpile offered the best cover within the circle.

There was no sign of any strange horses. Paul's and his were not in the barn corral or the pasture but they could be out at the straw pile. The wagon sat perfectly naturally, by the barn, as it always did. Paul would have driven up to the house to let Mildred and Jimmy off before going to unhitch. The split barn door was tightly closed and that warned Carl. In this weather, Paul always left the upper half open.

The yard was deceptively tranquil until the bird chorus turned to alarm, then stopped deafeningly with Carl's predator-like approach. That worried him. Surely they heard. He gained the cover of the woodpile and saw no one. He could smell the food cooking. Was everything alright? His faithfully accurate instincts told him otherwise.

He had to be sure and the only way was to look in, but how? He squirmed back to the others to tell them of his intention. He'd try the root cellar chute and he couldn't wait for dark. Anything could happen.

Alexsay and the Ghost would have to watch and create a distraction if he needed one to get across the gap from the woodpile and around the house to the chute on the east side. It was too close to the kitchen door for his liking so he might need the help. The Mauser wasn't the most delicate weapon for the crawl but that's all there was and he'd surely need it on the inside. Lord, how he hoped the Karmadys weren't hurt already.

He was dismayed by the brazen courage of the deceptively passive-looking giant of a man. Carl had expected a noisy reaction, not this! Alexsay walked as casually as on a Sunday stroll, up the lane toward the house, just as though he knew or suspected nothing. He beat with his usual vigour on the door while waving Carl over from the woodpile with only the palm of his off hand before anyone got to it.

Carl shadowed along the wall as he heard Mildred respond after an uncharacteristic delay. The third voice was harsh and certainly not Paul's.

Carl couldn't hear what it said and he didn't know what was done before the door slammed hastily shut.

Carl rounded the corner and his heart flipped until recognition kicked in. The Ghost crouched under the bedroom window. He held up one finger and then cradle-rocked his arms to indicate young child and pointed in. One of them had Jimmy.

Carl squirmed past and indicated the Ghost to hold his position. He crawled around to the chute lid. It would take time and noise to get it free and open. It was around the corner but only feet from the house door. He could hear Alexsay's big voice booming and he hoped the courageous fool wouldn't push it too far. Carl knife-splintered the wood and pried the inside catch free. He knew exactly where it was; he'd put it there.

The hinges screamed into their agonizing turn. Carl froze and listened. The noisy confrontation within continued. He slipped into the dank, earthy blackness and screamed the lid back, wriggled down the narrow passage and felt his way along to the foot of the ladder. The cellar door lurked in the shadows just inside the small, blanket-covered, heavily used pantry. Carl prayed it was clear enough for him to open and slip through. Mildred had often warned Paul about the possible consequences of his failure to replace the leather straps with proper hinges on the trapdoor. Carl hoped Paul's obligation remained derelict.

The door refused to move. Carl shoved much harder. It gave with great effort then slapped back noisily.

"Gadamm ya'! I'm warnin' ya! Next, it'll be a bullet through yer head!" Carl heard the wire blanket rings screech back shut and the heavy feet pounded their way back to the fray near the kitchen door.

"Paul!" He listened for response ... more urgent suppression, "Paul, can you slide off the door?" The only response was a gentle, almost inaudible shuffle as the bound man attempted to find the room in the confined space.

With silence above, Carl once again carefully coaxed the heavy door upward. It responded easily. Paul's work boots shot into the vertex, drove down to open it and held. Carl slithered himself through, ever so slowly, into the drear of the tiny, multi-shelved room. His bout with the root cellar darkness made visibility a guarantee. Paul, bloodied and bound, lay angled into the corner under the bottom shelves, Mildred's habit of putting things higher up was a salvation.

As Carl drew the Mauser up after him, the long, unwieldy firearm found little travel room and despite Carl's caution, prodded into the upper shelf and loosed a deafening avalanche of pottery. He had no time to contemplate a diplomatic alternative.

"Ga'bye ya' stoopert bastard!" Mildred's frantic lunge ended in a resounding slap and Carl heard her hitting the floor and Alexsay's insane roar.

The blanket, ripped clear of its wire loops, had not yet hit the floor at the report and blinding flash. The startled, hair-covered face, at the end of the muzzle, disappeared into a mass of bloody pulp and catapulted backward across the kitchen, knocking the second marauder backward and over the prostrate Mildred, into the ministering arms of the enraged giant. The crunch of snapping bone left one more and he held the child.

The bedroom window crashed and the child screamed. In the few seconds it took Carl to get around through the living room and the closed bedroom door, the scream turned into a constant wail and followed its source around the house, toward the door. The third marauder lay beneath the shattered window, gurgling blood, in the throes of terminal agony. Before Carl could get back into the kitchen, Jimmy was back in his mother's arms, terrified but unharmed. The kitchen scene would haunt Carl for the rest of his life.

Mildred and Alexsay, both splattered with gore, were at Paul and had him freed before Carl had Jimmy away from the horror and out into the yard. The Ghost had vanished again, as mysteriously as he usually appeared, this job, matter-of-factly finished.

Carl was retching violently when half the anxious village raced into the yard. Milly lifted Jimmy, now silent, free of Carl and cradled his tear-stained cheek against hers. "Are they alright?" She moved toward the door as blood- spattered Mildred burst out supporting limping and equally bloodied Paul. Alexsay was beyond description. Flakes of gelatinous gore stuck to his clothing. The tremendous muzzle blast of the heavy calibre weapon had disintegrated the marauder's skull. It was hard for the observer to comprehend the gore as impersonal. Surely, they all had to be seriously injured.

The villagers swarmed in and assumed immediate control. Although the sight was neither new nor unique to some of the veterans of the same, it was nevertheless, an initial shock. The Marshal came back out and leaned against the veranda post. Chris and Milly, alarmed at the expression on the hard and experienced face, rushed to him. "Jeez, thought I'd seen it all! ... that close? ...Ain't much head left!"

"No ya' don't!" To Milly's amazement, Carl jerked her away from the open door with uncharacteristic force. "Believe me, you don't want to remember this!" Milly had relived the horror of her own near-experience over hundreds of times, surely this could be no worse but she needed no more to haunt her.

Milly returned to look to Mildred, who leaned over the wagon wheel, trembling. Her boy was frightened but unhurt. She wasn't so sure about her battered husband, who now held her.

She'd treated the three marauders; all with wounds serious enough to make escape for them nearly impossible. She hadn't been given an opportunity to check Paul and she feared the possible consequences of a second blow to his head. She didn't know anything had happened until they'd burst through the door, dragging Paul with them. They'd been waiting in the barn.

Paul lay bound, in the pantry, all this time and she didn't even know if he was still unconscious until Alexsay got in and she heard him move. All she knew was they were going to kill Paul when she attacked. She remembered little of the fury until she regained her senses and with Alexsay's help, dragged herself free of the tangle.

Paul was bloody, but then so were she and Alexsay. Her head throbbed angrily, from the blow that had felled her but surely, not as much as his. She turned her attention to him. At the well, she cold-splashed the blood off to reduce the seeping. It wasn't the best but she wasn't going back in there to get her bags. His ear was cut through and the skin behind it torn open. It had already swollen and would need stitching as quickly as possible. The injury to his skull didn't seem serious. Other than the pain at the impact site, he seemed perfectly coherent and normal. Only time would tell her more. Carl brought her bags.

"You look awful! Best get you patched up too." Milly swabbed the side of Mildred's face and found nothing more than bruising and swelling. Mildred could tell better herself when she got to a mirror. "Better get the three of you back to the village and cleaned up, you'll more than likely be a bit uncomfortable here tonight anyway. This is awful! How can God allow such animals loose in his world? I'm beginning to wonder if any of us are ever going to see old age!"

The most diligent efforts got the blood and gore away but nothing could eliminate the stench of gunpowder and death. They'd taken the dead back to the village to ready them for a semblant Christian burial. The Marshal was the authority here and a firsthand witness to the circumstances and results; he'd complete the paperwork with Hugh's advisement.

Milly insisted that she was going to stay right here with her husband. He hadn't lived through anything close to the terror she'd experienced and she was emphatic; "Seeing it ain't near as bad as being it!"

They found the teams at the straw pile, cut free the remnant of a urine-soaked saddle that slung under the belly of one of the Buechler "greenies" and simply left them there. Carl hoped that the fool had actually tried to get on the animal's back.

The marauders had left their horses tied in the barn. They were a bit on the lighter side but they'd serve well for transportation and the lighter chores. One of the animals had a sizeable cut to the flank that probably determined the attempt on the youngster. "Looks to me that you got yourself three more horses!" was all the Marshal would say when Paul asked what to do with them. The cow and calf came willingly. No one was sure how they got to where they were; they weren't habitual escapees.

Tension and exhaustion dropped all of them into a shallow, fitful sleep and back to stark consciousness when they heard the distant, joyous bark. Carl and the Marshal were both up and out instantly and concealed to the approaching rider; the night was clear, warm and bright.

The Ghost dropped the squirming animal to its feet and followed him into the yard. Boone was unhurt. The trackers had found and recognized him wandering and confused, miles to the south, driven there by the near-miss consequences of his instinctive self-preservation. He was as much a part of the family and even Carl's love as any of the two-legged. They'd be overjoyed.

The trackers had warned most of the near community and had sent several farther afield. They hadn't found another circumstance at any, like at the Karmadys'. Most of the marauders were running to the southwest, to the rougher, unsettled terrain, with the hope of seclusion and escape. "We catch! Policemans come! You come sun for talk?" He denied the invitation to rest and food and was gone.

The Indians could easily have their way, judge, jury, and executioner. Yet, they too wanted it open and above board and like everyone in the close community, wanted to know the truth and see an end. They, like the Marshal, were extremely suspicious and wanted hidden motives revealed before the police came. The Marshal wanted to tell, not ask. He would have gone right then in his younger years but not any more.

They found sleep a lot easier now that the natural alarm was back in the yard. Nothing got in, out, or around without his ear-splitting commentary.

The Karmadys caught the three of them at breakfast and Mildred would have given them a royal feast if they'd allowed her. Both Paul and Mildred displayed the swollen consequences of the encounter but they seemed to have little serious, lasting injury. Jimmy was back to his usual, vocal self although he did explore the house and particularly the bedroom where he'd been held, before he returned to perch on Milly's lap.

Mildred packed the Marshal off with as much of everything as he'd need for several days. His parting advisement was to get on with their work, with an eye on every movement around them. He warned them to expect the police at any time and reminded Carl that both he and Paul had the responsibility of law enforcement and that authority remained in effect at his determination. Hugh had seen to its validity, so they could react whether he was there or not. He ordered Chris to lean on his employers' good graces and to "...work some of that soft muscle back into shape! You found them a big market out here, it won't hurt if you take a few more days to hammer a few more things together."

Milly smiled happily. She knew Chris had come for two reasons and one of them was to take her back. She felt instinctively cold, hard, and mean; she was no longer the demure little girl who screamed at a spider dropped on her. This was her place and these were her people. Nobody was going to drive them from it! She knew now what Carl meant and how he felt and how he could do so easily, with a clear conscience, all the terrible things he'd had to do this past winter. She'd do exactly the same. That's the way it was with them.

XIX
"Damn 'em ta hell an' their dogs an' rotten souls!"

"They hurt like hellfire!"

Sean was nearly in tears. "Had ta get 'em out! Ever seen a livin' animal burn?" The exposed hair under his hat, his lashes, and brows were burned off and his face was beet-red from the searing heat. Mildred had given him a soothing ointment that helped the burn, but amplified the lustre.

She'd unwrapped his scorched hands and looked worried; they were beginning to fester and they looked and felt hot. "These are getting worse! They could be getting infected! This is going to take everything I've got here. What have you been trying to do? You can't be using them like that and expect them not to! You're darn lucky I've got all this experience," Mildred scolded.

"You seen my place! What am I gonna do? We're havin' one hell of a time just keepin' our heads over. Thanks be ta Christ we still got the house an' none a' us are bad hurt. I gotta find them cattle or I gotta pack my bags! I been huntin' for days an' I ain't found a livin' one of 'em. Scared 'em sa bad they must'a run from here ta Hell! They're all I got an' I was sure countin' on 'em ... cows are milkin' an' what's gonna become of 'em? How 'm I gonna rebuilt with these an' no money? How 'm I gonna seed?" He held up his painful hands and choked back angry tears. "Ten years out a' our lives and nowhere else ta go! Damned near starved back East 'til we found this place! Bin hard but we were happy an' gettin' somewhere. Now they do this? Rotten buggers! I ain't never hurt 'em! What 'n Hell da they want? What's it gonna take ta stop 'em? Bloody miracle none a' us got killed!"

"Your cattle are what they want. I've read a lot about rustling back in the big cattle states. Grandpa knows a lot about such things. You've got a big herd and so have the Carlsons and why didn't they hit Paul's? Bet every other place they hit has cattle missing. If August hadn't run across them, yours would be gone too." She acknowledged the listening villagers. The small group had dropped their work and walked over when Sean rode in as agitated as they'd ever seen him. "Just who knows where the bigger cattle farms are? And you can bet that all of them owe money!" Milly's voice trembled with steely agitation.

Milly was right and they all knew it. "They went after both yours and Sven's real mean, because, you helped the Doukhobors. Bet they did most of the others too. They'd have butchered the families if they were after people. Why can't you find the cattle after all that hunting? Got to move fast, or we may never find 'em."

Alexsay scratched his incredulous head. "Findying Grand-paw! Vwe looking! Follow foot! Dough-wash ee-dyoit. "(rain's coming) He pointed out the ominous clouds on the western horizon.

"Better take plenty along. Heavens only knows where this can lead you. Grandpa won't be easy to find if he's on a trail. He'll know better by now, just what they're up to. We'd better feed you quick!" They were one step ahead of her and already on their way.

———

The yard was a chaotic shamble and sickeningly rank. Of the recently constructed barn, which had sheltered Carl for a night a few months ago, only a stinking ruin remained. A maggot-infested lump defiled the air with the stench of death; the heat of the ash made its removal impossible. A blackened, smouldering mound marked the site of the once full granary and the ash of hay and straw not consumed by the cruel winter, blackened the surface of its former location along with the rail fence which defended it.

The flames had crept along the debris and smouldered on, indefinitely, in the manure-filled corral. The railing of its west wall splintered into insane fragments and the hoof-churned surface, pattered over with the pug marks of the hounds, screamed the desperate escape path.

Sparks or burning debris had propelled the flames to within inches of the front wall and the turmoil, clearly visible, displayed the valiant effort of the family to salvage their home. The shattered, blanket-covered windows and the bullet-pocked wall marked Sean's determined battle line as he had crouched in his front yard and levered round after round into the fire, smoke and chaos of his farmyard. They could have all become maggot-infested lumps if he hadn't.

"Ain't seen Dad for three days, since he went after the rest a' the cattle." Twelve-year-old Jim staggered into the yard under a load of wire and tools, soot-blackened, yet triumphant in his attempt to re-establish confinement of the few head he'd found and herded back. "Mom'n the kids are in the house 'er garden somewhere ... ain't seen 'em all day." The words came haltingly and fearfully at first. He wasn't sure of anybody anymore but he knew Carl and Alexsay. His bloodshot eyes, sunken cheeks and haggard dishevel displayed the stress, desperation and fear of the past several days. Either the boy or his mother had stood sleepless guard every night since Sean left so the others could rest safely.

"He's alright!" Chris assured. "Down at the village 'cause his hands are hurtin' so bad. Mrs. Karmady wants to keep an eye on 'em to be sure they aren't infected. He'll be back, maybe tomorrow. You aren't goin' to have to be afraid no more. We'll find your cattle and bring 'em back. Can't help my boy or Al's, but as long as I'm alive and can do somethin' about it, it ain't goin' to happen again."

———

Fifty-two terrified animals, driven by the dogs over the light-brush prairie, left a swath that a blind man could follow. Alexsay insisted on finding the Marshal and the trackers, hoping to avoid needless duplication or a confrontation with any of the rustlers and maybe getting somebody hurt or killed. He followed for only as long as it took him to get a sense of direction. Sean had tracked until the trail deteriorated into a maze.

Their pace had obviously tempered to a casual walk and the herd began to spread and wander, grazing after their forced run and maybe mixing with other herds. Obviously, the rustlers left the cattle to wander in the unfamiliar country, likely hoping to round them up later, then headed off to steal more.

Alexsay followed a heavy drag-trail, flecked out with animal hair and blood-smear, into a densely brushed ravine, then nosed his way to the hide fragments and the skull, spine still attached. The remnant of the camp-fire, the bone fragments and the charred sticks told of the slaughter and feast. The fire had escaped its feeble boundary and smouldered through the heavy humus until the damp, sun-deprived interior smothered it. The blackened ash, swirled off by the breeze, left the site print-clear and obvious. The riders and hounds then headed northeast toward the village and the encounter site with August. There was no point in reviewing that, so Alexsay led the four of them west in the hope of crossing the trails of the Indian trackers or the Marshal.

Cattle tracks came and went at will but the over-riding horses ran one way; the rustlers were running for cover and escape, oblivious to their former ambition. The Indian trackers had been over-run, so Alexsay couldn't distinguish. They were heading for the rough, hilly country miles to the south and west.

———

Consuming darkness was the least of Alexsay's frustrations. They were now in a wilderness maze so fraught with jigsaw frenzy that he had no idea of trail, track, or purpose, and the rain began to fall. He led them off the barchan, into its lee, and away from the howling wind. The slope and the dense, well-leafed vegetation deflected the force of the driven rain but showered a soaking mist down through. Paul secured the horses as close to the lee as possible, to avoid the back-swirl and afford the most protection in the rain vacuum. The wind ripped most of it over the top.

Alexsay hunted a strong, light, dead-fall and had crutched it across two close, heavy tree branches of nearly equivalent height, then packed or pulled the underbrush and draped the horse blankets along its length. Carl tented it out and secured the corners of each with heavy stones and more deadfall. Alexsay snapped off sizeable, well-leafed, branches, that only his stature made matter-of-fact and propped them into the windward open end to deflect the blow-through. Max and Chris hauled everything there was room for under the shelter, while Carl hunted for anything he could prop against the ridge-pole, under the blankets, to reduce the snap and flutter that worked the ends of the blankets free of the pinning rocks. They crawled into the low, dark, interior, as wet as ship rats.

A fire would be made to order but was as impractical as it was unlikely in the saturated environment. They hauled out, each from his own, whatever the women had packed and pooled their resources ... bread, perashky, cheese, hardboiled eggs, even a dozen cold, baked potatoes. Hot would have been better but the honey-sweet tea, carried under the mackinaw, stayed luke, and worked better than cold rain water.

Darkness was never a problem. The night rocked and reverberated. Every few seconds the dismal interior erupted with blinding light and the envisioned flash stayed in the mind's eye until the next. They moved about with stuttering interval.

They'd removed their saturated exteriors for the semi-dry of their unders and huddled, wrapped in blankets, into a warming pack. Fortune favoured them with moderate temperature but sleep was as unrealistic as comfort and talk carried far into the tumultuous night, until dampened exhaustion overcame them.

Carl's hyperactive mind often disallowed him the absolute of undisturbed sleep. This night was no different despite his exhausting day. He sensed, more than heard, the repetitious, inhalant snuffle. Yet, lying next to Chris Hallvarson that was not unusual. Carl's dreamscape often painted strange and unique imagings and occasionally he'd wake in their aftermath, mildly entertained. But this time it grabbed the toe of his socked foot and pulled forcefully. He sprang like a coiled rattler and nearly nose-flattened himself against the rock-hard forehead of the inquisitive heifer. The startled creature, having recently absorbed so many terrifying inconsistencies from the normally passive humankind, bellered with surprise and lashed backward. The surrounding bush erupted with like snorts and blats and tendon-snapping hooves. The interior of the makeshift shelter was no less tumultuous.

Alexsay's uproarious laugh did little to dampen the apprehension. The agony of his arthritic arm tortured him throughout the night and robbed him of much-needed rest. He'd already heard and seen the cattle. The five tumbled out into the charm of early morning sunshine.

Chris chuckled as he wormed his way into the disgust of his cold, damp trousers. "We're huntin' them and they find us?" The cattle, seeking shelter from the storm of last night, had found their way into the same sheltered bluff.

The air was fresh and clean and quiet and thankfully warm, with the bird chorus as enthusiastic as the first warm day of spring. They had bread soaked in warm milk for breakfast. The domestic creature, balloon tight, stood with relief and gratitude while Carl simply walked up and milked her. Her less fortunate companions bawled their demands but there was no milking or oats forthcoming so they returned to their grazing.

The surface of the violently rolling, brushed-over landscape, roiled by the turmoil of so many hooves in the recent past had been washed clear of any specific direction. They drove, instinctively, southeastward, out of the natural puzzle, until they hit the rails, then followed east toward York. None of the group had ever been this far out in this direction.

———

The rails trestled across a cavernous, rock-strewn ravine with a deep, roaring stream that made passage with the herd impossible, so they left the security of the road and paralleled the embankment for a gentle slope. Alexsay had abandoned the well-marked trail some distance back, for the direct security of the track and he cursed his stupidity and the time wasted but the afternoon was gloriously warm and the rolling, greening countryside was as beautiful as any they'd ever seen.

The tranquil beauty would have been far more relaxing and enjoyable with full stomachs. Their fare was depleted and they'd have to find something. They hadn't seen a single human being or any sign of settlement since they'd left Sean's. This was as wild and as natural as anything Carl had ever imagined in the adventurous dreams of his childhood. He was glad he was here to see it before humankind spoiled it. It took his mind off the agonizing concern about his land and his personal ambitions.

They found a crossing on the former trail and learned to trust the accuracy of animal sense. It was getting late and the crossing site was flat and pleasantly warm. The stream, too, had flattened and gentled to a murmur, leaving sandy banks, warm, dry and secure. Nobody had any idea how far they'd come or how far they had to go and they were very hungry. This would be it for the day.

They devoured the last of the potatoes before Paul, the hunter, and Chris, his enthusiastic student, left to scout the stream for game. Deer usually came out to graze and water in the security of the evening. This was an opportune time and a promising location.

They planted their camp at the foot of the slope so that any attempt at escape would require the cattle to trample over them. They'd simply blanket out on the sand and draw the water-repellent horse blankets over them if they had to. Paul ordered them to avoid lighting a fire until they'd had a chance to scout for game; wood smoke was a dead giveaway.

The ravine to the north, the direction Paul and Chris had taken, flattened further into a grassy bank that provided grazing. The animals, deprived by the days march and confined by the steep banks, arrowed for it and could remain and rest without a problem.

Carl was sound asleep when the report echoed and re-echoed down the ravine and the cattle, unnerved by recent events, charged, in terror, toward the hapless camp. Frantic blanket waving appeared to be intimidating but only the experienced horses, running with the cattle, prevented a trample. They reached the camp first and stopped abruptly, the prayerful blanket wavers leapt into the gaps between and formed a fragile wall.

The very domestic nature of the cattle raced them to the security of human-kind and braked them to a stop while looking frantically behind for the source and ahead to their human protectors with wild, frightened eyes. They walked, passively, past the line, circled behind it, ears perked, tails arched, coughing and blowing their fears away, always watching to the north.

By the time Chris and Paul reached the camp carrying supper, the three had a roaring fire going and the pacified animals, a bit questioning of the smell of blood and the dead doe, wandered back to the grass and settled down.

Other than the coffee pot and a few cups, they had nothing, so they called upon the natural, prodded the meat unto green, forked, willow sticks and cooked their immediate fill. Alexsay, the experienced survivor, drove heavier forked posts into the ground on either side of the fire, then skewered thinly sliced strips of the remaining flesh on a heavier shaft of willow and hung them well over the fire to cook and dry slowly. In the wild, today's certainty would guarantee only more uncertainty tomorrow.

They were all very tired and the evening was warm. The sand beneath, warmed during the heat of the afternoon, radiated up through the blanket against the chill of night — they slept in comfort

Carl lapsed, if only in his sleep, back into his boyhood. He dreamed himself back at the very beginnings when everything was pure and clean and new, when there was nothing but space, time, and creation — he could anticipate plenty. Everywhere was an opportunity with none of the cares, trials and deprivation of later years. Youth didn't see the work and worry and terror and pain, neither did the dream. He awoke to what seemed an entirely new world. It was very early and it was very fresh. Chris snored determination! The others had either gotten used to it or were exhausted beyond comprehension. They slept on, even Alexsay. The sun hadn't risen yet and a mist draped over the shadow.

He rose and climbed carefully out of the shadow to the crest. He didn't want to wake the others. This time was his alone, to see and to feel the world the way God meant it to be, just the way Mama used to tell him it was. He resolved to love it in spite of what it might yet throw at him. He'd never seen a panorama so big and bold and breathtaking, as far as his eye could see ... green, shrouded in early mist, not a pillar of chimney smoke in sight.

The sun rose as beautifully as ever. He had no idea how long he'd stood.

The distant echo of gunfire shattered the dream and brought back the Caine-world. The camp awoke and began stirring.

Without a sweetener, "chawyee" (tea) was lousy, even Alexsay opted for good, strong hot coffee. Carl didn't like it black but the cattle were too restless and uncooperative so he didn't even try. The venison, thoroughly smoked and overly cooked toward the brittle side, was a bit of a challenge to chew, yet it was delicious and filling. Carl had never eaten it in such a primitive fashion and it was rare, at best, in any fashion back in Iowa.

They crossed the shallow stream and climbed back into the world. Alexsay, much the wiser, chose to follow the animal instinct. It would surely lead to the necessities of the livestock, the human would have to look to itself. Only the omen-gunfire warned that all was not well in the "Caine-world."

They moved steadily, at a good stride, most of that morning, with Alexsay on point, well ahead, luring the herd and upping the speed. Sensing a purpose, the cattle moved steadily and quietly. They remembered home, feed, security, and the addictive daily portion of grain.

They stopped abruptly, with sharp alert and their ears perked. They tested the air and blew alarmingly, yet remained transfixed, staring into the deep, heavily bushed gully, some distance to the left. Alexsay rode back quickly, off to their right to block the retreat that he anticipated in that direction. Carl whirled his rifle off his saddle and saw the others draw theirs. Alexsay waved a silent, meaningful, "Nyet!"

The clear, bovine bawl, brought with it a violent jostling of the obscuring bush as the cover broke and the cattle raced to the welcome of their own kind. The riders dropped their guard, yet were puzzled by the lack of response from their own spellbound herd.

The answer appeared only momentarily as a rapidly retreating glimpse. The figure of the huge animal, so familiar to Carl, was a first timer for all of the others, as the moose crossed an unavoidable gap in the bush. Paul got his longtime wish; he saw the beast that had escaped his determined search for five years. He saddled his 30-30, satisfied that his hunt was finally a success.

The Indians were right. The animal had a deterrent and overpowering majesty about him. Why he allowed the lost cattle to shadow him was a mystery of natural compassion that puzzled Carl.

Their herd had more than doubled. With the disappearance of the moose, the cattle lost their inhibition and a raucous greeting and intermixing consumed a great deal of patience. Their charge had become barely manageable and movement was severely restricted. It slowed to a crawl and sunset found the noisy enterprise still within view of the encounter site.

The campsite was not favourable. The herd, unless watched carefully, could wander into heavy cover and the hunt would begin again. They had to be watched all that night.

Carl dozed a bit, but he and Alexsay spent most of it hawk-eyed and talking quietly, away from the others.

Alexsay inflicted upon Carl, an understanding of the deceptive Doukhobor psyche. Simmering just below the tranquil exterior, lay a major dissension, largely the consequence of what Alexsay described as several decades of hypnotic leadership and a divisive national purpose inflicted upon their powerless circumstance. Carl was well-enough acquainted with the insidious tactics of corrupted power. What Alexsay told him of the inner workings was even more disturbing.

Many of the older Doukhobors worshipped their spiritual leaders with God-like reverence. "Why?" was well beyond Alyosha's Christian comprehension. Exploitation, both physical and financial, was not unknown.

Carl felt the same pain as he did for Paul and Mildred, when Alexsay, with trembling emotion, bitterly told him that Loosha's only-born, a son, was a consequence of an "immaculate conception."Alexsay was powerless, under the threat of ostracism and banishment; certain death in their cruel environment.The circumstance of the birth was difficult.The child had not survived and it left Loosha barren. It had destroyed Alexsay's soul and made of him, a bitter man.

The revelation explained Alexsay's often violent, explosive outbursts toward evildoers. He openly declared that his life meant little to him. He'd remained with Loosha throughout, largely because she was as powerless as he but it made of them, an arrangement, more than a marriage.

————

Only instinctive recognition prevented gunfire as the herd and their drivers rounded the bluff, dropped into the steep ravine and all but ran into the trap.The Ghost, with the Marshal, John McPherson, and several others had seen and heard and they simply lay in ambush for the approaching stock and riders until Alexsay's dress and massive demeanour identified them.

"Got a couple more of 'em early mornin'.Wasn't much fight left, as cold and wet and starved as they are.The whole country is out huntin'. Lucky there ain't more gettin' killed or hurt. Everybody's up tighter'n a fiddle string and just as snappy! Damn! I been at this so long I should have caught on sooner ... don't know how they expected to get away with it. Not many of them know the country, that's plain, so they ain't locals. Nobody seems to recognize any of 'em an' lots of 'em were carryin' Thorland cards and papers on 'em. Most of 'em come up from the States, I'm sure of it, but they sure ain't no cowhands or country folk. They're lost in the wilderness! Money trail led back to Des Moines until Max took Lars down. It stopped then, but picked up with the lumber shark until somebody dropped him and since then they ain't been paid. What else could I expect them to do?

"We found several of them carryin' Land Title maps. Now, just how do you suppose they got their hands on those? If they ain't filed, why would they be carryin' 'em? You can bet Hugh is lookin' to a pay trail to or from somebody on the inside there. Won't be much paper but there'll be big cash withdrawals in somebody's name. Land Titles ain't hired anybody new here that I know about and even if they did, why ain't it handled like regular payroll? Hugh and McArthur will find out and you can be sure somebody'll have to answer. Wouldn't you know, the chief registrar is a York councillor and Hugh will sure be lookin' into him. How else did they know where?" The Marshal laughed sarcastically. "Been a few cash transfers in from Winnipeg and out 'a the local bank. From who? To who? Ain't nobody around here with that name. Some bank records! Some police investigation! Local authorities huh?"

They drove the large herd, at the Ghost's direction, to the northwest and into the crowded corrals of an old, established yard, a large livestock operation, well back into the bush and far from realization and prying eyes. Carl envisioned shy, withdrawn, bachelor brothers, but nobody was around so he didn't bother to ask.

———

"You did what?" the Marshal thundered. "Well you sure guessed wrong!"

The three young officers indicated that they were more than aware of the attempted cattle rustling. They'd run across three Indians herding fourteen head a good twenty miles west of York and had arrested them.

"No they sure in blazes ain't! From what you say, bein' Indian makes 'em thieves? If that's what you think, I can see how things around here got so out 'a hand. Well you're dead wrong. In all my years a' this work, I've only seen Indians take an animal if they were starvin' an' it sure as hell wasn't no fourteen head. We been huntin' 'em for days and them three fellas are the ones that found most of 'em, but then ya' didn't ask did ya? You get, and let 'em go right now! We need 'em! Got the jail an' the hospital an' the grave-yard at York, full a' the crap that done it! Them boys hunted 'em down the last four-five days. Should be givin' 'em a reward for what they done that you fellas couldn't seem to do, instead 'a lockin' 'em up. Don't they teach you greenhorns nothin'? And where's them cattle at now?"

"Left 'em where we found 'em."

"'T'a hell ya' mean ya' left 'em? We got a bunch of 'em rounded up in Mike Wiwchar's corrals and, far as we know, there's still a bunch we ain't found. Got the whole bloomin' country huntin', tryin' to find their own cattle, instead a' seedin' like they should be, or rebuilding what they got burnt. Don't give me any more a' your bull-crap! If I got to listen to any more a' this, I'll let them out an' put you in! You're in my territory now an' if ya' were under my watch a while, I'd make real policemen out of ya. Ain't no cure for dumb!" the Marshal grunted to himself, as he turned in disgust to rejoin Carl and Chris.

"Sure can't figure this Force out ... got plenty of experience and they send in kids to do a man's work?" The fact that, with a full knowledge of the degree of the problem at York, only three of the youngest and most inexperienced recruits had been sent to investigate a crime of this magni-tude displayed either ignorance or open contempt and an ulterior purpose. Eight rustlers were dead, over two hundred head had been driven off and at least twelve, that the Marshal had seen, or knew about, were dead and likely more by final count. "That's sure costin' somebody!"

———

The Indian trackers, who'd earlier followed the large group of marauders to the southeast, watched them building the makeshift fence, in the heavily bushed valley a few miles from the peaceful little village that Carl had piloted Hank's charge through last fall. There was a waiting wagon loaded with wire and posts.

The Indians waited until the job was complete and the builders, think-ing they were unobserved, left, back for the post. The Indians simply tore the fence down before they returned and encountered the running night battle. How the rustlers planned to round up such a large herd and drive them that great a distance across the populated territory around York to the corral without detection, lay testament to their naive purpose.

———

This had been a long, hard drag and he was in no mood. The Marshal, more than twice Carl's age, showed signs of the ordeal. Carl himself couldn't remember a time when he'd been more saddle sore. In his entire life he'd never spent so much time over a horse. He appreciated the poor fellas back on the big cattle spreads in the States, making their living in the saddle every day of their lives. He'd slept outside, or called it that, under a damp blanket, for the last week and he'd eaten about as well. He earnestly wished he could have been walking behind Dan and Ben and the plough but it was worth the effort, because the scum weren't going away by themselves.

Surprisingly, for his size and deceptive shape, his overweight father-in-law was a tough son-of-a gun. He appeared as tired and hungry as Carl and just as riled but he could hit the ground and be asleep instantly. Carl wished he could do that!

Chris hadn't even thought about the need to get back. He'd wired home to tell "Mom." She returned:

"That's our only child,
Go get them!
Charles paper full! "

"How'd they know?"

Alexsay's arm pained him terribly during the damp, sleepless nights, so they'd sent him back. His impressive endurance was beginning to fail him.

Paul had taken another five head they'd found this morning over to Mike's and would be on his way home. His recent injury was bothering him so the Marshal had ordered him back and he was grateful. Mildred had been through a lot and there was a lot hanging on her.

This was much rougher country than around theirs. How in blazes Mitchell had ever found his way through the storm, into this, was a pure miracle. He was very lucky he'd found Mike's.

Wiwchar and his boys were as hard and experienced as any Carl or the Marshal had ever seen. Mike had shovelled his way across, then worked and wagoned out here with nothing, not even a word of English, over thirty years ago, when there wasn't a single white out here and he'd toughed it through.

It was still better than the old country. Mike's experiences in the old country, like Papa's, had earned his total distrust of everything but mostly human. He could trust his solitude. Yet, the forces that he so detested, had driven the innocent boy into his yard and because of that, Mitchell lived.

———————

Carl'd had enough! His patience and temperament were wearing thin. He'd get to Al's tonight. "Thank God!" John McPherson had been in the saddle for eight days, since this all started. Carlson had stopped in and told him to look out, well before any of the others, even the Marshal, knew what was going on. The Marshal had asked Carl to ride back with "the stubborn old fool!" because he wasn't sure John could make it. Carl was certain that McPherson'd had a lot to do with many of those in the hospital and the graveyard but he looked like he wasn't just too far from one of those places himself.

Carl knew there were still a few of the cattle and the renegades out there somewhere, running scared but they'd got the biggest part of them. There'd be no more danger. He didn't know if any of the settlers or natives had been hurt the last couple of days; none of them he'd seen were. Maybe this thing would be wrapped up in another day or two. There was a lot of sorting and herding to do but the owners would have to do that without him. He had to get back or there'd be no crop or home. Alexsay'd let them know but Milly'd still be worried sick. Three of the most important people in her life were out facing "God-knows-what!"

The entire country was up in arms, "Madder'n hell!"

Grandpa McPherson was so far gone when they rode into Al's yard that Carl and the lecturing Grandma had to help him in and put him to bed. He needed rest more than food. He'd learned to respect the circumstances that had driven his work-worn son.

Carl wasn't too far behind but he had to eat first and he went to sleep happy. Alice had informed him that the Buechler boys were now the proud owners of an extended family of two heifer calves and a healthy bull, all born, miraculously, trouble-free. The one left would be a while yet. Carl was too tired to even go and look. Max had ridden back a couple hours before and was "dead-out".

Carl was barely up and out to help with chores, when the very agitated Marshal rode in. "Damn bastards bumped McArthur off the bench in this district! Hugh woke me up to tell me … said he'd compromised his authority because he'd gone out to the village himself and wasn't qualified to sit the hearings an' the trials of this mess with an unbiased view — just a trump! Mark what I say, they're goin' to send in a hand-picked pigeon to sit on this one an' they might try comin' after Al an' you an' the rest on any excuse they can find. You an' Paul should be okay because you're deputized legally. Hugh didn't date it so they won't know when. He's one smart boy! Even the Council don't know just when; I didn't tell 'em. I knew there had to be a reason I didn't trust all of 'em … might try to come 'round it by jumpin' territorial jurisdiction with federal statutes to override the councils an' me. Alpert's called a public meetin' tonight, at the hall. Jeez I'm sure sorry! I sure know where ya' got to be but we got to fight this one out to the end. The orders are comin' from a way on up top an' they're scared because we still hold all the cards an' they ain't sure what."

———

The air bristled! The mass could have filled the building to the rafters and would have spilled out into the yard so the mayor suggested they move out into the yard where there was light now and room. Nobody worried about a seat; they'd brought some chairs out for the old folks. Mayor Alpert, with a huge voice of experience, chaired it and had his hands full.

The Marshal knew the crowd was mixed with ears so, on Hugh's advice, he bluntly laid it out and it was mind bending. They had witnesses enough to tie the court up for a year. They had a paper trail "from here to Christmas!" They'd requisitioned all the bank records and had them locked away. They had railroad records and employee witnesses and they had telegraph operators with legal exemptions from the obligation of confidentiality. They had victim's statements complete with the ability to identify the perpetrators. They knew a lot of the sources all the way back to Des Moines and they'd found a lot of interesting information on some of the rustlers they'd just put away. They had seen and heard most of it.

"Carl?"

"They've been hitting the Doukhobors until they found that they're too close-packed in the villages and will fight back. It's easier to hit wide-spaced farmyards who are just hanging on and owe big. Banks can kick 'em off or land titles can pull it on some of the unlucky ones or fool lots who just don't know and ain't got nobody to help 'em. They'll have all the developed land they need! It'll bring 'em big money, both east and back in the States. Lars Thorvaldson wasn't the only one with big fortune making plans at our expense. Now, we know where and who to look for."

"Hugh?"

"McArthur or no McArthur, they're not going to be slippery enough to slide around this one! If the pigeon they'd replaced him with, tries in the district, we'll just appeal it further. We've got the eyes and ears of all the news hounds clear across the country and in the States. We've the best legal minds in the same, along with a few surprises that we're not telling and best of all, just look around you. We got the people!"

"Ya' damned right! An' a graveyard full, over twenty, near as I can tell, innocent, decent, hardworkin' folk, an' a dead McPherson boy, an' the Carlson girl, just hangin' ta life; tore up so damned bad had ta hunt up the pieces! May never be right agin. Seen her this afternoon ... still can't talk with her throat an' mouth tore all ta hell!

"Damn 'em ta hell an' their dogs an' rotten souls! Brother-in-law a' mine back ta' Bismarck told me all about this fella." The nameless face, familiar to Carl, acknowledged him and shook with rage. "Hunted down his missus, all the way back ta Charles City an' would a' kilt her an' the Marshal, here, if his brother, there, hadn't 'a kilt ta animal first; they're that big an' mean! Ain't nobody safe, nowheres! We're standin' here talkin' 'bout laws an' courts' an' crooked judges an' maybe losin', an' some of us maybe goin' ta jail. 'Ta hell for? Me an' the Carlsons come up ta this country from Dakota. Me an' Cal an' Helga growed up in the same place an' she an' Sven come up 'fore I did. She looked ta my girls, an' me, when the missus took sick an' died ... teached my girls the only cookin' and sewin' they know. I

ain't standin' for 'em hurtin' or killin' no more a' our kids an' folks as long
as I got a damned good piece a' rope an' a loaded gun on my place!'"

His booming voice raged and Carl watched a crowd of passive, frontier
farmers become an enraged mob. He felt with them and he felt like them.
He agreed with every sentiment but he knew this couldn't be, or they'd be
doomed legally. Both he and Hugh roared above the din but sensed only
the futile vibrations in the pits of their throats. Max, again the instinctive
man of action, drove his way through the belligerence to race to the head
and the jail. Carl feared for him.

The Marshal's old service .45 roared upward toward empty, so close to
Carl's ear that it left him deficient to the din. It must have died, because he
heard, clearly, the Marshal's high volume rasp.

"By the livin' hell, you stop right there! Because if you don't, I'll have
to empty the next right into the lot a' ya'! An' ya' can be damned sure, as
much as I'd hate to, I will! There's a thousand more of ya' out there who
ain't crazy mad, who are goin' to suffer right into the hands of the animals
who are up ta' this. You're givin' 'em all the right reasons that they ain't got
now, to pull this out of our hands, throw whoever they want into jail and
send the army in to quash the 'Uprising at York!' and roll over all of us.

It ain't more'n a couple a years since Batoche. Did you forget that
already? They called it 'Rebellion!' an' they hung Riel just over a hundred
miles away from here. They'll do the same to us, and what you're tryin'
here is just that! We're tellin ya', we got everything on our side now an'
we're still governed by the law. What we got here is 'right reason.' We'll
have nothin' because, even the smartest a' lawyers won't have a leg ta' stand
on. The courts just won't listen, if ya' do what ya' intend ta do. Now settle
down and cool off, before they come in here and kill a thousand of us.
Won't the land tycoons both here an' stateside just love that? They'd have
just what they wanted an' those of us who get killed'll be the lucky ones."

The roar had drifted, into silence, with the deafening reports of the
heavy calibre weapon. The march braked and turned to hear the words of
experience and the only law they'd grown to respect, since his arrival.

"Much as I hate to admit it, he's right. Thet's jest what they'd do."

"He's a good one! Sure in blazes made a difference in this place since
he come."

"I sure don't need any more trouble. Western Loans an' Trust are just waitin' for that. They could sell my place for one helluva profit with what I put there."

"I'm gettin' title to mine this summer. I want to live on it 'stead a' gettin' buried on it!" The volume rose to a rumble as everyone talked at once, more to themselves then to each other.

"There! That's better! Now, Bill there, says he's got a barrel a' coffee on the house an' there's plenty a' sittin' room on down the street from The Hotel. Now let's go there an' think an' talk an' plan this out. We still ain't got all of 'em an' there's all those cattle to deal with an' get back. Let's go! Oh! Bill said he ain't got enough cups an' stuff for all of ya', so if ya got some at home, get 'em' an' get back here so we all know what'n hell we're goin' to do."

The town folk hustled off for the cups and the rural rounded the corner to The Hotel, all breathing easier after their near-fatal reaction.

———

"Yessir! He sure is! Cal's Pa an' mine come up ta Dakota after the war, both, hurt pretty bad. Paw got shot 'n' Frank caught a bayonet ... had a helluva time, been like brothers ever since. My youngest sister's Cal's missus. Ol' Frank died last fall, tough old bugger — eighty-seven year old! Pa's eighty-four an' still goin' strong, helped carry ol' Frank ta his rest. Pa's back at Cal's now, figured I'd best get back this spring to see 'im one last time. Sure'd like ta get up here ta see this country, but I don't think he can. Cal'd read everything he could 'bout what's happenin' here, 'cause a' me an' you — name's all over the papers down there. Couldn't say enough about ya, that's how I found out.

"Frank an' Pa's hurts made things awful hard for 'em so they stuck together. We, me'n Cal, growed up pretty hard, not much schoolin' an' lots a' damned hard work. He's sure one hard-nose sonuvagun! Neither a' us got much stock in this kind 'a bullshit! ... call it like it is! Said ya' was a man after his own heart an' said ta say 'Hello!' Sure'd like ta hear from ya sometime when things settle down ... wondered if yer head was serious hurt?" Carl leaned over to show Henry the scar. "Didn't explain it — figured maybe he thought ya was nuts fer doin' what ya bin doin' here!"

He laughed uproariously, at the simplistic interpretation and Carl laughed too, more at his boisterous guffaw than the rustic inference. Carl'd found another Cal, in the guise of Henry.

XX
"Welcome to our home!"

It was cool and blustery. The old, weatherworn mackinaw hugged in the warmth, almost out of gratitude. Years before, he had resurrected it from a nail in a leaky toolshed. It had been discarded there through disuse rather than overuse because it carried an antiquated cut. Yet its quality far exceeded its appearance. Appearance didn't really matter to him until now. He wanted to look nice for Milly; she always did.

The horse under him had become a part of him. His saddle sense was gone; he blended down through the trail-worn beast as if they were on his legs. He rode with deliberation and a sense of gruelling endurance. Dismount felt unnatural; his saddle-legs bowed and sponged under him and he decided he preferred to be on the plough seat.

He was nearly home. He'd agonized for a week over his needs and ambitions yet he recognized that everyone's well-being was his well-being. He'd accomplished more in a few months then any Buechler had in living memory. He had what he wanted, what Mama and Papa wanted, more than what they expected. He had Milly and they were both very happy about that too.

The weary animal, anticipating home as much as Carl, transported him over the rise with a renewed vigour that surprised him. Carl was selfishly glad it wasn't one of his own because the footsore beast would be useless without a week's rest and feed. Seeding was becoming an urgent necessity. In Maynard, they'd be done by now.

Carl's spirit soared! The once barren makings of his yard still supported the mounds of dirt, but rising well above them, a white lumber structure, rough-edged and unfinished. Minute, board-waving, figures crept with cautious deliberation along the skeletal roof and its extent crept rapidly skyward, above the waving bush, at a rate that determined its imminent completion. He knew Milly's determination and purpose and he was very pleased and happy; she'd so wanted to be a part of its makings.

A burst of joyous acceleration raced him into the bush-gapped approach to his yard as the roofed figures identified themselves, levelled the ridge-boards into place, and the hammers roared.

She flew down the approach, rough-clad and dirt-smudged, the most beautiful thing! Her look always amazed him. She'd been watching the crest all morning with anxious anticipation and, nearly felling her opposite, she dropped her end of the board with no announcement and raced away when she saw him. Her greeting easily equalled their meeting at the station. She loved being the creative one and he loved her spirit.

"Welcome to our home!" she beamed.

"But how ...?"

"I know I've got to go soon, so do they. We did all of this in the last three days. Gosh, these people know how to work and they certainly know what they're doing. I've read a lot about building bees, but I didn't think they still happened."

"They'd do anything for you! You've impressed them almost as much as you always impress me." That was as good as "I love you!" to her, because it was Carl's style.

"I didn't really believe them when they said, '... a few days', but there it is. The cement and stone took the longest. By the time it set properly, they had the walls framed, squared, boarded in and laying on the ground. Yesterday we had a lot more help to set them up and nail in the rafters and joists. Today? Well, you can see for yourself. There's the floor joists but no floors yet, come look. It'll be nailed in by this evening if we don't waste any time and we're not going to! Come on!" she hurried him. "I'm absolutely determined to make love to my beautiful husband under our own roof before I have to leave and I'm demanding his total cooperation, understand?" Carl blushed; she wasn't the least bit discreet about the volume of her statement. "Oh you silly! I haven't taught them that yet! Not that I have to," she added. "That's universal!"

Work stopped for hot tea and for Carl. Everybody wanted an update on the running reports that kept trickling back as the searchers returned. Alexsay had them fairly informed but he knew nothing about the displacement of the favourable Justice McArthur. That news brought a startled response from the people whose very existence suffered so terribly under such deliberate deceptions. They trusted very few and Justice McArthur, since his visit, had been given their faith.

Anastas shook his head with doubt when Carl told them that the hearing would likely be soon and deliberate, to inconvenience them as much as possible. "Nyet! No hear! Minoha zny-you!"

"He doubts that there'll be any hearing. You know too much!" Milly's voice steely hardened. "What you've got scares them; they're afraid you'll get too close to high places. Alexsay said he'd seen it too many times in the old country. It's no different here. Don't expect justice in this circumstance. I was scared for you but Anastas told me not to be. There are too many people who know too much; they can't come after all of you. Still, I'm really worried. Be very careful. I don't want to get a telegraph like you got, or worse." Milly and August, with Helen's help, had thoroughly discussed the circumstance with Anastas and the others. The Doukhobors had borne the nature of the system through too many sorrows.

"How's August? What's he been doing?" Carl asked.

She pointed to the obvious; the beautifully blackened field that Carl's anticipation had failed to notice. "It's ready for the seed. He said he couldn't walk behind the plough but he could surely sit a seat and handle the reins if somebody helped with the harnessing so I learned that too. He disked it both ways and it sure is nice. He did his potatoes yesterday with our plough, just like we did. He's disked what little he's got turned and he's probably at Paul's right now but he wants to try turning more with Paul's sulky, if Dan and Ben can pull it in the sod and if he can stand it.

"Mildred's been on the land pretty steady all these days but they haven't got enough good machinery. Even I can see that they need the help. That woman's a wonder ... handles the teams like she was born doing it and she's strong!

"I sure learned a lot about looking after livestock and an active little boy. I'm not very secure with milking yet, but their cow is a real dear, a perfect animal to learn on. She must know I'm a greenie; she fidgeted but never kicked once. Paul's back now and Helen's over helping with their garden while we're at our house. Paul's using our gang and they'll go with both disks if we can arrange more horse power. It's sure hard with all those horses gone. They don't want to over-push the heavy pregnant mares either ... sure need those colts!

"I sure learned a lot about machinery and working together," she continued. "We'd have nothing done anywhere if everybody went their separate way. Lots of the guys on the machines at the village are those doing the same as August. Should be taking it easy but how? I've never seen so much get done so fast. They plan to pull over and give Sean a hand within a few days. They're using his good seed drill until then. We can broadcast the little we've got and August's, because there just isn't enough time or equipment to do it all. Got to love these people! They sure pull together in a pinch! Don't see too much of that in the cities. Everything there's for money and too bad for you if you ain't got any. God I love it here and I know how much they appreciate me. I've never felt so good in my entire life. I still don't really understand what I'm doing to deserve it." She stopped for breath.

Carl thought he was listening to a veteran. He smiled at her rapid grasp of the concepts and terminology. "Are you sure you haven't been fibbin' to me?"

"No! I've never been anywhere near a farm but it's so full and active and exciting. There's so much to see and know and do. That's what I love about it. I can see the result of every move we make and it's all our own. There's something showing already in our peas, onions, and radishes. We'll be well fixed by the time I get back. I'll have to get some canning equipment and jars. Mom said we can have lots of hers because she won't need that many anymore but that won't be enough." She stopped again to catch up.

"That's why Papa sent me here." said Carl. "It's for ourselves, not always for somebody else. It's the first time in our lives that it's been ours."

"That's just about what Wilbur said when he was thinking about it." She choked back, switching her thought away. "We'll have to give August a hand." She suspected that she wouldn't be here to do it but she was worried about August and Helen. She was openly glad that Chris didn't seem overly hurried.

Carl knew his way around a hammer but he wasn't party to the systematic mechanism of the crew. Recognizing this early, he contented himself with handing in the boards. It was a bit harder for the handlers than the roof because they had to carry around through the doorway. The windows weren't sawed open yet.

At noon, rather than haul everything over, they all piled onto a hayrack for the quick ride to the village and not just to eat; there were so many things going on at once and they needed to plan.

By afternoon tea, the ground floor was done and they'd ladder-nailed a few boards on the upper floor for a work base. A few early-finishers hauled a sizeable pile of lumber in so Milly and one of the other women could hand the boards up while Carl busied himself with the construction of a door. He took his time because it would later serve as the storm door.

———

Milly held him in the darkened seclusion of the upper story of the first Buechler-owned home on Buechler-owned land for as long as records could determine, on any side of an ocean. He felt embarrassed at her seeing him like that. A meagre eight months before, he'd had nothing, not even her. Now the heart of their new home was beating.

They suppered with Loosha and Alyosha. The bawnyah smoked merrily so Loosha directed them to its warmth and comfort; just the two of them. Nobody else would appear until they'd done. Somebody'd overheard Milly's wonderment when she'd first come, and made it happen.

It was nearly dark when Alyosha wagoned them up to their door. He wouldn't hear of them walking. He'd packed in one of the home-made mattresses to help soften their memories and left without a word. Besides, they understood English better than that.

"I was sure getting tired of the trail. I'd make a lousy cowboy. I was just dying to get back to you, but ... "

"Oh shut up! I've got ya now! Com'ere!"

———

"What time is it?" she asked. Carl tried to slip away quietly but she was awake, just lying and watching him in the diminished light of their windowless, early sunrise.

"Not sure! I'm just going to start a fire and put some water on. Stay here; I'll be right back. Brr... it's chilly!" He struggled to get into his trousers in the fractious light that filtered through the careless gaps left where the windows would eventually be. She ran her backhand gently up and down his marvellously muscled back. He turned and kissed her hand then bent and kissed her lips before he pulled on his shirt and boots and left. The sun was well up as he opened the door.

"What's the word for today?" she asked loudly.

"I'm not really sure. I've been gone so much, I should be asking you. We've got to get the shingles on but I ain't got 'em. That'll take a trip to York."

"Maybe we should see if we can get some of the wheat in. Anastas said we can get some seed from them if you can help them back. That's what we'll do. I want to do some of that before I have to go." She disobeyed his order, rose and dressed quickly, and was out by the time he had the fire going and the water on. "I want to get our clothes washed before that too. Everything's filthy and I don't want you or anyone else doing my duties after I'm gone."

They breakfasted on what they'd brought from the village; soft boiled eggs and toast that Carl had improvised on a clean grating somebody'd brought over to screen some of the gravel for the chimney grouting. The bread had come out of the "pyetch" yesterday afternoon and smelled as fresh as the beautifully promising spring morning. Tea was a necessity because they had a coffee pot but no coffee. Somebody'd put in a jar of liquid honey as a sweetener or a spread.

By the time they'd finished, a wagon with Ivan and Nicholai rolled in with a creaking that determined a load. They were a bit short of the brick they'd need themselves but theirs could wait until more wagoned in. Carl's chimney had to be there to build around. The single-story kitchen portion of their home would come a bit later, when the rush was over. The chimney would sit between to accommodate both the cook stove and the living room heater without the need for any long, poor-draft, stovepipes.

The small rectangle, still uncut, over the future heater, determined a grating to allow heat through to the upstairs room and the stairwell would lead along the north wall from near its base to the back bedrooms. They'd also determined a stovepipe opening up there for an eventual upstairs heater to supplement in cold weather. The chimney support structure would sit in the future kitchen, on the square concrete block that Carl wondered about, just outside the door to the living room.

Nicholai, a skilled bricklayer, politely denied Carl's offer of help, went to work immediately on the heavy beam structure that would support the chimney, and eventually an enclosed, small kitchen storage area beneath, that would be near the cook stove, both warm and dry.

Carl and Milly walked to the village to get a buggy ride with Helen and August over to Paul's. They'd need the wagon for seed and to bring back Carl's remaining bundles but the teams were all employed. Paul's two were on the gang, Dan and Ben on the sulky at August's and with Helen there, Mildred would disk behind Paul. August, still multi-coloured but physically improved, wagoned back to the village with them to take back the team after they hauled the seed.

Chris rode in with the Marshal to a surprise as great as Carl's. "For two cents, I'd like to tell American Oil to fly their kite but I suppose I need them more'n they need me. I haven't spread seed since I was a kid and I know you haven't either, so where's a bucket or a bag and let's have at it!"

The field was larger than it looked and lacking the practice of familiarity, progress was slow and tiring. "Step! Cast! Step! Cast!" Ivan, observing their progress, came and showed them how to cover the ground with more speed, an even spread, and a far less exerting flick of the arm. Many still spread their crops in the tried and true manner; the village antique seed drill worked well but too slowly for their growing volume. The loan of Sean's more modern, larger machine was opportune and fortunate to their frantic, belated efforts. Sean's burns made the exertion of seeding an over-burden from which he would not recover without help and a large part of his indebtedness was the machine. They would not see him helpless. He counted desperately on their experience and dependability.

By mid-afternoon, a dust cloud appeared out of the village and the team ahead of it pulled Anastas astride a light cart chained to four harrow sections. He said nothing, dismounted, checked the concentration of the wheat seed spread, shook his head with approval and began the process of covering the seed. He stopped after a short time, again checked the consequence, shook another satisfaction and the team stepped into a lively tempo. In no time he'd have the afternoon's effort covered and secure; seed could not be left exposed over the night. Wind, heavy rain, a belated flock of geese, all could do severe damage to exposed seed.

The afternoon was hot and draining; again Chris's endurance matched his girth. Carl had broadcast lots of grass seed, never wheat, but Chris had the practice of youthful experience. He'd grown up doing this and he not only knew the practice, he smiled all afternoon with the joy of reliving it. This was for his girl. They were both his children. Carl helped fill the void left in their lives.

Milly, knowing the Marshal's bull-headed determination, rested and drank often to encourage him an excuse to do the same. He knew and was grateful for it. His age and the wound would no longer allow him the practice of endurance.

As the afternoon shadows lengthened, their pace shortened with the weight and wear. Carl didn't realize that a field this size would take so long and be so exhausting. He had envisioned a casual afternoon's work. Chris smiled at the enlightenment. "Forty acres was a big crop when I was a kid. It's an awful lot of work when there isn't the kind of help you've got here. You boys'll have to do something about a seed drill or you won't be able to handle it all."

———

The chimney stood, straight and tall, as its builders climbed down, picked up after themselves and waved Milly and the Marshal over for a brief discussion. They took up the bags and marched out into the remaining field and the pace picked up. Milly waved to Carl and pointed to the village as she toured the grateful Marshal through the house and future farmstead.

The sun touched the horizon as the exhausted men crawled onto the brick wagon for the ride back to the village. They were dirty, very tired, and hungry but the first Buechler crop, as small as it was, was in the ground. Chris, as tired as anyone, smiled with pleasure. He knew Carl's story and he knew all that it meant to the boy. He armed around his new son's broad shoulders.

It was late and nobody had the time or the ambition to fire up the bath. They would have it ready before the actual departure. Nobody, especially one so important and admired, would go home unwashed and hungry. For now, every house sported lots of warm water, homebuilt soap, and a large basin.

It was beautifully warm and the crowning sunset spirited its display into the souls of the observers. They were all very happy with the results of their intensive labours. More had been done than they'd imagined possible. Even the recovering injured found a new lease and purpose. If they couldn't dig or chop or hoe or carry a bucket or milk a cow, they peeled and sliced and boiled and baked to free up the women who could; they forgot pride and gender. They pushed their limits and, just like "Mee-lee" said, they could reach further every day.

Soon she was going to leave them for a while and they knew they would miss her almost as much as Carl would. They were going to see her and her wonderful father off with, if nothing more, good fellowship and best wishes until her return and a very good meal. They all needed that after the labours of the last weeks.

Mildred, with Milly's and Helen's help, had taught four of the younger women, all with beautiful voices, the English Lord's Prayer and they delivered it with as much rehearsed finesse as they could muster. Many of the elders sat through it with tear-filled eyes. These people, not of their race or calling, were as good and Christian as any they could imagine. Maybe they would bring the peaceful life that the world so relentlessly denied?

"I'm simply not leaving without you seeing me off and that's final!" She stamped her foot in mock refusal, yet she really meant it. We're just going to have to dig in and get the work done. Let's get at August's today. It's not that much. Dad says a day or two isn't going to matter. I think he likes it here! He hasn't said anything but I can tell by the way he acts. He's got a taste, just like I have. He's a bit worried about Mom; she's there alone but she's got Bertha. She's a bit worried though, Dad said, from her telegraph. She seems to know pretty near everything that's happening up here. I wonder how the papers there are getting all the information. I haven't seen anybody that looks like newspaper people.

By the time August's was done, Carl's reluctant legs told him not to pace behind the walker so he rode Paul's sulky to turn more for a few more acres; there was still time. Chris wandered off, afoot, to "have a look" and the others walked August's for a suitable yard site.

Duty rode the Marshal back early that morning. The gruelling, week-long ride had exhausted the older man and Milly was growing worried about him. She'd asked Carl to try to get him to back off a bit and to talk to the councils to try to get him some permanent help. She knew he'd never quit as long as the circumstances were unresolved. When he said he'd "die tryin'," she was afraid he meant it.

————

The smell emanating through the opened kitchen door was fantastic. The girls returned from the field to a well-wrapped quarter of fresh venison, tied to the clothesline post, well out of the reach of the exuberant Boone. Nobody'd seen the discreet delivery yet they knew the source. Mildred willingly acknowledged Milly's superior kitchen experience while she went at her grimy son and her neglected house.

The beautifully-done roast, floating in a meaty, gravy-inducing broth and surrounded by potatoes and carrots, sat mercilessly on the kitchen cupboard. Fresh meat at this time of the year was as much a luxury as it was a blessing. Large portions of it simply wouldn't keep and often promoted painful illness. When it was a fresh rarity, like now, it could anticipate a hasty over-consumption. Usually the only predictable summer meat dish ran around wrapped in feathers until a few hours before supper. Ice cellars weren't new but most settlers were only too glad to be housed. Scarce resources portioned out the priorities accordingly. They'd happen with time.

Chris, whose girth justified his consumption, found stiff competition and prevailed by only the smallest of margins. Since his youth, he'd never exerted himself to the degree he'd done since his arrival and especially the last three days. Though tired and sore, he couldn't remember feeling so good and alive, almost like he was living for two. He loved his children dearly and now regretted his long, duty-bound separations during their childhood. Since the death of his son, he had lavished his attention on the care and well-being of his daughter. He wanted the very best for her and he was more than grateful for her choice of a life-mate. Yet Carl's immediate resources were thin and despite his ambitious, determined nature, life would be hard. In the short time Chris had known Carl, he'd come to love him like his own and he was often amazed at the reaction.

The enormous distance disturbed him and he wanted to be near his girl. On many occasions over the winter, he'd altered his duties in the direction of Des Moines just to see her and to be sure she was recovering well. He had suggested the current excursion into the Canadian wilderness and the company enthusiastically responded; it was a good business move.

He was both grateful and amazed at the degree of progress on a home and the respect and admiration his child generated in the hearts of these unfamiliar people. They seemed to regard her with reverence and even displayed admiration for him. He was very glad the circumstance took him out into its wilds and his confined spirit loved its pure, uncluttered beauty. He was determined to capitalize on the opportunities in the burgeoning petroleum industry and he was even more determined that, somehow, it would be out here. Wilbur would want it. He would go back to Iowa grudgingly, yet confident that he could negotiate a return. He knew that Phyllis would offer nothing but support.

Both Chris and the Marshal saw and mutually agreed that the possibility of a successful future for the children was far more likely here then back in the States. They'd resolved that despite Carl's independence, they'd see to it that the basics were not wanting. Mary Pawlowich's gratitude and generosity gave Carl a foothold with the livestock and the machinery and Max was in the opportune position. They admired the sense of purpose and the co-operative principle of the Buechler clan. That was something that Chris had never known in his own youth. The Marshal would do everything he could to guarantee security. Carl's actions over the last winter could put him in harm's way if the criminals weren't cleaned up.

Milly was elbow-deep in Carl's large washtub. What Loosha's homemade soap lost on the aromatic side, it added on the hygienic. The nature of the work out here ground the dirt right into the fabric and made the harsh reality of the detergent an absolute necessity. Milly was well versed in the art of laundry but a machine did it and it was never quite this engrained.

Although the harsh cleanser did little for her manicure, it quickly eliminated the filth and in short order, most of the wash decorated the surrounding shrubs. Some of the older folks, back home, used to make soap but her childhood had been denied the privilege of grandmotherly wisdom.

She was singing happily while pailing more water to do the whites up from the run into the big fire-hung pot when a team and wagon rolled over the crest. The sole occupant was a stranger and so was the team. When the wagon turned into the yard, she became a bit apprehensive. She was familiar with the use of the firearm that leaned against the wall just inside the door and Carl had instructed her not to take any chances. When the wagon rolled up to a "Whoa!" beside the fire, she stood in the open doorway, well within its grasp.

"This the Buechler place? You Mrs. Buechler? Boss sent me out with this load a' shingles an' stuff fer ya'." He didn't ask where but assumed, pulled the load up beside the south wall of the house, and proceeded to unhitch.

"Water 'em down there?" he asked, acknowledging the run, the only visible source.

He was older and grandfatherly. The wagon was heaped with the bundles of cedar so Milly decided he was passive and left her security to follow him down with her pail. "Marshal yer grandpa?" he asked. "Bought these and wanted 'em here taday 'n here they are ... Lotsa stuff. Anybody around ta give us a hand?" he asked. "Sure are a talker ain't ya'?" He smiled. Milly had said little more than "Yes! No!" or "Maybe!" He hadn't given her an opportunity. "Got a grand-girl 'bout yer age, says she knows ya ... Carol, down ta The Hotel?"

Before the horses were watered, two men from the village had rushed over to investigate. The watch was up at all times and nothing happened around them without their immediate reaction. "Meelee" was there alone!

By sundown, Carl, Chris, and August found the large stack of shingles with all the necessities, sitting beside the house. Milly, despite the fact that she'd had nothing to do with the delivery, had seemed to perform her magic again. The older deliverer had wagoned over to the village with the two guardians for a good feed and had been convinced, willingly, to rest over for the return tomorrow.

The huge pile of clean clothing lay folded, passively, on the mattress. Milly had been well suppered and hoe in hand, was still at the volunteer grass that was beginning to offend her garden.

Mildred and Helen had once again overfed the three. They'd thrown their entire resource into the preparation of Paul's land and they had it ready for the drill. The villagers were nearly done and were preparing to move to Sean's — their old seed drill would be freed to Paul's. Barring the unique characteristics of the antique mechanism, Paul's too, would be finished in a few days. Tomorrow, they'd throw their efforts into the shingles while the beasts pastured. Then Milly and Chris would have to leave.

———

Carl was no novice to the art; many of the roofs in Maynard and surroundings carried the consequences of his youthful labours. Chris was a bit heavy for the scaffolding and August's best efforts evaded success, as he wasn't yet healed enough to endure the necessary bending and lifting. Helen witnessed his determination and all but physically removed him. Milly picked and laid the shingles while Carl aligned, nailed and roped up the heavy bundles as required. The width of the pieces varied and she had to learn to judge, selectively, each shingle, to allow it to best achieve the required coverage of the split below. It took a while for her eye and hand to gain the required precision.

By the time the alignment exceeded their reach from the scaffolding, the sun had peaked and they stopped for the prepared lunch.

The afternoon found August the sole groundling. The best he could gratefully manage was to tie the rope to each bundle for the lift. He couldn't even imagine an attempt to shoulder-carry any up the shaky ladder. Carl had tacked a two-by-four cleat to the bottom row over the risk of penetrating through the coverage, to secure a foothold on the steep slope. Because of Chris's weight, he guaranteed a rope on each end, to a spike driven securely into the rafter on each end at the peak. It would require several time-consuming moves of the cleat to achieve the ridge; that couldn't be helped. Shingling was slow, careful work.

Helen joined Chris and the two pairs went to work. Carl was a bit worried about Chris' size, and was once again surprised by his agility. The roofing climbed steadily. By the time they stopped for August's improvised tea, Chris had clawed his weight to the peak and rope-held Carl as he pried free, then pulled the two-by-four cleats to their next placement and secured them.

Evening found them with the southern slope completed and the scaffolding in place for tomorrow's efforts. They should be done early. Chris smiled broadly and gave the girls each a crushing hug. His forced movements displayed a brave face but a restricted, painful, mobility. The others, too, found muscles they didn't know they had and none of them exceeded August's restrictions by any great degree.

Only Loosha's huge supper exceeded their good cheer. Alexsay's arm pained him yet he laughed at it and them; he was happy. His last seed was in the ground for another year and he once again placed his mortality into the merciful hands of the Lord. It was like a huge weight had been lifted from his overburdened spirit. They would again evade the pain of hunger. The pain of man's cruelty was another matter. He'd deal with that when it arose, as he was certain it would.

Carl and Milly walked home slowly and quietly; their cramped legs needed the stretch but they were very tired. Tomorrow would once again be their last full day together for the next two months. It was a short time in a lifespan and it was to their benefit yet it really hurt. She'd been here building their home and both were eternally grateful for the privilege. It had fulfilled her burning desire.

———

Their new home stood wrapped in the marvellous fragrance of fresh cedar; its tan brick chimney, straight and tall. In the three weeks since her surprising arrival, she'd accomplished miracles beyond imagination and earned the love and admiration of the entire community.

The area was desperate to educate their kids at least to "read 'n write 'n figure." Because the country was so vast, she'd have to travel some but she'd promised and they were ever so grateful. For those too far away, she'd bring with her a multitude of prepared correspondence material at a variety of levels; compliments of her Des Moines training staff. There wouldn't be enough — she'd have to spend days, pen in hand, recopying more to go around. She'd need help, but who?

Many came to bid her a farewell and to encourage her flagging spirit until they could welcome her back once more. How they all knew was a mystery but they took the time.

The small bouquet of early wildflower crocuses and dandelions, picked and delivered by beautiful little Samantha Murphy brought her to tears. Milly didn't do that very easily. "Vhat's awright teacher! I wait you come back!" and she delivered a huge wet kiss to Milly's cheek.

Helga Carlson asked Milly to please stop at the hospital and try to instil some of her miraculous will into the badly dispirited Carlie. "She lays and cries all the time and won't talk to any of us. We don't care what she'll look like. We want her back. Please help us! She'll trust you!" Carl and Milly knew the feeling only too well. Helga too, had promised to open her home to Milly when necessary, if it helped her teach the kids.

Mildred cried openly. Jimmy, planted in her lap, watched Milly with straight-faced understanding and wouldn't leave her until he had to. The injured hobbled up in turn to express their blessings and pleaded for her safe return in the broken English they'd learned so rapidly from her. The children came shyly. "We'll get a school real quick; I heard my daddy say."

They ate the buns and cakes they'd brought. They drank the tea that August and Helen hauled over, they hugged and kissed and shook hands and pleaded for her rapid return.

"Dasvidanya!" (Until we meet again!)

By the time the horizon disappeared into the dark, Carl and Milly were alone again. They slept peacefully and comfortably. This would be their last parting. This was home and they'd be together in it, soon, for as long as life would allow. After the last few weeks they were both more secure and more determined than ever.

That's the way it was with them.

———

August could do little else until Paul got enough seeded for him to harrow, so he rode along. He and Carl would try to bring back a couple of the cows with calves. They could box the calves and encourage co-operation that way, but it would be slow and tedious and it was very far from Carl's mind. At least August and Chris kept a conversation going. Milly and Carl didn't feel much like talking. The bird-filled morning and the glorious sunrise only added to the emotion.

They stopped briefly at the McPhersons' and Milly said her good-byes over Grandma's lunch. Max had spent nearly a week with Al and John. Mitch was doing an amazing job of keeping the land harrowed behind the drill and they were well advanced. Max had railed out for Winnipeg yesterday, to organize and escort a large order of machinery. He'd have to see to the deliveries and the company technicians wouldn't follow to help the novices with their operation, so he'd be back and forth for most of the spring. Alice, with her artful hand, burdened herself with multitudinous copying of the "Whys, Wheres, and ...How tos!" in their stead and Max hauled them with him, everywhere.

Chris would arrange for the necessary storage facilities and the equipment to handle the fuel and oil. Al'd need them soon because Max's sales demanded it. Time and man-hours would be a scarce commodity.

———

The Marshal had seen and spoken to her as much as she was able and knowing both their natures, had warned Carl and Chris to control themselves in her presence. The heavily bandaged, ashen face of the once robust, pretty, fifteen-year-old, ignited the flame of anger. He was well justified. The girl could speak haltingly and only in a whisper. She cried bitterly but at least she talked to Milly.

When they returned an hour later, Milly met them just inside the door of her room. A smiling Carlie was trying desperately to swallow the broth her mother spooned to her, the first she'd taken down her badly injured throat without the feeding tube, since the attack.

"I have to go now, but I'll be back in a few months. Write to us as soon as you can and I'll mail you all of their letters. They're all anxious to know what's going on up here and they'll want to hear from somebody right in the thick of it. I'll get your picture to them as soon as I can and we'll send ours back, I promise. You'll be in all the papers down there; the kids will see to that. You'd best start writing as soon as you can, everything you've heard and seen and done and thought since all of this started. I'll get it all printed. You're a real heroine! They'll love you! Bye 'til I get back. We'll make a real book out of your story!"

Carlie threw up her arms and struggled to a sit. Milly returned to the long and affectionate hug.

"Hurry back you wonderful girl! I can see why the Doukhobor folks can't say enough about you." Helga and Sven wrapped her collectively in an embrace and kissed her, one on each cheek. Chris teared-over when he saw his girl in action. He knew why she was so well admired by these people.

"What did you do in there? Just look at her! A book? Her story? Who'd 'a thought of it? Put it together the right way, and I guess it will make a great story and not only for kids."

"And we'll do it too! I'll polish it up and I know the papers will push the story but I'm not too sure about the print thing and the book promise. I'm not kiddin'! ... *Carlie's Story!* I can see it now. It's really good. Right up there next to our story. Well guess what! We're living all the things that some of the best stories are made of."

They had a light lunch at The Hotel and bought food for the unpredictable ride back. The rush was beginning but all in this direction.

The train was on time and the seats were largely empty. The freighters were loaded with produce for shipment east. The return luggage was minute; almost everything stayed with Milly's home and husband. Even the parting was different; they were occupied with instructing each other what to remember and what to bring and what to do. Carl pushed the thirty dollars that the shingles would have cost, into her cardigan pocket and held her hand as she stood on the step for as long as his foolish legs could safely match the acceleration, then they shouted instructions until beyond hearing.

"Hey! How long did you say you've been married?"

She was gone again and Carl missed her already. He walked quietly, ignoring all the acquaintances who tried to good-humour him, back to August and the Marshal.

XXI
"In the hands of the Lord!"

"Hiya lover!"

Carol's voice rang above the throng outside the station and it embarrassed August. "Oh my God! What on earth happened to you? Did they do this? This is awful!" She ran her hand, with affectionate concern, over August's still discoloured cheek as he explained. Carol had heard about Carlie and the natives but had no idea anybody else had been hurt. He was, without doubt, the best looking piece of young manhood she'd ever laid eyes on. Their contrived romance had established a fast friendship and she'd worried about him throughout his courageous subterfuge.

"Come on, I've got something different baked for you and your long-faced brother. Ain't love grand and painful too?" she teased.

"But we just ate."

"Well you're goin' to eat again. I have to ask you a favour. Let's go." To Carl — "That's good! I hope you miss her like that all the time. In case you haven't noticed, you got the grand prize in that one." She pulled Carl along by his lapel. To August — "Since you were largely responsible for priming my fella and I guess I'm somehow responsible for yours too, we, Hal and I, don't have too many old friends around that we're both close to. You're about as close as we can get. We've decided to get married this fall and we want you and that blond you dumped me for, to stand with us. What do you say?"

"When?"

"We haven't decided on a sure date yet. It'll be after harvest sometime. Why?"

"Well, Max and Alice asked us for July. I'm sure she'll be happy to do it but only if you promise to do the same and we'll see who does whose first." To Carl — "We weren't goin' to tell anybody just yet until we're sure we can have something around us to count on, so you keep quiet for a while." August turned to Carol. "And you too; you've got such a big mouth!" She slapped him playfully, then wrapped him in a delightful hug and kissed him, this time with no deception, on his unblemished cheek. "She's scared that something'll happen to spoil this for her too. My gettin' hurt scared her I guess."

"I'll be golldarned!" Carl whooped with glee, grasping August in the traditional Buechler handhold. August was his flesh and blood yet his reaction was out of joy for Helen. He knew she'd have everything that her pain-filled life had denied her because he knew August. "Thank God!" He clenched his hands heavenward and heard Mama's gleeful laugh.

His depression was gone. Wouldn't everybody be surprised and happy; especially Papa and the kids. He had no idea if they even knew about Helen; August was tight-lipped and wouldn't write much about such things. Carl was certain one of the first people Milly would see when she got back was Papa and he knew that she would surely tell and just wait until Papa met her! ... His three oldest, matched with such fantastic girls! Carl would see to it that she'd meet the train with August.

All the lunches since their arrival made an early supper unnecessary but they knew it wouldn't escape them at the McPhersons'. They rolled into the yard at five and announced their arrival to Grandma and Alice. They knew enough about the workings of the place so that the choring was all done by the time the men came in to do it. Alice's morning sickness sometimes rolled over into the afternoon and Grandma wouldn't allow her out of the house until she knew things were safe. She still grumbled about the wisdom of Alice's premature pregnancy and the willful girl obeyed the older woman's superior experience; both surely didn't want to hurt the baby. Grandma, despite her traditional grumbling, anticipated the birth with absolute delight.

John, who hadn't yet seen August, cursed openly at the sight of the bruises. Grandma regretted the reaction but didn't comment on it because she knew the emotion of the old man. His temperament was hair-trigger after Michael and she was seeing a side of him that forty-two years hadn't yet shown her. She felt a lot like he did when it came to defending the kids.

Early next morning, Carl and August bumped two rambunctious calves into the high box, behind the tight new rolls of barbed wire, left a tail board out to maintain eye contact with the anxious, rope-led, mothers and headed home. The cows certainly weren't the hurried kind and the road back was long and frustrating.

The move over to Sean's was completed by the time he and August crawled by. Frantic arm waving was the only indulgence because some were already out in the field and others were at corral repair and a clean-up of the ruin. The recovered cattle were held only by young Jim's hasty barbed wire enclosure. There was still extensive pasture fence damage from the wild escape, despite the family's effort to get it repaired in time. The boys felt guilty at passing, but then, they didn't have even that much to contain theirs.

They watered, then tree-tethered the cows with whatever rope length they had along so the animals could graze to its extremity. August walked over to his, then Paul's, to see the progress there. He'd be useless to Carl anyway; the prospect of bar-punching a posthole was beyond him yet. Grandma's huge packed trip-lunch would keep them for the afternoon.

———

Sunset found Carl very tired and very pleased with progress. He'd punched, hauled, and posted the entire south side of his yard site. He had holed the western side down to the water run, then wagoned the posts and spread them along its entirety. He'd lost some time walking to the village, to Alexsay's, because his post maul was still over at Paul's. He liked Alexsay's because it balanced better. He tested the question and realized that August and Helen had indeed kept their intentions unknown.

He wasn't really hungry but Anastas walked over after sunset with some curiosity and fresh food for him and it tasted so good that he downed all of it. The team was hitched so he wagoned the old man back. Because of her English, Helen had gone over to Sean's to help with the cooking and August would night over at Paul's for an early start, so Anastas prevailed on Carl to night over with him. The cattle re-tethered to a post with plenty of grass were secure. Besides, he could actually see them through Anastas' kitchen window.

The next full day saw the posts all in around the yard and had the perimeter wrapped by two loose wires. Carl had dropped the tailgate out of the box, re-bored the binding rod holes larger, and shoved the crowbar through the roll of wire and out the other side, then simply let the team unroll it. He'd anchor-wire and brace the fence corners, then tighten to a finish tomorrow and let the cattle graze the yard until he could get a pasture fenced. They wouldn't be much of a nuisance if everyone watched where they stepped.

As soon as the yard was fenced, Carl planned to turn more land with the walker and maybe seed a few acres of later oats for the livestock. He could cut and stack some of it whole and get grain to them that way. There weren't too many hay sloughs on his and he wasn't sure where he'd find enough feed. Most of the sloughs stayed too wet, except in unusually dry summers and most were heavily willow-bunched. Maybe he'd cut some on open, unfiled land. Others did it and nobody had complained about the practice yet, that he knew of.

And what about a barn and corral for the winter and a place for August and Helen and what would the rest of them need? "Jeez! I'd better not think about it!"

By noon, the corners and the wires hummed tight. He had only the entrance gate at the road to finish, so he turned the cattle loose to enjoy their gleeful ramble before he ate. Instinctively they seemed drawn to the opening, so he lunched in the gap while they explored and observed him with shy resentment. Carl loved fooling with them at feeding, when he had time and when they were calves. The trust made them easy to handle.

With the fence finished, the cattle secure and a large part of the afternoon ahead of him, he teamed over to Paul's to see what action required him and the team around there. The seeding had advanced to more than half the acreage with frustrating creep. August and the harrows sat idly much of the time because the old shoe drill kept a constant ritual of minor infractions, wiring and pinning and tightening. Paul didn't seem worried; that was the familiar nature of the creation. "That's alright! ... couple days, she'll be done. How'd you make out with 'em?"

They hitched Carl's fresher team to the drill and retired one of Paul's to the pasture. The young Buechler team objected a bit to the unfamiliar hitch but Paul's superior horse sense offered them little option. The other youngsters that August used on the harrow, rested half the time anyway and the blacks got the afternoon off.

Carl tooled up and went at Paul's pasture fence. The passive cow had achieved a secret escape route and Carl went out to find it. The heavy weight of the unusual winter's snow had raised absolute hell with tight wire. The southwest corner, still bushed in, had allowed the snow to pile and pull the fence down with it. The enterprising cow had unrestricted access to the entire countryside. Fortunately, she was a homebody and she returned each evening on the wrong side of the fence, requiring a lengthy walk to herd her and her uncooperative calf around through the gate. Mildred was getting a bit irritated. Carl had to come back to get more to repair the breakage. The posts were good but the wire damage took time. Paul had already repaired the evident damage south of his yard, committed by the escaping rustlers.

August was alright but Carl was Jimmy's favourite and he'd latched on most of the evening. Carl was the only one to put him to bed and talk him to sleep. Jimmy had lost a disagreement that evening, with his mother, over the issue of Boone's unauthorized admission into the house and the ragged disappearance of half a large loaf of fresh bread.

Carl curled up on Anastas's re-padded seat. His place would have allowed more comfort but it was so cold and lonely with Milly gone. August needed the saggy, old bed to rest his aches. It could hold both of them but they'd be crowded and August had some rude sleeping habits. Carl smiled with wondrous humour. "How's Helen going to break him?" He certainly hoped he didn't have any; Milly hadn't complained yet.

The next morning was calm and beautiful. The temperate atmosphere encouraged exertion. Dan and Ben walked with comfortable ease and the fresh sod ribboned out. Alexsay told him that he could safely seed the kind of crop he wanted, to the middle of June. He'd have a lot more in then he'd ever imagined and the reason for that was cooperation and the efficient use of manpower. Paul was right when he said that Carl couldn't go wrong with these people. The Buechlers' first crop would be an impressive acreage.

———

Everything happened at once. The parade of men, machines, and animals converged at the same time, just two days later. Sean's was done, the villagers were done, and Paul was done. August and Paul rolled in with the disk and drill, just as the village parade rolled over the crest. The meeting at Carl's gate was jovial and high-spirited. August and Helen hadn't seen each other for nearly a week and the men giggled at their enthusiastic reunion. Both were definitely losing their inhibitions.

They'd all done their part, now it was in the hands of the Lord. There'd be no more work this day; it was home to care for the horses, rest, cleanse and feed body and spirit. The bawnyah smoked, the pyetch baked, the kitchens boiled and the people smiled with renewed energy and hope. In the last three weeks, they'd achieved more than they'd ever imagined possible. Since "Pavlowa," and now "Car-roll" and "Awoo-goost," the prospect of a barren, unfriendly, landscape was peopled with promise and hope. With the terrors of the past winter, even the old aloof neighbours warmed to the "Brotherhood and Community." In their generations of deprivation and pain on both sides of the ocean, they found it hard to understand that good people remained. Only God could have sent them.

August went with Helen, while Paul took his team back and would pick up his family. Sean and his were extended an invitation and would be there soon. Mildred would have to check his hands again; she had the impression that she'd mastered the infection and she wanted to be sure. Her warning had scared him into caution and the timely intervention of his neighbourhood and the recovery of most of his livestock had earned his undying gratitude.

Exhaustion and the warm and cleansing steam subdued the common chatter of the bath. Everybody was physically as well as spiritually grateful. Carl heard portions of whispered prayers of thanksgiving. Most of these people put their faith where their mouths and hearts were. Yet, in every group there are always marginalizers.

The only rehearsed portion was the request for the group to sing again, the "Lord's Prayer" as before. It simply fascinated them! The meal was simple and unelaborate, wholesome and filling; the atmosphere more solemn than celebrational. The prayers, totally spontaneous and unrehearsed, were of thanksgiving, a request for the Lord's blessing on their crops and forgiveness of their sinful nature, a request for the security and the rapid, safe return of Mee-lee and blessings on the unions of Max and Crasna Hallawvaya, Awoo-goost and Hawnya. The pair blushed; somebody knew! Anastas beamed with joy.

The singing was general; everyone indulged and it re-echoed the prayers. Carl could see Mama smiling and Papa's happy contented face. Papa would be very happy here. To find peace, he too had run from conflict.

Paul's oats, raised on new land, required only a gentle breezing to blow out the chaff and dust. He and August went at the newly turned land on Carl's, while Carl and the blacks rolled more on August's. By the tenth of June, they decided they'd done far more than they'd anticipated or hoped for and considered their efforts nothing short of miraculous. The first Buechler crop ever, was in the ground. It was time to concentrate on other essentials.

———

The mill was already in action but there was very little August's month-old injuries would allow him to do, so he'd help Paul wagon in more of the oats. How they'd manage the loading, Carl wasn't sure. He helped with the first loads and then headed for the bush. Village and neighbour teams rolled back and forth to York every day so they were in good, safe company. The trail was packed and solid and the temperature was jacket stripping. Paul's teams and the work-hardened youngsters would haul while the black heavies went into the bush with Carl.

Circumstances at York told him that the mill would have to run full-out to come anywhere near the demand of York alone. The logs would have to roll. The mill, barring a major breakdown, could easily handle more than it had over the restrictive winter. Chris and Al promised all the necessary fuel and Max had already laid up a good supply of the parts that the engine had proven necessary. John McPherson would rebuild the air intake on the engine to eliminate the dust problem.

The contractor at York had promised August and Carl more teams and even a man to haul if they could meet his demand. His volume alone would more than pay off the engine and they were already thinking of a second, smaller unit to run the planer, like the mill, in colder weather. The steamer would then be free to thresh and saw the wood without the necessity of a shutdown. Manpower was the prime difficulty.

The farther they cut into the bush, the heavier the logs got. The first arrivals had concentrated on building up a suitable load site and the size of the logs made canting them on beyond the ability of human muscle. They'd built around a sizeable spruce and had devised a winch system to it that required a team to hoist the logs onto the wagons. Four or five logs made an enormous load, too heavy, so most loaded with only three of the big ones and got back a little sooner; it averaged out better and saved horsepower, breakage and down time.

Dan and Ben skidded the giants out to the load site. The size amazed Carl … nothing at all like what he'd ever seen in Iowa. How did the cutters get the giants down and trimmed so fast? Carl never had to wait. The team had to strain with the effort of some of the biggest but most would allow a two-log pull. The load wasn't constant so they certainly weren't prone to tiring.

At the load site, he tried to skid them as close as he could, to get them where they should be for the winch. He soon learned to exert a bit more effort with placement and save the back muscle.

He rarely got to the mill during the day but he could hear the angry snarl and the sharp bark of the engine off in the distance. Each evening, when he returned, the pile of lumber seemed to double. They were doing extremely well and there were few repair or service stops.

The cabins weren't much above crude yet but they were functional. The men likened them to the block housing prepared for them during their first winter here before they got anything built … certainly better than the caves and thatch-covered holes some lived in.

The weather held moderate with a few good showers but the heat was beginning to climb. John McPherson's modified air intake solved the dust problem and the shed over the machine required hinged modification to allow a cooling breeze through the structure to prevent overheating of both men and machine.

The entire crew wore broad smiles. They were nearly doubling their production from the best of last winter but the strain on the reduced manpower was telling. The steamer and the planer-shaper, now back and in action, was hopelessly outmatched and certainly suffered the lack of August's youth and vitality.

The two teams hauling to York were soon supplemented with another and John McPherson at the reins. He fuelled in and lumbered out but the haulers still lost ground. When Paul and August had the rest of the oats hauled in, August and a few village teams began a steady daily trip to the village and the York teams could load a lot heavier from there for the much longer York relay. The word from York was "Keep it coming!"

Carl was again becoming anxious. August would need a place built and they'd need a barn or shelter of some kind. They'd need at least two good granaries and the house needed a lot of work before everybody got here. But money was so scarce that the opportunity to work it off was not an option. August kept an eye on the cattle but what was the garden like?

Milly's letters were brief and busier. Carl had written only one that told her of the circumstance. Time was passing so quickly that there never seemed to be enough. He'd worried about being lonely and now he wished he had some time to be. Bertha's single letter told him of the glee and anticipation at the prospect of Helen and Alice and seeing their new world.

Because the mill and the bush crew had far exceeded the planer and the transport, they decided to shut the mill down for a while to catch up with both and allow the men to get some time to pull things together and get a bit of their own work done. Carl hadn't been out for three weeks and he hadn't seen Max in a month — neither had any of the others.

———

The yard looked forlorn and lonely. It was cow-trimmed yet awash in a sea of yellow dandelions. Where they came from, Carl had no idea; there weren't that many there last fall and the cattle surely wouldn't eat them. There was easily enough grass for them. With the rapid growth, all the two pairs could do was suppress it. He'd get the other two pairs here as quickly as he and August could, then get them and the teams into their own pasture so he could have the yard back for the human rush to come.

The wheat, shallowed by the broadcast and harrowing, flourished in the abundant moisture to a vibrant, green carpet and in so short a time! Carl'd never seen it so luxuriant in Iowa. The oats flourished in an orderly fashion after the disciplined drill and sat well above the ground with an equivalent enthusiasm but there'd be a bit more volunteer grass in the inter-rows.

The village promise, to keep an eye on the garden, was good. He could readily see the consequence of the disciplining hoe. The waving grasses along the edges, displayed the natural intent. A large area supported some of Carl's surplus cedar shingles, pushed into palisades at regular four-foot intervals around the transplant tomatoes and cabbages. Lengthy, oval dikes surrounded the moistened cucumbers and Carl hadn't done any of this. He could easily see that in future years, the garden would have to translocate somewhere nearer the water source. The potato patch emphasized its enormity now that they waved a foot in the air and the corn and beans, seeded later, supported both outside leaves and centers, well above the ground. The peas were blossoming and sprouting pods.

He wished he had a stove but Milly would be bringing one so he'd manage with the campfire. Some of the old timers had lived that way for years.

The house still smelled fresh-lumbery on the inside, the first new anything he'd ever had in his life, except maybe clothes that Mama built. Ingmar had given Mama the solid, new sewing machine that kept everybody covered and Carl couldn't remember too many winter evenings without its sequential clatter. He realized that his status in the family put him in both a fortunate and an unfortunate position. As the eldest, he was, most often, at the head of the hand-me-down chain and got more new then any of his siblings. On the unfortunate side, a lot of the responsibility for his siblings fell on his early childhood. Yet for both, he was grateful. It had taught him far in advance of his years. The rest grew up as kids largely because of him.

Once again the responsibility for the family fell upon him. They'd be here soon and he'd have to accommodate them. He'd have to partition off the rooms and get a stairway in somehow. He'd been around construction a lot and had seen them done but stairs and windows were a bit beyond his expertise. Carl opened the door and went at the partitions. Milly's modified plan even held the dimensions and he had Papa's good, old folding-measure.

The eventual stairway, along the north wall, would cover a storage closet adjacent to the master bedroom. Carl would leave the actual stairway open for better heating but that would take a well-finished, costly banister. He'd do something temporary until he could. The closet would have doors from the bedroom and the living room; it was large enough for both. The living room would L-shape the full length of the south side, around the bedrooms, up to the closet-stairwell. The short side would accommodate the doorway to the first bedroom with the kitchen door directly across, between the heater and the base of the stairs.

Carl squared off the bedrooms and cut the rough-thickness two-by-four wall studding. He'd put them at twelve-inch centers, because the upper floor weight would be carried by the wall and he wanted it strong. He made sure they were long enough by the outside-wall height measure, to fit a double upper plate and a single lower. By that evening, he had the walls framed, complete with doorways and post-mauled tightly into place to take up the existing upper floor sag.

He began boarding it in diagonally, like the outer walls, for more strength. It took a lot more cutting so he was surely glad of the old crosscut. Like his mackinaw, Papa found it abandoned and rusting and had revived it to its superior quality. The sharpening of last fall held to the hard steel. He worked slowly and accurately because he didn't want the wall finishing, likely paper, to trace the diagonal marking.

The outer walls would be boarded in, after the insulation. What that would be, Carl wasn't sure. After the hellish winter past, he recognized the need for considerable substance.

Carl had tea, radishes, lettuce, and soon peas and a few mini-spuds. He'd have been independent but for the bread. It lacked variety yet, but then, mankind was built as a vegetarian and he could live quite nicely on veg-etables. However, Helen wouldn't allow it. She said she had helped to nurse him twice and she wasn't going to let him sneak back again. He was going to get at least one good meal every day and that would be at supper, "So don't be late! Somebody's got to look after you 'til she gets back!" Lonely old Anastas just loved having all of them around as much as possible.

The master woodworker walked over with August, and measured the windows and stairwell. It was he who had reprimanded the builders to back away more to allow the stairs a more gentle slope. "You comink. I show how bwill-ding!" Milly and Helen had been at his English.

August's overenthusiasm soon petered and Carl rip-sawed the framing from the superior planking Anastas had hand-selected for these jobs. Anastas made sure they had enough of the material prepared for all of the windows and more. He and August worked the windows, while Carl built the stairs himself, under Anastas's close scrutiny. Carl loved to learn and enjoyed the challenge to prove as much to himself as anyone else, that he could. This was his, he wanted to do it right!

Within two days, both the stairs and windows lay complete. Anastas smiled at their pride and Helen translated his sly remark: "Why work when all you have to do is teach somebody else to do it?" All the windows needed was glass, they didn't have any of that here.

The stairs fit very tightly into the allotted space. Alexsay ordered the stairs placed into the upper dimension at a far steeper angle than they would ultimately fit. He handed the postmaul up to Carl and instructed him to drive the high side down slowly and carefully toward the joist. It went into place with little difficulty, forcing the well framing over enough for a tight fit without cracking anything. Then Carl drove the entire unit down until the upper stair-edge matched the upper floor-level exactly. The treads were tight and glue-nailed, so Carl would likely have a squeakless set of stairs, at least until the house settled.

The windows consumed all of one day and most of the next, sawing the openings, setting them in loosely, shimming them to fit. Allowing some flex room as the house settled, was a time consuming, painstaking job. The bottom panel had to open or close without binding and the trimming had to be neat and finished looking; the old master would tolerate nothing less.

———

August and Helen left for York early that morning with a load of lumber. They didn't say anything and they went alone. Everybody knew of their plans and anticipated preparations. They'd bring back glass for Carl's windows.

Carl hauled over the makeshift heater he'd thrown together in Paul's sleigh but the villagers thought it wasn't safe so Ivan and a few others brought over the old wood stove from the village shop. It flat-topped so Carl could cook on it. With the direct draft the homely implement performed excessively and Carl had to fuel it with caution. Both Carl and August had developed the habit of throwing on any dry wood they ran across in their wagon travels and had accumulated a fair pile.

Carl apportioned his time between the house and the garden. Never in all his years had he seen such a crop! In time for the family, a lot would be ready. He picked a sizeable handful of seed-revealing peapods. He loved the whole fresh pods almost as much as the confined seed ... just beautiful in a mixed vegetable salad. He fumbled in the soft dirt under some of the mature-looking plants and found to his satisfaction, a goodly number of silver dollar-sized spuds. He rubbed the delicate skins off and boiled the firm whites.

Paul and Mildred did not want for meat. Every week or so a fresh variety of game or fowl appeared and the bearer remained discreet. Carl and the Karmadys wandered back and forth every day or so to see how things were going and he usually came away with some, always roasted or fried and all he did was reheat it.

Often, at sunset, when he knew Helen was gone, he wandered over to Anastas's and the old man always welcomed him. Throughout his entire life, Anastas had lived amongst these people, who respected him and looked to his wisdom and experience yet he was a very lonely man and had grown close to very few people. He loved Helen and the boys as his own and was honoured by their admiration, respect, and company. Milly had brought his Anastasia back to life. Even if only in his memory, she was real to him and she'd soon be back. He had very little in the way of good, close, fellowship throughout his youth; most hadn't survived. He could identify with these young people almost as if he were young again.

The wagon crested the rise late the next evening, with more than Carl expected. He'd been watching the hill all afternoon and was beginning to wonder why Helen and August weren't back yet. Two cows followed lazily behind, they'd brought the other two pairs with them. Carl was driving posts along the south side of the quarter, the lowest and roughest land on his, for the coming pasture and he was nearly the full half-mile down. By the time he got back to the yard to greet them, they had the calves out and the cows loose and a glorious reunion was under way. It was a good thing Carl had as much done as he did because they'd need the pasture very soon. In a week's time when the folks came, there'd be all kinds of people around.

There was a letter. Mother Hallvarson would be coming with them. Young Bertha had broken her arm a month before and although she felt very sorry for herself, she was as giddy and silly with anticipation as Carl would expect her to be. Herman and Arnold were readying themselves to tame the wilderness. They resented the fact that they couldn't be there that long because there was a crop in the offing that they'd have to get off much sooner than the one up here. Papa was beside himself with joy and found it hard to contain. Everybody was just dying to meet Helen.

Mary Pawlowich was in a state of agitation. They weren't really her family yet they were so much a part of her life that she wanted desperately to come and see but didn't think she should. Everybody was trying to convince her and she looked like she just might. Almost everybody close to her around Maynard would be gone and she'd be desperately lonely; she so loved the Buechler kids. She doted over young Bertha like her own and was making a proper young lady out of her.

They'd be bringing more of the cattle because they weren't putting up any feed but they needed the teams for harvesting. They were bringing the mower and the hay rake with them too.

Well, I'm now, a certified teacher, Oh yes I am! And I'm going to be a published author too — well not just me. The newspapers around here are just nuts about the stories coming out of there. They are actually starting to annoy me with their persistence. As far as I can gather, the Charles paper sourced a certain redhead, who was in on just about everything around there, and has a real flare for a good story line.

I've done much of what I promised Carlie, and the publishers, with all that's going on up there, are going for CARLIE'S STORY just as soon as I can get back to her and we can finish. The kids are excited over it and I'm sure she must be drowning in letters from them. She's written a few back, because she's at home

now and much better. The kids are screaming to meet a real live heroine of the frontier! I don't know how that can happen, but it surely would be something for her.

This letter will take a week to get to you, so I'm saying that I'll see you in a week's time.

Your love,

Milly.

———

They posted their way back to parallel the south edge of the waist-high, heading wheat, back toward the road allowance. They'd leave a fenced-in pathway along the west fence of the yard, down to the water run for when the pasture sloughs dried up. It would mean the inconvenience of opening two gates to get in or out of the yard but what else could they do? For now, the south edge of the pasture, straddling the slough on the neighbouring quarter, held plenty of water so the run wouldn't get used for a while and without the cattle in the yard, the gates didn't have to be closed at all.

Carl couldn't believe it! With August's now more capable help, they completed the posting that day, and the next found most of the wire up and tight, the corners and gates done. They were a bit short of wire but the village had a few rolls of older used, that they didn't need immediately, so the boys could replace it when they got more.

By ten the next morning, the inquisitive creatures nosed their way with a bit of trepidation, through the passage, and into their new pasture. They looked questioningly into the ten-fold expanse, viewed the fenced perimeter and slow-witted their way to the realization that this wasn't a security risk at all, then lapsed into juvenile prematurity with a hoof-snapping race to the far end. They drew to an abrupt halt at the far fence, nose gauged the extent, then heaved and panted their way back as enthusiastically, to a sod-ripping stop at the boy's feet, nosing them with seeming gratitude.

The emotion was mutual. Had the boys the physiology, they would have accompanied the gambol. A very short time ago, this place hadn't even existed; they'd been nowhere. Now, in a few days, they'd all be here with three very special ones that hadn't existed then either. Neither of the boys could wrap their thinking fully around the extent of what had happen in so short a time. If the Buechlers ever did own land in Europe, they certainly hadn't owned as much as the two of them held here. Surely, there'd soon be more! With every step accomplished, they'd always think back to Mama's prophetic, final words. She always knew.

"Where we gonna put 'em all? I don't know what they're bringin' for bedding. Sure hope it don't turn cold or nothin'. There'll still be a few days before the wedding and I know that they're all goin' to want to be out here to see our places before they head back to help get ready. There's goin' to be an awful lot of running back and forth and we'll have to get the livestock here, after they rest a bit. That'll be slow goin'. We're sure goin' to need the mower and rake pretty quick. I don't know what the folks at the village are planning but you can bet it's somethin'. They're goin' to run them all through the bath too, you can count on that!"

"Well, if there ain't nothin' better and the boys want to rough it like they think, we'll haul in some straw, nail together a frame to hold it in, horse blanket it and they can sleep on that ... done it lots of times. Let the older folks have the mattresses but we should get the rooms upstairs boarded in if we can."

"We're goin' to need more than one team with all the stuff they're bringing. Milly alone's got the stove and Lord knows what else by now. We'll need all of it right off, too, just to keep everybody fed and watered and comfortable. I can just see the kids now ... so excited! They ain't been nowhere; I know I sure was. I'm just as excited now, just to show 'em, with Helen now and all."

They went at the rooms and by sundown, the upstairs was an enclosed series of cubicles.

"Ain't very proud of ourselves are we? But, God ain't we good?" Helen came up the stairs to see what they'd done for the day, smiling at their arrogant humour.

"This place sure changed from last fall. Come! Supper's ready and I'm trying to keep it warm. I've just about got it finished and I want you to see." She smiled quietly to August.

"What?" Carl questioned the subtle remark. It was really none of his business but he was so excited that he didn't think.

"Well, you're not going to see until it happens. The folks are all going to be here and everybody is going to be ready anyway. We don't know why we should drag it all out. We're very sure of what we want, and we'll get set up somehow. We're going to get married now. We've told Max and Alice because we didn't want to take anything from them and they think it's just great. The folks at the village know and are getting things ready anyway, so why not?" The very practical Helen stated everything so simply and matter-of-factly. But both the boys knew the turmoil of emotion that had to be swirling beneath the perfect exterior.

"God, I'm sure happy for you; both of you!" Carl felt her trembling in his gentle hug. She smiled perfectly as usual. The tears were in his eyes.

"Your words are always so accurate. Thank you for my life. It means so much more to me now."

August smiled and said nothing. Helen and he shared everything. He knew what Carl's influence meant to her and he was just as grateful. She was days away from having something she'd so longed for; she'd have a family. She was in an emotional frenzy; she loved them, yet she'd never even met them. Would they love her?

The End of Book One

About the Author

Gerald Benneke is a graduate of the University of Saskatchewan's College of Education and has taught History and English at a number of locations in Saskatchewan before returning to the land as the fourth-generation operator of the family farm. The author's farmstead lies in an area immersed in personal, territorial, and national history. A short drive takes him to the historic sites of Fort Riviere Tremblante, Fort Pelly, Fort Hibernia, Fort Livingston, the Crowstand Mission, and nearly forty of the  sixty-one old world Doukhobor village sites. A bit further takes him to Cannington Manor, the Qu'Appelle Valley, Fort Carlton, and the battle sites of Duck Lake, Fish Creek and Batoche. A mile and a half from his door puts him on the old Fort Pelly-to-Yorkton trail.

The author's maternal grandparents did indeed walk out of Siberian exile and were indeed aboard one of those trains that "bleak December" day of which he writes. His paternal great-grandparents did indeed board a train out of Maynard, Iowa that cool October evening to establish the homestead, much of which he and his wife still own today.

Photos also available of author at Fort Livingston and Fort Pelly Sites.

Printed in Canada